D0408170

A
SINISTER
SPLENDOR

A SINISTER SPLENDOR

Mike Blakely

A TOM DOHERTY ASSOCIATES BOOK

New York

This is a work of fiction. All of the characters, organizations, and events portrayed in this novel are either products of the author's imagination or are used fictitiously.

A SINISTER SPLENDOR

Copyright © 2019 by Mike Blakely

A Forge Book
Published by Tom Doherty Associates
175 Fifth Avenue
New York, NY 10010

www.tor-forge.com

Forge® is a registered trademark of Macmillan Publishing Group, LLC.

Library of Congress Cataloging-in-Publication Data

Names: Blakely, Mike, author.
Title: A sinister splendor / Mike Blakely.
Description: First Edition. | New York : Forge, 2019.
Identifiers: LCCN 2018045273| ISBN 9780765328380 (hardcover) |
    ISBN 9781429943611 (ebook)
Subjects: | GSAFD: War stories.
Classification: LCC PS3552.L3533 S53 2019 | DDC 813/.54—dc23
LC record available at https://lccn.loc.gov/2018045273

Our books may be purchased in bulk for promotional, educational, or business use.
Please contact your local bookseller or the Macmillan Corporate and Premium Sales
Department at 1-800-221-7945, extension 5442, or by email at
MacmillanSpecialMarkets@macmillan.com.

First Edition: February 2019

Printed in the United States of America

0 9 8 7 6 5 4 3 2 1

For my grandchildren,
London, Norah, and Ford

TO THE READER

Left to my own devices, I might never have sought to write a novel about a subject as broad and mysterious as the Mexican War. But my esteemed publisher, Tom Doherty, suggested through my indefatigable editor, Robert Gleason, that I might consider fictionalizing this long-ago clash between neighboring nations. At the time, I have to admit, I knew few details about the war. However, a modicum of research turned up scores of harrowing events and generated familiar names such as Ulysses S. Grant, Antonio López de Santa Anna, Zachary Taylor, and Jefferson Davis, to name a few.

I could not turn down the project, though I knew it would involve an enormous amount of research. Luckily, I had traveled throughout Mexico for decades, so most of my geographical research had already been accomplished. Delving into scores of histories, diaries, memoirs, military reports, old newspaper accounts, and other sources, I decided that too much information existed for one novel. Accordingly, for this volume, I have focused on the first, or northern, phase of the war under the leadership of General Zachary Taylor.

Militarily, the Mexican War served as a training ground for many future generals of the Civil War. Culturally, it grew from "Manifest Destiny"—a grassroots obsession among many American citizens in favor of expansion to the Pacific coast. Politically, it redrew the map of North America. Yet, for all of its sweeping historical significance, the war was fought and endured by *individuals* from both sides of the border—most of them average, some destined for greatness.

To tell this story, I have chosen some of those real people to use as my characters. In fact, all of my point-of-view characters in this book are actual historical personages. I have done my best to fictionalize their thoughts, emotions, and words. I have created a few minor characters to move the story along as a work of fiction. I have also left out many real people for the sake of brevity. (For example, General Taylor had about forty officers and men on his staff who remained near him almost constantly. For the most part, I have condensed all of these staffers down to one man, Taylor's adjutant, William Bliss.)

Each chapter of this book represents a fictionalized account of historical events that actually happened. I have gone to great lengths to stay as close to the truth as possible. However, the chronicles of many historians differ. Even contemporary eyewitnesses disagreed on the details of many events. Men who stood shoulder to shoulder often remembered the same incident differently. My job as a novelist has been to choose the version that seemed most logical or to combine various recollections.

Accordingly, this is not a history. It is a historical novel. My hope is that the reader will enjoy this book while learning about the war—not by memorizing names and dates and places but by experiencing the times through my fictionalized versions of the actual men and women who lived them. It was an era not so unlike our own—a period of controversy and partisan politics, of great promise and frightening uncertainty, of dangerous ambitions and delusions of glory. The results of the Mexican War still shape and haunt us to this very day.

Northern Theater of the Mexican War

AUGUST, 1845–FEBRUARY, 1847

"The enemy . . . set fire to the grass . . . the fire began to spread. Its *sinister splendor* illuminated the camp."

Description of the battle of Palo Alto by
Mexican officer Ramon Alcaraz.

Part I

BUGLE, FIFE, AND DRUMS

The Strains of War

SAM GRANT

Gravois Creek, Missouri
May 20, 1844

The Gravois roared at Lieutenant Grant from a quarter mile away. He reined in his cavalry mount and listened to the din of the tributary over the patter of raindrops peppering his felt hat brim. He had not counted on this. Gravois Creek typically did not carry enough of a flow to run a coffee mill, as the old-timers would say. The rain must have fallen in a much heavier deluge upstream. No matter. There would be no turning back.

He touched his spurs to the mare's flanks and trotted onward toward the familiar creek crossing. The horse, excited by the approaching noise, pranced nervously yet gracefully under him. Grant reveled in the sensation of such power beneath him, barely gathered to the restraint of spurs and reins.

He rode near enough to find the flooded stream spilling over its bank. The mare, catching sight of a dead tree floating down the Gravois, shied and wheeled back toward Jefferson Barracks, then returned to the creek bank at her rider's insistence. Grant stared in awe at the raging stream. This little prairie rill, this brook, this trickle had gone as mad as a rabid pet turned man-killer.

"Damn, Sam," he said to himself, indulging in the mild profanity only because no one other than his mare would hear. Though it was not really his name, he had grown accustomed to calling himself Sam. Born Hiram Ulysses Grant, he had arrived at West Point only to find his name erroneously recorded as Ulysses Simpson Grant. It was an honest mistake made by the congressman who had arranged his appointment to the academy. The congressman, Thomas L. Hamer, knew that Grant's family called him Ulysses, so he assumed that to be the young man's first name. He further assumed that Grant's middle name was probably Simpson, as it was common for a son to take his mother's maiden name as his middle name.

Ulysses Simpson Grant's fellow West Point cadets would soon take note of his first two initials, U. S., and begin calling him both "United States" Grant and "Uncle Sam" Grant. Sam would stick. He didn't mind. He rather liked the simplicity of it. And it was a relief to have won such an innocuous moniker. He had long harbored a dread that someone during the course of his life would realize that the initials of his actual name—Hiram Ulysses Grant—spelled *hug*. He much preferred answering to Sam rather than to "Hug" Grant.

The Gravois crossing, well known to the young officer as a peaceful ford, had turned nightmarish—a slip-sliding descent into a crashing, growling, flotsam-choked torrent of muddy runoff. Often he had ridden from Jefferson Barracks—on the outskirts of Saint Louis—to White Haven, the plantation home of his former West Point roommate, Lieutenant Frederick Dent. It was a coincidental convenience that his former roommate should have been raised so near to the first duty station of both West Point graduates. Grant had often ridden with Dent the few miles from the barracks to the plantation to partake in the joys of family life, as his own kinfolk lived several days' travel to the northeast, in Ohio.

But this was not the Gravois which had so often beckoned his crossing on his visits. Usually ankle deep, it had now swollen beyond mathematical calculation. Yet Sam Grant felt his jaw tightening, for he knew he was going to swim it. He would not be denied this journey. He had realized, even as a boy, that he inexplicably possessed a peculiar superstition that now served to lure him into the raging death trap of Gravois Creek. The superstition was this: If ever he should start upon a road or a trail or a course of action, he could not and would not backtrack. Even should he accidentally take the wrong fork in a road, only to realize it a mile on, he would find some long way around to his destination rather than retreat even a single step.

In this case, it was not the superstition alone that drove him. Ahead, at White Haven Plantation, he had business to attend to—fearsome business of a most personal and urgent nature. To this purpose, he had dressed in his best uniform and had even had his boots polished. He would not turn back now, or ever, from his destiny.

Enough hesitation. He spurred a firm command to the mare to enter the swollen stream. She obeyed in spite of her fears, having absorbed the insistence of her rider. In fact, she plunged in, seeking the solace of the far bank. In a moment she was swimming, the muddy bottom having dropped beyond reach of her hooves.

As the horse sank deeper, Grant slipped from the saddle, but he held firm to reins and mane. Cool water soaked through his uniform and he smelled the odor of rotten debris. He had chosen his moment well, as he saw no rafts of driftwood near enough to tangle in a cinch or stirrup and rake him under. As the mare stroked powerfully, her nostrils spraying great blasts of breath and raindrops, the current carried them downstream and around a bend that provided a beneficial eddy and a lucky gravel bank, gently sloped. He scrambled atop the saddle as the mount found her footing.

The mare, winded, managed to climb the opposite bank to safety. Grant reined his mount to a stop to let her stand and breathe. He looked back at the thing he had traversed and shook his head. Now he turned his attention to himself. Silt and dead leaves covered his uniform. A number of twigs had tangled in the braids of his epaulets. Mud mocked the work of the bootblack back at the barracks.

No matter. He would borrow a suit of clothes. He waited, somewhat impatiently, for his horse to catch her breath. Suddenly, a fit of coughing doubled him over, causing him to wheeze uncontrollably. *Damn cough.* It had come over him at West Point, three years ago, and he had been unable to completely shake it since earning his commission as a second lieutenant.

Second Lieutenant Ulysses S. Grant. It still stunned him to think about it at times. Grant had never intended to become a soldier. His father had surprised him with the appointment to West Point, which he had arranged through his acquaintanceship with Congressman Hamer. The very idea of reporting to the military academy had struck young Grant with an almost overwhelming dread. Having received schooling of only the most rudimentary stripe in a one-room schoolhouse, Grant had feared he would disgrace his family through utter academic failure on the banks of the Hudson. He had been stunned, in fact, when he passed the entry exam quite handily.

It was as if by providence that his father's decision had led him to this place where he now stood, sopping wet on the west bank of the Gravois, facing a challenge as daunting as any he had ever encountered in his twenty-two years. He forced one last cough from his chest, spat, and spurred his mare.

Outside of White Haven, he saw an elderly slave known as Old Bob trudging up the road toward him, carrying an ash bucket, his hat pulled low against the drizzle.

"Hello, Bob!" he shouted from a distance, so as not to startle the old black man by riding up on him in a storm.

Old Bob raised his eyes from the muddy ground. "Sir," he answered. "My fire done burned down. I'm goin' to the neighbor's for a coal." He seemed shocked to find Grant riding on such a day.

This did not surprise Lieutenant Grant. Besides the weather, the slaves would be well aware that the Fourth Infantry had been ordered south to Louisiana some three weeks ago, en route to Texas to prepare for war with Mexico. Grant was a second lieutenant in the Fourth Infantry, and as such should have already departed. He had been left behind only because he had been away in Ohio on leave when the orders came down from Washington.

"Very well," Grant said. "Tell me, Bob, is Master John home?"

Bob nodded. "Yes, sir. I seen him on his porch no more than a hour ago."

"Good. I'll need to borrow a suit of his clothes."

Old Bob took in Grant's mount and the condition of his uniform. "Sir, if you don't mind me askin' . . ."

"Not at all."

"Did you swim that crick?"

"My mount did the swimming. I held fast to the pommel."

Bob chuckled, his eyes twinkling honestly. "You a brave man."

"Foolhardy is more the case. Oh, Bob . . . Is Miss Julia home, as well?"

Old Bob smiled and nodded. "Yes, sir, she is sure enough to home, all right."

Grant rode to John Dent's house, a small cabin located two miles from

White Haven's main plantation home and headquarters. He looped his reins around a hitching rail, stepped up on the porch, and used an iron knocker fixed on John's door. He waited. Then Sam spotted a bootjack on the porch and decided to muscle the wet leather from his feet, not wanting to track in any mud. He knocked again. Finally the door opened to reveal young John Dent, who burst into laughter at Grant's appearance.

"Did you fall in?"

"Plunged," Grant said.

John was about the same age as Sam Grant. Next to his former West Point roommate, Lieutenant Frederick Dent, John Dent was Grant's closest confidant at White Haven Plantation. Frederick had already gone south with the Fourth, so Grant was relieved to find John present to help him with the ominous task at hand.

"I'd ask what brings you here, but I think I know."

Grant nodded. "I need to borrow a shirt and a pair of tongs," he said, using army slang for trousers.

"Come on in," John ordered. "You're a bit taller than me, but my clothes will have to do."

An hour later, Sam Grant, now escorted by John Dent, arrived at White Haven's main plantation house. They tied their mounts outside the front gate and walked up to the large frame home, John Dent carrying Grant's sodden uniform.

Before John could reach the door, it opened to reveal the housemaid.

"Hello, Kitty," Grant said, removing his hat and tugging at his ill-fitting garments.

"Mr. Grant? I declare!"

"Kitty, take Sam's uniform and clean it up. He went swimming in the Gravois."

The slave woman glared at Grant incredulously as she took the damp clothing.

"Wait downstairs, Sam, and I'll announce your arrival to Julia."

Several minutes later, Grant found himself sitting uncomfortably in the dining room, his borrowed pant legs drawn halfway up his boot tops.

The shirtsleeves, too short to secure at the cuffs, were instead rolled up to his elbows. His wet hair was pressed to his scalp and combed back in waves that danced above his collar, dampening the fabric. At least he was wearing his own boots, which he had cleaned back at John's cabin. He held his hat in his lap.

He was more nervous now than when he had plunged his horse into Gravois Creek. He tried to rehearse something to say. Julia would be here any moment. How would he greet her? Where would he begin?

Back when Grant had first started coming to White Haven with Frederick, Julia had been away at a boarding school in Saint Louis. When she returned to her family home as an eighteen-year-old beauty, Sam's visits had taken on a new purpose. He secretly sought any chance to walk or ride alone with Julia and had found her company quite agreeable. She, too, seemed always to enjoy his company and conversation.

But, what if . . . , he thought. What if he had misinterpreted her feelings? Was he about to make a colossal fool of himself, sitting here in clothes too small for his frame, having risked his life in the Gravois for nothing? He put the thought aside. He would forge ahead. He would always forge ahead. Anyway, the timing was good. He would soon leave to catch up to his regiment. Should he find himself a brokenhearted soldier in the near future, he would not have to endure the looks of pity from the folks around White Haven, Jefferson Barracks, or Saint Louis.

"Sam?" she said, stepping into the room. Then she burst into laughter at the sight of him sitting in John's clothes. Her ringlets of brunette hair danced behind her ears, and she placed her hand over her full lips as she chuckled at his expense.

Sam rose to his feet, his face flushing. He smiled and shrugged. "I got soaked in the creek crossing. I borrowed a suit of clothes from your brother."

"I can see that." Her bright eyes twinkled in the lantern light of the dining room. "Sam, what are you doing here? I thought you had gone south to join the regiment."

"I couldn't go without . . . without saying . . . good-bye. Among other things." His heart was pounding, his stomach twisted in a knot.

She seemed to float toward him on a taffeta cloud. "Is there going to be war with Mexico?" she said, real worry kneading her brow. "The newspapers are full of all sorts of incongruous rumors."

"I don't know," Sam admitted. He could talk about this confidently, for he had thought it over. "It's likely, I'd say, given the public attitude in favor of immediate annexation for Texas."

"Oh, but Sam, why does it all hinge on Texas? I've heard it's covered with Indians and rattlesnakes, anyway."

"Mexico still claims Texas, or at least the part between the Nueces River and the Rio Grande del Norte. Mexico has long promised war if the Republic of Texas becomes a state."

Julia sighed. "There are so many politicians ranting over it this way and that. What is your opinion of what should be done?"

Sam shrugged one shoulder, a bit surprised at what seemed like Julia's sudden interest in politics. "I rather agree with Senator Benton. Texas should become a state someday, but only after the dispute over the border with Mexico is settled diplomatically rather than on the battlefield."

She nodded, as if in agreement. "Then there's the other question," she said.

Sam realized that she had caught him dancing around the other obvious issue. He had grown up in the free state of Ohio. Julia had been raised by a slave nanny. Would this matter to her? Could she love a northern man?

"You mean the slave issue," he said.

"Exactly. Will there be slavery in Texas, or not?"

"That should be settled prior to annexation, as well. Not to prevent war with Mexico but to preserve our own union."

"Perhaps cooler heads will prevail," she said, "and compromise. Perhaps we will avoid war, to say nothing of the possibility of war with England over the Oregon boundary line."

Grant bowed his head. "That is my fondest hope. But I am a soldier, Julia, and I will follow the orders of hotheads if I must."

She nodded. "Duty."

Just then, Julia's younger sister, Nellie, burst into the dining room.

"Lieutenant Grant!" she said flirtatiously. Then, noticing his garb, she burst into a fit of giggling. "How funny!" she declared.

"Oh, hush, Nellie," Julia said. She turned to Grant. "Lieutenant, how long do you expect to remain?"

Grant shrugged. "I am going to try to stay a week."

Nellie gasped. "Oh, my, Julia! Your dream! Last night!"

Julia placed her hand over her mouth as it opened in surprise.

"A dream?" Grant said.

"Heavens! Yes, I dreamt that you came to visit, wearing civilian clothes." She gestured at his apparel. "When I asked—in my dream—you said you would try to stay a week!"

"So, you've been dreaming of me?" Grant smiled.

"Well," she said, blushing, "I suppose I did last night."

Nellie seemed barely able to contain herself. "You said the very words Sister dreamed!"

Julia now looked rather befuddled. "You must excuse me, Sam. I must write this in my diary this very moment." She turned and disappeared toward her room, with Nellie in tow.

Abandoned in the dining room, Grant felt crestfallen. This was not going as he had planned. When would he have a moment alone with Julia?

"Oh, Sam," she said, stepping back into the doorway. "I must go to Saint Louis tomorrow to stand as bridesmaid for a friend. Will you ride with me?"

Grant came to attention. "Of course."

She smiled and disappeared.

Well, that's better, Grant thought. He and Julia had spent many hours together riding, talking, laughing. He could stay with John tonight and practice his proposal. He could wear his own military plumage. They would ride.

By the afternoon of the next day the sun had dried the landscape around White Haven Plantation. Sam Grant and Julia Dent took the new wagon road into Saint Louis on two good saddle horses. Grant approved of the road, which was covered with small pieces of stone broken off of larger rocks by hand. His military schooling made him appreciate how easily an army might move down such a modern roadway. He and Julia chatted incessantly as they rode the first few miles toward Saint Louis.

"Sam, I have so missed our rides together," Julia said. "It really didn't occur to me until you went away on leave to Ohio."

Grant saw his opening. "I felt the same way, Julia. In fact . . . I must tell you how I feel. Not just about riding together. But about *being* together."

"Oh?" Her perfectly plucked eyebrows rose inquisitively.

"Julia . . . since we met, I have enjoyed every moment in your presence."

She smiled innocently. "As have I, Sam."

"In a way I never experienced before."

"Really?"

They rode stirrup to stirrup, their mounts plodding lazily along. Grant rode to her left, as it was more comfortable for her to face that way on her sidesaddle.

"Yes . . . and . . . well, when I learned that the regiment had been ordered south, something came over me. A feeling hard to describe. I felt . . . I knew I had to act, however ill prepared to do so."

Her brow furrowed and she smirked with one corner of her mouth. "What are you talking about, Sam?"

His heart beat like the drums of war and his right hand trembled as he reached out to her. Enchanted, she pressed her fingertips into his palm.

"Julia, life without you would be insupportable. I must ask you . . . Will you . . ." He choked back the sudden urge to cough. "Will you wait for me to return, and . . . join fortunes with me?"

She looked puzzled. "What is it you mean by 'join fortunes'?"

Sam flushed. "We will have to wait. Only God knows how long. But, when I return, I would be imminently pleased if you would consent to joining me in matrimony." The urge to cough became excruciating, but he fought it off. "Julia, will you be married to me?"

She snapped her hand away as if stung. "Married? No!"

"No?" His hopes sank and he felt painfully foolish.

"No! But, Sam, I think it would be quite charming to be *engaged*."

His mind scrambled to make sense of her reply. "You would like to be engaged?"

"Yes."

"To me?"

She scoffed daintily and gestured to their surroundings. "Yes, to you. Whom other than you? Your horse?"

"Engaged to be married?"

"Engaged, yes. *Married?* No!"

He mulled this over, still holding that aggravating cough deep in his chest. This was a setback. But . . . at this point, engagement seemed like a logical step to his ultimate goal. He reached into the pocket of his tunic and found his class ring. "Then, will you wear my West Point ring?"

"Oh, no," she said. "I can't wear your ring. Everyone would notice. We can't tell anyone, Sam. What would father say?"

"But your father likes me."

"Sam, you know my whole family adores you. Even father. *You. A northerner.* But he has warned me that he would never consent to my marrying a soldier. So we can't tell anyone, can we?"

This was befuddling. Yet she was not completely rejecting his proposal. She was young, sheltered. She needed time to let the idea settle.

"Then we shall be engaged," he said, almost as a question.

She smiled and offered her hand back to him. "Lovely. Secretly engaged."

"Secretly," Sam said. "For now."

The wedding of Julia's schoolmate in Saint Louis was excruciatingly bothersome to Lieutenant Sam Grant. The unmarried young men in attendance swarmed around his secret fiancée in flocks.

The next few days, at White Haven, were better. Sam spent his nights at John's cabin. By day, he and Julia took long walks and longer rides. She even made mention of their engagement a few times, mostly to remind Sam that it had to remain a secret, especially from her father. This proved easy enough to accomplish, as the elder Colonel Frederick Dent spent most of his time overseeing the work of his slaves on his plantation.

When the day came to leave White Haven, Sam rode from John Dent's cabin to Julia's home to say good-bye and—hopefully—to reaffirm their engagement. The maid, Kitty, answered the door, invited Grant in, and summoned Julia. Sam greeted Julia just inside the front door.

"Lieutenant," she said. "You're going away?"

"I must."

"Kitty, you may leave us," Julia said.

The woman frowned protectively but withdrew toward the kitchen.

Julia's eyes brightened. "Come, Sam. Step out onto the piazza, where we can talk privately." She reached for his sleeve and tugged him toward the door.

As Julia pulled him outside, Grant spotted sister Nellie loitering about the bottom of the staircase, looking sheepishly away, caught in attempted eavesdropping. Julia led him out onto the broad porch and shut the door behind them.

Grant knew he had to seize the moment, before a sister or brother or servant or a coughing fit interrupted. "Have you thought more about our engagement?"

"Yes, I have. I have decided that it only makes sense for us to remain engaged. I mean, rather than be married."

"What do you mean?"

"You're going away, Lieutenant. Even if I thought it would be pleasant to be married, it's not as if you could take me with you. Our engagement is the most logical course of action—for now."

For now, he thought. That was slightly encouraging. By this time, the young officer understood that he would have to win this campaign by increments. He had already decided upon his next objective. He took his West Point ring from his pocket.

"In that case, you will want to wear my ring."

She smiled. "I will cherish it, Sam. And I will wear it when Papa is not looking."

He had slipped the class ring into her hand and had started leaning forward, bowing his face toward hers, when Kitty opened the door to the porch.

"Everything all right, Miss Julia?"

"Yes!" Julia sang. "Lieutenant Grant was just leaving. I'm seeing him off." She pulled the door closed, leaving them alone again. She looked up into Sam's eyes. "We must not tell anyone until you can return to speak to Papa."

Sam nodded and smiled. Facing Colonel Dent did not intimidate him half as much as the ordeal he had just survived. "And I will, as soon as I can secure another leave of absence."

She nodded and stepped invitingly close to him. "Are you going to kiss me before you leave?"

"Yes. But first I want to tell you . . ."

"Yes?"

"I want to tell you that I am in love with you, Julia. I love you."

Her smile spread like the northern lights. "And I love you, Sam Grant, my soldier."

His lips touched hers and he smelled sweet scents and felt wanton desires. He slipped his hand behind the small of her back and pulled her closer, emboldened by her lack of resistance. He heard the door latch rattle and broke away from her.

"I will write every day that I am able."

"I will reply to every letter I receive."

The door cracked open. "Miss Julia, it's time to dress for dinner," Kitty warned.

Julia rolled her eyes as her hand slipped from Sam's, taking the ring with her as they parted. "Good-bye, Sam," she said aloud, then mouthed the words *for now.*

The lieutenant grinned and stumbled down the stairway as he placed his hat on his head. He tripped down the walk and through the gate. Gathering his reins, he mounted his horse with the fluid ease of a boy born to ride. He returned Julia's wave and rode in the most buoyant of spirits back toward Jefferson Barracks.

SARAH CHILDRESS POLK

Sarah Polk turned the metal knob on the parlor lantern to lengthen the wick and cast more light on the nine-day-old copy of the *Baltimore Sun* that she held in her hand. She had already read the paper several times over, front to back, often using her quill pen to draw ink circles around tidbits of political developments that were already old news back East.

As she turned to page two, she came across a side story in the *Sun* that described how Samuel Morse's invention, called the "telegraph," was sending news of the 1844 Democratic Convention from Baltimore to Washington, DC, almost instantly, the copper wires having been strung between the two cities so Morse could demonstrate his new device. The inventor himself tapped out the news in his peculiar code, according to the *Sun*.

Oh, if only those wires could reach Columbia, Tennessee, she mused. Or even Nashville, four hours' ride away. She and James would have learned days ago what course their political future might take. But, as it was, news took nine or ten days to reach Nashville from the nation's capital—via railroad, riverboat, and horse-drawn hacks. She knew the Democrats had convened ten days ago, and she had hoped that they might receive news of the results earlier today. But the sun had set and no rider had come galloping from the Nashville post office. Another anxious night seemed in store for her and her husband, James K. Polk.

Sarah sighed and set the newspaper down beside her on the sofa. She looked for something else to do, her eyes scanning the interior of the small cottage—the tidy little refuge she and James enjoyed away from national and state political centers of Washington and Nashville. She hoped to find a chore in need of doing, but she had been cloistered inside the cottage for days and had attended to every task imaginable. The oiled pine floor was swept, the chinaware washed and dried, the bookshelf feather-dusted. Even the doilies for the morning coffee cups and saucers were in place on the colonial-style dining table.

She got up from the sofa in the parlor and peeked through the doorway into James's study. The chair at the desk was empty, so she stepped into the study to find James napping on the settee. He had spent most of his time for the past ten days in his study, day and night, writing at his desk, pacing back and forth, snatching fractions of a night's sleep on the settee.

She tiptoed to the desk, a creaking floorboard making her wince. James so needed rest. She did not want to wake him. Once again, she looked over the most recent notes he had made at his desk. She could see what he was doing. One pile of papers represented the issues of the day—Texas, Mexico, Oregon, England, the U.S. Treasury, tariffs—and also included James's recommendations for possible cabinet appointments, should the Democrats prevail in the upcoming election.

The second stack of documents involved the less attractive prospect of James hanging out a shingle as a private attorney in Columbia, should the news from the Baltimore convention disappoint them.

True to his nature, James K. Polk was preparing for all likely possibilities. Either he would be nominated as Martin Van Buren's vice presidential running mate or he would become a political castaway, relegated to a private law practice in Tennessee.

Sarah's calm, intelligent eyes drifted from the desk to her husband, asleep on the settee. She so loved that little man. He was such a good, decent man. She remembered meeting James here in Columbia, twenty-one years ago. He had just won his first election, taking a seat in the state legislature. He was a captain in the Tennessee militia. A devoted follower of General Andrew Jackson, James Knox Polk had followed the general's advice when Jackson suggested he marry Sarah Childress.

James had pursued her with relentless purpose and had won her over.

Though he was a man of slight proportions, she nonetheless admired his strong jaw, noble forehead, and serious nature. He had virtually no sense of humor, which she found ironically amusing. Because he thought of himself as merely average in terms of his intellect, James felt he had to treble the work and study of his political opponents. Sarah, however, considered him her equal in intelligence—an opinion she reserved for very few men.

After they married, it became clear that they would produce no children. So Sarah turned her nurturing instincts toward James's political career and made it grow, slow and steady, like a pampered son. After serving in the state legislature, James won a seat in the U.S. House of Representatives. He served seven terms, gradually earning better committee appointments and finally becoming Speaker of the House during Andrew Jackson's presidency. He became Jackson's right-hand man, always up to the task of carrying out Old Hickory's wishes. He even became known as "Young Hickory." While other politicians caroused, dined, and bandied their reputations about town in Washington, James worked. He learned the ruthless game of politics, forged only the strongest and safest of alliances, absorbed the public sentiment nationwide, manipulated the press, and cut backroom deals with a cunning that few power brokers could master.

Then, a wrinkle: due to the nation's economic troubles in the thirties, it became clear that the Whigs would win a majority in the House and that James would lose his position as Speaker. Rather than bear that indignity, he had chosen to run for governor of Tennessee. He had won, of course. But two years later he lost his bid for reelection, by a handful of votes, to a Whig challenger, a glib country lawyer who had yarned himself into office. James was no raconteur, but he ran again to regain the governorship, in forty-three, and again lost to the same Whig opponent, however narrowly.

Now James K. Polk, former Speaker of the House and governor of Tennessee, was a two-time loser—a dark horse gone astray. He and Sarah held to one hope that would revitalize his political career and spare him from a life of obscurity in private practice. They hoped to secure for James the Democratic nomination as the vice presidential candidate for the 1844 election. For this reason, James had stayed at home rather than traveling to Baltimore. By long-standing custom, it was considered unseemly for presidential and vice presidential hopefuls to attend their party's conventions. He had sent his agents, particularly the loyal Cave Johnson, to represent his interests and secure the nomination for him by any and all means necessary.

Sarah knew this decision had already been made, probably nine or ten days ago, at the convention in Baltimore. It was past time for prayer, which she and James had indulged in at length when the time had been appropriate. Now, all she could do was hope and wait for the mail to arrive from Baltimore.

If James was denied the nomination for VP, Sarah knew whom to blame. None other than Martin Van Buren. For months before the election, Van Buren had been favored for the nomination as the presidential candidate. And since James controlled the Tennessee delegates, he held leverage that would aid the New Yorker in his bid to regain the White House. He would deliver Tennessee to Van Buren, but only if Van Buren would promise to add him to the ticket as VP. Van Buren had seemed agreeable.

Then the issue of Texas statehood had arisen out of nowhere and Van Buren had, astonishingly, spoken out against annexation, placing his nomination in dire jeopardy. If Van Buren failed to get the nod to run for president, James had little chance of running as vice.

After that, things didn't look good for Van Buren or James. But one incident kept lingering in Sarah's ever-optimistic mind. James, along with some other influential Nashville-area Democratic strategists, had been summoned to the Hermitage to meet with the great General Jackson. Old Hickory's health had declined in recent years, but he still wielded more political power than any living American. Sarah remembered James returning from that meeting and telling her, in his own words, how the conversation had progressed:

"Van Buren has committed political suicide," the general had announced. "We can't win the White House by opposing Texas annexation."

"Let us look at the alternatives," James had suggested.

This they had tried, but Jackson had found a flaw of some sort with each likely presidential candidate in the party, until the field seemed exhausted. Then the old warhorse had looked James in the eye.

"You would be the best candidate for the job," he had announced.

"Who?" James had replied.

"You."

"Me?"

"Yes. We'd choose a northern running mate to fill out the ticket—hold the party and the Union together."

James had chuckled nervously about this when he told Sarah, and James rarely chuckled.

"Why are you laughing?" she had asked. "It makes perfect sense."

"General Jackson wasn't serious. James Polk is not exactly a household name. It's not my time yet, Sarah. Not yet. Vice president is the next rung on the ladder. Then we shall see."

All this had swirled in her head for nine days now, making her feel downright dizzy. She knew she should lie down and attempt to sleep, so she kissed James's forehead and went to the parlor to recline on the sofa. Curling up with an embroidered pillow under her head, she felt as if she could very possibly fall into deep and much-needed slumber. She was almost there when she heard the faint ring of spurs on the stone landing outside.

The polite rapping of a knuckle on the door made her spring to her feet, hoping she could get there before another knock woke James. Opening the door, she found a young man holding a package wrapped in twine. His horse, well lathered with white sweat, stood in the street, illuminated by the lantern light from the open door. The young man appeared haggard from a hard ride, yet he gallantly swept his hat from his head.

"Good evening, Mrs. Polk. I'm sorry to disturb you at this hour, but I've come from the post office in Nashville." He handed her the package.

"Thank you," she said. "Would you like some tea? Coffee? You may stay the night if you wish."

"Thank you, ma'am, but I have to ride back. There is much to do."

She placed her palm on the package, as if to divine the essence of its contents. "Do you know the outcome of the convention?"

He forced a smile. She couldn't tell if it was an expression of pity, or fatigue.

"It's not my place to say, ma'am. Good evening, and good luck."

After he turned away, she closed the door and carried the package into James's study. She would cut the twine and open the package first, then wake him. She didn't intend to open the letters from his political operatives, of course, but she could prioritize them for him. After she snipped the string with her sewing scissors and pulled back the thick brown wrapping paper around the bundle, she could not help reading the headline on the Washington *Globe*.

Sarah actually gasped. She read the headline again, astonished. Then she quickly read the first few paragraphs of the article.

"Oh, my," she whispered. She dragged James's chair over to the settee where he slept, indifferent to the noise the chair legs made scuffing across the floor. She saw him begin to stir as she sat in the chair next to him. Gently, she shook his shoulder.

"James . . . The news has arrived from Nashville . . . about the convention . . ."

His eyes opened and he drew in a deep breath that seemed to lift him upright into a seated pose. "It's about time," he said, rubbing his eyes.

"I didn't open the letters, of course, but I couldn't help noticing the headline of the *Globe*."

"Is it good news, or bad?"

"Brace yourself, James. It's not what we hoped for."

His shoulders slumped, but his eyes searched her face for clues. "Out with it, Sarah. I've waited long enough."

"You're not going to run for vice president, James. But . . . you could very well become the next president of the United States of America." She held the newspaper up in front of his face.

He read aloud, slowly: "*Democrats unanimously nominate James K. Polk for White House bid.*"

She tried to keep herself from absolutely gushing. "Congratulations, James. What do you think?"

"I think . . ." He rubbed his face and raked his graying hair back over his head. "I think the Lord sometimes humbles us by granting us more than that for which we have prayed."

She thought it better not to tell him that this was *exactly* the outcome for which she had prayed.

He got up and kissed her on the cheek. Then he stepped over to his desk and opened the lowest drawer. He picked up from the desktop the stack of documents that represented the scenario of a private law practice. This he shoved deep into the open drawer before kicking it closed with his foot.

"Now," he said, turning back to her. He smiled slightly. "Let us read that article and try to determine how in the *world* James K. Polk ever became the Democratic nominee for president of the United States of America."

JOHN RILEY

John Riley left his boardinghouse at the end of Market Street and strode east on Huron toward Charles O'Malley's trading post. Feeling the cold, he turned up the collar of his coat and tugged on the front of his Donegal tweed cap. He left the coat unbuttoned to reveal the green wool sweater that, along with the tweed cap, proudly identified him as, by the grace of God, *Irish*.

His breath steamed from his lungs on the cold north wind that whipped across Mackinac Island from Lake Huron. The weather here was not so unlike his boyhood home of Galway, on the western coast of the Emerald Isle. Here, hundreds of Irishmen like himself had come to find work, their familiar brogues a comfort to his ears. Yet he felt so far away from his home, his dear wife, and his beloved son.

Saturday was payday for Charles O'Malley's employees and, as such, a day to gather in the trading post for conversation and drink. Riley had been here over a year, working on the docks for O'Malley. He had quickly risen from a common stevedore to a foreman but had yet to save enough money to bring his family across the ocean. At four dollars a month, the wherewithal proved slow to accumulate. It would take a fair sum to sail his kin here. He refused to book passage for them in a coffin ship like the one he had sailed on, where immigrants were crammed together in the dank hold and not even allowed a breath of fresh air above decks for the duration of the voyage. He would not subject his lad and his wife to such rigors. They would sail on a proper vessel when their time came to follow him.

As he walked on in long strides, his boots pounding the boardwalk under his 210 pounds of muscular bulk, he glanced out toward Haldimand Bay and noticed the domelike wigwams along the lakeshore on Windermere Point. These were the birch bark homes of the Ojibway Indians, who had lived here for untold generations before Frenchmen and Englishmen invaded their paradise. Riley could empathize with a people dispossessed of their homeland. As long as he could remember, his Ireland had suffered the indignities of living under English rule. He dreamed of returning someday to run the bloody bastards into the sea and reclaim the Ould Sod for himself and his people.

Like many an Irish lad who hated England, Riley had nonetheless volunteered to serve in the British Army. How better to someday defeat them than to infiltrate their ranks and learn their strategies? With the Brits, he had fought as a regimental pioneer against Afghan tribesmen from Kabul to Jellalabad, acquiring the rank of sergeant major. He had also served as an artilleryman and knew his way around cannon.

Returning to Ireland, he found his home in the grips of a deepening famine and struck out for America to find better prospects for his family until the day came when they could return to drive the hated English from the Emerald Isle. His very reason for immigrating here, to Mackinac Island, Michigan—instead of to Boston or New York—was to position himself nearer to the despised English troops in British Columbia, as war between America and Canada was likely, over the boundary dispute out West.

As he marched on toward O'Malley's trading post, past the fish markets at the head of the docks, he saw an American shop owner weaving toward him, already Saturday night drunk at four in the afternoon. The man stumbled into Riley's shoulder and bounced off of him, into a butcher shop wall.

"Hey, watch where you're goin', you big mick!" the man said, the words slurring all over the American accent.

Riley stopped and turned to face the drunkard. "The name's John," he said.

The man's eyes widened, then blinked nervously. "Oh, John Riley. I didn't recognize you with your collar up."

"You don't own the whole boardwalk," Riley grumbled.

"Of course not. My apologies. Good day to you, Riley." The sorry sot turned and staggered on his way.

Riley felt his fists unclench as he, too, resumed his walk. Known as a brawler with a short fuse, he enjoyed his reputation as a man not to be crossed. He stepped off of the boardwalk into the mud of Fort Street, wending his way between ox-drawn carts, mule teams, and a few fellow pedestrians. He glanced up the steep street at Fort Mackinac, perched on the rocky bluff, now garrisoned by Company K of the Fifth Infantry, U.S. Army.

More than once he had considered walking into the fort to enlist. A private could earn seven dollars a month. At that wage, he could save enough to sail his family to America by the time his five-year enlistment had ended. And the army was recruiting. War fever was in the air, with the presidential election at stake. In fact, the elections had already occurred, a month ago, but the final results had yet to reach John Riley's ears here on this frontier island in Lake Huron.

He strode on between the sloping vegetable gardens of Fort Mackinac to his left and the docks lined with fishing boats to his right. He spent six days a week on those docks, making sure O'Malley's goods got loaded onto the right steamers. The bulk of the trade was in hundred-pound barrels of salted whitefish bound for Chicago, Detroit, Cleveland, and Buffalo. Additional traffic in jugs of maple sugar, bales of furs, and kegs of fish oil had to be sorted and shipped on the appropriate vessels. He also had to receive and sign for merchandise imported for O'Malley's retail enterprises on the island, including everything from cloth to ink, potatoes to candles, French brandy to oriental spices. As a dock foreman, he bossed two dozen men, but he often bent his own back to loading and unloading alongside his subordinates.

Charging on down the boardwalk through the cold, Riley came to the red brick blockhouse that served as his boss's trading post. He glanced up at the gold letters on the emerald background of a sign that read "Charles O'Malley." He grabbed the door handle and looked through the glazed glass windows to find the interior jammed with fellow Irishmen.

The moment he opened the door, an unusually boisterous hum of voices—even for a Saturday—assaulted his ears. Men sang, yelled, laughed.

A young stevedore who worked under Riley removed his dudeen pipe from his mouth. "Top of the day, John," he said, a whiskey slur on his smoky breath.

Riley nodded and watched the crowd part for him as he made his way to the sales counter where O'Malley typically sat on Saturdays, conversing with his countrymen about Old Ireland, world affairs, and new American developments. Behind the counter, Riley admired the shelves stacked with bolts of cloth, reams of paper, tins of smoked oysters, kegs of gunpowder, bundles of fishnets, bars of lead . . . He removed his coat, breathed in the tobacco smoke, and pulled his tweed cap from his head.

"If it isn't John Riley!" O'Malley said, his voice booming above the hum of voices in the trading house. "Pour the man a cup of *potcheen*!" The Irish boss of Mackinac Island, O'Malley wielded substantial authority on the docks and remained ever partial to his kinsmen from Ireland. He was a few years older than Riley, who was himself a well-traveled twenty-seven.

"To Ireland!" Riley said, taking a sip of the homebrew whiskey handed to him by a compatriot. He did not drink much, but he knew how to ingratiate himself among his countrymen.

"*Erin go Bragh*," O'Malley replied, punctuating his toast with a swallow. He then handed Riley a stack of gold and silver coins he had counted out for the foreman's weekly wages.

As he dropped the specie into his pocket, Riley signed for his pay, his ornate script standing out among the rude *X*s slashed on the ledger by most of his colleagues.

"Pray, what's all the fuss about in here today?" Riley asked, returning the quill pen to the inkwell.

O'Malley slapped a newspaper down on the desk in front of him and pointed to the top of the left column. "You can read the news for yourself, John, unlike these unlettered *spalpeens* around you!" He waved his hand in fake derision at the men surrounding him, all of whom took the good-natured jest as intended. Only an Irishman could get away with calling another Irishman a *spalpeen* without causing a fistfight. Many of these men had, indeed, worked as itinerant farmhands back in Ireland, as the term suggested.

John Riley glanced at the newspaper: the *Daily National Intelligencer*, the mouthpiece of the Whig Party, published in Washington, DC. He noted the paper's date: November 26, 1844—just eleven days ago. This issue of the *Intelligencer* must have sailed on the swiftest of steamers through lakes Erie and Huron.

His eyes moved down to the first column, where he scanned through the verbose journalistic styling for the crux of the news held therein: *"It is now certain that at the late elections . . . electors have been chosen of whom a majority will cast their votes . . . so that, in effect, JAMES K. POLK, of Tennessee, has been chosen President . . . The disappointment and pain with which this result has filled our breasts . . ."*

The news, however disappointing to the defeated Whigs, stirred the fighting blood down in John Riley's viscera. So this was the reason for the commotion in O'Malley's trading post today. Polk, against all odds, had won the election.

Though still an immigrant who had no vote, Riley had followed the campaign closely. He thought back on the Whig's flippant campaign slogan, "Who is James K. Polk?" Indeed, most Americans he had overheard discussing the race early on could not answer that question. But Henry Clay, the Whig candidate and founder of the Whig Party, was a well-known politician and a household name. His election was supposed to have been inevitable. Apparently the Whigs had underestimated James K. Polk, the Democrats, and the attitude of the citizenry.

Polk had run on expansion for the country—into Oregon and Texas. Rumor held that he wanted California, too. However bold and arrogant his Manifest Destiny platform, it seemed a narrow majority of American voters agreed with Polk on his expansionist schemes.

It was Polk's campaign cry that had first gained Riley's approval. "Fifty-four forty or fight!"—a reference to the border dispute between the United States and England, out West in the Oregon country. In his campaign, Polk had demanded that the Brits give up their claims in the West as far north as 54 degrees and 40 minutes of latitude—all the way up to the southern tip of the Russian colony of Alaska. The Brits wouldn't go along with that, of course, but Polk was threatening to take the soil by force if elected.

War with the bloody British!

Now that the dark horse, James K. Polk, had pulled off the upset, war with England was a virtual certainty. *Imagine!* Having once served *in* the queen's army, now taking up arms *against* the bastards!

"What are you thinking, John?" said O'Malley. "That menacing look on your face would frighten the devil himself."

The men around him fell into silence, awaiting his reply.

"Polk has won the election. There will be war with England out West in the Oregon country. I'm thinking the time is nigh for John Riley to kill some bloody Brits. I'll swear to Saint Patrick that I will attain my former rank of sergeant major, or die in the trying!"

A cheer of approval roared around him.

"As God is my witness, John Riley, if you join the army, I'll join with you!" said a red-haired youth standing at Riley's elbow.

"I'm not your recruiter, lad. Choose your own path. If you follow me, you'll march straight into the jaws of bloody hell, where a man is more likely to get buried than brevetted."

"I'll march with you!" the youth insisted.

"If we're to fight the Brits, I'll enlist as well!" another man promised.

"Careful," O'Malley said. "There's another war brewing down on the Texas border. What's to keep the U.S. Army from sending you to Mexico instead of Oregon?"

Now the whole room quieted as illiterate dockworkers listened to O'Malley and Riley—perhaps the only two men present who could read a newspaper.

"What threat is Mexico, compared to the almighty British Empire?" Riley argued. "There will be plenty of troops from the southern states to march to the Mexican border. The regulars in the north will stay in the north to fight the Brits. It's only logical."

"Military logic?" O'Malley said.

"We can almost see the bloody redcoats across Lake Huron from here," Riley said, jutting a finger northward. "What sense would it make to march men from here to Mexico when the real threat is just across Saint Mary's River in Canada?"

"What makes you so sure the Americans will go to war with England?"

"Polk's promise: 'Fifty-four forty or fight!'"

O'Malley scoffed. "The words of a politician carry the weight of a gnat! If England offers a reasonable compromise, Polk will take it. You don't really think he wants to fight two wars at once, do you?"

"War over Oregon is more likely. The Mexicans can be bought. You've heard the rumors that Mexico wants to sell her northern frontier."

"Bah!" O'Malley exclaimed. "Mexico won't sell anything without a fight."

Riley shook his head. "Mexico is racked with debt. She is more likely to treat with the United States than England. The war will be here, in the north."

O'Malley sighed. "If you're wrong, you'll end up in Mexico, fighting your fellow Catholic brothers. Don't rush to enlist, John. Wait and watch things develop."

Riley pounded his fist on the bar. "The wheel has been set in motion. I'm damned if I can stop it now. I'll not miss a chance to take a shot at a redcoat!"

O'Malley tossed back a shot of *potcheen*, slammed down his cup, and squared his shoulders to Riley and the whole crowd in his store.

"Service in the U.S. Army is no stroll across the glade for an Irishman. Here on Mackinac, you lads live on a frontier island where the Americans have not yet learned to hate your guts. You've heard of this movement spreading across the states, haven't you? The so-called nativist movement? It's anti-immigrant, anti-Catholic, and especially anti-Irish. It's infected the army, too. You're likely to be serving under nativist officers who would just as soon give you fifty lashes as return your salute."

Riley set his jaw and arched his back. "I survived service in the British Army. The Americans can do no worse."

"They'll march your Irish arse straight to the front lines."

"I am well aware of the dangers. I, too, am a danger to any bloody British redcoat within reach of my rifle, my sword, or my bare hands!" He lifted his half-full cup of *potcheen*, eliciting huzzahs and cheers from his fellow sons of the Emerald Isle.

Charles O'Malley shook his head and smiled, as if to say he had tried. "You're a hard man, Riley. I suppose you've got reason." He yanked the jug of homemade whiskey from the arm of a teamster and poured himself another drink.

SARAH BOWMAN

The skiff caught a small wave that lifted it and sped it toward the broad, sandy beachhead off the bow. Sarah Bowman, army laundress, sat at the stern, looking forward, anxious to get her feet on solid earth again.

The oarsman facing her was a rough frontier sort. He wore a slouched Mexican palm leaf sombrero, tattered clothing, and holey leather shoes. His beard grew long, dark, and unkempt. He rowed much too languidly for Sarah's approval.

Ahead, on higher ground above the gentle slope of the beach, she saw rows and rows of tents erected by infantrymen who had arrived before her. Having seen her share of army camps, she guessed that a thousand men had arrived here on the Texas shore. She knew a couple of thousand more were likely to follow. Beyond the tents, she made out a formation of soldiers marching at drill on what must have been designated as a parade ground.

"Put your back into it, sailor," she said to the oarsman, the only other soul aboard the small vessel, which was otherwise filled with her laundry cauldrons, cooking vessels, and personal effects.

"I ain't no sailor," the man said. "I just own a boat, that's all. And I don't take no orders, especially from no woman."

The skiff had stalled in a swell. Facing the man with the oars, she drilled his eyes with hers beneath the ruffles of her bonnet, though she had to blink at the afternoon sun glaring down, glimmering off the waves.

She was bigger than the boatman, but then again, Sarah was bigger than most men. Standing just over six feet tall, she weighed 195 pounds, according to the Fairbanks scale she had stepped on a couple of years ago at a cotton gin.

"Well, ain't you some kind of Blackbeard," she said to her shipmate. "Let's dance."

"Huh?"

She grabbed him by the shirt and, using the rocking of the boat to her advantage, lifted him from his seat amidships.

"Hey!" he protested, losing hold of his oars.

Whirling her weight forward in a counterclockwise circle, she deposited the smart-mouthed boat owner where she herself had recently sat at the stern and in turn took his vacated seat between the oarlocks.

"Now, let me show you how to row a boat, you lazy scalawag."

Shocked at his sudden ouster, the deposed captain quickly scanned the beach and looked over his shoulders for other skiffs, hoping no one had seen a woman so easily unseat him aboard his own vessel.

"Don't get her turned sidewise or she'll flip," he warned, trying to recoup some dignity.

"Just sit still and watch, Commodore." She smiled at the befuddled look on his face.

"I ain't no commodore."

Looking aft now, beyond the boatman and back out to sea, Sarah took in some two dozen dories and skiffs ferrying soldiers and supplies to the beach. Farther out, the smoke plume of a shallow-draft steamer marked the sky—the very vessel that had carried her from the sailing ship, anchored offshore, to Blackbeard's skiff for her landing.

Taking hold of the oars, she thought about her voyage, happy to have it nearing an end. After leaving New Orleans, the three-master had sailed for two solid days and nights, beyond sight of land, across water a shade of purplish blue the likes of which Sarah had never seen. Fish with wings would leap amazingly from the prow of the vessel and actually fly farther than a bobwhite quail.

Many if not most of the soldiers on the sailing ship had become seasick from the first day, vomiting uncontrollably over the gunwales, day and night. Her husband, Sergeant John Bowman, had been one of them. Sarah, somehow unaffected by the rolling and tossing of the ship, had spent hours carrying freshwater to the debilitated men, some of whom slept on the decks, curled up like sick little puppies.

The oceangoing vessel had anchored in deeper waters, outside the bay, for the pass leading into Corpus Christi Bay was too shallow for big ships. The seasick men were sent ashore first. Sarah's husband had been too ill to say good-bye to her. Off-loading men, wagons, artillery, weapons, ammunition, tents, tools, and her own laundry cauldrons from the ship to the smaller steamer in roiling seas had been accomplished, in spite of the difficulty and peril, by lowering one load at a time from a boom on the ship to the deck of the steamer. Shifting her goods from the small steamer to Commodore Blackbeard's skiff had been somewhat easier, in the protected waters of the bay.

Glad to be looking back on all this, she now gazed beyond the scowl of the boatman and caught sight of the next wave swelling up behind the small craft. She dipped the oars deep and pulled hard, getting a head start on the rising wave curling shoreward. Pulling again, and again, she caught the wave at the moment it broke, sending the skiff skidding up onto the sandy beach, white sea foam frothing her landing like a welcoming carpet.

"There," she announced with satisfaction, shipping the oars. "*That's* how you beach a skiff, Blackbeard." She hiked her skirt up and stepped over the starboard gunwale, finally setting foot on terra firma, albeit knee-deep in surf.

"The name's Baker, and you caught a lucky wave, that's all."

"My husband always says, 'Give a man luck, and shit'll do for brains.'" She trudged out of the bay waters, oddly feeling as if she were still riding on a rocking vessel. Looking between her feet, she saw a perfect sand dollar, which she picked up and studied with a smile.

"Husband?" Baker said, as if shocked.

"My husband's a soldier. Do you know that I make more money than he does, doing laundry and cooking for the officers?"

"Do tell? I guess that makes him a lucky man. Give a man luck . . ."

"And shit'll do for brains." She laughed. "You're all right, Baker. My name's Sarah, by the way." She shook his hand.

"Pleasure," he growled.

"Help me unload my things. I want to get my camp set up and wood gathered before dark."

"Yes, Your Highness," he muttered, grabbing a large laundry cauldron and lugging it out of his skiff.

"How come you own a rowboat in a place like this?" Sarah asked, carrying a heavy trunk up above the tide as cool water lapped around her ankles.

"I'm a smuggler," he announced. "Or was, before I hired on with the army to land men and supplies ashore."

Sarah raised her eyebrows with approval. The life of a smuggler somehow appealed to her. "What all do you smuggle?"

"Tobacco mostly."

"To who?"

"Well, the Mexicans, Your Majesty. Who do you think?"

"Don't they grow their own tobacco in Mexico?"

"Yeah, but the government buys it all and taxes the hell out of it. We smuggle in American tobacco here, at Kinney's Ranch, and sell it to Mexican mule skinners a lot cheaper than they can buy it from their own government."

She added a couple of Dutch ovens to her growing pile of equipage on the beach, watched a brown pelican dive for a fish near the shore. "Well, you're a damn fine pirate, Mr. Baker. I'm impressed. You know, you ain't bad lookin', either, aside from that missin' tooth. If I wasn't already married . . ."

He looked up at her and chuckled. "Don't start that kind of talk. My senorita would cut your throat, if she should reach it."

"If she couldn't, she'd have to settle for yours."

"That's what worries me. A man's got to sleep sometime."

She laughed with the boatman and finished unloading her things. By now, a number of soldiers had noticed that a woman had come ashore and were standing at a distance, leering, talking, and laughing. She expected no less. Most of them would recognize her from Fort Jessup or Jefferson Barracks. Sarah tended to stand out in a crowd of men or women or both.

A gull swept over her head, causing a small crab to scuttle up under her cooking equipage. She scanned the bay, the dunes, the orderly rows of army tents, trying to get her bearings on this unfamiliar shore.

"How far are we from the Nueces River here, Mr. Baker?"

"Look here," he said, taking her by the arm, and pointing to the north.

"See that cut around the bluff? That's Nueces Bay. The Nueces River empties into it. Mind the gators up in there, you hear?"

She ignored his warning and his rough palm caressing her upper arm through her sleeve of calico. You couldn't blame a man at this lonely smuggler's outpost for a little polite groping. "You mean this camp is south of the Nueces?"

"That we are."

"You mean, this is it? This sorry, sunburnt patch of sand and cactus? This is what the Mexicans are willing to face the U.S. Army for?"

"Loco, ain't it? They call it no-man's-land, but seems like every son of a bitch in the world wants it."

"Explain something to me, Baker. They say Mexico still claims all of Texas."

"Yeah, that's what they say."

"But, at the same time, they say Mexico only claims this strip between the Nueces and Rio Grande."

"Yeah, they make that claim, too. The Nueces River was the border between the old states of Tejas and Tamaulipas. So the Mexicans claim it's always been the southern border of Texas, since the Spanish times."

"So what are they claiming? Just the Nueces Strip, or the whole damn state?"

Baker shrugged. "They make both claims. Whoever the hell 'they' are."

"How can they claim all of it with one breath and just part of it with the next?"

"Don't try to make no sense of it. Nobody's got control of anything south of the border, wherever the hell the border even is."

She turned her face seaward so the wind would blow back the strand of wavy auburn hair that had escaped her bonnet. "Well, if anybody can settle it, Old Rough and Ready is the man for the job."

"Who?"

"General Zachary Taylor, that's who."

"Oh. Well, I wish he'd get on with it so I can get back to the simple life of a smuggler. This army contract is hard work. I'd better get back at it, Your Majesty, Queen Sarah." He winked at her and flashed his gapped row of crooked teeth.

"See you around camp, Baker." She returned his smile.

After Baker shoved off, she turned and scanned the beach. She saw soldiers swimming naked down the way. Others tried fishing with improvised tackle. She spotted a cluster of strong young men not far away, staring at her as if she were some kind of mermaid washed ashore.

"Hey, boys!" she yelled, her voice carrying over the Gulf breeze and the rush of the surf. "Don't just stand there; get your rear ends down here and help a lady ashore!"

By the time the sun stood just above the rim of the high sand bluff to the west, Sarah had located her husband's regiment—the Seventh Infantry—and had chosen her campsite near the officers' tents. She had set up her laundry cauldrons and cooking vessels and had cajoled some loitering soldiers into gathering firewood for her.

She was driving the last of her tent stakes deep into the Corpus Christi sand when she looked up and noticed a rider approaching on a crow-hopping horse. She recognized the horseman as Lieutenant Grant of the Fourth Infantry. She considered him one of the more likable young officers from Jefferson Barracks and had heard a rumor that Grant had become engaged to his best friend's little sister. This "army of observation," as President Polk had labeled it, was a close-knit community.

She admired the way Grant stayed with the Texas mustang, which he must have just purchased and begun to train, judging from the antics of the mount. "Stay with him, Lieutenant!" she cheered, though the horse bucked precariously close to her camp.

She had noticed, over the months, that young Grant's health had improved. He had looked like a scarecrow back in Missouri. Then, at Camp Salubrity in Louisiana, he had begun to gain weight and to look more like a man than a gangling boy.

Grant succeeded in getting the pony stopped without landing on the sand. He loosened his reins to let the beast relax.

"That's some nice trick ridin', Lieutenant!"

The officer tipped his hat. "Thank you, Mrs. . . ."

"Bowman. Sarah Bowman."

"Just arriving?"

"Just this afternoon, sir."

"Make sure to check that tent for rattlesnakes before you crawl into it."

"Any rattler I catch will make fine stew, sir."

He smiled. "No wonder the officers of the Seventh look so well fed."

She laughed with him. "Sir, if a lady needed to buy some supplies, where do you think she might find the nearest store?"

"Ma'am, I am sorry to report to you that there is no marketplace within a hundred and fifty miles of here." He pointed to some shacks up on the bluff. "The village of Corpus Christi numbers only a hundred souls, and everything edible there has already been purchased. But we have supply wagons coming from Austin soon. And you might ask around about fish or venison to be had."

"I will do that, Lieutenant. One more question, if you please, before you get on with your pleasure riding."

"Yes, ma'am?"

"Would you be so kind as to direct me to the infirmary? I'll be needing to look after my husband."

He pointed southward. "All the way to the end there, Mrs. Bowman."

"Thank you, sir."

The lieutenant touched the pony's flanks with spurs and the green mount moved off sideways toward the dunes. Oh, well, she thought, if he got bucked off, at least he'd have soft sand to break his fall.

Sarah started walking south between the beach and the rows of tents. She noticed her shadow on the smooth, wet sand to her left. It stretched across ten feet of ground, due to the low angle of the sun. She hadn't seen a mirror in days, but she admired her own hourglass figure moving gracefully over the lightning whelks and patches of seaweed washed ashore. She might be a large woman, but she was all woman, by God. Even now, at thirty-two years old, her figure looked so shapely and lean that a man might think she wore a corset.

She glanced to her right to see the reddish ember of the sun melting into the bluff. The fife and drum players, up ahead, found a terse ending to their march, and Sarah heard a sergeant shouting orders for the men to form a hollow square from their columns. She stopped to watch the maneuver as the snares resumed the marching beat. Always impressive on any parade ground, the troop movements seemed even more magnificent here on this desolate beach. The companies moved in swinging gates and shifting blocks to form the defensive square. Within a minute, the soldiers stood two ranks deep, shoulder to shoulder, with bayonets jutting outward from the hollow formation.

The regimental commander yelled an order, dismissing the men on the parade ground. Sarah smiled. She loved military life.

Then she saw him. General Taylor! Old Rough and Ready himself! Though aging and portly, sitting atop his white horse, he still made her heartbeat quicken. There was something very attractive about a man who wielded that much power. He had been watching the men at drill, and now he was joshing with them as they walked near Old Whitey, his horse.

Turning her attention back to the beach, Sarah noticed a party of men ahead, lugging a long, rectangular seine net ashore. When they lifted it laboriously above the water, she was astonished to see dozens of fish flopping crazily in the net—each big enough to make a meal for a man. In addition to the larger creatures were hundreds of small baitfish an angler might skewer on a hook.

"Hey, where'd you boys get that net?" she said, walking past.

"Bought it in New Orleans," the man nearest to her said.

"Them fish for sale?"

"You can take as many as you want," the soldier said, smiling.

"Leave me half a dozen right there and I'll gather them up on my walk back."

The private nodded and politely touched the bill of his campaign cap.

Striding on down the shoreline, she noticed a few buildings standing up on the bluff to her right, some distance from the houses of Corpus Christi that Lieutenant Grant had pointed out. That must be the place Baker had told her about, she reasoned. Kinney's Ranch, the smuggling outpost for American tobacco.

The camp she passed before reaching the infirmary was Major Ringgold's unit, Company C, Third Artillery. She hoped to get a glimpse of the dashing Ringgold. He was something. He spoke French and rode fast horses. Ringgold had revolutionized artillery tactics, even writing a new army manual about it that was in use at West Point. He had traveled abroad, learning the best strategies from U.S. allies overseas and then improving upon them. His guns were called "flying artillery." Unlike the old foot artillery, his gunners all rode horses when on the move, giving the batteries never-before-seen mobility. His textbook theories had not been proven in battle yet, but they certainly looked impressive enough at drill.

Finally Sarah approached the tents of the infirmary, where she heard the coughs and moans of men sickened by the typical camp maladies—

diarrhea, measles, scarlet fever. It was peculiar, she thought, how some individuals—like Lieutenant Grant, and herself, for that matter—seemed to thrive on the hardships of marching, sailing, and camping, while others—like her poor husband—suffered miserably under the same conditions.

She approached a surgeon and asked after her husband, Sergeant John Bowman.

The beleaguered sawbones swept his arm in a gesture toward the pallets of men laid up under tarpaulins propped above them for shade. "You'd know him better than me, ma'am."

So Sarah started strolling among the men, recognizing John's sallow face after searching for a few minutes. She knelt over his sleeping frame and touched his stubbled face, unshaven for several days now. He opened his eyes and focused on her.

"Hello, Sarah," he said in a croak.

"Are you all right, John?"

He coughed, then caught his breath. He looked gaunt and weak. "I will be, as soon as I get off this goddamned boat."

"You're off the boat, John. You're on land now."

"How come I still feel the boat rockin'?"

"It'll pass, husband. Are you hungry?"

He shook his head. "Can't hold nothin' down. Not even a drink of water." His eyes closed, and he seemed to be slipping back to sleep.

"I'll be back tomorrow morning," she promised. "And I will shave that beard of yours for you, and bring you something you can eat."

"Thank you, Sarah." His eyelids fluttered but did not open.

She kissed her husband's feverish brow as he fell asleep. Sarah left the infirmary and trudged back up the beach. She worried about John, feeling somewhat dejected. She decided to thank the Lord for her own health and to pray for the best for her husband.

Passing Ringgold's flying artillery, she noticed some commotion around one of the six-pounders and realized that the men had found an unusually large rattlesnake coiled under the gun. They were daintily prodding at it with bayonets and other implements. Trotting over to the artillery piece, Sarah noticed a broken oar that someone had thrown on the woodpile. She grabbed it and ran at the circle of men.

"Step aside, boys!" she ordered. She charged between two soldiers and used the splintered end of the oar to flip the huge diamondback out from under the gun, its tail buzzing a warning, causing men to scatter. Whirling the oar around, she used the blunt end to whack the snake over the head three times, silencing the vibrations of the tail. Pinning the fanged end of the animal to the sand, she deftly reached down and grabbed the viper close behind its battered and bloody head. She lifted it triumphantly, letting the six-foot length of the snake dangle beneath her fist.

"I don't know what you boys are havin' for supper," she said, "but my boys are dining on fish and rattler stew!" She marched back on up the beach, taking her broken oar with her in case she encountered any other reptiles venturing out for the evening.

Brigadier General
ZACHARY TAYLOR

Corpus Christi Beach, Texas
September 29, 1845

His men called him "Old Rough and Ready." He was feeling more of the former and less of the latter just now, hunched over the portable writing desk in his command tent. At least the weather had cooled enough that soldiers could drill without a tenth of them falling out from the heat. The nights were becoming downright brisk, which only reminded General Zachary Taylor that his quartermaster's requisition for three thousand woolen blankets had not yet arrived. Washington was some two weeks away by steamer, so communications came and went slowly, especially through the hands of bureaucrats. Taylor was accustomed to that, having served on many a frontier during his military career. But now the stakes were higher, here on the verge of an all-out war with a foreign nation possessed of an army superior in numbers and experience to his own.

It was becoming clear to Taylor that on this frontier he would frequently have to adapt, forage for provisions, purchase rations from the locals, catch wild horses, and perhaps even capture enemy supplies.

As he pored over his pitiful excuse for a map of the region between the Nueces and Rio Grande, a mosquito whined into his ear. He stuck his thick index finger into his ear to smash the insect, only to feel sand grinding in his aural canal. Sand. Sand everywhere. Sand, sand, sand. And more sand. He longed to receive his marching orders away from these dunes on Corpus Christi Bay.

He heard the tapping of the West Point graduation ring on the wooden tent pole—the habit of his adjutant, Captain William "Perfect" Bliss, in announcing himself.

"General Taylor, sir, if I may?"

Taylor turned on his camp stool to face Bliss at the tent flap. The captain wore an impossibly immaculate uniform. His dark eyes peered urgently from a handsome, youthful, clean-shaven face.

"You may, Captain, if it's good news."

The general knew that Captain Bliss had been sent by President Polk to keep an eye on him. Taylor's politics as a Whig did not exactly dovetail with those of the current administration. What the president had not counted on, however, was the friendship that would develop between Taylor and Bliss. The rapport had begun the moment they met, and the trust between the two men had grown daily. Bliss was, as his nickname suggested, as close to perfect as a young army officer could hope to be. He had been accepted into the academy at the age of thirteen, for heaven's sake.

"I think you will be pleased," said the ever-optimistic Bliss. "That Texas Ranger has arrived. Captain Samuel Walker."

"Oh?" Taylor stood, his knees cracking, and bolted from his tent. "Where, Bill?" He narrowed his eyes at the bright autumn sunshine.

Bliss pointed. "Tying his mount, there, sir, at the picket line."

Taylor focused on the man in civilian clothes loosening the saddle cinch, his back turned. His build was thick but lean, his posture somewhat hunched. He looked sturdy enough. Two pistol grips protruded from a leather belt, along with a short sword, a bowie knife, and some sort of pouch—probably for ammunition. He wore a Mexican sombrero.

Taylor reached for his panama hanging just inside the tent.

"Captain Walker," Bliss called. "General Taylor will see you immediately."

Taylor saw Walker turn to reveal a broad, fair face devoid of expression, two light gray eyes gazing like chunks of ice from under his hat brim. Shocks of light reddish hair shook like flames on the Gulf breeze. At twenty-eight, he seemed traveled and troubled beyond his years.

The two men strode together and shook hands.

"Captain Samuel Walker, at your service, sir." The man's face remained a blank canvas.

Taylor smiled. "We've been anticipating your arrival since receiving your letter. Thank you for making the long ride from San Antonio."

"It was a nice trot, sir."

"Would you care to take a stroll with me? You must be weary of sitting in the saddle."

Walker nodded. "A saunter down the beach might loosen the knots, sir."

Taylor tossed his head toward the south and the two men left Bliss behind for their walk.

"Captain, I might have expected you to stand nine feet tall, given your reputation in Texas."

"Only a-horseback, sir."

The general chuckled. "Tell me about yourself, Captain. I've only heard wild rumors of your career. Start with where you come from."

"I was born in Maryland. Joined the Washington City Volunteers when I was nineteen and went to fight the Creeks, then the Seminoles under your command in Florida, sir."

Taylor liked the Ranger's efficient style. One breath covered two decades. "Did we ever meet in Florida?"

"No, sir, but you signed my promotion to corporal."

"For meritorious service?"

"It was worded 'For exceptional courage at the battle of Hacheeluski.'"

"A hot little skirmish."

"Yes, and I've seen hotter since, sir."

As they strolled past the Fourth Infantry's headquarters, Taylor noticed the junior officers craning their necks, trying to figure out who the civilian visitor might be.

"When did you come to Texas?"

"I landed in Galveston in forty-two, about the time the Mexican Army under General Woll invaded San Antonio. In answer to that affront, I volunteered to fight the Mexicans at the Battle of Salado Creek. From there I rode with General Somervell and the Texas Army to the border, in retaliation for the San Antonio raid. We took Laredo and Guerrero without a fight. You probably know what happened next."

"Not from the horse's mouth. Tell me about it."

"Somervell got cold feet and went back to San Antonio. But a couple hundred of us were not yet satisfied that Mexico had been punished, so we quit Somervell's command and went on downstream to capture another border town."

"Mier?"

"Yes, sir. The day before Christmas I was scouting ahead with two other men. We were ambushed by Mexican cavalry. Two of us were captured and put in a jail in Mier. As you know, our main force was surrounded at Mier the next day and had to surrender, but I was not in that fight. I could only listen to the shooting from my prison cell."

"Quite a soldier's Christmas for all of you."

"You might say so, sir. After that, we were marched deep into Mexico. One morning we overpowered our guard, capturing arms and mounts, and made our escape. We then set out for Texas."

"A long trek."

Walker nodded. "Too long. We had to kill our horses for food. We ran out of water in the mountains and most of us had to surrender. You know what happened after."

"Yes," Taylor said, quietly. "The notorious Black Bean Incident. A cruel lottery."

"Every tenth man was to be executed, by order of President Santa Anna. The beans were in a covered mug. White beans, mostly, but every tenth one was black. We were down to one hundred seventy men, so there were seventeen black beans in that mug. I overheard Bigfoot Wallace say that the black beans looked a little bit bigger. They all felt the same size to me. I drew a white one. Seventeen of my comrades were not so lucky. They were stood against a wall and massacred."

"Another wartime atrocity by Santa Anna," Taylor said, shaking his head. "What was next for you and the survivors?"

"Most of the men were marched to the prison at Perote. My group was taken to Tacubaya. They forced us to work on roadways around the city of Mexico. After months of hard labor, starvation, and some rough treatment and such, I escaped with two others. Seeking out American and French citizens who were fain to help us, we made our way to Tampico, where I boarded a ship for New Orleans. I had no money, but the ship's crew needed a carpenter, so I signed on to work off my passage in that capacity."

Taylor thought of Walker's knowledge of the country and cities in Mexico as he shot a smile at the Ranger. "Ah, New Orleans."

"Yes, sir, it was a balm for the soul to be back among free men."

"I read the newspaper accounts. I believe it was in the New Orleans *Picayune*. You vowed vengeance on Santa Anna."

"That was an accurate quote and I fully intend to live up to it."

"You've quite likely come to the right place if those are your intentions, Captain Walker. Now, tell me about your Ranger service."

"After I fattened up a bit in New Orleans, I went back to Texas and joined the company of Captain John C. Hays. The boys all call him Captain Jack. I knew him from the Somervell expedition. When I signed on with Jack, he gave me these." Walker drew his two pistols from his belt. He lay one across his open palm and extended it to the general.

"Colts?"

"Yes, sir. Model five, made in Paterson, New Jersey."

Taylor took the arm and studied it. "I've never actually held one of these in my hand. I've only seen one or two." His eye for weaponry quickly noted the innovation—a revolving cylinder that served as a magazine for five rounds that could be preloaded into the five chambers of the cylinder. "I've tried some cumbersome pistols with four or five revolving barrels," he said. "This seems far superior, as long as the chambers line up perfectly with the barrel."

"It's very well machined," Walker said. "I've never had one fail in that respect."

"That kind of failure might blow a man's hand off." Taylor stopped on the beach, turning the pistol from side to side. "Pray tell, Captain." He laughed. "Where the devil is the trigger?"

"Cock the hammer, sir," Walker suggested.

Taylor thumbed the hammer back and saw the trigger swing into view from the underside of the frame, where it awaited his index finger. "Brilliant design."

"It's a might too fragile for campaigning. I'd rather it had a real trigger and a sturdy brass trigger guard. Feel free to fire it if you'd like to, sir."

Taylor smiled and pointed to a chunk of driftwood beached at high tide. "That stob sticking up amidships," he said, announcing his target. He executed a left face, assuming the pose of a pistol duelist, elbow bent, muzzle skyward. He lowered the barrel, sighted, and fired. A spray of sand flew up short of the log.

"It takes some getting used to," Walker allowed. "Shoot all five rounds if you'd like, sir."

Taylor cocked the Colt and adjusted his aim. He shot long. The third attempt blew a chunk of waterlogged wood away a foot to the right of the target. The fourth round sailed high and wide, but the fifth shattered the knot serving as his bull's-eye.

"Bravo," Walker said.

"It has a right smart little kick to it."

The Ranger shrugged as he took the empty pistol back from the general. "It's thirty-six caliber. I'd rather it were forty-five."

"Care to show me how it should be done?" Taylor asked, pointing at the second pistol on Walker's left hip.

In a blink, Walker whipped the revolver from his belt and fired two shots into the log, the bullets fitting into the same hole. He shifted the Colt to his right hand and repeated the feat with two more shots. He reached his left hand downward to the beach and scooped up a sand dollar, which he handed to Taylor. "If you please, sir, toss this in the air."

The general took a grip on the intended target—a large, perfect specimen the size of a tea saucer. "Ready?"

"*Listo.*"

Taylor flung the sun-bleached sand dollar into the sea breeze. Before it had flown a dozen feet, Walker blasted it to fragments with the last live round in his Colt. A cheer rose from the officers of the Fourth, just up the beach.

Taylor gestured down the beach for the stroll to continue. "Brilliant shooting," he said, though he felt bested by the exhibition. He noticed that Walker had somehow removed the barrel and the cylinder from the Colt. The Ranger reached into the pouch on his belt and produced another revolving cylinder, already loaded with powder and bullets, percussion caps fixed in place over each of the five steel nipples. He slipped the loaded cylinder into place and reconnected the barrel of the Colt with a familiar ease.

"Are those the exact arms you carried at the Sister Creek fight?" Taylor had heard of the legendary battle—the first clash in which Rangers used the five-shot revolvers against Comanche warriors, surprising the braves with superior firepower.

"The same," Walker said.

"Do you remember the fight well? I've heard you were wounded severely."

"I carry the memory of the battle of Sister Creek right next to my heart." He pulled the top of his shirt open to give the general a peek at the scar on the upper part of the left side of his chest.

"Is that where the Comanche got you with his spear?"

Walker nodded. "Ran me clean through on that bloody battlefield. We were outnumbered five to one. I remember shooting my tenth round and drawing my bowie knife, but when I wheeled my mount, the warrior was almost upon me. I still recall the way he twisted his wrist as his pony bore down on me. He turned the flat of the steel blade horizontal so it would slip between my ribs."

Taylor didn't press for further details on the Sister Creek fight. He knew Walker had been so badly wounded that his recovery was considered miraculous to many. "Your service to Texas has been trumpeted far and wide, Captain, and your courage is unquestionable. I consider your visit to my camp an honor."

"I am equally honored to enjoy your hospitality."

"Now, about your letter of last month. I seem to recall you wished to make an offer of some kind to my command."

"I am here to volunteer my services, sir. I know this border. I know the interior of Mexico and I know the enemy. I would like to raise a company of Texas mounted rifles. A spy company. My men will serve as your eyes and ears, carry correspondences, and track enemy troop movements. And when the war starts, we will serve as cavalry."

This man is a godsend, Taylor thought. *His mere presence in camp will bolster moral.*

"How many men do you hope to recruit?" he asked.

"No more than thirty, sir. An elite corps. Only the best and bravest."

"How quickly might you be able to assemble your company?"

Walker looked out across the Gulf of Mexico. "Even if you were to march for the Rio Grande today, I promise you my company would overtake your army before you arrived."

Taylor raised his eyebrows. "But you still have to ride back to the settlements to gather your recruits."

"I stand behind my claim. These men ride hard."

General Zachary Taylor could no longer hold the smile back from his face. "I ask that you and your men enlist as privates. Just a formality for payroll purposes. You can wear your civilian attire and your title will remain that of captain."

Walker bowed slightly in acceptance of the offer.

"Captain Bliss will write your orders and provide you with a payroll for your men. I am most pleased to welcome you into the United States Army of Observation." He stopped and offered his hand.

"Honored to serve, sir." Walker shook his hand with some vigor.

Taylor heard hoofbeats down the beach and looked up to see a team of four horses pulling an 1841 model twelve-pound howitzer at a gallop. A gunner rode atop each of the horses in the team, while other artillerymen rode on the limbers, caissons, or saddle horses. A few of the men carried ramrods or sponges like flagstaffs.

"Ah, it appears we will observe a gunnery drill by the flying artillery."

"Is that Major Ringgold?" Walker asked.

"That's him. The well-traveled author." Taylor thought of himself serving in various frontier outposts while Ringgold dined with foreign dignitaries from France to Prussia. The general stood shoulder to shoulder with the Texas Ranger and watched the gunner rein the team to a stop. Men leaped from saddles to sand. The gun was quickly unhitched from the limber.

"With spherical case shot, load!" shouted Ringgold.

"To your posts!" a sergeant ordered.

As men scrambled to their positions around the cannon, Ringgold yelled, "Load by detail! Load!"

A gunner checked the vent hole of the weapon with a slender steel pick.

"Sponge!" shouted the gunnery sergeant.

A gunner with a wet sponge on the end of a pole swabbed the inside of the barrel to remove any fouling or embers from the previous shot.

"Load spherical case shot!" the sergeant ordered.

Taylor watched as a man holding the twelve-pound load in both hands slid it into the muzzle.

"Ram!"

A soldier with a ramrod stepped forward and shoved the load all the way down to the breech of the gun, while another used the steel pick to puncture the seal on the cartridge down the vent hole. Taylor nodded in approval of the way the men moved in crisp maneuvers that rivaled a ballet.

Ringgold moved in to aim the gun at some target on the sandy bluff a half mile away. He motioned for the gunners to move the muzzle left by grabbing the trail spike and turning the carriage wheels in opposite directions while he turned the elevating screw under the breech to lift the muzzle higher.

"Prime!" the sergeant shouted.

A private inserted the friction primer into the vent hole and carefully uncoiled the long lanyard attached to the primer.

"Ready! Fire!"

The cannon roared as it spewed smoke and sparks and wheeled two feet backwards in the deep sand. A moment later its load of spherical shot case exploded just above the bluff, its shrapnel kicking up puffs of loose soil.

"Limber!" Ringgold ordered.

In seconds the six-pounder was hitched behind the team. The artillerymen mounted their horses and the detachment went charging back down the beach whence it had come, to set up for another practice shot.

"So that's Ringgold's famous flying artillery," Walker said.

Taylor nodded. "Quite impressive at drill, no?"

"Yes, sir. But what do you think of their combat potential?"

Taylor smirked. "Too much flying and not enough artillery, I suspect. But . . . we shall see, Captain Walker. We *shall* see."

President
JAMES K. POLK

Washington, DC
November 2, 1845

It was just another Sunday, Polk told himself as he stepped out of the President's Mansion and into the cold, damp morning. Sheltered overhead by the north portico, he stood alone and watched the rain. He turned up the collar of his woolen coat and pulled the silk top hat firmly down over his prominent brow. He saw the presidential carriage turn down the drive toward the mansion.

He could think of no reason to avoid attending church simply because of the inclement weather—or the fact that he had been born exactly half a century ago on this date. A mere five decades of his trifling existence on earth scarcely warranted an absence from worship services. Let the glory be to God Almighty, Creator of Heaven and Earth. Polk was merely a president, creator of controversy and debt.

The black carriage, pulled by two black horses, rattled up under the porte cochere and stopped. The driver sat on his seat, exposed to the elements, wrapped in his raincoat. He nodded at the president and Polk forced a smile as he touched his hat brim. He turned back toward the door of the mansion. Where was Knox? Why couldn't people be prompt? He was forever waiting for someone to show up on time. Cabinet members, senators, foreign dignitaries. His personal secretary, Colonel J. Knox Walker, was more reliable than most, but Polk now found himself waiting on him, too.

Knox burst from the door as if aware of the president's frustration. "My apologies, Mr. President. I couldn't find my gloves."

"Precisely the reason God gave us pockets."

"Yes, sir. By the way, Mr. President, many happy returns on your birthday."

"Thank you, Knox. Come along now, we must hasten our pace or we will arrive late for church and have to sit down front." Polk charged forward and climbed into the carriage. "Take us to the Foundry church," he said to the driver, before ducking his head into the enclosed cab.

Knox climbed in behind him and sat on the seat across from him. "Sir, don't you usually attend the Presbyterian church?"

The coach lurched forward, the horses excited by the brisk climate.

"Mrs. Polk is Presbyterian. I am a Methodist."

"I am aware of that, sir."

"Mrs. Polk did not care to step out into the rain on this fine day, so I am going to attend the Methodist services at the Foundry church for a change."

Knox, a fellow Tennessean, smiled at him. "Of course. Very well. Sir, while we have a moment, I wanted to remind you of Secretary Buchanan's scheduled meeting with you tomorrow to discuss the diplomatic mission to Spain . . ."

Polk nodded as his mind drifted. Knox was forever reminding him of things. The mission to Spain was among the least of his worries on this day. Weightier concerns burdened his thoughts. In fact, Secretary of State James Buchanan, whose name Knox had just uttered, was among them.

One might think that a man would find utmost satisfaction in serving as secretary of state for four years. Few loftier positions existed in government. But Buchanan had recently become enchanted with the idea of being nominated for the vacant seat on the Supreme Court.

"I would rather be chief justice of the Supreme Court someday than to be president of the United States," Buchanan had said in a private meeting on the matter.

Polk cared very little for what Buchanan would "rather be," but he did not say so out loud.

"You know I rely upon you," he replied, instead. "I need you in my cabinet. There is much to be done."

Buchanan had resigned himself to his role as secretary of state, but

Polk would often wonder if he should not have *encouraged* Buchanan to seek the seat on the bench. Buchanan often disagreed with him, notably on the issue of the tariff, and especially on the Oregon question.

"We must not take the hard line with Great Britain over the Oregon boundary," Buchanan had insisted in a recent cabinet meeting. "Heaven forbid we find ourselves at war with both Britain and Mexico!"

"We will do what is right on both fronts," Polk had argued. "One issue has absolutely nothing to do with the other. We must not give Great Britain the slightest hint that we fear fighting two wars at once!"

Polk had the memory of General Jackson behind him on this. In his last letter to Polk before his death, Jackson had written, "*War is a blessing compared with national degradation. To prevent war with England, a bold and undaunted front must be exposed. England with all her boast dare not go to war.*"

Knox was still going on about the challenge of finding an able ambassador to Spain. Polk tried to look out at Lafayette Park through the window, only to find the glass fogged over. His thoughts drifted to the problems with Mexico.

Mexico had warned for a decade that if the United States were to annex the Republic of Texas as a new American state, she would consider such a move an act of war. President Herrera had broken off diplomatic relations with the United States soon after the annexation was approved by Congress. Polk had been attempting to reestablish relations to avoid a war—or at least to foster the appearance of avoiding war. But the anger in Mexico toward both Texas and the United States was rooted deep in years of border warfare.

It was well that he had become president. Who but James K. Polk could be trusted to carry out the dream of his departed mentor, the great General Jackson? Texas had been a secret obsession of Jackson's for decades. It was Old Hickory who had quietly urged Sam Houston down to Texas to create an independent republic that would one day become a state. That day had come. General Sam Houston was now a Texas hero and a new U.S. senator. He had done his job and garnered his reward.

Polk saw no reason to complicate the issue. Sam Houston had defeated President Santa Anna at the Battle of San Jacinto a decade ago, capturing the Mexican head of state as he attempted to flee the battleground. Santa Anna—the captured president of Mexico—had signed the Treaties of Velasco, establishing the Rio Grande del Norte as the border between

Mexico and the new Republic of Texas. To the victors go the spoils. The Del Norte, as Polk preferred to call the river, was the border. Period. Texas was now part of the United States. Polk would defend that border until the last foot soldier fell.

But that would only be the beginning. Vast opportunities beckoned here. *Nueva Mexico. Alta California.* The place names rang in Polk's dreams. The map of America he saw in his mind extended all the way to the Pacific Ocean. If Mexico could be provoked into a conflict, justification could be found for an all-out offensive war. Reparations were already due. American citizens had been mistreated in Mexico—robbed and murdered without recourse.

Examples were manifest. Polk used two of the more extreme ones when defending the issue of indemnification. In one, an American investor had bought over half a million dollars' worth of fine port and shipped it to Mexico for sale. When the shipment arrived in Veracruz, harbor authorities seized it. The entire shipment simply disappeared, and the investor was never compensated or allowed a court hearing in Mexico.

In one of the worst examples Polk knew of, an American ship captain—owner of a sailing vessel and employer of his own American crew—won a contract to transport Mexican troops up and down the Gulf Coast. One day, the Mexican soldiers murdered the captain, threw his body overboard, and impressed his crew into service without pay for months. Again the Mexican courts offered no justice.

Mexico clearly owed huge settlements to the United States for these abuses, Polk mused. Had not France invaded Veracruz in 1838 for the same reason? And yet the Mexican treasury held no money with which to pay reparations. So Mexico would pay with land—her northern frontier, to which she clung ever so tenuously. Mexico City could not protect it.

Polk recalled that General Jackson had warned for years against foreign powers grabbing California and New Mexico. What empire would not covet the harbor at San Francisco, the silver mines and trade center at Santa Fe? It was known that England, France, and Spain wanted Mexico's northern borderland; it was suspected that Holland and Portugal might have fanciful designs upon it, as well. Even the Russians up the coast in frozen Alaska had to desire a more temperate port.

Why shouldn't America snatch the prize before some other nation did? No foreign power in possession of that frontier could be trusted to remain friendly to the United States. The survival of the republic depended upon seizing it! If there was a way to add New Mexico and California to the map, Polk would pursue it. He had been trying, secretly, to purchase the region from Mexico. His envoys had offered twenty million dollars, but he was willing to pay as much as sixty million. He knew President Herrera wanted and needed the money but feared the political backlash he would suffer for selling.

No matter. If Mexico refused to sell, war could be provoked. All that was required was to order General Zachary Taylor southward to the Rio Grande del Norte.

Polk felt the coach come to a stop and heard Knox rambling on about the vacancy at the Spanish Embassy. ". . . and I'm certain Mr. Buchanan will present a list of capable candidates for the mission." His secretary scrambled out to hold the carriage door open.

"Thank you for the briefing, Knox." Polk stepped down from the vehicle and onto Sixteenth Street. "I don't suppose listening to a briefing on the day of rest would incur too much wrath from the Almighty." He glanced up through the fat raindrops at the cut stone facade of the church—its carved masonry and stained glass.

Entering the vestibule, he hung up his hat and coat. He and Knox found seats in the back row just in time for the service to begin. He soon realized how much he missed the Methodist rituals. The familiarity of the invocation served as a fitting birthday gift to him on this, the fiftieth anniversary of his first breath. A faint smile lifted a corner of his mouth as he remembered Sarah's wry comment to him this morning.

"So, Mr. President, how does it feel to be entering your sixth decade?"

"My dear," he had replied, "you make me sound even older than I am."

She had laughed. "You must take solace in the fact that you are the youngest president ever elected."

It was well that Sarah had a keen sense of humor. Her wit compensated for the fact that he possessed almost none whatsoever.

The cavernous sanctuary rang with comforting incantations that could not, however, compete with the burdens of the presidency. Polk went on musing over Oregon, Texas, the tariff, Mexico, even that trifling mission to Spain . . . *Alta California* . . . *Nuevo Mexico* . . .

When his mind snapped back to the service, he heard the pastor reading from the Acts of the Apostles: *"Because He hath appointed a day, in which He will judge the world in righteousness by the man whom He hath ordained; whereof He hath given assurance unto all men, in that He hath raised him from the dead."*

"Assurance unto all men," Polk thought. Yes, this is what he needed to hear. He would do what was right by the laws of God. God had raised Christ from the dead as a sign of assurance. Of this, Polk had no doubts.

But all this talk of rising from the dead only reminded him of his own mortality. He was fifty years old today. In another fifty he would be sleeping with the generations which had gone before him. The vanities of this world's honors would profit him little half a century hence.

Like a thunderclap the epiphany hit him. Sand through the hourglass fell without pity. He had said from the beginning that he would not run for reelection and he had meant it. He would have only four years to accomplish his goals. Months of his presidency had passed and he had yet achieved very little. In this, he found a new resolve. "Who is James K. Polk?" the citizens had asked. He would show them. It was time for him to start putting his house in order.

Private
JOHN RILEY

Riley knew now that he should have ignored the recruiter's promises at Fort Mackinac and heeded the warnings of his former employer, Charles O'Malley. It had been a year since the presidential election. A year since war fever had infected Riley's heart. A year since his hatred of the bloody British had driven him to enlist in the U.S. Army.

"Fifty-four forty or fight," Riley muttered under his breath as he trudged through the sleet toward the mesquite brush in search of firewood. He had no idea what the latitude was here on the wretched Texas coast, but it was a far cry south of fifty-four forty.

Soon after Riley enlisted, President Polk had backed down from that campaign threat and had begun to work with the Brits to find a compromise border line. But by then it was too late. Riley was on the muster rolls. Soon, Company K was ordered to vacate Fort Mackinac and journey south to join the rest of the Fifth Infantry on the wild shores of Texas. As O'Malley had warned, the Fifth would not be taking up arms against the British but against the Mexicans. Fellow Catholics. This did little to assuage the enmity that Private Riley felt for the pompous, Protestant, English oppressors his people had hated since before he was born.

Still, he was a soldier and would do his duty. At least, this is what he kept telling himself he would do. But the U.S. Army did not make this an easy task for an immigrant soldier.

"Oh, you'll make rank quick enough," the recruiter had told him. "A man with your gunnery experience? You'll transfer to artillery and make sergeant major again in no time."

He wondered now if that recruiter had known just how big of a lie he had spoken. It was obvious that immigrants in the U.S. Army had almost no chance of earning a promotion.

Riley rubbed his hands together for warmth and strode on toward the mesquite. He had not expected such bitter cold this far south in Texas. Apparently the army had not, either, for it had failed to provide decent coats and blankets, and the canvas tents had not arrived to replace the flimsy summer enclosures of deteriorating muslin.

Down here on this lost coast, he could sense the indifference of the faraway bureaucrats. The army was going to conquer balmy Mexico, no? Why would they need blankets or canvas? The soldiers here at the smuggler's outpost called Kinney's Ranch would just have to endure these icy blasts from the northwest. The Texans here called the storms "blue northers." They barreled down from the arctic on enormous clouds ranging from gray to blue to purple, laden with sleet, freezing rain, and whistling winds.

As he marched on across the makeshift parade grounds through the foul weather, he now saw the brush through the sleet and so quickened his pace. Then, near the mesquites, he saw a man sitting on the ground. No, not sitting. Tied. "Bucked and gagged" as they called it. John Riley was no stranger to strict military punishment, having served under the British. But this bucking and gagging had gotten out of control here on Corpus Christi Bay.

Walking up to the tree line, Riley stopped to urinate on the sand within talking distance of the unfortunate soldier. The private sat on his rear end on the sand, his knees bent, thighs drawn up to his chest. A stout wooden tent pole ran under both knees. The man's arms passed under the pole and his wrists were bound tightly together in front of his shins. His ankles were also tied, and a rag had been stuffed into his mouth. Bucked and gagged. The man shivered uncontrollably in the cold. Snot ran from his nose. Each breath came out as a piteous groan.

Even the slightest offense—or no offense at all—might have led to this cruel punishment, and Riley knew the poor bastard may have been sitting there for hours in the sleet, his joints aching, his muscles cramping.

This was the lot of the immigrant soldier in the U.S. Army. O'Malley had warned of this, too. He had told Riley of the nativist movement that had swept America and infected the U.S. Army. Now Riley knew how truly that admonition had been expressed.

He looked over both shoulders for signs of any officer who might be watching. "Are you Irish, lad?" he asked.

The young soldier nodded, his body convulsing with the effort. This came as no surprise. A quarter of the soldiers under Zachary Taylor's command had been born in Ireland.

"You know I cannot free you, or the punishment for both of us will be greater even than that which you now endure."

The man blinked, blew mucous from his nose, nodded again.

"You cannot cross yourself bucked and gagged there as you are, but I can make the sign of the cross for you." To disguise the holy ritual, he reached up with his right hand and tugged the brim of the shako hat, touching his forehead in the process. Then his hand reached downward to button the fly of his trousers. He completed the holy gesticulation by pretending to brush away an unwanted object from his left shoulder, then by tugging at his leather shoulder strap toward the right shoulder. He didn't dare make the sign of the cross in any sort of more obvious way, for fear of some hateful nativist officer looking on through the sleet.

The man on the ground sighed his appreciation.

"May the Lord watch over you and give you strength on this day," Riley said. "Do you know the twenty-third psalm, lad?"

The soldier nodded again.

"Say it again and again in your mind, and you will survive this day. 'The Lord is my shepherd . . .'" He heard the soldier grunting the cadence of the familiar verse along with him. Riley continued to recite as he stepped into the mesquite thicket to gather wood. "'Yea, though I walk through the valley of the shadow of death, I will fear no evil . . .'"

He found the pickings almost nonexistent, as the chaparral had been combed for three months now by thousands of troops. He broke off a few green limbs in order to look productive and wended his way out of the brush. Continuing along the sand dunes to the next patch of chaparral down the beach, Riley encountered another man being punished in a way even more sadistic than the buck and the gag. This man was "riding the horse."

Made to straddle a tall sawhorse with his arms bound behind his back and weights hanging from each ankle, this luckless private had probably been in agony for hours. Two guards had been assigned the duty of watching him to make sure he didn't try to throw himself off of the painful implement of torture. And that's what it was. Discipline was one thing, but this was torture.

Here in the U.S. Army, Riley had seen punishments he had never even dreamed of in the British Army and had never heard of among any European armed forces. There was one inhumane punishment in which a man was bound near the shore of a river or pond, or even by the sea. A dozen soldiers with buckets were ordered to throw water in the man's face incessantly until he almost drowned. Men had been known to die from this treatment—or to go mad afterward. One that Riley knew of had slashed his own throat with a bayonet.

On another occasion, Riley and four other stout soldiers had been ordered to hold a drunken man down on the ground so that his forehead could be branded using a red-hot iron with the letters *HD*, for "habitual drunkard." The man, of course, had been an immigrant soldier, and the nativist officer who had ordered the mutilation had whiskey on his own breath at the time of the punishment.

Walking forward toward the unfortunate soldier on the sawhorse, Riley suddenly noticed that a rider on a large white horse was also approaching the man, from the other direction. This was General Zachary Taylor himself. Riley knew Old Rough and Ready immediately by his toad-like build atop the pale horse, his common civilian clothing, and the wide-brimmed planter's hat he habitually wore about camp. Riley stepped into the edge of the chaparral and pretended to pick up a stick of mesquite as he listened and observed.

"How long has that man been on the horse?" General Taylor asked one of the guards.

"Since assembly, sir."

Riley was close enough to see the general's thick lips move with his next question. "What was his offense?"

"Wal, that soldier is Dutch, sir," the other guard answered. "He don't talk English real good. He didn't git what the captain ordered him to do."

"Take him down and carry him back to his tent," Taylor ordered. "You men need to teach your messmates the English words they need to know to follow orders. We have to make an army out of this rabble."

"Yes, sir!" The guards rushed in to remove the weights from the German's ankles so they could lower his pain-racked body from the cursed sawhorse.

Having heard this, Riley picked up his firewood and continued along the edge of the brush. When the general drew near, he dropped the few sticks he had gathered, stood at attention, and saluted.

Taylor returned the salute. "As you were, soldier." He rode near enough that Riley could feel and smell Old Whitey's warm breath on his face. "What do you know about that man bucked and gagged back yonder?" the general demanded.

Riley decided to tell the only truth he knew. "He's a son of the Emerald Isle, sir."

"Like you?"

"Yes, sir."

"What was his offense?"

"I did not witness the event, sir, but I overheard talk about its character."

"What did you hear?"

"I heard he stumbled in drill, sir." Riley didn't know this to be true, but he had seen other Irishmen bucked and gagged for that trivial infraction.

"Stumbled? That's all?"

"To my knowledge, sir, yes, sir."

"Get him up and take him to his tent."

"That I will, sir!" He saluted again.

"Carry on, private." Taylor then turned his mount and rode back the way he had come.

Riley ran back to his countryman sitting bucked and gagged on the cold ground. "The general himself has ordered me to free you!" He pulled the gag from the young man's mouth and threw it aside.

"Thanks be to God," the soldier muttered.

Riley drew a knife from his boot top and sliced through the knotted rope around the man's wrists. "Now, stretch out slow. Take your time getting up, lad."

After a minute or two, Riley was able to lift the soldier to his feet and turn him toward his camp. "Where are your mates, lad?"

"Battery E. Third Artillery."

Riley groaned. Since coming to Corpus Christi, he had identified most of the nativist officers who preyed on immigrants. First Lieutenant Braxton Bragg, of the Third's Battery E, was one of the most vicious.

Still, he threw the young man's arm over his shoulder and walked him to the artillery camp, not far away.

Just as Riley was giving the lad over to his messmates, Lieutenant Bragg himself confronted him, having seen him carry the young soldier to camp from the officer's mess.

"Who the hell are you, soldier?" Bragg demanded in a high, harsh voice. Except for the hateful glare in his eyes, his features were quite handsome.

Riley came to attention and saluted. "Private John Riley, Fifth Infantry, sir."

The lieutenant slapped Riley's salute away from his forehead. "You're stinking Irish shanty trash! I can tell by the whiskey slur on your lips!"

Riley stood at attention and remained silent, though he hadn't had a sip of alcohol since leaving Mackinac Island.

"Who told you to free this piece-of-shit papist?"

"General Taylor, sir."

Bragg's face darkened. "You big Mick cropper. You stick out like a jackass among the other men, don't you? I won't forget you, Riley. If I find out you're lying about General Taylor, you will have hell paying the piper!"

"Sure, it's the truth, so help me, sir."

Bragg slapped Riley on the side of his head, the unexpected blow staggering Riley a step to one side. Though his temper boiled and he longed to strike back, he stood at attention and looked beyond the officer.

"Do not speak to me unless you're ordered to!"

Riley stood fuming as the abusive lieutenant turned away.

The men of the Third Artillery dared not thank Riley aloud for returning one of their own, but one patted him briefly on the back as he left, his temper still fuming. As he plodded back to pick up his firewood, Riley hoped for a moment in the coming war to settle the score with Lieutenant Bragg. For now, he prayed for the good sense to hold his temper. At this moment, the clouds broke over the dunes. A shaft of sunlight beamed down on the village of Corpus Christi, perched on the bluff to the west.

Riley thought back to a Sunday, not long ago, when he and a few other Irishmen had risked nativist retribution to attend mass being administered by an itinerant priest from Matamoros. Padre Alfonso did not speak English, but the Mexicans and Irishmen alike who gathered in the

makeshift church—a trading house in the village—knew the Latin incantations by rote. Having been deprived mass for weeks between
Mackinac Island and Corpus Christi Bay, Riley felt his heart warmed
and his conscience soothed. He gathered that his fellow Catholic soldiers felt the same way.

But before dismissing his congregation, Padre Alfonso had passed out
printed handbills to each of the U.S. soldiers. Outside, the men gathered around Riley as he unfolded the circular the priest had given him
in order to read it in the sunshine. He found the type thereon well arranged and ornately rendered by an experienced printer.

"Is it English?" one of the men asked.

"Aye, that it is," Riley replied.

"What does it say, John? You're the only man of letters among us."

Riley read quickly and silently through the pamphlet, then looked
grimly at the lads surrounding him. "Hand over those dodgers," he ordered. "Every one of you. You're ne'er to get caught in camp with this on
your person."

"But what does it say?"

"It says, 'Good for fifty lashes at the nearest whipping post.'"

"I'm not giving mine up until you read it to me," one of the soldiers
protested.

Riley snatched it from the soldier's hand before he had time to resist.
"I will read it but once, so you'd all better listen well."

The men nodded.

Riley shook the leaflet out in the cool Gulf breeze and the sunshine,
and began to read:

"Sons of Ireland. Listen to the words of your Catholic brothers. Our
religion is the strongest of bonds. If you follow the doctrines of our
Savior, how could you take up arms against your brothers in faith? Why
do you rank among our wicked enemies?

"Come over to us. You will be received under the laws of Christian
hospitality and good faith which Irish guests are entitled to expect from
a Catholic nation. Our hospitality tenders toward you what you can
possess and enjoy: military rank, glory, and as much property in land as
you require, and this under the pledge of our honor and holy religion.

"May Mexicans and Irishmen, united by the sacred tie of religion and
benevolence, form only one people!"

"Speak not a breath of this," Riley had warned, tossing the pamphlets into an outdoor *orno* that some senora had stoked for the baking of her daily bread. "Now, march back to camp, you *scalpeens*. Ignore this propaganda."

But now, weeks later, on this cold day in December, with the singular shaft of sunlight beaming down through a break in the clouds, illuminating that same makeshift chapel atop the bluff, John Riley could not help longing for the tolling of bells in a proper cathedral, the chanting of priests, the aromas of incense, and the love of fellow Catholics in a nation under the cloak of His Holiness, the almighty Pope Gregory XVI.

President
JAMES K. POLK

The president sat at his desk with his back to the window. He could feel the winter chill gnawing at his elbows through the glass. He was listening to a rather coarse gentleman from Pennsylvania laud his own efforts on behalf of the Democratic Party in his congressional district. He had come, of course, to seek some office as a reward, but he had not gotten around to saying as much just yet.

"I near wore out the goddamned cobblestones in Harrisburg!" the man declared. "Knocking on doors by day and knocking heads together in the taverns at night!" He guffawed as he brandished a meaty fist. He smiled, revealing tobacco-stained teeth. He wore a threadbare coat with a patch on one elbow. He used its sleeve to wipe his nose. He was bald and had a neck like a bull.

It was Polk's habit to see all manner of visitors most mornings from eight until noon. This open-door policy attracted politicians, foreign diplomats, common citizens, admirers, detractors. But by far the most typical class of unannounced visitor was that of the office seeker.

". . . and when it came to 'Fifty-four forty or fight,' I was always ready to fight, Sir President . . ."

This pugilistic boast, which Polk did not doubt, made his mind drift to the Oregon situation, which weighed heavier on his mind than the Pennsylvanian's self-congratulatory diatribe. Negotiations with England were still at an impasse and, when it came to dealing with John Bull,

Polk believed in leverage. He now favored terminating the 1827 agreement of joint occupation of the Oregon country, signed by the United States and England. Many fainthearted members of Congress feared this would lead to war, but Polk believed Lord Aberdeen and Sir Robert Peel would compromise. In spite of the campaign demand of "Fifty-four forty or fight," Polk was beginning to accept the forty-ninth parallel as a workable settlement.

". . . and it seems that I spent so much time on the campaign, Mr. President, that my employer—the Whig bastard—booted my arse out of the foundry! Me! The one man jack who worked the hardest!" The man paused to slurp some tea.

To remind himself of the good Democrat's name, Polk glanced at the man's calling card on his desk.

"Mr. Runnels," he said, springing from his chair, "I assume you have come seeking some office in return for your much-appreciated service to the party." He scooped up the calling card as he came around the desk.

"Why, as a matter of fact—" Runnels said.

"Come with me."

The burly office seeker sprang eagerly to his feet and followed Polk to the office door. There, the president turned to face Runnels and handed his card back to him.

"I'm afraid there are no paying positions to offer at this time. There are only volunteer opportunities."

"Volunteer? I just told you of my volunteer service."

Polk opened the door and snapped his fingers at his personal secretary. He turned back to Runnels as Colonel J. Knox Walker joined him at the door. "Mr. Runnels, I invite you to give your card to my secretary, Colonel Walker. If some salaried position should arise for which your abilities would prove suitable, I am sure you will hear from him." Polk smiled, quite pleased with himself at the diplomatic ways in which he had learned to say no.

"By all means," Knox said to Runnels. "Perhaps as a postmaster at some new outpost on the Indian frontier."

"The frontier?" Runnels complained. "I live in Harrisburg."

Knox held out his hand. "Your card, sir, if you please."

The crestfallen Runnels handed over the card. "Well, I was hoping—"

"We'll be in touch." Knox pushed the man out of the president's office and shut the door, leaving himself and Polk inside. "I apologize for that one, Mr. President."

Polk sighed, his head wagging. "It's not your fault, Knox. It's my policy." He looked at the clock. Half past eleven. "Who's next? I suppose I have time for one more caller."

Knox smiled. "Someone a bit more interesting has come calling, Mr. President."

"Oh?"

"Colonel Atocha. The Spaniard. Perhaps you remember him?"

Polk searched his memory. "Atocha. Yes, he was here last year. A crony of General Santa Anna's."

"The same," Knox replied. "He has, in fact, just come from Cuba, where he visited with Santa Anna in exile outside of Havana. He would like to speak to you on behalf of the general."

Polk gave a single nod of his head. "Very well, Knox. See him in. And stoke the fire, if you please."

"Of course."

He watched as Knox placed two new logs—and the last visitor's calling card—on the embers in the fireplace. Knox left the office. Polk turned to the window. The glass was too foggy to see much of the scenery, but it was a dreary February day anyway. He waited until he heard the door open.

"Mr. President, I present to you Colonel A. J. Atocha." Knox withdrew from the office.

Through the initial handshaking and small talk, Polk admired Atocha's matching black trousers and frock coat, his silk vest, gold watch chain, and perfectly tied cravat. Last year, Atocha had come seeking the help of the president in forcing Mexico to pay damages for property lost. Atocha claimed he was Spanish-born but had become a naturalized American citizen. He had lived in Mexico and worked as an agent for then-president General Antonio López de Santa Anna. When Santa Anna was deposed and exiled to Cuba, Atocha's property had been seized and he had been ordered out of Mexico. Polk had simply told Atocha to join the ever-growing ranks of American citizens whom Mexico had abused.

Now he was back, and Polk gathered that this visit had nothing to do with Mexican reparations. They chatted about the weather as Polk offered Atocha a chair and took his own seat behind his desk.

"Your time is valuable," the colonel said. "I will not squander it. I have come from Havana, where I met with His Excellency, General Santa Anna. I wish to tell you of my discussion with him. But first, I request that our meeting here today remain confidential."

Polk stared at his visitor. Atocha was clean shaven and handsome in a devil-may-care kind of way. He was forty to forty-five years of age, Polk guessed. His dark eyes were alive and engaging but struck the president as shifty.

Polk shrugged and spread his arms. "Of course, Colonel. You may rely upon my discretion."

"General Santa Anna sends his warmest regards. He has been schooling the Cubans in cockfighting. His cocks have won more than thirty thousand pesos since he arrived in Havana. But the pit is a mere distraction for the general. He writes daily to his agents in Mexico and receives hundreds of letters by every steamer from Veracruz."

"He remains that well connected?"

Atocha nodded and smiled. "It is only a matter of time."

Polk shot a puzzled smirk across the desk. "Until what, may I ask?"

"The general wishes to return to power. And he wishes you to know that, when that happens, you will find him open to negotiations."

"What kind of negotiations?" Polk asked, playing the rube.

"General Santa Anna is willing to cede Texas to the United States, with the Rio Grande del Norte as the southern and western boundary. In addition, he would relinquish all lands north of the Colorado River of the West. All of this for thirty millions of dollars. With this sum, the general intends to return the government to solvency and—once again, as he has done many times before—save Mexico."

Polk raised his eyebrows but restrained his enthusiasm. The boast about saving Mexico was preposterous. Santa Anna had, in fact, nearly destroyed his country, almost single-handedly. But the offer to sell Mexico's northern frontier intrigued. Secretly, Polk had considered paying twice that much for the territories offered.

"Before any such negotiations could begin," Polk said, "Mexico must satisfy the many claims of American citizens abused by the Mexican government. Reparations are long overdue."

Atocha nodded his agreement and waved the idea aside as if fending off a mosquito.

"Then," Polk continued, "if the general should return to power and make such an offer as you have described, it would be considered at that time."

A wry grin sculpted perfect crow's-feet at the corners of Atocha's eyes. "Ah, but therein lies the rub," he whispered.

Shakespeare? Polk thought. "How do you mean?"

"Should any Mexican president propose the sale of Mexican soil to a foreign country, there would be another revolution and he would be overthrown. No. Mexico must appear to be *forced* into such a deal."

Polk did not know what to say, so he made a rolling gesture of his hand that said, *Go on . . .*

"General Santa Anna makes the following suggestions: One . . . assemble a large number of your warships within view of Veracruz. Two . . . move your army from Corpus Christi to the Rio Grande del Norte, across from Matamoras. Three . . . allow Santa Anna safe passage through the blockade to Veracruz. Four . . . order your minister, Mr. Slidell, to ask for his passports and compel him to board one of the U.S. ships of war at Veracruz. From there, Mr. Slidell should demand payment due to U.S. citizens, under penalty of invasion."

Polk frowned. Both Santa Anna and Atocha had certainly reasoned— or learned through espionage—that the said suggestions were already in motion, with the exception of allowing Santa Anna's safe passage through the blockade. Therefore, such safe passage seemed to be the one aim of Atocha's visit.

"You are suggesting," Polk said, "that since Mexico has no treasury to speak of, the only way she could pay the reparations due is by selling her northern frontier, and that the citizens of Mexico would allow this only if a large military show of force should frighten them into selling."

Atocha nodded. "Santa Anna believes it is the only hope for Mexico. And for peaceful relations with the United States into perpetuity."

Polk rose to pace the floor of his office, his hands clasped behind his back. "Colonel Atocha," he said, "is it true that General Santa Anna calls himself the 'Napoleon of the West'?"

Atocha chuckled and bowed his head, almost apologetically. "I know of only one occasion when the general flattered himself with that appellation."

"Napoleon saw himself as a conqueror. An empire builder. Why, then, would Santa Anna willingly cede almost half of his nation's territory to a foreign power?"

"Because he learns from his mistakes. After his disastrous expedition to Texas, Santa Anna came to realize that Mexico enjoys only a tenuous hold on her northern territories. With no money in her treasury and a debt of half a million dollars to the archbishop of Mexico, it only makes sense to sell a territory that otherwise will one day be taken by some superior military force."

Polk found his trust in Colonel Atocha lacking. Still, he knew enough about General Santa Anna to make Atocha's stratagem seem negligibly feasible. Santa Anna had ascended to the presidency of Mexico more than once through brief displays of courage on the battlefield and prolonged propaganda campaigns in which he took credit for victories he had not won and blamed others for his own defeats.

He had started as a young artillery officer for the Spanish Army, then joined the fight for independence. Polk's knowledge of Mexican affairs after her independence were lost in the confusion of the times—warlords toppling other warlords. Santa Anna seemed to be one of the luckiest and cleverest of the breed, managing to get himself elected president in 1833. Within a year, he had dissolved his nation's legislature and sent his vice president into exile. A dictator now, he began dismantling the Constitution of 1824, which had been patterned largely after the U.S. Constitution. A despot, Santa Anna announced, was what Mexico needed. Her citizens were not ready for democracy.

But the American colonists who had been living in Mexico's Texas for over a decade did not intend to suffer a tyrant. The Texans—of both Anglo and Spanish descent—declared independence. What followed was Santa Anna's march to San Antonio and the slaughter of the defenders of the Alamo. Then the Napoleon of the West ordered the unconscionable execution of more than three hundred Texas patriots who had surrendered honorably at Goliad.

For these atrocities, the Texans had exacted their revenge on the battlefield at San Jacinto, where President Santa Anna was captured and narrowly spared execution by General Sam Houston, who considered him a valuable pawn. A captive head of state now, Santa Anna recognized Texas independence by treaty to save his own life. After wearing a ball and chain for a time, he then traveled to Washington, DC, where Old Hickory himself finalized the treaty negotiations between Texas and Mexico, establishing the border at the Rio Grande del Norte.

Polk now regretted that he had not attended any of the dinners or balls in Washington where Santa Anna had been wined and dined as a foreign curiosity. The general was popular with northern abolitionists, who saw his recent enemies—the Texans—as slavery supporters. Eventually, General Santa Anna returned to Mexico.

He found himself quite unpopular at home, until he got his leg blown off by a cannonball while defending the Port of Veracruz from a French invasion in 1838. France had attacked to force payment of reparations for abuses of her citizens living in Mexico—the same thing Polk now demanded for the United States.

After Veracruz, Santa Anna had made the most of his amputated leg and was celebrated as a hero once again. Soon he joined Mariano Paredes in overthrowing President Bustamante. Santa Anna was then installed as provisional president. President again! But not for long. He spent massive sums on a statue of himself and a lavish military reburial of his amputated leg. He levied taxes on cart wheels and conscripted peasants and Indians by the thousands for forced military service. His popularity slid to the point that lepers dug up his leg and dragged it through the streets.

Near the end of 1844, Santa Anna was once again deposed—this time by José Joaquin de Herrera—and exiled to Cuba, whence Colonel A. J. Atocha had recently sailed to visit him and his fighting cocks.

"Mexico's debt to the archbishop," Atocha said, continuing his sales pitch, "will actually work in our favor. The archbishop wields enormous influence over the citizenry. If we assure him that he will be reimbursed his half million out of the thirty million, he will approve of the sale."

Polk could not restrain a scoff. "So, the Archbishop of Mexico must be in on your scheme as well?"

"All of Mexico will follow his example."

"*All* of Mexico?" Polk said.

"Yes," Atocha insisted. "In Mexico, if you go against the archbishop, you spend eternity in hell."

Polk allowed a smile to spread across his face. "Colonel, your counsel has been interesting and intriguing."

Atocha rose, sensing that the meeting was coming to an end. "May I carry your answer to the general, Mr. President?"

"I have no answer for you on this day, Colonel. Unlike your friend General Santa Anna, I have little desire to act without the consent of Congress." He strode to the door. "I will consider the intelligence you have shared with me here today and decide which course of action—if any—should be pursued through constitutional channels."

Atocha joined him at the door. "Mr. President. Will you grant General Santa Anna safe passage through the blockade on Veracruz?"

Polk turned the latch on the door but did not open it. "I cannot answer that question on this day, sir."

"When will you decide?"

"If I were to decide as you wish, Colonel, you would hear of it from Santa Anna, not from me." He swung the door open and gestured to the outer office.

Colonel A. J. Atocha, looking disappointed, bowed slightly and left.

Closing the door, the president shook his head at the audacity of the intrigue he had just encountered. Imagine! Allowing the self-trumpeted Napoleon of the West back into Mexico to return to power and sell a third or more of her territory to America. If the plan worked, it would amount to a stroke of clandestine brilliance that could prevent all-out war.

But what if it was a trick? What if Santa Anna had no real intention of selling territory and simply wanted entrée through the U.S. Navy blockade? What was the worst that could happen? Even if Santa Anna reneged on his promise to sell New Mexico and Alta California, how much trouble could he possibly cause once back in Mexico? He would be a one-legged rooster in a cockfight. He was considered a disgrace to his nation by most of the Mexican citizenry. Why not let him go home?

Polk thought of something his envoy extraordinary and minister plenipotentiary, the Honorable John Slidell, had told him before leaving for the U.S. legation in Mexico.

"Oh, Mr. President," Slidell had said, in an offhand way, "my brother has asked me to offer his services as a naval officer to your administration in any capacity you might find helpful."

"Your brother?" Polk had said, unaware that Slidell had a brother in the U.S. Navy.

"Commander Alexander MacKenzie, currently in command of the brig of war *Somers*."

"MacKenzie?" Polk had said. "Not Slidell?"

"His change of name from Slidell to MacKenzie was authorized by the New York legislature and the U.S. Navy."

"I see. But why did your brother desire a change of name?"

"MacKenzie is our mother's maiden name from Scotland. The name change qualifies Alexander to inherit her family property in the old country."

What had seemed trivial at the time now struck Polk with a ring of opportunity. Why not send Commander MacKenzie to Havana to offer Santa Anna safe passage through the blockade? As a brother of Minister John Slidell, MacKenzie was doubtlessly well versed on current events in Mexico. This would give him an edge in the negotiations with Santa Anna. Because his last name was no longer Slidell, Santa Anna would have no clue that MacKenzie was actually the brother of the former U.S. minister to Mexico.

Polk opened his office door to find Knox scribbling some document at his desk. "Knox."

"Yes, Mr. President?" he said, looking up, but continuing to scrawl on the paper.

"Send a note to the secretary of navy. I shall need to meet with him this afternoon."

"Shall I say why, sir?"

"Tell him he will know why when he gets here."

Second Lieutenant
SAM GRANT

Corpus Christi, Texas
March 9, 1846

Grant woke to the cold Gulf breeze blowing through holes in the tattered muslin fabric of his tent. His blanket, similarly ventilated, did little to retain the warmth of his own body. As he shivered, he realized what had wakened him. The black cook who worked for Grant and four other officers had begun to clang pots and pans. Soon the sun would rise over the Gulf of Mexico.

Now, remembering what lay in store for this day, he smiled, in spite of his lack of enthusiasm for the coming conflict—an imminent war he considered unjust and wholly avoidable. His regiment would leave Corpus Christi beach today and head south on the smuggler's trail to Matamoras. Nights would be warmer down south, and, anyway, spring was coming on. Along with just about every other able-bodied soldier in this gritty camp, Grant relished the idea of the march to the border. He had had enough of Corpus Christi beach.

It was his fondest hope that, once Taylor's army arrived on the Rio Grande del Norte, a border settlement could be reached by reasonable diplomats and a cruel war avoided. Perhaps the United States could buy the Nueces Strip from Mexico. He knew that clinging to this kind of unlikely fantasy was naive, but he could not help wishing. He wanted to go home, marry Julia, and start a normal life.

But the truth was, he could feel the war fever in the air among his fellow officers. He could read it between the lines of bellicose newspaper articles and editorials. Americans wanted more America. Only so many sons could inherit the family farm. The others would have to move west. West . . . Defending the border of the new state of Texas was only the beginning. Talk of taking California had become a daily topic in Taylor's camp. That would mean actually invading Mexico and forcing the forfeiture of her northern frontier.

Since the day he fell off the sailing ship, trying to get on the steam shuttle to shore, Grant had seen a heap of changes here at Corpus Christi. Lying in his tent, he chuckled at the memory of his fall into the Gulf waters. Luckily, he was a strong swimmer, and some sailors had eventually lowered a bucket for him to straddle and hoisted him back up to the deck. It served as an awakening to the toils and dangers in store. Yet the rigors of army life seemed to have greatly improved Grant's health. His cough had left him and he had put on weight. He had his own opinion as to what had brought on the change. It was that kiss from Julia. She had healed him.

He had returned to Julia only once since then. Before sailing from New Orleans, he had secured twenty days' leave and had traveled back to White Haven to ask Julia's father for her hand. Colonel Dent did not consent to the union readily. He doubted that Julia would enjoy the roving life of an army wife. Grant had told the elder Dent that if she did not like the army life, he would resign his commission. Julia's father then consented to allow the young couple to remain engaged and to correspond while Grant was away with the army.

Grant had spent several splendid days at White Haven, taking long horseback rides and leisurely strolls with Julia. They would sit and talk for hours on the piazza, serenaded by honeybees working among the blossoms of locust trees and jessamine. Now, he knew not when he might see her again, but he wrote often, and she always replied.

After landing at Corpus Christi, Grant had made the most of his arrival. He bought three green-broke mustangs and began to train them to his purposes. He had accompanied a payroll train to San Antonio and Austin and back to camp. Grant had also noticed a subtle adjustment in the nomenclature attached to General Taylor's forces. The erstwhile Army of Observation was now being referred to as the Army of Occupation in the chain of command ranging all the way up to President Polk. Grant suspected that the next step, after observation and occupation, would be invasion.

Along with the shift in military semantics, many other changes had occurred here at the formerly quiet hamlet of Corpus Christi since he arrived back in August. As only a few head of livestock had been imported from the States—primarily the dragoon mounts and the trained horses for Ringgold's flying artillery—the men had busied themselves breaking hundreds of wild Mexican mules purchased from the locals and training them to pull supply wagons. Yet there were not enough mules available to pull all the wagons, so oxen had been purchased to make up the difference. The soldiers, most of whom had never driven so much as a cart, had become experienced mule skinners and bull whackers over the winter.

Meanwhile, rations had dwindled. Fewer fish were available to feed the men, and the available game—deer, wild turkeys, alligators, and javelinas—had been killed off or spooked out of the area. Few cattle were available for beef, and those had to be herded in from San Antonio, 150 miles inland. No cattle ranchers yet occupied this Indian- and bandit-infested no-man's-land. Freshwater had proven difficult to haul to camp from a point upstream on the Nueces, above the brackish estuary at her mouth. Even there, the cottonmouth-infested waters tasted of alkali.

As new regiments arrived through the autumn months, Grant began to hear many foreign accents among the rank and file—chiefly Irish and German. This development had given rise to an ugly side of the army's corps of young officers, some of them West Point chums of Grant's. He had been aware of the anti-immigrant and anti-Catholic nativist movement among civilians back in the Eastern states. He had read newspaper accounts of the riots between native-born Protestants and immigrant Catholics in Boston and Philadelphia. But he had had no idea how vehemently some of his fellow officers had embraced the bigotry of the movement.

Grant himself singled out no soldier on account of nationality, but he had no authority to countermand the extreme punishments doled out by officers who had bought into the movement. Some of the immigrants had served in foreign armies and had seen more combat than most of the young officers in the Army of Occupation. The idea that green second lieutenants fresh out of West Point would abuse these experienced warriors based on their foreign accents alone was not only distasteful to Grant but also militarily unwise. When hostilities indeed commenced, the war-wise immigrants would prove invaluable, in his opinion.

As the size of Taylor's army grew over the winter, so had the village of Corpus Christi, now boasting a population of about a thousand civilians, most of them engaged in nefarious endeavors such as gambling, whoring, and whiskey peddling. Drunkenness had become such a problem that General Taylor had placed the camp under curfew after dark. Taylor had maintained strict discipline over his troops. The few bad examples of violence directed toward civilians had been quickly dealt with. By and large, the local citizens admired Old Rough and Ready, especially because he paid premium prices for goods and services needed to keep his army functioning.

Even so, as tents, blankets, and uniforms wore threadbare and sand dunes chewed leather boots to shreds, the coldest weeks of the winter came on. The few American locals at Kinney's Ranch claimed that the winter of forty-five and forty-six had been the coldest in memory. Along with cold and hunger came sickness. The ranks grew at the infirmary, as did the number of graves in the camp cemetery.

So, as an attempt to improve morale and give the soldiers something to do besides drink, whore, and gamble, Grant and several fellow officers had built, at their own expense, a crude theater that would hold an audience of eight hundred men. The officers themselves acted in the plays they produced. Charging just pennies at the door, they soon recouped their investment. In the long run, however, the theater only succeeded in attracting yet another depraved set of civilians to Corpus Christi: professional actors.

But now the time had come to leave all this behind and get on with the campaign. Resolving to rise and start this momentous day, he threw his blanket aside, pulled his boots on, and crawled out of the tent. A swath of crimson clouds far out to sea painted the eastern horizon. He took a long moment to admire the scene as he urinated on a patch of prickly pear cactus.

Throwing his jacket over his shoulders, Grant walked toward the campfire for a cup of coffee. Jacob, the black cook, saw him coming and filled an iron cup from the pot hanging over the campfire.

"Mornin', Lieutenant Grant, sir." Jacob had seemed uneasy in Grant's presence since the cook accidentally let the officer's three mustangs escape back to the wild. Riding one of the horses bareback while leading the two others to water, Jacob had been pulled from his mount when the two led horses spooked at some sight, sound, or smell. He had been dragged for some distance through mesquite and cactus before losing his grip. The horses hadn't been seen since.

"Thank you, Jacob," Grant said, taking the steaming cup of coffee.

"Sir, I'm sorry about them horses," Jacob said, repeating his apology for the umpteenth time. "I wish I'd've held on to just one for you to ride south on today."

"I'm an infantry officer, Jacob. It is well that I should march with my men."

"It happened all of a sudden, sir."

"It was an honest mishap that could have befallen anyone. I don't want to hear about it again. What's for breakfast?" Grant, whose own father had never so much as scolded him, usually treated the men under his own charge with leniency, sometimes to the point of drawing criticism from his fellow officers.

"Fatback and biscuits, sir. Best I could rustle up."

"That will do."

After breakfast, Sam Grant packed his belongings and ordered a couple of privates to carry them to the nearest wagon in the supply train. The soldiers assigned as teamsters were harnessing mules, so Grant decided to get a look at the mule team that would pull the wagon containing his personal effects. This would help him find his possessions later, as each wagon master tended to select animals of similar colors and sizes for his five-mule team.

Besides, it was always entertaining to watch the men hitch the ill-tempered Mexican mules. He stood back some distance as a sergeant picked a big, reddish mule from the picket line—a rope stretched taut between two stout mesquite trees. Two privates approached the mule cautiously, ready to avoid hooves or teeth. Each man put a lariat loop around the mule's neck, then untied the animal from the picket line.

With the beast lunging this way and that, the two privates managed at length to lead it to the wagon, where two other soldiers cautiously fitted it with its harnesses. Then, after pulling and prodding the mule up to the left side of the wagon tongue, they hitched the mule's harness leather to the wagon rigging. Just when they finished, the mule reared up in protest, then kicked the front of the wagon, tangling for a time in the straps and chains.

"You son of a bitch!" the sergeant yelled.

"Yeah, you son of a bitch!" a private echoed, holding to the rope around the mule's neck.

"I wasn't cussin' the mule!" the sergeant shouted. "Keep a tighter hold on that animal, private!"

Grant chuckled, standing akimbo, the sun rising to his back, finally warming his shoulders. He himself knew how to hitch a team. He had grown up working with gentle draft horses on his father's farm. But these wild mules represented an altogether different challenge. It took an army to harness these hell beasts.

He continued to watch as another red mule was hitched to the right of the wagon tongue, under similar exertions. With the wheel mules in place, the swing mules were hitched ahead of them. Finally, the lead mule was harnessed and placed ahead of the two swing mules.

"Well done, men," Grant said, realizing that the same struggle he had just witnessed had occurred, simultaneously, alongside scores of other supply wagons getting ready to disembark on this morning—not to mention the wagons drawn by oxen. The whole army wasn't leaving today. This was just the second wave. A vanguard of dragoons had left yesterday. Tomorrow and the next day, the third and fourth groups would depart. Scouts had determined that the few natural springs along the smuggler's road could not furnish water for all of Taylor's troops and their animals at once, so the Army of Occupation had been divided into four segments for the trip to Matamoras. In all, Grant figured that General Taylor's Army of Occupation included 307 wagons, eighty-four of which were drawn by oxen, the others by mules.

As the Fourth Infantry awaited orders to march, Grant saw his company commander, Captain George A. McCall, riding toward him at a trot. A slender man, handsome and well coifed, McCall represented the epitome of the U.S. Army officer.

"'Morning, Captain," Grant said.

"Grant, I've found you a mount." He pointed. "There is a horse for you."

Grant looked toward the beach and saw one of the black servants who traveled with the regiment holding a three-year-old bay with black points—a fine-looking mustang.

"Thank you, sir, but I've decided to march with the men," Grant explained.

"Grant, I want you to buy that colt. That colored boy purchased it for three dollars and he said he'd sell it to you for five. That is the only mount available for sale between here and Matamoras. The price is reasonable. I'll loan you the five dollars if I have to."

"Captain, I have five dollars. It's just that I thought it appropriate for an infantry officer to march afoot, like the men."

McCall rode nearer and spoke in a lower voice. "It's not appropriate for an officer in my company to march afoot when my own servant in my employ rides my spare mount. Now, if you don't buy that colt, I'm going to have to unhorse my servant and order you to ride my other mount in his stead."

Grant thought about the servant having to walk all the way to Matamoras because of him. "Well, sir, if I must ride, I might as well ride my own horse. I'll purchase the colt."

"Good. Carry on, Grant." McCall rode on down the line, inspecting the wagons assigned to his company.

Grant pulled a five-dollar gold piece from the pocket of his tunic.

"Sir!" said the sergeant in charge of the wagon that held Grant's possessions. "Let me take that half eagle and I'll lead your new colt over here for you. The men will help you get your tack out of the wagon."

Grant realized that the sergeant must have overheard the conversation with McCall and appreciated an officer who was willing to march with his men, even if he wasn't allowed to do so. "Very well," he said. He tossed the coin to the sergeant.

Returning with the colt, the sergeant said, "I asked the colored boy, sir. He said nobody's ever throwed even a blanket on this hoss, so my boys will ear him down for you and we'll get him saddled."

"I appreciate that," Grant replied. He stepped over to the wagon and pulled out the *bosal* he had purchased from a caballero in the village of Corpus Christi. Made by hand from leather and woven rawhide, with reins of braided horsehair, it was the Spanish version of a hackamore, used for training young horses. Fixing no bit in the mouth, it instead controlled the mount by means of the rawhide band over the nose, above the nostrils, which would effectively limit the amount of air flowing to the animal's lungs, affording the rider some control over the untrained horse.

Next, he and a private muscled the Ringgold saddle out of the wagon bed. Grant admired the Ringgold's graceful lines, the pleated seat, the brass trim. Designed by Major Samuel Ringgold of the flying artillery, this was the most comfortable and serviceable saddle Grant had ever ridden. He had borrowed a spare from the flying artillery with the understanding that he would return it, should Ringgold's company need it back.

By the time the enlisted men had adorned the three-year-old bay with Grant's *bosal* and saddle, a shout could be heard coming down the line of supply wagons. A sergeant up ahead turned to pass the order down through the ranks: "Wagons, forward, *ho!*"

"You boys hold on tight, so the lieutenant can mount up," said the sergeant.

"Point him toward the dunes," Grant said. "I don't want him running among the mules." When the men had turned the colt west, Grant put his left foot in the stirrup, stepped up, and swung his right leg over the high cantle. He settled into the saddle as deep as he could and nodded at the soldiers to release the bay's ears.

The colt bolted forward and began to buck but soon got into sand deep enough to hinder his gyrations. Though he jolted along in the saddle, Grant held a tight rein and felt confident that he could stay in the middle. Even should the bay fall, the soft sand would help prevent a disaster.

The real catastrophe, in fact, seemed to be back at the wagon. Still atop his crow-hopping colt, Grant nonetheless saw the lead mule lunge ahead so suddenly that it pulled the breeching up tight against the rumps of the wheel mules, causing them to sit down like pet dogs. Meanwhile, the swing mules were bucking harder than Grant's colt, tangling harnesses.

As his new pony tired, Grant glanced up the line of wagons and witnessed other teams of mules making similar protestations as the entire supply train somehow began to lurch unevenly southward. He kept his mustang plodding through the deep sand, hoping to tire the beast before he got on the solid ground above the dunes. He had little control over the direction his mount took, but the colt seemed to want to follow along with the mules, so Grant went along for the ride.

Time seemed to slow down, and the sounds around him diminished, leaving him in a momentary state of enlightenment. His modicum of control over his new colt and the halting progress of the supply train made a rare and unexpected sensation well up in Grant's interior regions, ranging from his guts to his heart to his brain. He felt a glow of pride within, never before sensed.

The regular soldiers in this little army were largely refugees from American slums or immigrants from foreign cities. Few had ever hitched a team before joining the army. The impossible idea that this many wagons might be harnessed to wild Mexican mules by these previously inexperienced enlisted men and actually driven in a chosen direction with any amount of success amazed him beyond his ability to comprehend the odds overcome.

It was something to remember—something to consider again, in the future, in times of dire necessity. Ranks of disciplined men under able leadership could accomplish what twice their number acting individually could ever hope to do. These average men, through training and military pride, were somehow achieving the unthinkable.

Grant's reverie faded when that Amazon laundress attached to the Seventh Infantry trundled past, driving a cart behind a burro, all her equipage piled around her. Grant remembered her real name—Sarah Bowman—but couldn't help thinking of the nickname she had acquired here at Corpus Christi. The men had begun to call her "the Great Western." He found this amusing. The famous vessel the SS *Great Western* was the biggest, most beautiful steamship in the world. Both big and beautiful, the woman seemed to fit the name and, in fact, sometimes called herself by the moniker.

"That's a right smart colt you're riding, Lieutenant!" she said, tapping her burro's rump with a stick.

"Thank you, Mrs. Bowman. I thought you would have sailed with the other laundresses down to Point Isabel."

"You know I can't let my boys go hungry on the march," she said, referring to the officers for whom she cooked.

Grant suspected that she wanted to miss out on neither three weeks' pay as a cook nor the adventure of driving south with the column. "Yes, of course. How's your husband?"

"No better, but still alive. They put him on a ship yesterday to sail south."

"I hope and pray for his recovery." At this moment, Grant's new mount decided to bolt ahead with such suddenness that he was unable to offer a proper farewell to the Great Western. At least the bay was running instead of bucking.

The trail led up the bluff past Kinney's Ranch, then angled toward the Rio Grande, some 150 miles south. Loping over the brink, passing oxen and mules, Grant's mount afforded him a view across the prairies and patches of chaparral alongside the old smuggler's road. Up here above the dunes, the terrain rolled gently away, inland. From the back of a horse a man could see over the mesquite brush for miles and miles.

It felt good to be out here, riding this mustang. The chill of dawn was long gone, but the sea breeze still carried a crisp, springtime edge to his nostrils. On the open swaths of prairie ahead, Grant saw explosions of blue and orange wildflowers flowing in lavalike shapes, surrounding islands of white and yellow blossoms that added to the great, colorful patchwork quilt. As the bay loped on ahead, the lieutenant rode for a furlong through air so fragrant that he almost choked on it.

Passing the head of the column, out of the dust, his mount finally tired and slowed to a trot, then a walk. The road in front of him was cut deep by the wheels of wagons and the hooves of cavalry horses that had led the way south yesterday. Riding more than a rifle shot ahead of the column now, Grant suddenly began to feel vulnerable. Bandits and Indians were said to prey on smugglers along this road, and here he was alone. What if Mexican cavalry had outflanked the first wave sent south yesterday and now lay in wait over the next roll in the prairie?

"Whoa," he said in a firm voice, pulling with steady pressure on the horsehair reins. The tired bay colt stopped, and Grant released the tension on the reins, rewarding the colt with air.

He imagined the eyes of enemies peering at him from the thorny chaparral. Clumsily, he felt for the hilt of his saber, then put his hand on the saddle holster containing his army-issue single-shot percussion pistol. He vowed to drill more with his weapons—to make himself familiar with the process of drawing them and using them, even at a full gallop. He thought he'd better wait here for the column to catch up, lest he should become the first combat casualty in a war that Mexico, or the U.S. Congress, or both, might already have declared, for all he knew.

Four days later, Lieutenant Grant found himself riding through an open prairie, along the windward side of the column. No one cared to ride on the downwind side of the wagons. Hooves and wheels stirred up a thick cloud of dust that mingled with ash from a recent grass fire. The fine particles of ash blackened the faces and knuckles of soldiers who had no choice but to drive their wagons through it. Grant surmised that the Mexicans had set fire to the grass to deprive the U.S. Army teams of graze.

Now, up ahead, he noticed the procession coming to a halt at the top of a high roll on the coastal plains. He decided to lope his pony forward to investigate. The bay colt, behaving quite properly after four long days of training, sprang to the task. Riding to the top of the rise, Grant saw the reason the column had halted. A few miles away, the open prairie crawled with horseflesh—a moving carpet of hides, manes, and tails—the great mustang herd of no-man's-land.

"Look, Grant," said Captain McCall, riding up next to the lieutenant. "That's the very herd from which your colt was captured."

"I wonder how far and wide it extends," Grant said.

"There's a vantage point a mile or so ahead, on that high open knoll." McCall pointed toward the place.

"Let us have a look, then," Grant said, smiling at his company commander.

They spurred their mounts together and began the race. Grant looked back to see half a dozen other mounted officers joining in the adventure. Within two minutes the heaving horses stood atop the highest roll in the prairie for miles around, yet the end of the mustang herd still could not be seen, lost in the dust of its own making. He had no way of calculating the size of the herd.

Grant stared with his mouth hanging open as some other officers pulled rein to his right and left, forming a line on the knoll. The bay colt backed his ears and nipped at a sorrel with a Spanish brand that was standing too near.

"Good heavens, Captain . . . Do you think that many horses could all fit inside the state of Rhode Island?"

"Perhaps," McCall answered. "But in a day's time not a blade of grass would be left and they'd all have to move on to Connecticut for fresh pasturage."

Some officers chuckled at the captain's assessment, then they all just sat astraddle their mounts and gawked for a time.

"We must remember this, boys," McCall said. "Those of us who survive this war will tell our grandchildren about the great Texas band of wild horses in 1846."

Just then, Grant's mount let out a long, plaintive whinny, his whole body shuttering under the Ringgold saddle. The men laughed.

Grant stroked the bay's sweat-soaked neck. "Sorry, boy. You've joined the army. There will be no going back to civilian life until your enlistment is done."

SARAH BOWMAN

Arroyo Colorado
March 19, 1846

For the past two weeks or more on the smuggler's road, the average daily death toll for rattlesnakes seemed to have been about a dozen, give or take a couple. Soldiers bludgeoned and hacked the poisonous reptiles indiscriminately, leaving the small ones lying and draping the larger trophies over mesquite limbs. As she plodded along with the column, Sarah's burro approached a headless four-footer left by the side of the road. The burro lowered his head for a better look and stomped on the diamondback without breaking stride as they trundled ever southward.

"You sic 'em, Pedro," she said, scratching the tireless beast on the back with her long, thorny mesquite stick.

The numbers of rattlers represented quite a minority compared to the herds of wild horses and deer, the huge flocks of turkeys, and the packs of wolves and coyotes she had witnessed on this trek. This was a wild and peculiar land where javelinas snapped their tusks at invading humans, panthers screamed at night from the chaparral, and tarantulas scurried across her face in her sleep.

Sarah remembered wondering, with the smuggler Commodore Baker, why the Mexicans would want to fight for this frontier at all. She had since learned why, by listening to the talk of the army officers for whom she cooked and mended uniforms. Mexico favored the Nueces for a border because it was a relatively short river, extending only three hundred miles or so inland. The idea was that the western border of Texas would end at the head of the Nueces and, from there, extend due north, limiting the westward sprawl of the new American state. The Texans, and most Americans, preferred the Rio Grande del Norte as the border. It reached almost two thousand miles inland, heading into the great Rocky Mountains, providing for a huge state, including the old Spanish settlements on the east banks of the Rio Grande—El Paso del Norte, Albuquerque, Santa Fe, and Taos.

This dusty, thorny, fang-infested hell between the lower valleys of the Nueces and the Rio Grande really was worth fighting for. It was like the toothy mouth of a gator. It was hazardous, but if you could subdue it, you could lay claim to all the riches beyond. You could feast on its meat and go into the suitcase business. No one really knew the extent of the resources that might lie inland to the north and east of the Rio Grande. Rich farmlands? Timber? Cattle ranching empires? Silver? Gold?

She mused over the ambitions of men in power. How hastily they sent poor soldiers into battle to carry out their lofty whims. She thought of her husband wasting away in the hospital tent. Though she prayed for him daily, she doubted God would spare him. John never would have become this ill back at Jefferson Barracks. This campaign was killing him. She knew it. Yet she knew the Lord worked His ways through many mysteries, and she found some good in it all. Besides laundress and cook, Sarah had become a capable nurse, having spent all of her spare hours caring for her husband and the other sick or injured men.

Ahead on the trail, she saw two soldiers attempting to lift an unconscious comrade into a wagon. Heatstroke and fatigue had taken its toll on many a man during the march. The two men, themselves exhausted, were trying to hoist the limp body over the sideboards of the wagon bed when an officer rode up. It was First Lieutenant Braxton Bragg of the Third Artillery, known as the sternest of the West Point disciplinarians.

"Lift that man in there, you dirty Dutch bastards!" He drew his saber and beat one of the soldiers over the back with the flat of his blade, as if whipping a beast of burden. "We haven't all day to waste over a dying immigrant!"

Sarah rolled up and stopped her cart. Jumping out, she rushed to help, getting her shoulder under the unconscious man's ribs to buoy him upward with her strong legs and back. The man was rolled onto a pile of tattered tents with a couple of other incoherent soldiers.

Bragg only scowled at her, then turned his fierce glare on the German soldiers who had stopped to help a countryman. "Get back in line! March!"

"You're welcome," Sarah muttered, as the lieutenant charged away on his mount. She didn't know if she had ever met a meaner son of a bitch than Lieutenant Bragg. The man possessed an outspoken hatred for the German and Irish soldiers, many of whom had seen combat with other armies in Europe, while Bragg had seen none.

"Git up, Pedro," she ordered, having climbed back into her cart. A half hour later, passing over one of those low rolls in the prairie, she could see that the column had halted up ahead. Through the dust, she made out a barrier of taller chaparral punctuated by bright green willows down in the next low swell. That meant a stream—the Arroyo Colorado. The entire column was drawing up and gathering here. Many of the officers had predicted a fight with the Mexican Army at this arroyo.

As her donkey cart bounced past some bull whackers, Sarah joshed with the men who forever gawked at her uncommonly large and shapely frame. "Take a break, you horny beasts!"

"You talkin' to us or the oxen?" a sergeant replied.

"If the shoe fits . . ."

"What are *you* gonna do about it?" a private asked.

"Take your bullwhip to your hide, if you don't mind your manners."

The men guffawed, and she joined in the laughter with them, until she saw a soldier relieving himself at the edge of the chaparral alongside the road. "Hey, Private, reel that in and button up your tongs. You're liable to get snakebit!"

"Ma'am, it *is* part rattlesnake!" the man boasted.

"Well, what in tarnation stunted its growth?"

The men roared, and she drove on past the ranks of the mule skinners, shouting encouragement and suggestive jocularities to the soldiers. She never feared any untoward advances from these men. First off, she was pretty sure she could whip most of them in a fair fight. And though not all were perfect gentlemen, the vast majority of them possessed a military code that honored womanhood—at least for white women such as herself.

Approaching the head of the column, she saw a stampede of dragoons galloping back up from the banks of the arroyo to the place where General Taylor was talking with his officers, about how to ford the stream,

she supposed. Sarah drove her burro cart up close to them, anxious to
listen in on the developments. She stopped near the place where Taylor
sat atop Old Whitey, jumped out of her cart, and strolled over near the
gathering of officers as the cavalry arrived from the arroyo.

"I want the artillery placements ready at dawn," Taylor was saying to
Lieutenant Scarritt, of the engineers. "I don't care if the men have to work
all night." The general angled his eyes toward Captain Mansfield, who
had just ridden up from the stream. "Report, Captain."

"The enemy is waiting across the stream, sir."

"How many?"

"We were unable to determine their numbers. They're hidden in the
chaparral brush and the timber."

"Artillery? Cavalry?"

"We couldn't see any guns, General, but we did see some lancers moving about. And we spoke to a Mexican officer across the water."

Taylor's eyebrows lifted casually. "The man spoke English?"

"Very fluently. He identified himself as a captain. He said any attempt
of the Army of Occupation to cross the arroyo would be considered an
act of war."

"Very well, Captain. You're dismissed. We'll camp here for the night
and prepare to cross at dawn." Taylor swung laboriously down from his
tall, white horse. "Bill!"

"Yes, sir!" shouted Captain William Bliss, the general's adjutant.

"I want all of the regimental commanders and the engineers at my
tent at sundown for a council of war."

"Yes, sir!" Bliss barked.

Sarah admired the dashing adjutant. Known as Perfect Bliss, the captain was the quintessence of an army officer. He reined his mount away
to carry out his orders.

"General Taylor!" shouted Captain Charles Smith. "I respectfully request the honor of leading the infantry crossing in the morning!"

Sarah heard a hush fall over the men within earshot, many of them
Smith's own infantry soldiers, who were sitting or standing nearby, listening. She glanced at their faces and found many stunned at their commander's offer to lead them into what everyone expected to be the opening
battle of the war.

Suddenly she felt honor bound to speak up. "General Taylor!" she
shouted in her loudest voice, so as many of the men as possible might

hear her. "Give me a strong pair of tongs and I'll wade across right now and whip every scoundrel I can lay hands on!"

Taylor's broad smile broke across his face and his shoulders shook with mirth, though Sarah heard no laughter. The laughter came, instead, from the enlisted soldiers within earshot.

"That won't be necessary, ma'am. The rest of you get back to your companies and await your instructions."

Satisfied that she had raised the hackles of this fighting force, Sarah withdrew to tend to her burro. She unhitched her cart and took Pedro to water, then staked him in some tall grass. She would set up her kitchen right here. If her boys wanted to dine tonight, they could come and find her, because she didn't have the time or the inclination to track them down just now.

In her deep sleep, the night seemed to pass quickly. Sarah rose before dawn to prepare breakfast. Her boys ate quietly in the dark, their minds on the battle they expected to face at sunup. When she had finished the dishes, she loaded her things in preparation for the crossing and hitched Pedro to her cart. She then tied the burro to a mesquite tree.

Next, she checked the loads in the double-barreled .50-caliber percussion pistol her husband had won from a gambler two years ago while playing stud poker in Saint Louis. She tucked the pistol under her apron strings and found a trail that led down toward the arroyo. She didn't intend to miss the crossing of the army. But she had to hurry, for daylight had crept over no-man's-land, and four companies of infantry, under Captain Smith, had already formed up to wade the brackish stream.

As she approached the Arroyo Colorado, an unexpected noise caught Sarah's attention, causing her to stop. A bugle? She heard it again and recognized the familiar notes of Assembly. But this bugle had come from *across* the Arroyo Colorado. Looking south, to the other side of the stream, she caught glimpses of red-and-blue uniforms darting around in the chaparral. She even saw the long, shining blades of lances rising and falling above the mesquite branches. She heard orders being shouted in Spanish. Then more bugle calls.

A company of flying artillery raced by her, followed by General Taylor on Old Whitey. "Don't judge the enemy's strength by his noise, men!" the commander shouted to the infantry.

Rushing ahead now to get a closer view, Sarah twisted and ducked through the willows along a deer trail. She heard the Mexican bugler blowing the notes of First Sergeant's Call, indicating that the head enlisted man in the company across the way was about to form up his men—for what purpose, Sarah could only guess.

She arrived at the bank of the brackish stream to find the water several feet below her, at the bottom of an eroded bank cut vertically through the dirt. This cut bank extended up and down the arroyo in both directions. But at dusk last evening, men with picks and shovels had begun carving a slanted road through it to facilitate the crossing of the wagons and artillery. She could see this road to her left.

Now, as she watched, three six-pounders of the flying artillery under the dashing Major Ringgold drew up and unlimbered on the bluff to guard the crossing of the foot soldiers. These artillery placements had been cleared of thorny undergrowth overnight by soldiers with axes. She heard the officers calling for spherical case shot to be loaded. For all she knew, Mexican cannon might be aiming back her way at this very moment.

Sarah found a fallen cottonwood near the water but far enough back in the willows to keep her concealed from Mexican snipers. She kicked at the log to roust out any snakes that might be lurking there, then took a seat on the horizontal trunk. With her pistol resting on her thigh, she would watch what just might turn out to be the beginning of a war.

With the artillery in place and a company of riflemen covering the Arroyo Colorado with double firing lines—the men in front kneeling while the soldiers behind them stood—the order was given to commence the crossing.

Smith's men waded in, holding their muskets and their ammunition pouches above their heads to keep them dry. They proceeded slowly as the artillerymen stood poised with lanyards in their hands, anxious to start the war with a yank of the cord. As the foot soldiers slogged across, a horseman plunged in behind them and overtook the wading men. It was the overzealous General William Worth. Apparently unable to restrain himself, Worth startled Captain Smith by joining him in the lead.

Mexican bugles continued to sing, and lance tips appeared here and there above the brush. But they were farther away now. The first soldiers floundered ashore on the far bank and Sarah began to see the whole lance-and-bugle show for what it was: bluff and bluster. Her hero, General Taylor, had handled it well. The Mexicans were withdrawing.

All signs of the opposing army vanished as Captain Smith waved *All clear* from the opposite bank. The fife and drums lit into "Yankee Doodle." Men cheered.

Sarah sighed. The thick grass at her feet seemed to beckon, so she slid off the log and reclined on the ground, face upward. The sun shone down through new green cottonwood leaves, illuminating them like stained glass windows. A spring breeze carried aromas of strange blossoms to her nostrils, mixed with the dank odor of rotten driftwood. She knew the men would take some time to cross, so she closed her eyes and drifted away, hearing the shouts of officers even in her sleep.

The curses of the mule skinners woke her, so Sarah sat up and climbed back up onto her log perch. She yawned and rubbed her eyes like a sleepy child. The first wagon was being eased down the steep slope the men had carved in the vertical cut bank. A group of soldiers behind the wagon held to a short rope tied to the rear axle to keep it from rolling too quickly into the water. Ahead, a long rope had been tied to the wagon tongue, passed between the swing mules, and then through the bridle of the lead mule. It led all the way across the arroyo, where a gang of twenty men pulled the mule team forward. In the middle of the stream, the wagon bed began to float, but the salty estuary moved sluggishly and the swimming mules easily pulled the load to the opposite bank.

She watched two more wagons cross before the process, although impressive in its ingenuity, began to bore her. Time had come to find her place in line and make her own crossing. Taylor had ordered a two-day rest at a spring on the south side of the arroyo. She would set up her kitchen and find a hunter who had bagged a deer or a turkey or one of those wild piglike critters called javelinas. She would purchase some meat and make some stew for her boys. The excitement in camp would run high tonight. The enemy had been spotted, and had turned tail.

Private
ANDREW SINGER

Rio Grande
March 29, 1846

"Some farmer done went to a lot of trouble for nothin'," said Private Andrew Singer as he pulled up another six-inch stalk of corn. "Any of you boys ever push a plow?"

"I learned to walk holdin' on to a plow," one private claimed.

"I plowed a million acres before I was ten years old," said another.

"Well, some corn farmer had him a nice crop comin' up till Zach Taylor's army moved into the neighborhood." Singer looked across the Rio Grande at the Mexican town of Matamoras, its gaily painted walls and wrought iron balcony railings visible in the afternoon sunshine. "That poor farmer's probably on one of them balconies right now, cussin' our sorry asses for pullin' up his crop."

"They sure plant early down here," said a farm boy from Ohio.

"You damn pumpkin rollers," said a soldier from Boston. "I'm glad I never had to make a living looking up a mule's ass."

"Well, you're in the cornfield with the rest of us now," Singer said, pulling up another plant and smoothing the furrows underfoot with his boot.

"That's the bitter truth," said the Bostonian, using his shovel to level the ground so the men could pitch their tents on this erstwhile cornfield. "Stuck here with you dumb hayseeds."

Singer threw a clod at the city slicker, which was answered with a shovelful of dirt hurled his way.

"Singer!"

The private cringed, having recognized the harsh voice of his sergeant at the edge of the field. "Yeah, Sarge?"

"Come here!"

Singer felt a touch of dread crawling about his skin as he wondered how long the sergeant had been watching. It was just a little clod. He marched quickly past uprooted corn plants and around a few tents his messmates in Company C of the Eighth Infantry were staking to the ground.

"Come with me," the sergeant said. "General Worth wants to talk to you."

"The general? What for?"

"You'll have to ask him."

"Am I in trouble?"

"Probably."

Singer's mind whirled back over the past several days, wondering what he might have done that would warrant an audience with General Worth. They had crossed the Arroyo Colorado without trouble from the Mexican Army. They had proceeded to march out of the rough chaparral country and into a land of pastures and croplands, many of which had been abandoned by the Mexican farmers in the face of the invading Yankee army. They came to this bend in the river across from the pretty little city of Matamoras yesterday and started making camp, fearful of an enemy attack at any given moment.

They had seen hundreds of Mexican troops across the river, drilling to martial music all day yesterday and today. Singer had to admit that their army band beat all hell out of the Americans' fifes and drums. Across the Rio Bravo, as it was sometimes called, the enemy army flaunted a marching ensemble with a whole brass section.

He had seen Mexican women, too, bathing naked on the far bank, causing many a man to gravitate toward the water when not on fatigue duty. It was Singer, himself, who had come up with the idea to teach off-duty "swimming lessons" to his messmates, and his classes had been well attended.

Thinking back on all this, though, he couldn't remember any serious mischief he had gotten into that might cause General Worth, of all people, to want to interview him.

When they arrived at the general's tent, the sergeant spoke to the adjutant, who spoke to the general. General Worth came out of his tent.

Singer saluted.

"Are you Private Andrew Singer, Company C, Eighth Infantry?"

"Yes, sir."

"Come with me. General Taylor wants to have a word with you."

General Taylor himself? Old Rough and Ready?

Singer followed Worth to the nearby camp headquarters, past guards who saluted General Worth. On a whim, Singer himself returned one of the salutes, then thought he'd better straighten up and act proper. They marched on, among officers from different regiments, who stood around smoking pipes, conversing, looking at maps, gazing across the river. Worth spoke to Taylor's adjutant, Captain Bliss, who leaned into Taylor's tent and said something to the general.

"Come on in, gentlemen," Bliss said.

Singer followed on Worth's heels, saluting left and right to every officer who looked his way.

"General, I have brought Private Singer to see you."

Singer stepped around Worth and came to attention, brandishing one more salute. He found Old Rough and Ready sitting on a trunk, darning a sock with a needle and thread. He had a boot on his right foot but the other was bare, the left boot lying beside the trunk on which the general sat.

"Forgive me for not returning your salute just now, Private."

Singer dropped his arm to his side. "Of course, sir. I wouldn't want you to poke yourself in the general's eye with that there needle."

Taylor looked up from his task, his calm, knowing gaze sizing up his visitor. Singer thought he might already have stepped in it, but then the general's thick lips formed a smile.

"You may stand at ease," Taylor said, resuming the mending of his sock. "Singer, I'm told you speak some Spanish."

"I understand more than I speak, sir."

"Where did you come by these linguistic skills?"

"My father served with the Duke of Wellington against Napoleon's forces in Spain, sir. He met a senorita and married her."

"Your mother."

"Yes, sir. She rarely spoke English to me. Mostly just Spanish."

General Taylor knotted his thread and used his teeth to cut it free from his sock. "How do you feel about the prospects for this war against Mexico?"

"I'm a soldier, sir. I don't feel; I just follow orders."

General Worth, standing by, grunted approvingly.

Taylor struggled to get the darned sock over his toes, for he was a little thick through the middle and, Singer concluded, a mite stove up from years of hard service on the frontier.

"I'm asking for your opinion, Singer. Speak your mind."

"Well, sir, I read the newspapers. Ten years ago, when he lost at the battle of San Jacinto, Santa Anna signed a treaty naming the border between Texas and Mexico at the Rio Grande. Texas being a state now, I'd say we're well within our rights to defend that border. I'd hate for them boys at the Alamo to have died for nothin'. Hell, that's the reason I enlisted. To defend American soil."

Taylor pulled on his boot and stood up, pushing at the small of his back. He smiled at Singer, apparently in approval of the private's answer. "General Worth tells me you have a knack for talking your way out of a bind when need be."

Singer glanced at Worth. "Sir, that may be true. But that might also point out a knack for getting into the bind in the first place."

The two generals laughed, and Singer began to relax. He still didn't know what the hell he had gotten himself into, but so far it was more interesting than being bucked and gagged on the parade ground—or pulling up some poor farmer's corn plants, for that matter.

"General Worth tells me that you are to be commended for teaching your messmates how to swim."

"Thank you, sir."

"So, you are a strong swimmer?"

"Oh, yes, sir. I was swimmin' before I could walk."

"Your lessons have nothing to do with the scenery across the river?"

Singer grinned. "Well that helped in recruiting pupils, sir. But it seems to me President Polk might want us to cross that river any day now, and I figured the boys in Company C ought to be ready."

Taylor looked at Worth and they nodded at each other.

"You've been handpicked to carry out an assignment, Private Singer. You can accept it or refuse it. If you accept it, and survive, you will be promoted to corporal and given an extra gill of whiskey. If you refuse, you will return to your company and continue to serve your nation."

"Sir, may I ask what the assignment is?"

"That I cannot tell you, unless you accept."

Singer mulled the matter over. This had something to do with understanding Spanish, being able to talk one's way out of trouble, and knowing how to swim. It sounded to him as if the generals were looking for a spy. "Corporal Andrew Singer," he said, mostly to himself. "Has a nice sound to it. My mother will be proud."

"Once you're in, there's no backing out," Worth warned.

Singer had had his fill of the boredom of fatigues. He could already see himself lording his corporal's stripes over the boys in his company. "Deal me in, sir."

Taylor smiled. "Bill, where's that circular?"

The general's adjutant, Captain William Bliss, produced the flyer from a stack of papers on the general's desk. He handed it to Taylor.

"Have you seen this?" the general asked.

"Yes, sir," Singer admitted. He had read a copy of it. It was a printed invitation, in English, from General Ampudia, across the river, for U.S. soldiers to desert. It was aimed at the immigrant soldiers, and the Catholic Irishmen in particular. It offered rank, pay, friendship, and farmland for the deserter who would cross the river to join Mexican forces.

Taylor gestured toward General Worth. Worth turned to address Singer.

"Your assignment is to feign desertion. Take this flyer with you and swim across the river. Pretend that you don't understand Spanish. Observe what you can of the enemy's forces. Stay a day or two and swim back over." General Worth thrust the printed circular at him.

Singer accepted the handbill.

General Taylor extended his thick palm toward his new spy. "Good luck, son. General Worth will explain the details to you."

Singer shook the general's hand, came to attention, and saluted. This time, Old Rough and Ready returned the salute.

After twilight, General Worth's personal guard escorted Private Singer to the banks of the river. Along this stretch of the undulating *rio*, the stream ran north to south, so crossing the river meant heading due west. The glow of the sunset silhouetting the cathedral belfry in Matamoras would guide Singer's way. Only a sliver of the waxing moon would appear tonight. It was the perfect hour to swim the river undetected.

As his guard withdrew, Singer clawed his way through the thorny underbrush and slipped into the cold waters of the Rio Grande. He reasoned that rain must have fallen somewhere upstream, for the current had picked up considerably since his last "swimming lesson" with his messmates. No matter. He really was a strong swimmer, and he had no weapons weighing him down.

The current carried him to his left as he dog-paddled his way across. Reaching the other side, he grabbed a tree branch along the stretch where the women bathed and washed laundry by day. He pulled himself ashore and immediately fished General Ampudia's flyer out of his shirt. There were trails here that the women used to carry their laundry to and from the Bravo. He followed one up the bank, his heart beating with the excitement of his lone mission.

Peeking over the brink of the trail, he found himself looking at a peaceful cobblestoned street fronting the river. Lamplight illuminated the windows of some houses, a café, and what appeared to be a busy cantina on the corner down the way. Couples strolled arm in arm. A small gathering of old men stared across the river at the campfires of the U.S. Army.

Singer caught himself thinking what a shame it would be to have to blast hell out of this pretty little town, should the stubborn politicians fail to agree on where the border ought to lie. But that was not his concern. He was a private on his way to earning his stripes as a corporal, and he had a job to do that might actually prevent his own friends from getting blasted to hell.

After watching for a minute or two, shivering from nerves and the chill water, he spotted four armed soldiers patrolling the street. When they had passed by, he slipped out of the riverbank timber and fell in behind them.

Might as well get on with it, he thought.

"*Por favor!*" he shouted, in the worst American accent he could muster. His mother would have twisted his ear for butchering the language that way.

As the soldiers wheeled around, he stepped into the light from a window and held his hands up and away from his body, his right hand clutching Ampudia's circular. This was the moment, he thought, in which he was most likely to get shot. He was wearing a U.S. Army uniform on the wrong side of the river. His heart beat furiously against his chest.

The four soldiers shouted all manner of Spanish orders at one another, and at him, but he pretended not to understand any of it. With the muzzles of ancient muskets pointing at him, he brandished the printed flyer.

"*Por favor*," he repeated.

The soldiers approached cautiously, one of them yanking the handbill from his grasp.

"Let's shoot him," one of the soldiers suggested in Spanish.

"He has no guns. No weapons at all. It would be cowardly."

"He wants to join us."

"Let's take him to Capitan Huerta," said the apparent leader of the patrol. "Huerta speaks English." The soldier thrust the muzzle of his musket toward Singer. "*Habla español?*" he demanded.

Per his orders, Private Singer pretended to understand nothing.

He was marched around the corner and down a street to the west, a guard to either side, one leading the way, one guarding his rear. Pedestrians turned to gawk and point. He felt the worst part was over. Now he simply had to convince the *capitan* that he wanted to join the Mexican Army.

Walking into the town plaza, where restaurants and cantinas carried on a lively trade, Singer passed a woman sitting at an outdoor café table, smoking a cigarette. A woman! Smoking! And no one seemed to mind. He noticed two artillery pieces across the square—antique six-pounders aimed in the direction of the U.S. camp. He had to remember to take note of weapons, troop numbers, horses, wagons, supplies.

Citizens gathered closer, shouting their excitement over his arrival.

"They have captured a Yankee!"

"He's soaking wet!"

"Will they hang him, or shoot him?"

"Save bullets," an old ranchero shouted at the soldiers. "A single noose can be used many times!"

A crowd laughed.

His guards escorted him to a two-story hotel at the corner of the plaza, where many soldiers languished. The Spanish language hummed all around him. This was a different kind of Spanish from that which his mother had spoken to him as a child and it began to overwhelm him, to the point that he deciphered very little of it.

Singer found the inside of the hotel lobby clouded with tobacco smoke and crowded with exquisitely uniformed officers of all ages gathered around painted jugs of what he thought must be tequila. He was ordered to halt here as one of his guards ran up the stairs. After Singer endured the cool-eyed stares of the officer corps for a long minute, the guard whistled down at his comrades and Singer was hustled up the steps and pushed into a lavish suite overlooking the plaza.

Singer found a man at a desk, writing a report of some kind, his face bent over his work, his fingers clutching a quill pen. A dark blue tunic with captain's bars on the epaulets was hanging on the back of the desk chair.

The captain looked up from the paperwork. "So, you are the deserter," he said, his English perfect.

Singer came to attention and saluted. "Private Andrew Singer at your service, sir."

The captain brushed his fingertips across his brow. "Of course, you know my name already."

"I'm afraid I do not, sir. We have only now just met."

He scoffed. "I am Captain Emilio Huerta."

"Thank God you speak English, sir. I didn't know what these fellers might have in mind for me." He tossed his head toward the guards who had captured him.

The captain drilled him with a cold stare. "You are a deserter. Is this true?"

"Sir, I think of myself as a recruit, not a deserter. I found myself on the wrong side of the fight, so I come over to the right side."

The captain jabbed his pen into an inkwell and left it there. "Why do you want to join the Army of Mexico?"

"A lot of reasons, sir."

The captain leaned back in his chair. "I am 'all ears,' as you say in your country."

He decided to start with a lie. "My father was Irish. My mother is Spanish. I am an American by birth only, sir. My folks were both Catholics."

"Irish and Spanish? How did this come to be?"

Singer told the true story of his father's service in Spain with the English Army.

"If your mother is Spanish, why don't you speak Spanish?"

"My father died when I was young. My mother married one of them heretic Protestants. He wouldn't let her speak Spanish no more. Wouldn't let her go to mass, either."

"How did your father die?"

Singer had thought this story out in advance. "A pine tree fell on him, sir."

The captain's brows revealed his skepticism. "In the forest?"

"No, sir. It rolled off a wagon at the sawmill."

"I see. My, uh . . . condolences."

"Sir, my recruiter lied to me. He told me I was going to fight the Brits in Oregon. He told me I'd make rank and be a sergeant by now. The American officers have got it in for us Irish—even a half-Irish boy like me. I just can't see taking up arms against Catholics and Spanish speakers."

Huerta seemed a bit stunned by the outburst. He looked at the guards waiting at the door. In Spanish, he gave his order: "Corporal, go downstairs and find a rope so we can hang this spy in the plaza."

The translation came gradually in Singer's mind, and that was good, for it gave him a chance to mask his reaction to the shocking directive. General Worth had warned him that the Mexicans would test his knowledge of Spanish in this way. He knew the captain was studying his facial expression, so he took care to appear clueless.

"Capitan?" the Mexican corporal asked. "*Seguro?*"

"No, not really." Huerta replied, in Spanish. "I was only testing him. You are dismissed."

The guards smiled, elbowed one another, and left the room. Captain Huerta got up from his chair and walked slowly around the desk, looking Singer over from head to toe. He came face-to-face with the spy. "You are my size, more or less. You should get rid of that uniform before you get shot. I have some dry clothes you can put on. Then I'll show you around town. Tomorrow you will meet General Mejia. Are you hungry?"

"Starved, sir."

The captain smiled and slapped him on the shoulder. "Welcome to Mexico."

Brigadier General
ZACHARY TAYLOR

Rio Grande
March 30, 1846

"General? Sir?"

General Zachary Taylor found himself staring at the map of the lower Rio Grande Valley, but he realized that his mind had drifted far away, to his Cypress Grove plantation in Louisiana. A slow rain pattered hypnotically on the tent canvas above his head.

"Sorry, Bill," he said to Captain William Bliss. He rubbed his eyes, feeling the fatigue of his commandership sinking deep into his bones. He had been wondering how his overseers and his servants—as he called his slaves—were getting on at Cypress Grove. Had the last frost come and gone? Had the rains loosened the rich, black soil for the plowshares?

"Sir, perhaps we should continue in the morning." Bliss rolled the map into a perfect scroll and tied it with a blue ribbon. He pulled a watch from the pocket of his tunic. "It's almost midnight, after all."

Taylor nodded at Bliss. The indefatigable young captain sometimes forgot that normal men needed sleep now and then.

"Yes, we'll take this up again after breakfast, Bill. Good night."

Bliss reached for his lantern and had begun to leave the commander's tent, when General Worth appeared.

"I saw your lamp still burning, Zach."

"The general was just turning in," Bliss protested.

"It's okay, Bill. You may leave us. What is it, General?"

Worth sneered at Bliss as he left the tent. "Our spy has returned from Matamoros," he said.

"Do tell? Bring him in."

Taylor saw Private Singer step into the lantern light, shivering in a soaking wet Mexican officer's uniform. The intrepid soldier saluted.

"Capitan Singer reporting, sir!"

Taylor grinned appreciatively, realizing that he hadn't felt a smile cross his face all day, until now. He saluted the spy. "I see they granted you a commission, Singer."

"Shortest military career in Mexican history, sir."

Taylor handed the man a blanket to wrap around his shoulders and invited him to sit. "Tell me about your adventure."

Singer went on about his capture, meeting Captain Huerta, dining on beef and incredibly hot peppers, attending a fandango. This morning, he had met General Mejia, had been granted his commission, and had been promised 320 acres of farmland after the war. His translator, Captain Huerta, had then taken him on a riding tour of the military camp outside of Matamoras.

"They have about three thousand five hundred troops," Singer reported, "and I heard rumors that more were coming from the south. About five hundred of the troops I saw were cavalry and looked like right smart fighting men. They carry lances, sabers, and *escopetas*. Sawed-off muskets, sir."

"I'm familiar with the term, Singer. Continue."

"Most of the men were infantry. The regular army infantry wear sharp blue uniforms and look capable. But there are thousands of conscripted troops. Peasants and Indians with old Brown Bess muskets. Dressed in white cotton tongs and shirts that hardly pass for uniforms. Some wore sandals or even went barefoot."

"Artillery?" Taylor asked.

"I saw about twenty guns, none larger than a twelve-pounder. I gathered that they don't have much in the way of ammunition to ram down the barrels, other than solid cannonballs and grapeshot consisting of busted-up iron. But I saw a couple of mortars that could do some damage."

"What was Mejia's idea in making you a captain? Captain of what?"

"Well, sir, he intended for me to raise my own company."

Taylor scratched at his chin stubble. "Of what?"

"Deserters. He thinks the Catholic immigrants are going to swim over in droves."

Taylor looked at Worth and read the grim concern in his face that Mejia's thinking might have some validity. "You've done well, Private Singer. You're dismissed."

Singer rose from his seat. "Begging the general's pardon, sir, but don't you mean *Corporal* Singer?" The likable spy gave him a grin.

"Of course. General Worth will see to your promotion. It's a far cry from captain, but you've earned it."

"Sir, I'd rather be a corporal in this army than president of Mexico." Singer saluted.

"Wise choice, soldier. Presidents of Mexico usually don't last as long as American corporals." He returned the salute.

Singer, Worth, and Bliss left his tent. General Taylor twisted the wick wheel on his lantern and lay down in the dark on his cot, fully dressed. He thought he would go to sleep quickly, but he lay there for some time thinking of politics, supplies, spies, religion, old battles fought, and the war to come. Finally, he drifted away to Cypress Grove and fell asleep to the imagined music of crickets in the cotton fields.

Private
JOHN RILEY

Fort Texas
April 11, 1846

He put the weight of his shoulders on the handle of the shovel, adding the muscle of his left leg on the back edge of the blade to drive the steel deep into the loamy river-bottom soil. Private John Riley scooped up pounds of earth from what had been a farmer's cornfield to deposit in the wooden bucket he had been issued. All around him, hundreds of soldiers—perhaps a thousand or more—were engaged in a common task: building a massive fort made almost completely of dirt.

Like most of the laborers, Riley had volunteered for this extra duty for the gill of whiskey promised to every man willing to dig and haul soil. He drank very little liquor himself, but he knew the lads in his company would not let it go to waste. Most of the diggers employed a shovel and a bucket. Others used picks, wheelbarrows, carts drawn by donkeys or oxen, and even their bare hands to scoop up soil loosened by others.

War was increasingly likely on this disputed border, any day now. Across the Rio Grande, Riley could see artillery moving into place behind the Mexicans' own earthworks. On this side of the river, General Taylor apparently intended to be prepared for the worst, should the cannonade begin.

The engineers had surveyed and staked the fort just four days ago and already the walls were higher than Riley's head. The design was simple enough: a six-sided structure with artillery to be placed on round battlements protruding outward from each angle of the hexagon. Because of the shape, some called it a star fort.

"I bet it's still cold up in Michigan," said one of his fellow infantrymen as he used his sleeve to mop the sweat from his brow. "This valley is a paradise."

"It won't be when the cannon begin to fire."

"What do you know of it?"

Riley glared. "I was a sergeant major in the British Army against the Afghans. A regimental pioneer in the Forty-Fifth Queen's Foot."

"Pioneer?" the Michigander said. "Queen's Foot? What the hell does that mean?"

"I was an advance scout. I would enter enemy territory to prepare lines of march for the regiment. And I was a gunner. An artilleryman. I've killed a hundred enemy, lad, and more. I've seen men standing as nigh as you and I torn to shreds by a single blast. This fort will be bloody hell when those cannon across the river begin to bark."

The green Michigan boy blanched and moved away from Riley to continue his digging.

What little timber could be obtained in the valley had been used to fashion small rooms around the inside of the fort walls. These would be covered with several feet of dirt, supposedly making them bombproof. The bases of the fort walls were fifteen feet thick, angling in toward the top. Around the outside of the wall, a dry moat had been created by all the digging. Riley estimated the diameter of the hexagon at some 250 paces. This was a sorry substitute for the medieval castles of stone he had admired in his native Ireland as a lad. It was nothing more than a temporary redoubt upon which to mount the two eighteen-pounders and the smaller guns in Taylor's arsenal.

The gill of whiskey notwithstanding, Riley felt deeply troubled to be engaged in the building of Fort Texas, as it was being called. Those were Catholic souls abiding across the river in the town of Matamoros. One day soon, shells and mortars would arch gracefully from these dirt walls and rain down on the citizens and soldiery there. Not even the cathedral would be spared. He felt he had been duped into waging a holy war upon people of his own religion.

A rumor among the ranks held that some Texas Rangers had ridden into the Mexican town at Point Isabel, at the mouth of the Rio Grande. The little village, called El Fronton, had been set on fire. Even the chapel

had burned. In his head rang echoes of stories his parents and grandpar-
ents had told of the awful days of English invasion in 1798, before his
time. These self-satisfied Protestant Anglos were forever burning
Catholics out of their homes and cathedrals. And now, he, John Riley,
had allowed himself to become a pawn of the Protestant war machine.

How have I come to this?

Another rumor maintained that General Taylor planned to divide his
forces soon and take most of the army to Point Isabel to receive supplies.
This idea concerned the war-wise Riley. Though he knew supplies were
needed, he could also see that the Mexican ranks across the river were
growing daily. Earlier today, among much ringing of chapel bells and
ceremonial cannon fire, General Ampudia and several thousand troops
had arrived at Matamoros. Plumes of campfire smoke now ringed the
little Mexican town. And Taylor planned to divide his forces?

Though he sympathized with the Mexican soldiers across the river,
he had no desire to be overrun, shot, and bayoneted by them.

At Kinney's Ranch, Riley had developed a high opinion of General
Zachary Taylor. That favorable view had recently come to an abrupt
end. A fortnight ago, Taylor had sent a spy across the river to pose as a
deserter. That man had returned, telling tales of lavish Mexican hospitality. He said the Mexicans had made him a captain! In addition, two
dragoons, captured earlier, had been released, and both had related treatment that far surpassed common courtesy. These accounts had spurred a
new trend. Men—especially Catholic immigrant soldiers—had begun to
desert in ever larger numbers.

To discourage the practice, General Taylor had ordered sentinels to
shoot any man swimming the river to Matamoros. Yes, deserters were
often executed in times of war. There was just one problem here. There
was no declared war. Not yet, anyway. To Riley, this practice amounted
to legalized murder. It was a blatant violation of the Articles of War.
Taylor was a military commander, not a king!

Dozens of men had deserted in spite of the shoot-to-kill order. Only
two were shot to death, though four others had drowned in the swift cur-
rents.

Then, new leaflets had begun to appear in the American camp. The
author of the flyer, General Pedro de Ampudia, encouraged all foreigners among the Americans—especially Catholics—to desert and join the
Mexicans. While collecting firewood, Riley had found one of the printed

circulars blown into a thicket. He had secreted himself in the brush to read it.

The Commander-in-Chief of the Mexican Army to the Irish, Germans, French, Poles, and individuals of other nations under orders of the American General Taylor:

Know ye: That the Government of the United States is committing repeated acts of barbarous aggression against the magnanimous Mexican nation; that the Government that exists under the flag of the stars is unworthy of the designation of Christian.

Now then, come with all confidence to the Mexican ranks, and I guarantee to you, upon my honor, good treatment, and that all of your expense shall be defrayed until your arrival in the beautiful capital of Mexico.

Separate yourselves from the Yankees, and do not defend a robbery and usurpation which, be assured, the civilized nations of Europe look upon with utmost indignation. Come, therefore, and array yourselves under the tri-colored flag, in confidence that the God of Armies protects it, and will protect you.

Though he had burned a similar flyer back at Corpus Christi, he'd slipped this one inside his shirt and gone about the task of gathering wood.

"I'll carry that bucket, John," said one of his messmates—another Irishman who had enlisted at Fort Mackinac. "Here's an empty one you can fill."

"You're welcome to dig awhile, lad," Riley said, the sarcasm thick in his Irish brogue.

"That I will, then. With the next empty bucket I bring."

"Mind you don't get lost."

He prepared to dig up a shovelful for the empty bucket, when the chimes of a cathedral bell across the river caught his attention. He straightened and pushed his hand against the muscles in the small of his back. Gazing across the river, he caught sight of a procession of holy men blessing a cannon hitched behind six black horses. Even from this distance he could see wisps of burning incense trailing from swinging braziers and the motions of the priest's arm as he cast holy water upon the cannon. It all served to stir his Catholic soul. How wonderful it

would be to live in a land where he could attend mass openly with his
wife and his son. Someday . . . Maybe someday—

"You!"

The voice jolted him back to Fort Texas. He turned to see a familiar
officer stalking toward him down the slope of the unfinished earthen
wall. It was Lieutenant Braxton Bragg, Third Artillery. He had been
looking over the fort's gun emplacements and had spotted Riley gazing
across the river.

"Sir!" Riley said, standing at attention. Being a big man was sometimes a curse. He could not help being noticed in a crowd. There were
weak men in the world who resented a larger man simply for standing tall.
This was particularly true in military life, where a man of smaller stature
could hide behind his superior rank in order to abuse a soldier larger than
himself. Right now, John Riley was the larger man of lower rank.

"I know you, you lazy Irish bum!" Bragg came close enough to spit
the words up at Riley's face. "Dig, you stupid mick!"

Riley renewed his assault on the moat.

"This is the second time I have suffered your insolence, Private! The
third will get you bucked and gagged in view of those idolatrous priests
you've been gazing at." He leaned closer. "And I *will* catch you a third
time, so help me God. It is only a matter of time." The lieutenant picked
up the bucket and threw its contents in Riley's face.

"Lieutenant Bragg!" The shout came from one of the ranking engineers atop the earthen wall. "If you please! We haven't the time!"

Riley was grateful when the lieutenant stomped away, for he had already taken a new grip on the handle of the shovel—one with which to
use the tool as a weapon to brain the abusive officer in front of the whole
army. Braxton Bragg had no idea how near he had come to death. But
Riley knew how close he himself had come to hanging for murder.

Now the artillerymen across the river began to drill with their newly
blessed fieldpiece, whipping the horses to a trot, galloping across the open
bank. They unlimbered the piece and prepared to fire at a distant practice target. Though he continued to dig, Riley could not resist casting
glances across the river at the Mexican artillerymen.

"Ignore that bastard," said one of Riley's fellow soldiers from the Fifth.
"Such is the lot of an infantryman. It's a soldier's life."

"This life," Riley growled, as he stabbed his shovel into the dirt, "is
not fit for a convict."

Across the river, the artillery fired. Spectators on the railed balconies of Matamoros cheered the marksmanship.

"That . . ." the Irishman said, pointing his shovel briefly toward the Mexican gunners, "*that* is the life of a soldier."

Riley woke the next morning to the rhythm of raindrops pattering against his tent canvas. He had gone to sleep in full uniform. He had only to grab his shako hat before he crawled out into the mist. This was Sunday. Riley had no assigned duties today, and he did not intend to volunteer for more dirt work on Fort Texas. He marched through the mud to the tent of Captain Moses Merrill, the commander of Company K of the Fifth Infantry.

"Sir!" he shouted outside the officer's wall tent. "Private John Riley, asking a moment of your time."

"Step in, Riley."

He found the captain at a small wooden writing desk designed to fold up for travel. "Sir! Requesting a pass to leave the camp."

Merrill looked up from his paperwork. "For what purpose, Riley?"

"I have been seized with a desire to go to church, sir. A priest is holding mass at a farm north of camp."

"So I've heard. You're the first to request a pass, though."

"Sir, the war might begin any day. I'd like to go to confession." He kept his eyes on the canvas wall over the captain's head, but Riley knew the officer was studying his face. He knew Merrill as a good officer and a fair man.

"You know Colonel Cross disappeared outside of camp two days ago, don't you?" his commander asked.

Riley saw his commander reach for the pass with his left hand as he dipped his pen into the inkwell with his right.

"Aye, that I do, sir." Colonel Trueman Cross was General Taylor's quartermaster. He had gone for a ride, alone, outside of camp, and had failed to return.

"Odds are he was captured by the Mexican Army or waylaid by rancheros. See that you don't suffer the same fate, Private Riley. Attend your mass and return with haste." He held the pass out for Riley to take.

Riley took the pass and saluted. "Thank you, Captain." He turned and stomped through a puddle outside the tent. At the edge of camp, a sentry hailed him. Riley presented his pass and was allowed to walk.

It was true that a rumor had been going around about a mass at an abandoned farm to the north. It was also true that Riley himself had started the rumor. He had no intention of confessing to a priest on this side of the Rio Grande. He continued walking north, with the river to his left. He heard the cathedral bells ringing in Matamoros. He had made his decision and felt no regrets.

As the rainfall increased to a downpour, shielding his movements from the eyes of sentries back at camp, Riley slipped into the brush and slid down a muddy arroyo to the banks of the Rio Grande. He would hide here for hours. The only men to have been shot in the river had attempted to desert in daylight. Riley would wait for dark.

A Mexican patrol found him in Matamoros with his leaflet from General Ampudia. He had heard the stories of Private Singer's fake desertion and expected to be brought before a captain. Instead, he was hauled into the office of General Ampudia himself. An English-born Mexican Army soldier, a Captain Furlock, translated. At first, Ampudia was interested only in gathering intelligence about the U.S. Army, and Riley gave up all he knew, truthfully.

Next, the general pried into Riley's background, particularly his military experience. As he answered through the translator, Riley studied the features of the general. In his forties, Ampudia was no match for Riley's size, but he was of similar build, his barrel chest and muscled arms straining at his blue tunic adorned with medals. His goatee was immaculately trimmed, belying a continental polish. His full head of black hair swept over the top of his head in a thick wave. Riley knew that, as an artillery officer under Santa Anna, this man had laid waste to the walls of the Alamo a decade ago.

Finally, the Brit, Captain Furlock, translated a most pointed question from the generalissimo: "Why did you desert the Yankees?"

The deserter scowled. "The abuses of the Yankee officers on immigrant soldiers have reached a most dastardly level."

Furlock translated the remark, and the follow-up question from the general: "The general asks what your intentions are, now that you have deserted."

Riley drew himself up into a most soldierly posture. "I seek an officer's commission to form a company of Irishmen. An artillery unit. Those of us who have deserted—and the hundreds to come—have scores to settle."

General Ampudia considered the offer only briefly, then nodded and spoke to Furlock.

"Congratulations on your promotion, Second Lieutenant Riley." Furlock offered his hand.

Riley, an officer now, never thought he would feel so elated to shake the hand of an Englishman. His thoughts whirled back to Mackinac Island. He had promised Charles O'Malley that he would attain his former rank or die. The newly appointed Lieutenant John Riley may have broken his oath to serve the U.S. Army, but he had kept his promise to O'Malley. And, he had remained true to his religion and his heart. This border conflict was now a holy war to Riley. Let any man who would raise arms against the Catholic faith go to hell and face the devil.

WILLIAM J. HARDEE

Dawn broke over Captain William J. Hardee's right shoulder, a singular beam torching the tops of mesquites. He twisted in the saddle, looking back to see the orange glow through the thorns of the chaparral. Beautiful. It somewhat soothed his nerves, as he breathed in the aroma of horseflesh and the stinging odor of trampled weeds.

He sat listening to the heated conversation going on between the commander of his scouting party, Captain Seth Thornton, and the Mexican citizen who had been serving as his guide. The guide was shaking his head, looking worried.

"Capitan, I go *no más* from here. *No más*."

"You must go, senor. It is your duty."

"It is yours, Capitan. Not mine. My duty is to tell you this: Do not go on. *No más!*" The guide angled his glare from Thornton's eyes to Hardee's, as if Hardee might be able to do something. Then he spurred his little mustang back downstream and trotted away into the rising sun.

Hardee rode forward. "Captain, may I have a word with you?" he said to Thornton.

Thornton tossed his head toward a high roll on the trail ahead. They trotted that way together.

Except for a two-hour rest last night, the men had been in the saddle twenty hours straight and had meandered across twenty-five miles of the valley upstream of Fort Texas, making inquiries, through their guide, of any local residents they came across. A rumor had reached General Zachary Taylor's headquarters at the garrison yesterday. The rumor suggested that the renowned Mexican cavalry commander, General Anastasio Torrejon, had crossed the Rio Grande somewhere upstream with a thousand cavalrymen—lancers. Taylor had ordered Captain Thornton to ride upstream with a mere sixty-five dragoons to investigate the rumor.

Fifteen days ago, Colonel Trueman Cross, Taylor's quartermaster, had disappeared outside of camp while pleasure riding. A few days later, his body was found. Apparently he had been murdered. A week ago, Lieutenant Theodoric Porter, leading a patrol near camp, had been ambushed and killed, along with one of his soldiers. Captain Hardee realized that these foul deeds could not be proven to be the work of regular Mexican soldiers. Mexican vigilantes, militiamen, or bandits, all known collectively as rancheros, were suspected. In order to persuade Congress to declare a war, President Polk would require an attack on American troops by regular Mexican Army soldiers. On this morning, Hardee couldn't shake the feeling that he was riding into exactly what the president had been awaiting.

He pulled rein on the trail where he and Thornton could look over the rise and see ahead to the west. Being from Georgia, Hardee saw what he thought of as a plantation up ahead. The Mexicans would call such a place a hacienda, the village around it a *rancheria*.

"What's on your mind, Bill?" Thornton asked.

"Captain Thornton," Hardee said to his equal in rank, who was nonetheless his superior in the field at this moment, "should we take precautions?"

Thornton sat slumped in his saddle. He always looked a bit peaked. "We will go ahead, Bill. We will question anyone we may find at that *rancheria* ahead."

"Of course. But should we address the men? Send scouts ahead? Guard our rear?"

Thornton sighed. "I will ride at the head of the column. *You* guard the rear, Captain."

Hardee looked coolly at the Marylander Thornton. He didn't sense any disrespect in the order to guard the rear. But he had hoped Thornton might adopt his other suggestions. "The guide seemed to think the enemy waits at that plantation ahead."

"He was tired of riding and wanted to go home. He's been trying to convince me all along that the Mexican cavalry is always just ahead, beyond the next bend in the river. You have your orders."

Hardee nodded. They loped their mounts back toward the column, both captains riding fine American horses, for the Second Dragoons had ridden their own stock to Texas from their former post at Fort Jesup, Louisiana. Seth Thornton rode a huge red roan, while Hardee straddled a favored bay. Reaching the head of the column, Hardee continued his canter on toward the back of the formation, checking over the men as he rode.

They looked tough and ready. The dragoons traditionally cultivated a wild and fearsome look. They grew long hair and long beards and, to a man, seemed to have practiced a menacing glare. Each carried a saber, a Hall carbine rifle, and a single-shot horse pistol that could also be used as a club. The pistol was carried in a saddle holster aside the pommel of their Ringgold saddles.

Many of these men had been tested in skirmishes with the Seminoles and Creeks. Yet Hardee worried about how they would match up to true cavalry soldiers like the ones he suspected the Mexican general, Torrejon, had crossed over the Rio Grande. The dragoons could fight from the saddle, if need be, but they were more accustomed to dismounting and fighting afoot. They had just recently, in fact, been remounted, having been dismounted two years ago and designated as "dismounted rifles." Since being remounted as dragoons, they had had little time to drill in cavalry tactics. How would they match up to the battle-hardened Mexican lancers?

Captain Thornton seemed to believe that the Mexicans had not crossed the border at all, or that, if they had, they would not fight. Hardee had served some time with Thornton but could not say that he knew the man well. Some of the officers thought of Seth Thornton as a bit "tetched," as the term went in Georgia, or touched in the head. Thornton had survived the explosion of the steamer *Pulaski* off the coast of North Carolina several years ago. As the ship sank, he had distinguished himself by diving into the waters time and time again to rescue women and children who otherwise would have drowned. When the lifeboats were full, he had lashed himself to a floating hen coop. He was fished out of the sea three days later, ranting like a lunatic.

There were those in the officer's corps who believed a bit of the maniac still lurked in Captain Thornton's mind. Hardee did not agree. Thornton was recklessly aggressive, but he was not crazy. He wouldn't be able to claim insanity as an excuse for his actions, should something go amiss on this day.

"Check your loads, boys!" Hardee said to the men as he rode past them. "Watch the chaparral!" He took up his place in the rear, next to Sergeant Tredo, a reliable soldier and tough leader of the enlisted men.

"Stay alert, Sergeant," he said to Tredo.

"Like a hawk, sir."

The column started moving toward the hacienda a couple of miles ahead.

The sun had risen over the mesquite tops by the time the head of the column arrived within musket range of the tiny settlement. From the rear, Hardee peered through the dust kicked up by hooves. The Rio Grande, its riffles sparkling in the sunshine, flanked the dragoons to the left. The chaparral grew dense in the valley but had been cleared above the brink of the riverbank to make way for a pasture, some houses, and some outbuildings.

A virtually impenetrable fence made of thorny bushes, cacti, and stacked brush enclosed the field and the buildings. They called it a chaparral fence in this region. Hardee thought of it as a frontier answer to the European hedgerow. It was dense enough to hold wild cattle and too high for most mustangs to jump, yet a mounted man could see over the top of it.

The field enclosed by the chaparral fence measured about forty acres square, by Hardee's estimation. The houses and outbuildings were all located at the far end of the cleared pasture. He saw Thornton probing for an entrance through the chaparral fence. Finding none along the eastern approach, Thornton turned left around the first corner he came to, the column of dragoons snaking behind him.

When Hardee brought up the rear around this same northeast corner of the fence, he saw that Captain Thornton had found a gap in the thorny hedgerow about halfway along the north side of the enclosure. Two long timbers, suspended one above the other, spanned the gap, serving as a gate. A soldier had dismounted to pull these wooden bars aside so the dragoons could enter the enclosed field. Most of the company was already inside the chaparral fence.

This shocked and worried Hardee. He had expected that Thornton might send a platoon into the enclosure to search the houses for inhabitants, while leaving the main body of his company outside the chaparral fence, in the event escape should become necessary. Hardee brooded over Thornton's lack of precautions. If Hardee had been given command of this company, he would have already ordered sentries to the four corners of the chaparral fence to watch for trouble. Thornton had called for no such safeguards. He led the entire company of dragoons into the pasture, single file, heading for the houses at the far end of the enclosure, a furlong from the gate.

Has he never heard of shooting fish in a barrel?

As the last man in the company to pass through the gate, Hardee turned back to look about the dense chaparral forest surrounding the outside of the fence. He felt nervous, entering this place. As far as he knew, there was no other way in or out of this fenced pasture. The thought occurred to him that the dragoons' sabers could be employed, in a pinch, to hack a hole through a weak spot in the hedgerow.

"Sergeant Tredo!" he said, entering the field.

"Sir?" Tredo barked as he wheeled his mount to face the captain.

"Follow the column up to those buildings, but keep your eyes on this gate. I'm going to see about posting some guards, so have eight men picked for sentry duty."

"Yes, sir!" Tredo's nod showed that he approved of the idea.

Hardee loped forward to find Thornton. Many of the dragoons had dismounted. Some apparently had been ordered to search the buildings, which seemed abandoned. Others were lighting cigars or drinking from canteens. His eyes located Thornton near the largest of the houses, which was still nothing more than a cabin made of planks and roofed with handmade shingles. The captain was talking to an old man who had been found inside.

"Captain Thornton," Hardee said.

Thornton glanced at his second-in-command but did not answer. He turned back to the ancient ranchero.

"*Como se llama este rancho?*" he said, laboring through his limited Spanish.

"Rancho de Carricitos," the old man replied, his jaw jutting defiantly.

"*Donde esta* General Torrejon?" Thornton asked.

The old man cupped his hand behind his ear.

"I said, *'Donde esta* General Torrejon?'"

"Torrejon?" the old man said. "Torrejon?" He shrugged. *"Quien sabe?"*

"Captains!" The shout came from Sergeant Tredo. "The gate!"

Hardee, still in the saddle, looked back at the gap. A wave of panic swept through his innards as he saw foot soldiers wearing dark blue uniforms and shakos that resembled top hats entering the fenced field. Dozens of them had already poured in through the gate. Above the thorny summit of the chaparral fence, he saw lancers spreading out along the outside of the chaparral fence, the blades of the weapons glinting in the sun, the riders wearing plumed helmets and tunics of red, green, and blue.

"To horse!" Thornton ordered.

Everywhere, men scrambled to mount and groped for their weapons.

Hardee's jaw tightened angrily. This is what he had feared. The Mexicans were pouring from the chaparral where they had hidden and were now spreading out to encircle the entire *rancheria.*

"Charge!" Thornton ordered. "Charge the gate!" Laying spurs to his big roan, Thornton drew his saber and rode past his own company of dragoons to take the lead in the assault. There was no time to place the men in formation. No time for bugle calls.

Hardee found himself riding around the opposite side of the men who were turning to follow Thornton, some of them still afoot, trying to mount. He passed lieutenants Kane and Mason, both of whom spurred their mounts to follow his example. Now he was third in the charge, behind Captain Thornton and Sergeant Tredo.

As he galloped, Hardee drew his percussion pistol from the pommel holster and cocked it. His bay charged ahead bravely. Two hundred yards away and closing fast on the escape route, he saw more Mexican infantrymen streaming into the field to establish a skirmish line to the right side of the passageway. Outside the fence, more mounted troops in colorful tunics swarmed, brandishing *escopetas.*

Charging on, he hoped the resolve of the Mexicans would break, but they held, the soldiers inside the fence kneeling now to fire. A hundred yards, and nearer, nearer, ever nearer. Would they ever fire? He felt a battle yell welling up within and let it escape from his lungs. The dragoons behind him joined in with war whoops. Hardee was beginning to think the Mexican show of force nothing but a bluff. Then the first blossoms of white smoke hurled a volley of whistling balls past him. He heard the musket balls thudding into men and horses, and yet Thornton charged on ahead of him.

A well-timed second volley from the cavalrymen outside the fence rained death into the faces of the dragoons. Ahead of Hardee, Thornton turned aside to the right, directly in front of the Mexican skirmish line. Hardee could see him pulling reins, but Thornton's big roan had panicked beyond the captain's control. Hardee fired his single-shot pistol in the direction of the skirmish line as he wheeled to the right through a welcome cloud of smoke.

"Captain!" he yelled at Thornton. "We've got to cut through this fence. We're trapped."

"Cut through the fence!" Thornton ordered. "Use your sabers!"

Musket fire seemed to rattle from everywhere now as the dragoons milled in confusion. *Fish in a barrel.* Thornton's roan screamed and tumbled forward, slamming him to the ground packed hard by hooves. Thornton did not move.

"Follow me!" Hardee yelled. He continued to gallop to the right, away from the skirmishers, toward the river. He looked over his shoulder to find men riding after him. Beyond them, he saw a number horses and dragoons on the ground, some of them already in the hands of the enemy.

As he galloped toward the river, Hardee replaced his pistol in the pommel holster and drew his saber. The field inside the chaparral fence was large enough to ride beyond the effective range of the Mexican muskets and *escopetas*. His idea was to use sabers to chop through the hedgerow fence on the south side. If they could hack a hole, the dragoons could escape across the Rio Grande or find some cover from which to mount a defense.

His bay, heaving for air, reached the south fence. Hardee looked over the top of the chaparral fence and felt his one hope for escape sink as he saw the river below. A tangle of thorny underbrush on the riverbank protected a perfect quagmire of bogs and quicksand below. It formed a natural moat along this side of the rancho. There was no escape.

"What do we do, Captain?" a wild-eyed private yelled.

Hardee looked downstream. The southeast corner of the fence was a furlong away, and Mexican lancers were already lining it, all the way to the riverbank. He looked upstream and saw the red-and-green tunics of riders above the fence in that direction as well.

"Captain, we're trapped!" a dragoon cried.

"Form up!" Hardee ordered. "Form a line and face the enemy."

He inspected the dragoons as they obeyed his order. All of them were privates. Some had dropped weapons in the chaos. Many men and horses were bleeding from bullet wounds. He counted only twenty-five of the fifty-two privates who had left Fort Texas yesterday. The others had been captured, wounded, or killed in the last few terrifying minutes. Aside from Hardee, all the officers and noncommissioned officers were dead or taken prisoner. Hardee was the company commander now.

He turned around to assess the enemy's strength through the field of musket smoke. Mexican soldiers continued to march into the pasture while more cavalrymen streamed out of the chaparral to surround the hacienda beyond the fence.

"There's hundreds of them, Captain," a private said behind him.

Hardee looked at his options. Escape across the river was impossible. An offensive charge would prove suicidal. The idea of surrender was distasteful—but acceptable, considering the overwhelming odds against him. He turned his prancing bay back around to face his men.

"I will ride forward to secure terms. If I am murdered, I expect the men of the Second Dragoons to sell their lives as dearly as possible. If we must be taken prisoner, we will do so with dignity and live to fight another day." He heard no complaints from his men.

Returning his saber to its scabbard, Captain William J. Hardee reined his mount to face the Mexican Army and rode forward at a walk. A third of the way across the field, he saw a single Mexican cavalry officer coming to meet him.

Lieutenant
SAM GRANT

Point Isabel, Texas
May 3, 1846

Grant's eyes blinked at the inside of the tent canvas, strangely aglow with the pale light of the coming dawn. It heaved above him in the sea breeze as if he were inside the lungs of some beast. Something had wakened him, but he could not be sure what. From his cot he looked past his feet, through the opening of the tent, and saw rows of more tents, sand dunes, and an American flag on a pole bent to the wind.

He had ridden here with most of Taylor's army to receive supplies and reinforcements at this little Gulf Coast port, twenty-three miles from Fort Texas. Only 550 men had been left behind to guard the star fort. No true harbor, by any stretch of the imagination, the roadstead at Point Isabel merely offered vessels a place to anchor in the open water offshore. From there, supplies and munitions had to be painstakingly lightered to rickety docks that were completely inadequate for the purposes of an occupying army.

While men slowly brought supplies ashore, Grant's company, and others, had been ordered to build earthworks and other defensive structures to protect the coastal supply depot. A small guard would be left behind to garrison Point Isabel. Accordingly, Grant had been working long hours overseeing the construction projects designed by engineers. As a result of the heavy toil, he had been sleeping very soundly in his tent on the shore near the docks.

But something had jarred him awake. Had he heard something? Felt something?

The coming day's long list of duties began to weigh upon him, and he hadn't even gotten out of bed yet. Even so, he felt obliged to lie still in his blankets and try to determine why he had wakened with such a start from a sound sleep.

Then it came again. A rumble, far away. Thunder? Again, like hooves drumming a distant bridge. The reality struck Grant all of a sudden. Cannon. The artillery battle had begun at Fort Texas, over twenty miles away. The war he dreaded had come.

Outside his tent he heard the voices of excited men. Some even cheered. He threw his blankets aside, sat up, and ducked into the day. Officers and men strutted, smiling, spoiling for battle. Not Grant. He remembered the razed ruins of El Fronton, the burned-out village here at Point Isabel, or Santa Isabel, as the Mexicans called it. Some said Texas Rangers had torched the hamlet of El Fronton. Others claimed the citizens themselves had set fire to their town to deny its goods to the Americans.

Either way, Grant knew that peaceful citizens, mothers and children, old folks and farmers, had been forced from their homes by this unnecessary war—a conflict that could have been avoided through diplomacy. With the hotheaded Polk in office, he feared there would be many more El Frontons in the coming days.

Charles May, a captain in the Second Dragoons, ran up to Grant, his long hair blowing across his smiling face.

"Do you hear the cannon, Grant?"

"Yes, I heard."

"Isn't it glorious?" He ran off without waiting for an answer.

Grant did not think it so glorious. In fact, at this moment, he deeply regretted his enlistment. He should have stood up to his father the day the old man informed him that he would soon report to West Point. And yet, if not for West Point, he would never have met Julia. The irony of love and war bewildered him. Was this simply his unavoidable destiny?

He heard another distant peal of ordnance. Indeed, he thought he felt it through his stocking feet. He ducked back into the tent and sat down on his cot to pull on his boots.

Julia . . . He so wanted to see her now, to hear her sweet southern voice. The only recourse left to him was to write. The bombardment inland would demand even longer days here at Point Isabel. Taylor's army still had cargo to receive and fortifications to build around the harbor. These tasks would be rushed, now that shooting had started, for Taylor would soon need to hasten back to Fort Texas to rescue the 550 men left there to defend the star fort across from Matamoras.

There was much to be done, and Grant would see to his duties. But first he would write a letter to Julia.

SARAH BORGINNES

To the Great Western, the war had begun with a scream and a thud. The first Mexican cannonball to hit Fort Texas yesterday at dawn had howled over the river and slammed into the soft dirt of the sloped outer wall, causing little damage. Hundreds of solid balls, exploding shells, and mortars followed, falling like ungodly hailstones among the soldiers left there to defend the star fort.

The other women in Fort Texas were huddled in the bombproofs, sewing sandbags and nursing the few wounded men. But Sarah continued to tend her coffeepots over a fire that hugged the inside of the western wall, where Mexican cannonballs and mortars were least likely to hit. She felt relatively safe here. Soon, however, another pot would boil and she would carry it up to the artillerymen who fed the powder and iron into the mouths of the hell-beasts on the fort walls.

She thought back to the Arroyo Colorado, where she had hidden herself among the willows in hopes of witnessing the beginnings of a war—perhaps a right smart cavalry charge, some rifle fire, and a shot or two from the flying artillery. She had never dreamed up this scenario—stuck behind dirt walls, encircled by the deafening roar of artillery, trusting God and guardian angels to save her from shot and shell.

Even her name had changed since the Arroyo Colorado. She had received word from Point Isabel that her husband, Sergeant John Bowman, had died in the infirmary. Though she grieved, she also knew that the military establishment would eventually realize that she was now an unattached woman working as a laundress. The army frowned on the presence of unmarried women in camp. So she had promptly proposed the idea of marriage to Sergeant Henry Borginnes of the Fourth Infantry.

"I have a dowry of two thousand dollars and the firmest pair on the Rio Grande," she had said.

A chaplain had performed the ceremony, and she became Sarah Borginnes. Now her new husband had marched off to Point Isabel with the bulk of the U.S. Army and she was ducking cannonballs at Fort Texas.

Between blasts, she heard boiling coffee rattle the iron lid of a pot suspended over the bed of coals. Covering her palm with a folded rag, she grabbed the hot vessel from its S-shaped iron hook. The boys on the north wall were next in line for a steaming cup of brew, but walking across the open interior of the fort was dangerous, so she angled toward the south end of the tunnel that traversed Fort Texas.

Sarah herself had helped to build this protective tunnel, when not washing or cooking. Under direction of engineers, the soldiers had gathered hundreds of empty wooden barrels discarded around camp. These hardwood casks had begun to stack up everywhere, so it was logical to put them to use. The larger barrels were lined up on the ground, standing upright in two parallel lines across the middle of the fort. The two lines of containers were just far enough apart for two men to squeeze past each other. On top of these, the men had stood more barrels, creating the six-foot-high walls of the tunnel. Sarah had lifted many of these into place with the tunnel builders. She then helped the soldiers cover the top of the corridor with scraps of lumber, tree limbs, sticks, brush, and old canvas. Atop this, hundreds of men heaped tons of earth, one shovelful at a time, covering the thick walls and lighter roof. The resulting passageway was far from bombproof, but it provided some protection from shrapnel for troops angling across the interior grounds of the earthen fort.

Stepping in between the pickle barrel walls, carrying her steaming coffeepot before her, she moved slowly as her eyes adjusted to the dark within. The tunnel smelled of brine and vinegar, damp earth, salt pork, and mold. Its dirt cover muffled the muzzle blasts of the ordnance outside, lending her some solace from the ear-pounding percussion. Occasional pinpricks of daylight, created by shrapnel, gave her enough light to see. Soon she caught sight of a soldier heading quickly her way.

"Watch yourself, Private. Hot coffee comin'."

"After you, ma'am," the farm-fresh boy said, stepping aside.

"Any news?" she asked, switching places with him in the tunnel.

"Captain Loud's eighteen-pounders dismounted an enemy gun."

This explained the cheer she had heard on the west wall a few minutes ago. "Hell of a handle for an artillery officer, ain't it?"

"Ma'am?"

"*Loud!* Captain *Loud!*"

The boy laughed. "Hadn't thought about it! Good day, ma'am." He disappeared into the darkness of the protected walkway.

"Hot coffee comin' through!" she said, encountering more runners. Stepping out of the passageway on the north end, Sarah took a deep breath and marched up the slanted dirt wall to the northwest bastion of the star fort. A projectile screamed into the redoubt from above, landed inside the walls, bounced, and embedded itself harmlessly in the dirt embankment.

Amazingly, only one man had been killed in Fort Texas after the first day of bombardment from Matamoros. A well-timed fuse on a Mexican howitzer shell had exploded it in the face of a Seventh Infantry private making repairs on the fort, killing him instantly. Several wounded men were laid up in the bombproofs, but all seemed likely to survive. The 550 soldiers holding the fort maintained a proper respect for Mexican artillery, but many truly feared an all-out infantry assault. Since General Taylor had taken the bulk of the army to the coast to receive and transport supplies, the Mexicans outnumbered the Americans six to one around Fort Texas. Sarah had heard the Alamo mentioned more than once.

Reaching the top of the fort wall with her coffeepot, she glanced toward Matamoros. She saw no muzzle blasts and expected no enemy projectiles for the moment. Taking a few seconds to observe, she noticed some men muscling one of the eighteen-pounders toward some new target. Two infantrymen were busy repairing the redan with sandbags that gave the gunners some protection. Artillery soldiers swabbed the barrel of a siege gun with a wet sponge on a wooden pole as others pried open ammunition boxes and stacked cannonballs. A lieutenant sighted one of the guns with a tangent scale for a distant shot.

She located Captain Loud and was surprised to find him conversing with the current commander of Fort Texas, Major Jacob Brown.

"Major Brown, I have coffee for the boys!" she announced.

"Ah, good morning, Mrs. Borginnes." Brown picked up an iron cup from an ammunition box, knocked dirt from it, wiped it out with his finger, and held it under the spout of the coffeepot. Grime and soot covered his face, making the whites of his eyes look strangely alive.

Sarah had long felt a deep admiration for Major Brown. No arrogant West Pointer, he had come up through the enlisted ranks, winning his promotions and his commission in Indian skirmishes and frontier campaigns. This was by far the largest engagement of the major's career, but he seemed unfazed by the mantle of leadership entrusted to him.

"Any new developments, sir?" she asked.

Brown tested the steaming cup with his upper lip. "Yes, actually. The enemy came across the river in the dark and built a new battery emplacement overnight."

"On this side of the *rio*?" she said, feeling the shock on her own face.

Brown pointed to the northwest. "Not half a mile from here. They've been firing away with a battery of six-pounders. Come take a look!" He picked up a telescope from a field desk that someone had improvised from empty crates.

Sarah set her coffeepot on the desk and followed Brown to the sandbagged parapet. The major handed her the telescope and pointed upriver to the new earthen fieldworks hastily erected overnight by the Mexican gunners.

"Tell me what you see," he said.

She adjusted the focus of the optics and steadied the glass on the battlement. The muzzles of the guns came into view. "My God, I can see their faces!" she said. "Hey, them ain't no Mexicans!"

"They are now."

The realization swept over her. "That looks like the big Irishman, John Riley, wearing an officer's uniform!"

"The whole battery is Irish," Brown said. "Deserters."

"And now they fire on their own friends?"

"A traitor knows no friends," the major answered.

"The scoundrels!" She felt her anger flare as she handed the telescope back to the major. "I hope you make them pay, sir!"

Brown gestured toward the men wrestling with the eighteen-pounder. "We'll range them with that siege gun soon enough and drive them back across the river, if we don't blow them all to the devil himself."

Sarah saw a weary enlisted man empty the coffeepot she had brought with her. She retraced her steps to pick it up for refilling. Suddenly she heard the shriek of a shell. Major Brown grabbed her and pulled her downward to the dirt, throwing himself on top of her. A ball fired from John Riley's battery of deserters clipped the top of the redan and hissed through the space where she had stood seconds earlier. It dropped into the fort, tearing a section of the tunnel away when it hit.

The major sprang up and away from her, offering his hand. "My apologies for manhandling you so, Mrs. Borginnes."

But Sarah had found the encounter rather thrilling for more than one reason. She smiled at Brown. "I owe you for saving me, Major Brown." She thought she might actually be blushing. She took the officer's hand.

He pulled her to her feet, saying, "Not at all, Mrs. Borginnes. Carry on."

"Sir, if I may ask . . ." she said, feeling emboldened by her new familiarity with the fort commander.

"Yes? Go on."

"I'd like to be issued a musket. In case they attack the fort. I can shoot as straight as any man."

The major smiled as he looked about the parapets. "You, Private! Come here!"

"Sir!" the private said, leaping up from the place where he had been filling a sandbag with his bare hands.

"Go with Mrs. Borginnes to the armory. See that she is issued a musket and ammunition by my order."

"Yes, sir!" the private yelled, apparently anxious to leave the bulwarks.

"Thank you, Major," Sarah said. "I will make good use of it, if it comes to that."

Major Brown smiled, nodded, and turned back to his duties.

"Fire!" Captain Loud ordered.

Sarah had no time to cover her ears as an eighteen-pounder roared, its projectile arching across the river and exploding in a direct hit on a Mexican gun. Sarah actually saw the enemy cannon tube flip through the air, along with one of the enemy gunners. The men around her cheered the bull's-eye marksmanship.

In the midst of the celebration, she saw fear in the eyes of some of these soldiers. Then there were others who embraced the action and the danger with something akin to joy. The thought struck her that those whose eyes showed fear possessed a stripe of greater courage than the men who seemed oblivious to the danger, for they remained on their posts in spite of their terror. She realized that she belonged to the class of lesser bravery, for none of the danger concerned her very much.

She tossed her head at the private and slipped back down the sloped wall, flashing a reassuring smile at a soldier carrying a shovel and a bundle of empty sandbags up to the embattled parapet.

Lieutenant

SAM GRANT

Grant mopped his brow with a handkerchief as he strolled along the breastworks. He stopped to watch a soldier stacking sandbags around an artillery placement.

"Overlap the sandbags, Private. Stagger each course." He moved the bag the man had just put in place, to show how the wall should take shape.

"Yes, sir," the man replied.

As the parapet took shape, Grant turned an ear to the west. The distant din from the artillery battle at Fort Texas had a lighter ring to it so far this morning. The punctuating roars of the big eighteen-pounders were absent from the menacing drum roll of battle. He was pretty sure he knew why.

Captain Samuel Walker—a Texas Ranger acting as General Taylor's scout—had managed to sneak past all the enemy patrols between Point Isabel and Fort Texas. Incredibly, Walker had gotten into Fort Texas to talk to Major Brown. He had left the star fort immediately thereafter, snuck through the Mexican lines yet again, and dodged enemy patrols all night to bring intelligence from Major Brown to General Taylor. At a council of war called before dawn this morning, Walker had told what he knew.

In attendance at the meeting, Grant had studied the Ranger captain as he reported in a rather quiet voice. He had gathered that Captain

Walker was a famous Indian and Mexican fighter in Texas. Grant found him rather haggard. Perhaps he had been ill or was simply exhausted.

"Major Brown told me with utmost confidence," Walker had reported, "that Fort Texas will withstand the artillery bombardment from Matamoras. The Mexican batteries are no match for the U.S. guns."

"What about an infantry assault?" Taylor had asked.

"That concerns Major Brown more than the artillery, though he has made preparations. Hundreds of rounds of canister and grapeshot have been carried to the gun placements. If the Mexicans charge, the Rio Grande will run red with their blood. Buzzards will come from as far away as Chihuahua. Brown will not surrender. He will fight to the death. He told me this himself."

General Taylor picked his teeth with a mesquite thorn. "Yes, but we know from the Alamo just how many casualties the Mexicans are willing to take to breach the walls of a fort. Brown has 550 men inside Fort Texas. General Arista has six times that number."

"Sir, there's a way we will know if Major Brown observes Arista forming up his men for an infantry assault."

"How's that, Captain?"

"I told Major Brown that the bombardment can be heard quite clearly here at Point Isabel. Especially the eighteen-pounders. So, come dawn, if he sees Arista massed for an infantry assault on the fort, he will wait until precisely six-thirty in the morning to fire the siege guns, which he will unleash with a sudden fury. If Captain Loud's eighteen-pounders are silent until six-thirty, we will know that the Mexican infantry are prepared to attack the walls."

Taylor shrugged. "Arista might order his men in place for a charge just to scare the hell out of Brown—hoping for a surrender."

Walker nodded. "That's likely. At least we will know whether or not the Mexican infantry has moved into attack formation. But I tell you in all confidence, General, that Brown will *not* surrender. He has not faltered in the face of an almost continual bombardment for three days. His eyes are bright and his wits keen."

"Captain Walker," said General William Worth, a note of skepticism in his voice, "if you managed to ride in and out of Fort Texas last night, I would think the enemy guard around the fort rather light."

Grant watched Samuel Walker's jaws tighten, though his countenance otherwise changed very little. His light gray eyes blinked once, disdainfully, and cut toward Worth. *There*, thought Grant. *There is the menacing spirit of this legendary fighting man.*

"General Worth, sir, I did not *ride* into Fort Texas. I hid my horse miles outside the fort and walked. Then I crawled, sometimes on my belly like a snake. I crawled past Mexican guards whose throats I could have slit. I hailed our own sentries, had my audience with Major Brown, and crawled back out the same way I had crawled in. When I reached my horse, *then* I rode here. I assure you, Fort Texas is surrounded by a brigade of Mexican regulars."

As he had listened to all this talk last night, Grant had felt a dread of the coming carnage creeping into his heart and guts. It was odd. He didn't fear it for his own safety but for the impending loss of humanity—the boys who would never marry, the men who would never return to their families. The weeping of mothers, wives, and children. The moaning of men on bloody field hospital cots. He didn't understand why he could see this coming and others could not. Damn the warmongers in Washington, so far away and safe in their tidy houses.

Now, remembering the predawn council of war, Lieutenant Grant pulled his watch from his pocket as he stood on the docks at Point Isabel. The time was 6:29. Half of the signal from Fort Texas seemed already to have been sent, for he had not heard the big siege guns all morning. All around the docks and the fortifications, officers ordered men to cease their toil and stand at ease.

Grant stared at the face of his watch. The second hand passed its zenith and continued. *This watch has always run fast.* He closed his eyes and waited, then waited longer. At length, he heard the pronounced rumble of Captain Loud's battery. The signal was clear. The Mexican Army had formed up around the star fort for an infantry attack. Whether the attack had actually begun was unknown.

What Grant did know was that Taylor would be itching to head back inland at the earliest opportunity to rescue the defenders of Fort Texas. Oddly—though he disagreed with the necessity for this war—Grant also felt a certain sense of urgency for this maneuver. Duty called. He found himself aching to return to Fort Texas, even though he suspected that he would have to fight his way through.

SARAH BORGINNES

Fort Texas
May 6, 1846

The bombardment had now rattled the Great Western to her very marrow. She had almost reached the point where she hoped the enemy would just go ahead and attack the fort. For three nights now she had attempted to sleep in the bombproofs with dirt raining down on her face and hair. For three days she had carried coffee and food to the gunners on the walls, feeling the percussion of the powder charges rattle her skull. The hellish whistling of shells had become as common as the buzzing of bees or the chirping of crickets. The fort's latrines had begun to stink to high heaven and supplies were diminishing rapidly. Fort Texas had become a living hell.

Still, she smiled at the men she encountered. They needed her encouragement now more than ever. The defenders of the fort had wakened this morning to find that large numbers of Mexican infantry and cavalry had crossed the river overnight and had taken up positions just out of artillery range, apparently in preparation to rush the fort.

Oddly, Major Brown had ordered Captain Loud to keep his eighteen-pounders silent until well after dawn. Then, about 6:30, he had unleashed a barrage of exploding shells in the direction of the enemy formations. She guessed that this was to show the enemy what manner of hell they would have to charge through, should they attempt an all-out assault. It seemed to have worked, for the Mexican lines had not moved forward. Still, Sarah kept her issued musket handy at all times and wore her cartridge box belted over her shoulder and around her waist like any foot soldier.

As she began to cook a midday stew for the gunners, she heard a shell howling through the air, sounding more ominous than most. It wailed like the scream of a panther mixed with the shrill song of a steamboat's whistle. She looked up at the wall where Major Jacob Brown had been inspecting some damage. A solid cannonball struck his thigh and flipped him off of the fort wall like a fingernail flicking a bug aside.

"No!" she screamed, running toward the place where he had landed, on the sloping inner wall of the fort. She sprinted through a gap that had been blasted in the tunnel and slowed to a trot as a few soldiers reached the major before her. One had already tied a tourniquet around the thigh of the commander's mangled leg. As men lifted the major, one of them cradled the broken part of his limb that dangled in a blood-soaked pant leg.

"Take him to the surgeon, boys!" she ordered.

The major groaned as they jostled him along. She ran ahead of them to the section of the bombproofs being used as a hospital.

"Doc!" she yelled into the enclosure. "A ball hit Major Brown! His leg's damn near tore clean off!"

She stepped aside to make room for the men carrying the commander. Having done all she could do, she trudged back through the gap in the pickle-barrel tunnel to return to her cook fire. Something tugged at her bonnet as a dust cloud sprouted from the ground in front of her. She felt her bonnet to find a bullet hole in the fabric. Some sniper's shot—probably intended for a gunner on the wall—had fallen into the fort and almost hit her in the back of her head.

Angry now, Sarah cussed under her breath. She went out of her way to angle across the fort interior to the little foundry that had been built yesterday. This had, at first, appalled her. The foundry was used to heat cannonballs red hot. The glowing orbs would then be carried to the parapets by pairs of men wielding makeshift tongs. There, the balls were rolled down the muzzles of six-pounders so that they could be lobbed into the houses and shops of Matamoros to set the city afire. The Mexican citizens had abandoned the place, but the intentional torching of nonmilitary property still struck Sarah as unnecessarily mean.

The maiming of Major Brown and the bullet through her bonnet had changed her mind. She stalked up to the foundry, where half a dozen men labored in the heat.

"Give 'em hell, boys!" she shouted above the din of big guns.

The men looked at her with weary eyes.

"Yes, ma'am," one of them said, picking up a cannonball for heating.

Another threw a barrel stave into the fire. "That's what we're givin' 'em, ma'am. Pure-dee hell!"

She turned back toward her cook fire to tend her cauldron of stew. This day had started badly and gotten worse. The Mexicans had to have seen the major struck down on the fort wall. This would only encourage them. Soon they would send soldiers to cross the dry moat, she feared. She fixed her eyes on the musket that she had left near her fire. She was ready to use it, shoulder to shoulder with the men, but she prayed General Taylor would return to rescue her before the Mexicans charged. Otherwise, this might very well be her day to die.

General
MARIANO ARISTA

General Arista sat astride his charger, trying to think in American. He could speak English, for he had lived as an exile in Cincinnati for three years. But words were superfluous, particularly in English, and most especially during times of war. What he had to rely upon here was his knowledge of American *thinking*.

"Capitan," he said to his aide-de-camp, Jean Louis Berlandier, "send General Torrejon to cross the road and secure the left flank, then report back to me immediately."

"*Si*, General!" The captain spurred his horse to a canter.

Arista scanned the terrain ahead. Here, he would soon engage the Americans under General Zachary Taylor. His scouts and spies had ensured him that Taylor was on his way back from the port of Santa Isabel with a large wagon train of supplies to relieve the men he had left behind at the earthen fort across from Matamoros. At the very least, Arista knew he must prevent Taylor from getting through to the fort. At best, he hoped to rout the Americans and capture their supply train.

He smiled, anxious to tangle with Taylor. He knew the old American general as an Indian fighter who had never commanded artillery or cavalry in a battle. "Come, General Taylor," he said under his breath. "Bring to me my provisions."

Behind him stood the tall timber—*palo alto*—a noted landmark on the road from Santa Isabel to Matamoros and a good place to conceal his reserve forces and supplies. The open plain stretched out for miles before him, flanked on the left by the Matamoros Road. In the distance, he could see the dust cloud of the American army approaching from Santa Isabel.

The Americans called it *Point* Isabel. Typical. The Protestant heretics thought more of a geographic feature than the consecrated Catholic saint whose name blessed that little port.

Though he bristled at the arrogance of the approaching enemy, he had to admit that he admired certain aspects of American culture, including many agricultural innovations he had seen while traveling from Florida to Ohio. Not the abhorrent use of slaves in the South, of course, but the advanced techniques of planting and harvesting in the northern states made possible by metal tools and machines. He greatly envied the magnificence of the industrial complexes he had seen, particularly the iron foundries and steel mills. Oh, if only *Madre México* possessed such works. Agriculture and industry. Together they had bred an American instinct for expansion. From the halls of Congress to the meanest tavern, Americans lusted for lands beyond their own borders.

His smile wrinkled his fair, freckled face. Not much difference between Congress and a lowly tavern, but as much could be said of Mexico, as well.

The smile slipped away as he focused again on the chosen battlefield before him.

Think in American!

They would arrive all full of Yankee bluster. The Americans actually believed in their hearts that they owned this disputed land north of the Rio Grande del Norte, however outlandish that claim might seem to a native-born patriot like Arista. They would fight. But they were untested compared to the soldiers of his war-torn nation. Some of Taylor's troops had skirmished with *Indios*, but few—mostly European immigrants—knew anything of battle on a large scale with artillery, cavalry, and bayonet.

Arista knew that his second-in-command, General Ampudia, would soon arrive with reinforcements, for he had called off the siege of the Americans' earthen star fort. With Ampudia's troops, he would outnumber Taylor roughly 5,000 to 2,200. True, the enemy possessed better muskets than his troops, and even a number of rifles. But that would count for little after the first volley or two, when the battle became a hand-to-hand bloodbath. Here, the bayonets and lances of his profes-sional soldiers would wreak bloody havoc on the untested army of the United States of America.

The enemy's only real advantage lay with the spawn of the gringo ore mines: cannon. The artillery battle over Matamoras had proven that. The American guns were more modern and more powerful; their ammuni-tion far superior to the solid brass cannonballs and the metal scrap that Arista's batteries had to use as grapeshot. His spies had warned him of Captain Ringgold's flying artillery, but Taylor's two eighteen-pounders—each pulled by six yokes of oxen—concerned him more.

Arista knew his greatest advantage was in his cavalry. He commanded well over a thousand veteran horsemen. Other than a company of volun-teer Texas Rangers, Taylor had no men who knew how to fight at a gal-lop. The Second Dragoons were essentially mounted infantrymen. Their tactics had proven useless at Rancho de Carricitos, where Torrejon's troops could have cut them all down like lambs in a slaughter pen.

His battle plan, accordingly, seemed logical enough. He would attack with his cavalry and flank the enemy, capturing artillery batteries and provisions. His battle-hardened infantry would easily turn Taylor's coun-terattack. The Americans would abandon their slow-moving supply train and ox-drawn eighteen-pounders and retreat en masse to Santa Isabel.

Taylor was an old Indian fighter, nothing more. He was out of his ele-ment here, his strategies dated. Even now, Arista's spies had told him, the old plantation owner was riding to Palo Alto in a wagon driven by one of his slaves. Of real war, he knew nothing.

A Gulf freshet whipped into the tall timber, stirring the leaves and making the battle flag of the Tampico Battalion, to his right, snap smartly, as if anxious for combat. The tricolor banner, featuring the familiar im-age of the eagle and the snake, represented his most elite infantry unit. The Tampicos had been baptized in the blood of their comrades. Arista knew they would stand firm.

The general trusted that he could rely upon the rank and file above the loyalty of his own officers, for the politics of Mexico forever slith-ered through his army like that snake on the Tampico flag. Arista him-self had been a royalist, a rebel, and an exile. Sent to this northern frontier to lead the Mexican Army of the North, he was now a conservative serv-ing at the head of a liberal officer corps. He would be foolish to ignore the possibility of insubordination among his junior officers.

Despite these worries, Arista felt confident that his eventful journey had prepared him for this day. The son of a Spanish Army officer—born José Mariano Martín Buenaventura Ignacio Nepomuceno Garcia de Arista Nuez—there had never been any question about his path in life. He was to be a soldier, like his father. He had served honorably as a young Spanish officer during the revolution, helping to put down rebellion in Mexico. But after the liberals had succeeded in a coup d'état in Spain, he had switched alliances and joined General Iturbide to fight *for* Mexican independence rather than serve a liberal Spanish government. His service in the revolutionary army, helping to win and hold Mexican independence, catapulted him upward in the ranks to brigadier general.

His stand against the lawless despot Santa Anna had brought about Arista's defeat, capture, and exile to the United States. After Santa Anna's own defeat and capture in Texas, Arista returned to Mexico and once again resumed his service to his nation as a general. During the French invasion of Veracruz, in 1838, Santa Anna—having somehow secured his release from the Texans—summoned Arista. They met in Veracruz with the French Navy anchored in the harbor, threatening a ground invasion. Generals Arista and Santa Anna talked for hours into the night, hashing out old differences and agreeing to move forward as loyal Mexicans against the coming French attack.

Just before dawn, French soldiers snuck ashore and stormed the house where Santa Anna and Arista slept. Slipping out in his nightshirt, Santa Anna was mistaken for a servant by a French soldier.

"Where is Santa Anna?" the French invader shouted.

Santa Anna pointed up the stairs to Arista's room. "Up there!"

General Mariano Arista suffered the indignity of capture by the French. Santa Anna escaped to the barracks, rallied some troops, and drove the French invaders down to the docks, where a cannonball fired from a French warship shattered the former president's leg, making him once again an obligatory hero to the Mexican citizenry. Making the most of his amputation, he would become president again. And, again, he would be deposed by his enemies.

So Santa Anna was now in exile in Cuba, and this day—at Palo Alto—belonged to General Mariano Arista. He was forty-three years old. He had seen battle for more than two decades. President Paredes had named him general-in-chief of the Army of the North. His forces had covered more than fifteen leagues a day marching northward to Matamoras. His troops were inured to the hardships of the field, and they ached to repulse the pompous Yankee invaders.

Hoofbeats penetrated his musings. His aide-de-camp, Captain Berlandier, returned at a gallop.

"Sir, General Torrejon has moved to the left flank, as ordered."

"Very well," the general said. "Now, quickly, tell General Noriega to follow his written orders and place his cavalry to the right." Arista pointed toward what would become his right flank. "Do you see that tallest tree?"

"*Si*, General."

"Tell Noriega I order him to form up there immediately!"

"*Si*, General!" Captain Berlandier spurred and left.

Arista was annoyed that Noriega had not yet carried out his written orders to move to the right flank. He considered it an intentional act of insubordination. Envy and jealousy forever hobbled the Army of the North.

Reining his big gelding to his right and riding along the front lines of the Tampico Battalion, he looked sternly into the eyes of a few soldiers. They snapped to attention as he passed. Some of the men possessed the fair-skinned features of the Spanish elite, as did Arista himself. The general's red hair and freckles were especially unusual among men in the Mexican Army. But many other soldiers bore the dark features of mestizo blood. The differences in skin tone mattered little on this day. He had seen them all bleed the same crimson shade.

"*Listo?*" he asked, catching the eye of an enlisted man. *Ready?*

"*Siempre!*" the soldier replied. *Always!* Others nearby agreed.

Arista smiled. Unlike most Mexican generals, he had always enjoyed the admiration of the common soldier.

"Today you will see the faces of some gringos. Let them see no fear in your eyes. God stands with us against the heretics from the north. We will fight and defend the soil of Mother Mexico! Always!"

"*Siempre!*"

"*Viva la Republica!*"

"*Viva la Republica!*"

The general caught the eye of the regimental bandleader standing before his fifes and drums and section of brass instruments. "Play!" he commanded.

Captain
SAMUEL WALKER

Under a bright spring sun at its zenith, Sam Walker rode out of the chaparral and onto the broad plain that afforded the first glimpse of the Palo
Alto timber along the Matamoros Road. He expected to find Arista's
army here, and he did. He could see it strewn out a mile wide, already in
battle formation.

He had longed for this. Not since that ill-fated advance on Mier, back
in forty-two, had he found himself at the vanguard of an invading force.
There, he had been captured before the fight had even begun. Months of
captivity had followed. He was hoping for different results today, but he
did not fear any outcome that might lay in store for him.

"Boys, let's get a closer look," he said to the mixed band of volunteer
Texas Rangers and regular army dragoon officers who rode with him.
Before anyone could answer, Walker spurred his mustang forward to
canter down the road.

Tall stalks of saw grass covered the plain to his left, standing shoulder high to a man afoot. Walker had seen saw grass in Florida while
serving there under General Taylor. The plant tended to grow along
riverbanks and in swamps, indicating to the Ranger that the ground
might be soft in places where the saw grass grew. The blades of this grass
indeed sported jagged teeth like a saw, sharp enough to slice a man's flesh.
The top of each stalk was hard and almost as sharp as a darning needle.
This thick grass might slow down an infantry charge, he thought.

To the right of the road, a series of marshes and pools indicated boggy ground that could hinder an artillery or cavalry advance. But other than the saw grass and the bogs, the prairie seemed a perfect spot to practice the art of war.

He wanted to ride close enough to identify the various units under General Arista—horse, foot, and guns. Already he could make out the banner of the elite Tampico Battalion anchoring the center of the line.

"Walker, we're within artillery range," a dragoon captain warned from behind. It was Captain Charles May, whom Walker considered something of a braggart.

Walker smiled and spurred his mount on.

"I brought a spyglass," shouted a lieutenant. "No need to get so near!"

The Ranger finally pulled rein just out of the reach of enemy muskets. Now he could hear the Mexican Army band belting out a tune over the squeaking of his party's saddle leather and the heaving of their horses.

One of his Rangers arrived at his shoulder. "That's a right smart ditty. Them chili-bellies can sure blow them horns."

A puff of smoke from a cannon muzzle attracted his attention. Walker heard the report of the eight-pounder mixed with the whirr of the solid shot that sailed over his head, bounced down the road behind him, and splashed into one of the bogs, scattering a flock of ducks.

"We'd better git before they reload that piece," Captain May suggested.

Walker was still taking note of battery positions and looking for the pennons of the veteran Mexican cavalry and infantry units. "Better to set still a minute than to retreat right into their range."

The Mexican gun bucked and roared again, the ball sailing lower, but still overhead. "Now's a good time to report back to the general, boys." He took his hat off and waved a *hasta luego* to Arista's army before reining his pony around to the rear.

A canter out of cannon range and a trot of ten minutes delivered him to Taylor's army, which was lumbering down the road, encumbered by the two hundred supply wagons and two huge siege guns, each pulled by a dozen oxen. Back at Point Isabel, Walker had suggested leaving the supply train and the eighteen-pounders behind until the enemy could be cleared from the road by a more mobile force. But Old Rough and Ready had refused to further divide his army on the Rio Grande.

"My duty is to get these provisions to Fort Texas," he had said in his slow, methodical way. "I will not leave them behind to rush into a fight. We will all proceed together."

Now Walker spotted the general astride Old Whitey, holding a parley with some officers as the army plodded by. He was glad to see that Taylor had abandoned the seat of his wagon, which his slave had been driving. Some of the northern boys sneered at the idea of a slave owner carting his chattel to war. Besides, a general ought to straddle a steed in a battle.

"General Taylor," Walker said, reining in with his left hand as he saluted with his right. "General Arista sends his regards from the muzzle of a field gun."

Some of the younger West Pointers bristled at this mockery of decorum, but Taylor only smiled and returned the salute.

"I heard the reports, Captain. What lies ahead?"

"Arista's holding the road at Palo Alto. Torrejon's on his left. The Tampicos are in the middle. More cavalry to his right, under Noriega. Their batteries are scattered along the whole line. Other infantry regiments, too."

"How many men, total?" the general asked.

"I'd say about three thousand. They take up about a mile across the prairie. Arista's got the tall trees to his back. Probably has some reserve troops hidden in there."

"How's the ground?"

"Good in the prairie to the left of the road, but covered with tall grass. It's boggy to the right side of the road, but the men can fill their canteens and water their horses at the first pond. It's out of range of the Mexican guns."

"Good. Well done, Captain." Taylor turned to Lieutenant Jacob Blake, a combat engineer. "Lieutenant, ride ahead with Captain Walker and reconnoiter the field."

"Yes, sir."

As he reined away with Blake, Walker saw General Taylor swing his right leg over his pommel as he leaned back to prop his left hand on Old Whitey's rump, looking as calm as some old farmer at a county fair. He thought it well that the army's commander seemed relaxed, so long as the general was not *too* relaxed. Very soon, time would tell.

Lord, let this war commence.

Part II
HORSE, FOOT, AND GUNS

In Line of Battle

Brigadier General
ZACHARY TAYLOR

Palo Alto
May 8, 1846

Rounding a bend in the Matamoros Road and riding out of the chaparral, General Zachary Taylor beheld a glorious sight. A couple of miles ahead, across a level grassy plain, he saw an army stretching from left to right like a multicolored ribbon. The midday sun made polished steel implements of war glisten all along the ribbon like ripples on the water of the pond to the right of the road. The tall saw grass on the plain stirred on a mischievous breeze between him and his enemy.

"Captain Bliss," he said.

"Yes, sir," his adjutant replied, riding at his side.

"There is our foe."

"I see them, sir."

"Send couriers to the commanders of the regiments. Tell them to hasten ahead and prepare to form up in line of battle. The enemy will likely harass our line as we deploy. Then I want you, personally, to gallop ahead and tell Lieutenant Blake that he had better find some ground suitable for the Bull Battery in the next ten minutes. Go!"

"Yes, sir!" Bliss spurred his mount and wheeled away to follow his orders.

General Taylor smiled as he watched his adjutant part the saw grass at a canter. He felt grateful that his enemy, General Mariano Arista, had chosen the ground that he himself had coveted for this clash. Good, open terrain for heavy artillery fire followed by a bayonet charge. Even the weather could not have been scripted any better.

God must be on our side.

As the regiments moved forward and fanned out on the prairie to take their assigned positions, Taylor congratulated himself for sticking to his guns back at Point Isabel. There, his junior officers had urged him to leave the supplies behind, to rush forward and clear the road to Fort Texas before bringing up the wagon train. But General Zachary Taylor had only smiled blithely at the reckless impatience of the young West Pointers. The whole purpose of this march was to get the provisions to Fort Texas. Why would he leave them behind? Yes, the supply train would slow their march, but it was the supply train that had to get through. Some had even suggested leaving the slow-moving eighteen-pounders at Point Isabel. Drawn by lumbering oxen, they had been dubbed the "Bull Battery."

"You may rely upon the flying artillery," Major Ringgold had said. "I recommend leaving the Bull Battery behind to protect the works at Point Isabel."

Only Lieutenant William H. Churchill had disagreed, and that was because he commanded the Bull Battery and wanted to be in on the imminent engagement.

To Taylor the decision was a simple one. After decades of skirmishing with Indians, he finally saw a real battle shaping up before him. Leave his biggest guns behind? How ridiculous. Yes, they moved slowly behind the oxen, but the supply train would allow his army to move no faster anyway. He had no intention of leaving the provisions or the Bull Battery behind. Churchill's siege guns would give him the advantage of range and devastating firepower.

Taylor had refrained from scolding the younger officers bent on mobility, urgency, and a yearning for battle. He had politely rejected the advice to hasten upstream and ordered a methodical march, en masse. And now it had all worked according to his plan. He would soon face Arista's forces on an open field of battle with the advantage of the big guns on his side. The presence of their much-needed supply train would give his men all the more reason to fight.

Within minutes, fifes and drums from the various regiments were leading soldiers to their places in line of battle. Soon he saw Captain Bliss riding back with Lieutenant Blake.

"Lieutenant Blake reporting as ordered, sir!" the field engineer blurted as he reined his horse to a halt and saluted.

"Report," Taylor ordered, already fed up with the military protocol.

"Sir, I have found a solid path around the bogs and a good location for the Bull Battery to unlimber."

"At what range?"

"Nine hundred yards from the enemy line, sir. Well within the effective range of the eighteen-pounders. With your permission, sir, I will escort them forward immediately."

"See that you do, Lieutenant."

Over the next few minutes, Taylor rode casually ahead and kept an eye on the enemy line, expecting a cavalry charge that might complicate his plans. Meanwhile, the regiments formed a line of battle, just out of range of Mexican artillery. Finally, from his saddle atop Old Whitey, he watched as a team of oxen laboriously pulled the second eighteen-pounder into position a half mile from the Mexican line. Now all the pieces were in place on the chessboard.

"Bill," he said to his adjutant, Captain Bliss, "you would think that General Arista would have harassed us with a cavalry charge by now while we moved into line of battle."

"I was thinking the same, sir. Why would he allow us to deploy our regiments unmolested?"

Taylor shrugged. "He must be very fond of his defensive position against the timber."

He could see now that Lieutenant Churchill had the second siege gun in place and ready for firing. The Bull Battery was the last of his units to move into position for the coming battle. It was time.

The Gulf wind was upon his back, bending the broad brim of his palm leaf hat. Between gusts, he could just hear the Mexican band playing martial tunes.

"Bill!" he shouted to Captain Bliss.

"Sir?"

"Order the long roll."

"Yes, sir!" Bliss trotted to the line of drummer boys stationed nearby. In a moment, the long roll sounded, swelled, and ended with a shot of hardwood sticks on calfskin. All across the American lines came the rattle of bayonets being fixed to musket barrels. First sergeants shouted orders and men began to march toward the Mexican lines, trampling down the tall grass stalks, which only sprang up again behind the first in line.

The drummers resumed their cadence and the march continued. Taylor rode along at a leisurely pace, as if looking over one of his plantation fields back in Louisiana. For several long minutes his lines approached Arista's. Still, Arista ordered no attack. Taylor now watched as two flying artillery batteries, under captains Duncan and Ringgold, advanced ahead of the infantry—Ringgold to the right, Duncan to the left—their trained teams pulling the six-pounders at a long trot. With seven hundred yards dividing the two armies, Taylor turned to William Bliss.

"This is close enough," he said.

Bliss ordered the drummers to cease and told the bugler to sound a halt to the march. The army ground to a standstill. Taylor was amazed to see the flying artillery already unlimbered and loaded. He scanned the broad enemy lines for some sign of action. He did not have to wait long. A cannon muzzle on the enemy's right blossomed with smoke and sent a ball flying. It missed Duncan's gunners and fell short of the infantry but rolled into the ranks of the Eighth. Men scrambled aside to avoid it, for they could see the projectile plowing toward them through the tall grass.

Thank God the Mexicans had few exploding shells to hurl at his lines. Their ammunition consisted mostly of solid brass spheres, their grape-shot nothing more than bits of scrap iron.

Taylor looked over his shoulder at Churchill's siege guns, positioned between the front line and the supply train. The oxen had been moved aside to graze, and the gunners seemed to be in position around the eighteen-pounders. Certainly Churchill would respond to the enemy's opening shot, as his orders dictated. As if to answer the general's questioning mind, the first of the big guns erupted, bucking backwards, hurling a shell overhead and into the Tampico Battalion. The exploding shell tore a hole through the ranks, casting corpses aside as a child would blow away the tufts of a dandelion.

Now Duncan's six-pounders, in advance of the front line, added to the opening salvo as several Mexican guns also hurled shots. Duncan's load of canister howled toward the Mexican line and exploded just short of an infantry unit, taking down several enemy soldiers in one blast. The choice of target was by order of Taylor. He suspected the Mexican artillery would attempt to take out his own ordnance. He, on the other hand, would use his more lethal ammunition—like the dreaded canister—to demoralize the Mexican infantry. The general expected this battle to be won by the bayonet.

The Mexicans continued to lob solid shot short of his lines, the American infantrymen sidestepping the balls as they rolled in. It was almost comical to watch his soldiers break ranks for a rolling ball, then close ranks behind the path of the projectile. But Taylor refrained from smiling. Sooner or later, one of those hunks of metal was going to do some damage, and then the horrors of war would call for no laughter.

As the artillery battle continued, Duncan's and Ringgold's field guns fired and reloaded rapidly, slinging a hellish barrage into the enemy line. Taylor saw William Bliss cantering his way, holding his gold pocket watch in his hand.

"General, the flying artillery are firing seven rounds per minute!"

Taylor's eyebrows raised. This was unheard of. Perhaps Ringgold was on to something after all with his new methods of light artillery.

Now, in the growing chaos, a Mexican gun found its range. A solid brass ball whistled into the ranks of the Eighth Infantry, on the left, not far from Taylor's position on Old Whitey. It hit an infantryman in the shoulder. The soldier flew one way, his arm the other.

Taylor looked at his adjutant and saw the ghastly pale look upon the younger man's face. This was William "Perfect" Bliss's first taste of battle. "Watch for a cavalry attack, Bill. We will need to respond quickly when it comes."

Captain Bliss blinked, then nodded. "Yes, sir." The adjutant turned his eyes away from the mangled soldier and looked toward Torrejon's far-away horsemen, the glint of their steel lance tips sparkling at the enemy's far left flank.

General
ANASTASIO TORREJON

For over an hour General Anastasio Torrejon had watched the big guns of the Americans pour deadly fire into the ranks of the Mexican infantry. The canister and spherical shell shot of the gringos had mowed the foot soldiers down like shocks of wheat before the scythe, yet the blood-spattered survivors refused to break ranks.

It was Arista's fault, he thought. That idealistic fool had failed to mount a counterattack of any kind. The reason was clear to Torrejon. Arista's officer corps harbored little respect for their commander and his conservative political views. They had no intention of following his orders with any kind of urgency. The enlisted men admired the general, but Arista had never figured out that he must win the hearts of the officers first, above the rank and file.

In an odd way—for Torrejon himself held no great respect for Arista—this state of affairs made him anxious to receive his orders to attack. Torrejon had already distinguished himself at Rancho de Carricitos, where he had killed or captured the entire party of dragoons under the Americans' Captain Seth Thornton. He saw his opportunity now to win the day again, if only Arista would order the charge.

Finally, Arista's aide-de-camp, Captain Jean Louis Berlandier, came riding at a gallop to Torrejon's position.

"General Arista sends his regards," Berlandier said, saluting.

Torrejon ignored the regards but returned the salute as he took a folded leaf of paper that the captain had produced from his tunic. The terse note from General Arista ordered him to charge, turn the Americans' right flank, and capture the enemy supply train. He smiled. His subordinates had already been given their orders on how to form the companies up for the charge. He was ready.

Within minutes they assembled in columns. At the head of his regiment—eight hundred men strong—Torrejon led the advance at a long trot. He angled to the left of the Matamoras Road, where the chaparral would lend some cover. Though a cavalry movement of this magnitude could not go undetected by the enemy for very long, he knew even a minute or two of surprise could benefit the maneuver, and therefore he intended to use the cover of the brush for as long as he could. Looking back over his shoulder, he could see his entire regiment on the move, with two eight-pound artillery pieces trying to keep up in the rear. At this moment, in spite of himself, he admired the methods of the Americans' flying artillery, which he had witnessed for the first time today. Ringgold's tactics made his army's gunners seem to creep along like tortoises.

Otherwise, his horsemen presented a splendid sight, their hundreds of lance points jutting skyward as they rode.

"*A la lope!*" he shouted. "*Marcha!*" His mount knew the order for the canter and lunged forward, the columns behind him soon joining him in the quicker gait, the order having been passed back through the companies. On he charged, knowing the enemy must have seen him by now. Still, catching glimpses of the Yankee line through the scattered brush, he saw no opposing force moving to protect the American right. The surprise would devastate the enemy.

Suddenly, Torrejon's mount balked and floundered. He spurred, but the charger slung his head, then slipped in a soft patch of dirt, almost tumbling.

"*Alto!*"

The ground here, though covered with the same grass as the good terrain behind him, had turned into a bog he never could have seen coming. The units behind piled into the forward riders, causing horses to kick and rear. Men cursed; some were thrown and trampled.

Torrejon waved frantically to his right. "To the road! Use the road. Quickly!" He now regretted holding to the cover of the scattered chaparral. Any advantage he had won by the concealment had already been lost in this quagmire.

The young officer nearest to him reined to the right, but only found softer footing that sucked at his mount's hooves. He had led his entire regiment into an invisible bog that had surrounded him on three sides. He would have to back out, though the last of his men were still piling forward.

"To the rear!" he railed. "Damn you, fools! To the rear!"

Captain
EPHRAIM KIRBY SMITH

He could see that the enemy cannonade had rattled the nerves of his soldiers. He himself fought back the dread of death and violence. His company would look to him for leadership. He could not fail them, would not disgrace his family's legacy.

"Stand firm, men!" This was all he could think of to say, but it seemed to help. His men stood at order arms, awaiting the directive to attack.

"Sir, are we gonna charge or not?" a private demanded.

Captain Ephraim Kirby Smith, a company commander in the Fifth Infantry, U.S. Army, understood the soldier's anxiety. Anything was better than standing here, waiting for the next cannon shot to scream their way. He looked sternly into the eyes of the private.

"I have sent a request for orders to our regimental commander, Colonel McIntosh. I have expressed to him that we would rather advance than stand here and dodge cannonballs."

The soldier's eyes cut away from Smith to watch two infantrymen carry a wounded man to the rear. A cannonball had severed the victim's foot.

Out of habit, Smith looked toward his brother, Captain Edmund Kirby Smith, also a company commander in the Fifth. Standing with his troops a stone's throw away to the right, Edmund seemed to feel his brother's gaze. He looked back at Ephraim and gave a quick nod.

Ephraim Smith nodded back and scratched at sideburns that grew thick from his ears to the corners of his mouth.

"Captain!"

Smith's first sergeant came sprinting toward him. He slid to a stop and pointed down the Matamoros Road. "There's enemy cavalry riding out of the brush. Hundreds of them."

Through the artillery smoke, Captain Smith saw the enemy movement a half mile away. It struck him as a deadly but beautiful sight, like a gaily patterned viper slithering out into view. The gaudy colors of the uniforms and the fang-like lances made his heart leap.

"They aim to flank us, Captain," said the first sergeant.

"Report to Colonel McIntosh. Hurry!"

As he watched his first sergeant run toward McIntosh's position, Smith noticed that the Texas Ranger Captain Samuel Walker had arrived, horseback, at Colonel McIntosh's side and was already pointing out the enemy movement. *Good.* Captain Smith now noticed some twenty horsemen in civilian attire nearby: Walker's Spy Company of Rangers. The presence of these hard-riding men tendered some confidence.

He looked toward Edmund. Edmund glanced back and forced a smile.

Now Smith looked back to the Matamoras Road. Torrejon's cavalry were still pouring out of the chaparral. They seemed disorganized and took some time forming up for the charge. Some of the horses and riders looked as if they had fallen in mud.

Searching with his eyes across the battleground to his left, Smith could see that Lieutenant Randolph Ridgely, of Ringgold's flying artillery, had spotted the Mexican cavalry on the road. His gunners were busy limbering two six-pounders, hopefully in preparation to support the flank.

The artillery, like the Rangers, gave Ephraim Smith more comfort. Yet he knew the Fifth Infantry would take the brunt of the coming attack. Hundreds of veteran Mexican riders could only be turned by an equal number of muskets in the hands of trained foot soldiers. He feared that, if American bullets failed to stop the Mexican horsemen, the bayonets of the Fifth would prove virtually useless against the long lances of Torrejon's men—ten-foot poles with ten-inch razor-sharp blades and a triangular pennon below the blade to absorb and prevent the slick blood of slain men from running down the spear shaft and spoiling the lancer's grip.

Now Smith's first sergeant returned at a run, gasping, having over-heard the conversation between Colonel McIntosh and Captain Walker.

"Sir, the regiment is to make an oblique move ahead and to the right. We will form a hollow square to defend the flank, sir." The veteran noncom propped his palms on his knees as he bent to catch his breath.

The order to march came by drum roll, bugle call, and shouted orders. Smith's company advanced at double-quick time over four hundred yards with the rest of the regiment. Arriving at the far right flank, winded, they prepared to form a defensive square, as they had done scores of times at drill, each company aware of the movements required to create the square from column formation. Some marched forward, some back. Others wheeled and swung like hinged gates bristling with bayonets.

Smith listened as first sergeants barked orders to their companies:

"Platoons! Right half-wheel, march!"

"Left oblique, march!"

"Forward, left wheel!"

"Halt! Right dress!"

The square took shape between the Matamoros Road and the duck ponds to the west. Each side of the hollow formation was two ranks deep. Inside the square, a reserve unit waited to reinforce any breach in the ranks from any direction. The regimental colors and the commanding officer, Lieutenant Colonel James S. McIntosh, also occupied the center of the hollow formation. The entire five-hundred-man formation covered a patch of prairie no more than thirty yards square. A small target for distant enemy artillery, it bristled in every direction with musket barrels and fixed bayonets.

Smith felt reasonably confident that the square would answer any flanking attempt. No matter where the enemy cavalry swarmed, American muskets and rifles would aim—left, right, front, or rear. He found himself guarding the forward face of the square—the position most likely to take the initial cavalry charge. He stood less than a quarter mile from the enemy now, and he could make out the horsemen waving the tips of their lances in the air. He glanced at the men around him. Fear blanched the faces of some. Others visibly trembled. But none broke ranks.

Captain Smith thought of his forebears from Connecticut. His grandfather had fought at Bunker Hill and throughout the War of

Independence. His father, during the War of 1812, had charged at Lundy's Lane, later earning the rank of colonel. Service in the regular army was a family tradition. Smith himself was nearing forty years of age. Like his brother, Edmund, he had served in the army for almost two decades and had never seen combat. He was determined to meet it with honor.

"Stand firm, men!" he cried, hoping his voice would not crack. "We will not fire until they are upon us! Stand firm and prepare to fight!"

"Here they come!" his first sergeant announced.

My God. They are eight hundred strong. The colors! Such power! The gallantry! Can we stop them? Yes, we must. Trust the hollow square.

The enemy horsemen formed a broad line, several ranks deep. They galloped headlong at the Fifth Infantry's square, looming ever larger. At one hundred yards, they suddenly stopped, their forward rank drawing *escopetas* from saddle rings or scabbards. This front rank unleashed a hailstorm of lead toward the Fifth's square. Smith heard the bullets popping against U.S. uniforms. Wounded men screamed. Some fell. Others carried on as if mindless of their wounds.

"Hold your fire!" Smith ordered. He stepped aside so a soldier could drag a gutshot comrade into the middle of the square.

The front rank of the lancers veered right with muzzles smoking. The entire cavalry formation charged again, then halted, the second rank drawing and firing the old blunderbusses into the Americans' square, then curling aside to reveal the third rank, which also advanced, halted, fired, peeled away.

A few more men fell from the square, wounded or dead.

"Hold your fire, men! Stand firm!" Smith had never seen or heard of a cavalry maneuver like the one he was witnessing, yet the old flintlocks had not blasted any gaping holes in the hollow square. He heard an order in Spanish and saw the horses leap forward toward him, the lances leaning low to draw American blood. Fifty yards away now . . .

"Hold your fire!" He knew he could not let the men pull their triggers too soon.

Forty yards . . . Thirty . . .

"Fire!"

The front rank of infantry released a long-awaited barrage. Enemy riders fell and horses tumbled in earth-jarring wrecks, yet still more charged gallantly on, live mounts leaping over dead ones. Each soldier in the front rank, having fired, dropped to one knee and braced the butt of his weapon on the ground, bayonet jutting up and out. The second rank took aim behind the kneeling men of the first rank.

Twenty yards . . . Ten . . .

"Fire!" Smith yelled.

That did it!

American lead tore riders from Mexican mounts and turned others back, wounded. Scores of cavalrymen veered and pressed the far right flank of the U.S. line, only to find Captain Samuel Walker's Texas Rangers guarding the extreme right, west of the road. The Rangers fired rifles, Colt revolvers, and shotguns from their saddles, forcing the Mexicans to veer farther to their left, onto boggy ground. They milled in confusion as the men of the Fifth reloaded using paper cartridges holding powder, ball, and buckshot. Smith's men fired at will now, driving the riders out of musket range.

"Cease firing and reload!" Smith shouted. His heart was beating so hard that the words came out in surges.

A shout from Colonel McIntosh at the center of the square now ordered a side movement of the formation toward the middle of the battlefield. Wondering why, Captain Smith looked toward the rear and saw that Ridgely's two six-pounders were rapidly taking up a position behind the square. As the ground was too boggy to the right of the square, he could see that the Fifth would need to move left to open up a path for the flying artillery to blaze away at the rallying Mexican horsemen.

"Carry the wounded to the middle of the square!" Smith yelled. "Left face! Company, march!"

As his men tripped over dropped weapons and dragged wounded men, the entire regiment nonetheless moved haltingly toward the left. Glancing back over the battlefield as cannon roared between the two armies, he saw Torrejon's riders trying to organize a second charge. Behind them, the two fieldpieces at the rear of the Mexican charge were finally ramming home loads. The defensive square continued to slide toward the middle of the American line. Smith thought of draperies being pulled gradually from the edge of a window to reveal the dark pupils of two peering eyes. Only, these eyes shot fire.

The Mexican fieldpieces erupted, but fired high. Smith's relief was short-lived, as he saw the lancers charging yet again. They were either unaware of Ridgely's two guns or were simply too brave to falter. At fifty yards, the flying artillery unleashed two loads of spherical case shot, blasting a hole into the Mexican advance. Yet the survivors charged on.

"Fire!"

Smith's men resumed their musket fire, then Ridgely's two pieces—having reloaded with miraculous speed—slung another lethal dose of hell into the lancers, almost point blank. Finally, the beleaguered Mexicans peeled away. The soldiers of the Fifth cheered as the fleeing enemy riders picked up their dead and wounded as best they could under the withering fire of the flying artillery.

Ephraim Smith looked over his shoulder, across the inside of the square, and waved at his brother. Through thick gunpowder smoke he saw Edmund wave back.

Turning back to the front, Smith thought he might vomit, but he choked back the urge through sheer will. A fallen cavalry mount writhed just two paces in front of him, its entrails bulging from a wound in its belly. The paunch of the warhorse had been ripped open and the pungent odor of offal made him gag. As he wondered if he should order a soldier to shoot the suffering steed, the beast rolled its eyes and shuddered, releasing its last breath in a blessed death rattle.

Brigadier General
ZACHARY TAYLOR

Palo Alto
May 8, 1846

The long days of incessant drill on Corpus Christi beach had paid off, he thought. It gratified him to see infantry and artillery working together so smoothly under fire to turn Torrejon's attack, but he had expected such professionalism for months. What he could not have foreseen was the overall lethal efficiency of the flying artillery. Ringgold's batteries had been able to rush to any given position, sling shot after shot accurately at the enemy, then wheel away to new ground before the Mexican artillery could range them. This swarming offensive, coupled with the firepower of the Bull Battery's eighteen-pounders, had thus far made the expected infantry charge unnecessary.

Taylor knew this could change at any minute, depending on what Arista had in mind across the way. But for now, in this first battle of an infant war, he was content to let his artillery speak for the U.S. Army. That contentment ended suddenly when a Mexican ball hit a caisson behind one of the siege guns, rendering four gunners dead or unconscious.

"Bill!" he shouted.

"Sir!" Captain William Bliss responded immediately.

"Write a note to Ringgold. A Mexican gun has ranged the eighteen-pounders. Tell him to find that gun and destroy it."

Bliss was using an empty ammunition crate as his makeshift desk. He scrawled the note and handed it up to the general. Taylor spread the paper across his thigh to sign his rank and name with the plume Bliss handed to him. Bliss then carried the signed order at a run to a dragoon waiting nearby.

"Godspeed," Taylor said, as he watched the dragoon gallop into the maw of the battle. The messenger rode a light gray horse, making him easy to follow with the naked eye, even at a distance. Through the battlefield gun smoke, Taylor saw the mount arrive at the side of Major Ringgold astride his big bay horse he called Old Branch.

Another Mexican cannonball shattered the wheel of a limber and bounced through the ranks, finally hitting and mortally injuring one of the oxen used to pull the eighteen-pounders. Taylor watched as an infantry soldier walked over to the crippled ox, took aim at its head, and put the beast out of its misery with a single shot.

"There will be beef for supper," he said to Captain Bliss, who had just returned to his side.

"I don't know that I will have the appetite, sir."

"The war has begun, Bill. You must never pass up a chance to eat or sleep when the opportunity presents itself."

"Yes, sir."

Looking back toward Ringgold's position on the battlefield, the general saw the gunners limbering two pieces. Apparently Ringgold had already judged the source of the shot that had damaged the works of the Bull Battery. This would be interesting. Where would Ringgold move next to deal with the offending enemy cannon?

Within a minute, horses, artillery, ammunition, and gunners were racing toward the right flank of the battlefield to take up a new and advantageous position. Taylor thought Ringgold would move perhaps a quarter mile, but he kept going, galloping right. Four hundred, five hundred, six hundred yards. A half mile, and the flying artillery still had not slowed its pace.

My God, he's going all the way to the enemy flank. He's attempting to enfilade the entire Mexican line!

Bliss was looking through a spyglass. "Sir? Are you watching Ringgold?"

"Yes."

"He's going to flank them!"

Taylor shrugged. "Why not? The Mexican cavalry has fallen back in confusion on that flank."

"The order I wrote only said to eliminate the artillery hitting our siege guns, not to enfilade the enemy line!"

"I know, Bill. I read it before I signed it. Ringgold is seizing the moment. Perhaps he couldn't determine exactly which enemy gun had ranged us, so he decided to line them up and bring them all under fire."

This is gallantry beyond the pale of imagination.

"It's reckless."

"Yes."

The flying artillery swung into position and unlimbered before the Mexicans recognized them as the enemy. Tubes were swabbed and loaded. Canister and grape tore into the nearest infantry to hold them at bay, then Ringgold's men reloaded with exploding shells that they lobbed farther down the Mexican line, blasting enemy gunners away from their pieces and effectively ending the bombardment of the Bull Battery. It was astonishing how quickly Ringgold's men could reload and how accurately they could fire. Yet Taylor worried for the major's safety now. In his courageous maneuver, he had drawn the attention of Arista's entire army. From atop Old Whitey, Taylor could see enemy fieldpieces pivoting to fire back at Ringgold's six-pounders.

"Come on now, Ringgold," he muttered to himself. "That's enough. Get your little guns out of there."

"Sir!" Bliss shouted. "The grass has caught fire near Duncan's battery!"

The general tore his gaze away from Ringgold and looked toward Duncan, to the left. Flames were leaping, smoke spreading across the battleground. Maybe Ringgold could use the cover of this smoke to escape back to the relative safety of the American line.

Taylor narrowed his eyes as they swept right again. He strained to follow Old Branch through the thickening smoke. He blinked, and it seemed the mount and rider vanished. Then he saw the horse kicking on the ground. Men rushed to Ringgold's aid. A Mexican ball had hit Old Branch. The gunners were in chaos, and Taylor feared the worst for the gallant Ringgold.

Captain
JAMES DUNCAN

Palo Alto
May 8, 1846

"Fire canister to the front!" Duncan yelled, standing in his stirrups, pointing toward the Tampico Battalion through the grass fire smoke. "Aim at their colors, Sergeant!" A flaming wad from the muzzle of one of his six-pounders had ignited the tall saw grass, but he intended to get off one last round before the enemy target became completely obscured by smoke.

For two hours his men had killed and maimed the foot soldiers on the Mexican side, constantly dodging the counterfire of the enemy artillery by hastily limbering, moving, unlimbering, firing. This was his first taste of battle, but his training had served him well. *Don't think about the dead men on the other side. Follow your orders. Do your duty.* Like all of Ringgold's men, he felt a need to prove the mettle of the flying artillery to General Taylor and was willing to risk life and limb to do so.

Now, through the black smoke, a dragoon came galloping on a large gray horse.

"Captain Duncan!" the messenger yelled. "Major Ringgold's down!"

Duncan looked to the right, toward the place where he had last seen Ringgold's battery. He found nothing but smoke. "What do you mean, he's down?"

"A ball hit Old Branch. It hit Ringgold, too. Both his legs, broken at the thighs."

This news staggered Duncan, but he would not let his alarm show. "Is he killed?"

"Not yet, but . . . He looked me right in the eye. He said, 'Don't stay with me. You have work to do. Go ahead.'"

Duncan attempted to peer through the smoke. "Where the devil is he, Sergeant?"

"He rode all the way to the enemy's left flank to enfilade their line. His gunners are trying to hitch up and get him out of there."

A strange lull had fallen across the battleground. The smoke from the crackling grass fire had clouded all artillery targets, and both sides had ceased to fire for the first time in hours. There was no sense in remaining here, Duncan thought. Taylor had given the company commanders of the flying artillery batteries much latitude in decision making. They would go where they deemed themselves most needed, without waiting for orders from above.

"Company! Limber!" He turned to the dragoon on the gray horse. "We'll go to the aid of Major Ringgold."

The dragoon nodded. "With your permission, sir, I'll guide you there. There are a couple of boggy places to be avoided."

"Very well."

His men brought the horses around and hitched limbers to guns and caissons with a haste that filled Duncan with pride. Yet he reeled to think of Ringgold crippled and dying.

Just as he began moving toward Ringgold's position, he heard— and felt—the rumble of many hooves coming from the left. He slowed his men.

"What the hell is that?" his gunnery sergeant said.

A gust lifted the smoke for an instant and Duncan caught a distant glimpse of a large body of enemy cavalry cantering toward the U.S. Army's left flank. Now he knew he could not rush to the aid of Major Ringgold. If that cavalry assault got around the U.S. left flank, the Mexicans could capture the supply train.

"Turn about!" he yelled at his men. "To the left flank!" As his gunners wheeled, Duncan looked at the dragoon messenger. "Sergeant, go quickly. Tell General Taylor that our left flank is under attack by a battalion of enemy cavalry."

"Yes, sir!" The man on the gray horse left at a gallop.

Duncan spurred his own mount and caught up with his men, quickly galloping past them to take the lead. Charging in front of the Eighth Infantry's line, he rode all the way to the extreme left flank, where he pulled rein and raised a hand to stop his men. Swirling smoke still obscured him from the cavalry attack he knew to be approaching.

"Here!" he shouted. "Unlimber! With canister, load!"

"Sponge . . . Load . . . Ram . . . Sergeant, aim toward the timber at the far left of the battlefield!"

This was where he expected to see the Mexican cavalry appear, upwind of the grass fire smoke. The Eighth Infantry had been waiting to protect the left flank all day and probably knew nothing of the enemy cavalry charge bearing down on them through the cover of the smoke cloud.

"Prime!"

The rumble of hooves approached inside the smoke cloud. The cloud swirled toward Duncan's battery, concealing the Mexicans. Now, within musket range, the smoke thinned to reveal the colorful tunics of the Mexican riders, the pennons fluttering under the blades of their lances. They were attacking in line formation perhaps four ranks deep, so they presented a broad target, impossible to miss. The sight, as it emerged from the cloud, almost enchanted Duncan with its grandeur. They were riding directly into his line of fire and still seemed unaware of his presence. His four fieldpieces sat loaded and ready to answer their attack.

"Hold your fire," Duncan said. *We must crush the forefront of that charge.* "In battery, make ready . . . Fire!"

Gunners yanked on the lanyards that sparked the charges in the breeches of the guns. The six-pounders rocked back as they erupted and sent canister howling at the enemy horsemen. The four rounds of the first volley exploded just before the shells hit the ground in front of the charge, throwing horses and men back in a hail of lead balls.

"With canister, load!"

The second salvo fell in among the bunched cavalry mounts and blossomed with hellish smoke and lead. Two more rounds did similar damage. He thanked God for his lucky timing. He watched his men work with precision.

"Fire!"

The next four rounds completely staggered the enemy horsemen and sent them either tumbling to the ground or scrambling for the cover of timber to the left. Broken and bloody men and beasts lay still or floundered about on the battleground. Duncan's artillery had changed the imagery from grand to ghastly in less than a minute. The power his guns wielded both emboldened and horrified him.

"Load canister and be ready, boys!" he ordered calmly. "They may yet charge again."

Minutes passed. Saw grass burned. Smoke cleared. Captain Duncan caught sight of the cavalrymen retreating back to their lines through the cover of the timber.

"Looks like we whipped 'em, Captain," said a young gunner, his eyes shining bright from his soot-darkened face.

Now Duncan thought about Major Ringgold flanking the Mexican left, enfilading their line. The brave move had won the commander a horrific wound. Duncan knew what he was going to do next, but he could not bring himself to speak it just yet. He was going to move forward and flank the Mexican right, as Ringgold had taken the left. It was the best way to draw the fire away from Ringgold's position so that his men could get him and his guns out of there. At this moment, the enemy batteries were all trained on Ringgold. With the speed of the flying artillery, Duncan knew he could take the flank and unleash a modicum of hell on the Mexican line for a couple of minutes before the enemy gunners could swing their fieldpieces around and range him.

"Limber!" he ordered.

"Yes, sir!" his gunnery sergeant yelled. "Hook 'em up, boys! Where are we going, Captain?"

Duncan drew his sword and pointed it toward the fleeing enemy cavalry. "There."

General
MARIANO ARISTA

General Arista blinked at the smoke stinging his eyes. Even the grass fire had benefited the Americans. Through that smoke cloud, he had heard the eruption of cannon and knew from the screams of horses and men that Colonel Cayetano Montero's cavalry attack on the American left had been repulsed. The flying artillery of the famous Major Ringgold possessed impossible mobility. They fired and reloaded faster than men with muskets.

What else could go wrong?

Earlier, General Torrejon had failed on the left after charging needlessly through boggy ground. Why had he not held to the solid footing of the road? Meanwhile, the siege guns of the Americans had plowed great swaths of death and dismemberment through his infantry. His legendary Tampico Battalion had been decimated.

General Arista had ordered attacks that had never materialized. In one case, he knew it was because a messenger had been blown to bits by an exploding shell, but in other instances he suspected his junior officers simply ignored his directives. Did they *want* him to lose this battle so that he would be recalled and *they* could ascend? He found the depth of such treachery difficult to fathom. Finally, Montero had led a spirited assault from the right, only to be slammed back by cannon that had moved into place behind the cover of the smoke cloud. What more could possibly go awry?

"General!"

Arista turned to see a gory surgeon's assistant stumbling toward him. A bloodstained hand presented a salute.

"Report!" he ordered.

"The chief surgeon has disappeared. He ordered us to move the field hospital farther back. We don't know where he took the trunks."

"What trunks?"

"The trunks with all the surgical tools and bandages and . . . and . . ." He threw his hands into the air, unable to find words.

Arista felt the frustration of the day boiling. "Find the coward! Find the trunks! Accomplish this, or you will answer to me!"

The medic nodded, saluted. "Yes, sir."

"Take a horse." He pointed to some cavalry mounts that had lost their riders and had wandered back to the lines.

"I will do my best, General."

As the bloody medico stumbled wearily away, Arista thought of the wounded men awaiting attention. "*Pobres diablos,*" he whispered. *Poor devils.* It was a phrase he uttered often in war.

Now his attention turned to shouts coming from his right flank. A cannon belched smoke and a shell sailed into the beleaguered Tampico Battalion and exploded. Shrapnel sang past his ears as soldiers crumpled, corpse-like. Somehow, a battery of enemy artillery had emerged from the timber on the far right flank and unlimbered to enfilade his line. Four guns were now raining a devastating fire on his men, and all his artillery were aimed the wrong way.

Ringgold had hit him in the same way from the left. Counterfire had knocked Ringgold from his horse—about the only bit of luck to come Arista's way today. But now, with his guns still trained on Ringgold's battery to the left, another unit of flying artillery had succeeded in attacking his line from the right! Worse yet, he could see his infantry falling back in disarray. His right flank was crumbling.

"*Bastante!*" he yelled angrily. Spurring his mount and charging right, he stopped only to order a battery of his six-pounders to pivot about and find the range on the enemy guns.

"With what?" an indignant artillery officer replied. "We have no more ammunition." He kicked an empty crate.

"Find more! Do your duty!"

Regaining his gallop in a single bound, Arista rode all along the front line as the American shells whistled overhead. Now he could see that Noriega's shattered cavalry had retreated into the infantry and started a panic, and still the grape and canister flew through the troops like swarms of hornets.

Finally, he reined toward the rear to cut off the men who were falling back. "*Alto!*" he yelled at the conscripts. "Stand your ground! Load your muskets!" He used his boot and the weight of his mount to knock down the men who continued to flee. Yelling as he headed them off like a stampede of cattle, he was joined by a few subordinate officers trying to prevent an all-out rout.

Now he recognized the face of a reliable cavalry commander.

"Captain! Attack those enemy cannon with your lancers!"

"Yes, sir," the captain answered. "But, sir, they have already limbered their guns and they are gone!"

"What?" He stood in his stirrups and saw the flying artillery dashing away. "Pursue them!"

"Yes, General!" The captain rode forward to gather his riders.

Arista turned to an infantry colonel he found shouting at his men to stand and fight. "Colonel, march on the enemy left. Follow the lancers. Now! Attack them!"

"*Si*, General!"

General Mariano Arista heard a great roll of drums swell up from the faraway American right, followed by the clarion ring of bugles. Taylor was going to charge the other end of his line! It was well that he had already ordered an attack on this end of the battlefield. Now he knew he must ride swiftly to the left and order his troops to fall back into the timber lest they become overrun by the Americans.

He spurred and felt the power of the steed carry him back toward the left. As he rode, he glanced at the sun dipping into the upper branches of the trees. This was no time to lose this battle, on the verge of twilight. He would let the Americans advance unopposed on his left. Perhaps his lancers could do some damage on the right.

Come quickly, nightfall. Tomorrow we will fight anew.

Brigadier General
ZACHARY TAYLOR

Palo Alto
May 8, 1846

It was like trying to watch a play with the stage curtain constantly going up and down. General Zachary Taylor had been unable to witness all of the maneuvers through the cloud of grass fire smoke that forever swirled, lifted, descended, thickened, and thinned. He had seen Duncan's brilliant maneuver to protect the left flank with his battery, then marveled at the same captain's courageous decision to advance all the way to Arista's right flank.

That move had created the distraction that helped Ringgold's men get him out of the mess he was in at the other end of the battlefield.

As he had watched Duncan vanish in a swirl of smoke on the left, General Zachary Taylor had ordered an advance of all his units on the right. Distracted by Duncan, Arista would never see it coming. General Twiggs was marching three infantry regiments forward now, accompanied by artillery and led by dragoons.

Ringgold had been hauled to the field hospital on a caisson trundling up the Matamoros Road. That hard-riding dragoon courier on the big gray horse had said that Ringgold's wound was a bad one, with much flesh torn from both of his shattered thighs. Taylor hoped Ringgold would live long enough for him to express his pleasure in the performance of the flying artillery, in which the general had not, until today, held much confidence.

Now he was watching Captain Charles May of the Second Dragoons lead the charge on the right.

"That damn smoke," he said to Bliss. "Can you see anything, Bill?"

Bliss lowered his spyglass. "Captain May didn't get the dragoons close enough, sir. They rode up and fired their carbines, but they were not yet inside the effective range of the weapon."

Taylor smirked at the way that every word Bliss spoke seemed to come right out of an army manual. "We must keep our eyes on Captain May in the future. Maybe he doesn't judge distances well."

Bliss had the spyglass at his eye again. "Nonetheless, sir, the enemy seems to be retreating from our advance on the right without opposition. They're withdrawing into the timber."

"Maybe Arista wants to fall back and lick his wounds overnight."

"And live to fight another day?"

"Or maybe it's a feint, and he has something planned on our left flank."

Bliss's spyglass and Taylor's eyes swept together from the south to the east. He saw that the smoke had finally cleared from his left flank. Captain Duncan had returned, his battery intact, and had positioned himself on the left flank again. Then Taylor noticed the lancers approaching, followed by a regiment of infantry.

"Bill, get a note to Twiggs on the right. Tell him not to pursue the enemy into the timber. Tell him to capture the line the Mexican Army previously held but go no farther."

"Yes, sir."

"Then get word to the Eighth Infantry on the left. Order them to hold that ground at all cost!"

Bliss was already scribbling the first note. "Yes, sir."

For the first time today, Taylor found himself peering down on his battlefield from above—an impossible hawk's-eye view. This had happened to him at Fort Harrison on the Wabash against Tecumsah, and again at Okeechobee, fighting the Seminoles. He now saw everything from on high. However unreal, the vision did not unsettle him. He thought of nothing beyond the battle beneath his gaze. From his merlin vantage, he could even see the future trajectory of the fight. Both lines—his and the enemy's—were going to pivot counterclockwise but remain an equal distance apart. There, the day's struggle would end. Darkness would fall. Victory—slim but sure—would be his.

Lieutenant
SAM GRANT

Palo Alto
May 8, 1846

Lieutenant Sam Grant had watched the carnage from a distance all day, like some ghoulish spectator. But now his regiment, the Fourth Infantry, had received orders to march forward. The enemy's left flank was falling back, it seemed, and General Taylor wanted to occupy the ground the Mexicans were surrendering.

Drums rolled and fifes piped a march. As his company commander, Captain George A. McCall, gave the order, the fifty men in his unit began to advance. In an odd way, Grant felt something of a relief. Though sickened by what he saw as senseless death and mutilation, he had felt useless all day. As his men strode forward, he could see Mexican artillery still holding their ground, supported by some remnants of lancers and infantry.

The enemy guns commenced to fire on the U.S. advance, the balls bouncing and rolling among the soldiers. Looking to his left at the wrong moment, he saw the head of a foot soldier explode from the direct hit by a cannonball. The man's splintered musket stock, and even his very skull, became shrapnel that tore into and injured several men around him. After the ball bounced, it slammed into the side of Captain John Page's face, tearing away his lower jaw.

Stunned by what he had just witnessed, Grant could only march onward and hope the projectiles would miss his men. The sun had joined the horizon. He placed his hand on his saber hilt, expecting at any moment to hear the bugle call for a charge. Nerves twisted every muscle in his body into taut cables. He decided to pry his thoughts out of his own self-absorbed plight by looking at the battlefield as a whole. He was an officer, after all, and might have to lead men someday as commander of a company, or even a regiment. He had better learn to function through his fear, to think strategically.

Grant looked to the right for danger of the enemy flanking his regiment's advance. He saw no such threat. The Fifth and Third infantries also supported the flank, as did a battery of flying artillery. To the rear, Captain May's dragoons had reloaded their carbines and regrouped. Briefly, Sam thought about his former West Point roommate and future brother-in-law, Frederick Dent, marching with the Fifth.

Now, through sporadic musket and cannon fire, he heard faint drum and bugle calls from the faraway left flank. Looking that way, through a mile of smoky twilight, he could just make out a company of Mexican lancers harassing the U.S. left flank. Just as quickly, he saw the muzzle blast of Duncan's guns repulsing the enemy horsemen.

Now he felt the awesome strength of the advancing American line in its entirety. A mile of moving muscle and weaponry. Again he was impressed by the power coordinated groups of trained men could wield. The thought that one man—General Taylor—could control two thousand soldiers so smoothly struck him with wonder. He looked over his shoulder toward Taylor's position and saw him in the distance, riding serenely astride Old Whitey. He could not help shaking his head over the calm leadership of the general. Courage was one thing. The ability to make decisions under fire was quite another. He wondered if Taylor would order the long-anticipated bayonet charge. But as the light dwindled and the flying artillery found the range on the enemy units in front of Grant's regiment, the Mexican left melted away into the tall timber, leaving the Fourth Infantry holding the field.

Releasing his talon-like grip on his saber hilt, Grant looked down at the ground his company now occupied. He saw dried, black blood soaked into the dirt. With the next step he saw fresh, red blood dripping from stalks of grass trampled by the enemy retreat. Drumbeats signaled a halt to the advance.

"It looks as if we're to hold this ground," Grant said to the enlisted men near him. "Prepare to make camp while we still have the light."

His subordinates began breaking up empty wooden crates left behind by the Mexicans. Campfires flared as stars appeared. Each company formed up for roll call. In Grant's company, one man had been killed—the man hit in the head with the cannonball—and five wounded, including Captain Page.

Captain McCall pulled him aside. "Grant, send a platoon with all the canteens of the whole company. Order them filled at the duck ponds near the supply train. Send a sergeant and a guard with them. There may be sharpshooters in the chaparral."

"Yes, sir," Grant said. He winced at a scream from the surgeon's tent.

"Are you all right, Lieutenant?"

"Yes, sir."

McCall placed his hand on Grant's shoulder. "Today we saw the elephant."

Grant nodded. "We didn't order a volley all day."

"Perhaps tomorrow we will draw the claret," McCall said grimly.

Grant sent the canteen detachment to the pond and strolled about his company's camp.

"Sleep on your arms tonight, men. The enemy is still near at hand." He looked toward the southeast, at the flickering campfires of the Mexican Army six or seven hundred yards away, some of them camped in the open prairie, others tucked into the chaparral.

He continued to walk aimlessly about his company's camp. Some of the men ate heartily from provisions brought from the supply train. Others barely nibbled at hardtack or salted pork. One of the men offered Grant an ear of corn that had been roasted over an open fire. He took it, gnawed at it.

"Eat!" he ordered, shaking the cob at his men. "Tomorrow we will be of no use to one another in a weakened state."

Spotting a group of junior officers at a nearby camp fire, he trudged over to see what he might learn. As he approached, he recognized the face of his friend Lieutenant Frederick Dent in the firelight.

"Sam, the news is good," said Dent, shaking Grant's hand. "Well, not so bad, I should say. We lost only nine men killed, forty-seven wounded."

"The number of dead will rise," a captain said. "Some won't survive their wounds."

"Captain Page?" someone asked.

Grant's company commander, Captain George A. McCall, answered. "He can't survive long with no jaw. I know I wouldn't want to."

"What about Major Ringgold?"

Dent answered. "Still alive, but it's a miracle he's lasted this long. He's being hauled back to the navy's surgeon at Point Isabel."

Charles F. Smith of the Second Artillery shook his head. "That was something to behold. I've never seen anything so heroic."

A first lieutenant spat a stream of tobacco into the fire. "The enemy losses were no doubt in the hundreds."

"Should have been worse for them," Charles F. Smith muttered. "If Taylor had ordered the bayonet charge, we would have crushed the enemy on the field instead of allowing them to escape into the chaparral."

McCall looked at Grant. "Do you agree, Sam? You haven't said a word since you got here."

"It's not my place to second-guess a general," Grant allowed.

"Brevet general," Smith said.

Dent nudged Grant. "Speak your mind, Sam."

Grant stared at the fire as he thought about the troops still surrounded at Fort Texas. "The objective of the day was to get our provisions closer to the garrison, not to attempt to destroy the entire Mexican Army in a single engagement." He was a bit stunned to hear his own voice speak with such certainty.

"In my view," Smith said, "we should have destroyed the enemy today so that we *could* relieve the garrison in the morning. We're only a few miles away. Now we will likely have to fight our way through the Mexicans tomorrow while the garrison remains besieged."

"You're probably right," McCall said. "And Arista now knows better than to meet us on the open field, where our artillery can pick him apart. He'll be holed up in the brush next time. We'll have to go in after him."

Frederick Dent took Grant by the sleeve and pulled him a few steps from the gathering at the fire.

"Have you heard from home, Sam?"

"Not since we arrived at Point Isabel."

"Same with me. We must try not to alarm my sisters. Or Mother."

Grant nodded. "I agree. No need for bloody details."

Dent sighed. "I must get over to the field hospital. A few of the boys in my company took hits today."

"Do you want me to go with you?"

"No, Sam, you've got your own company to look after. Get some sleep."

Grant wandered back to his camp and lay on a blanket on the ground, using his rolled tunic for a pillow. He stared up at the moon. It was three days shy of rising full, and it illuminated the smoke plumes that rose from the campfires and the still-smoldering saw grass.

He thought about Julia and longed for the reassurance of another letter from her. How could he tell her about what he had seen today? In his next letter—as Frederick had suggested—he would gloss over the carnage and declare a tactical victory so that she might worry less. He wondered how long this conflict would keep them apart.

The breeze from the Gulf felt cool, yet when it lessened he could hear the moans of injured men in the field hospital. *There but by the grace of God go I*, he thought.

He remembered a Bible verse he had once memorized from the book of James:

> *"For what is your life? It is even a vapor that appears for a little time and then vanishes away."*

Eventually he fell asleep and dreamed of cannonballs rolling through White Haven Plantation.

MARIANO ARISTA

By the gray morning light, General Arista reined in his mount as he saw Captain Berlandier pull up and gesture down the road toward Matamoras. A league away, he could plainly hear the artillery battle over the Americans' earthen fort on the Rio Bravo.

"This is the place," Berlandier said. "Resaca de la Palma."

The general-in-chief studied the road. It dipped down into the *resaca*—a former riverbed the Rio Bravo had abandoned in its age-old meanderings. Where it crossed the *resaca*, the trace resembled the narrows of an hourglass. Thick chaparral crowded it on either side, pinching it to a wagon's width. Pools of standing water, one to each side, also flanked the road. The little gully was only shoulder deep to the average man, but it would provide some cover from attack.

"Why here?" he asked his aide-de-camp.

"The wagons of the Americans must cross the *resaca* here to get to their fort. No other wagon road exists through a hundred leagues of chaparral. Only goat trails. Hold this bottleneck, and the Americans cannot get their supplies to their fort."

Arista felt a glimmer of hope brighten his mood. Yesterday's battle had devastated his army's morale. More than five hundred men had been killed or wounded. Worse yet, a treacherous rumor had been started by some ambitious junior officers personally or politically opposed to him. The rumor held that Arista had committed treason, that he had made a

bargain to deliver the Mexican Army to the Americans. How preposterous these whispered accusations, and yet how readily swallowed by
doubting fools. Woe to the general who had to place spies within his own
ranks.

He nodded his thanks to Berlandier. "You have chosen well, Capitan."

Captain Jean Louis Berlandier was a man whose opinion the general
had learned to value. Since marching his Army of the North to Matamoras, Arista had found Dr. Berlandier's council so useful that the general had made him aide-de-camp and bestowed upon him the rank of
capitan. Berlandier had been living in Matamoras for several years, working as a physician, and knew the country well. But his expertise did not
end there. The journey of the forty-one-year-old Berlandier had not been
typical.

Jean Louis Berlandier had been born in France, near the Swiss border. He had studied botany at the academy in Geneva, in which city he
had also apprenticed under a pharmacist. It was as a young botanist that
Berlandier had journeyed to Mexico, twenty years before, to collect spec-
imens. He soon found himself working for the Mexican government as
part of a boundary expedition exploring the northern frontier as far as
the Rio San Saba. On the frontier, he had become familiar with soldier-
ing out of necessity.

He had since settled at Matamoras, where he became a pharmacist,
then a medical doctor. He was adventurous, worldly, educated, and accomplished. He spoke Spanish, French, and German. Arista relied upon
him, here along the Rio Bravo. His knowledge of medicine and surgery
had become indispensable just yesterday, after Arista's chief field doctor
had disappeared.

The general turned his mount about to look at the ground over which
the Americans would have to approach. He saw that the *resaca* hooked
forward to the left and right of the road, like the horns of a fighting bull.
Nearing the depression, the chaparral along the road thinned out a bit,
which would afford a field of view for his gunners and musketeers. Farther
out, the growth was so thick that the enemy would have to approach well
inside musket range to even catch sight of the Army of the North.

Berlandier guided his mount up beside the general's. "Resaca de la
Palma is your thorny moat," he said. "Believe me, I have collected bo-
tanical samples in this chaparral. It will scratch a careless man to bloody
shreds. A charge upon this place is possible only down the narrow road."

This was the best news Arista had encountered since he had begun his retrograde movement at dawn. Taylor had not followed as he withdrew this morning, but Arista knew the American commander would start for the earthen star fort sooner or later. Later, he guessed. Taylor would want to rest his soldiers and their horses today. He would attack tomorrow, giving Arista's *zapadores* ample time to construct breastworks on the already naturally defensible Resaca de la Palma.

He looked into the wizened eyes of his aide-de-camp. "I will establish my headquarters south of the *resaca*. Call the regimental commanders to my tent for a council of war within the hour."

"*Si*, General!" Berlandier saluted and rode away at a gallop, toward the Army of the North.

Arista waved at his personal guard, who had been waiting within shouting distance. The eight combat veterans came at a trot. Feeling confident in his army's ability to defend Resaca de la Palma, he began looking forward to a cup of midday tea. He had reports to write.

"*Venga, hombres!*" he shouted as his guard neared. "*Vamos a hacer campamento!*" It was time to set up camp.

Arista rode south through *Resaca de la Palma* and beyond. He chose a small meadow to the right of the road for his camp. Within half an hour his tent was erected and he was seated at his writing desk.

"Tea is ready, General."

Arista looked up at the camp servant at the open tent flap. "Come in, Pedro," he ordered.

The servant entered with a silver tea service, tiny loaves of sugar, and goat's milk from a nearby *rancheria*.

Arista looked through his tent door to see the pack mules and supply wagons kicking up dust on the road. "Pour a cup, then leave me," he said to the servant. "I have many correspondences to complete."

When the servant brought his cup, Arista took a sip and looked into the man's eyes. The servant took from his pocket a scrap of paper. Arista took the paper, nodded at the servant, and tossed his head toward the open door.

"The tea is good and strong, Pedro. You may go now."

When the servant left, the general unfolded the paper and looked at the names of junior officers written upon it. Pedro was loyal and had sharp ears. He was as much a spy as a servant, and Mariano Arista relied upon him. The general had charged him with the task of rooting out the rumormongers in his ranks. There were a dozen names on the paper.

This went beyond insubordination to the brink of mutiny. When he put his defenses in place for the coming battle with the Americans, these ambitious young hotheads might find themselves in very dangerous places. He put his teacup on the silver tray and sighed.

No . . . He would not stoop to their level of treachery. He would put the most able officers in the logical locations. The malcontents would eventually be rooted out or won over, but he would not offer them up as sacrifices to the Americans.

GEORGE A. MCCALL

Palo Alto to Resaca de la Palma
May 9, 1846

Captain George A. McCall stood shoulder to shoulder with Captain Charles F. Smith of the Second Artillery, facing General Zachary Taylor. Remaining at attention, he struggled to contain his excitement. His lungs heaved like bellows as his heart pounded out drumbeats of war. General Taylor had just given Captain McCall and Captain Smith their orders for the morning.

The sun had risen outside, but the coal oil lantern wick still burned inside the commander's dark tent. Taylor stood over his war map, bathed in the lamplight, with his finger still on the spot he wanted attacked—a place called Resaca de la Palma.

"Arista is wasting his cavalry advantage by holing up in the woods," General Taylor said. He raised the globe on the lantern and blew out the kerosene flame. "You have your orders. Proceed immediately."

Together with Smith, Captain McCall saluted General Taylor, faced about, and left Old Rough and Ready's tent.

"So, we shall take the fight to the Mexicans," Captain Smith said, a wry grin complementing his fiery eyes.

McCall nodded. "How long will you take choosing your hundred and fifty men?"

"I will have them formed up within the hour."

"We will rendezvous where the road enters the chaparral."

"Agreed." Smith peeled away for his unit at a trot.

McCall consciously maintained the set to his jaw. His long legs carried him quickly to the company he commanded in the Fourth Infantry. Glancing about, he saw men cleaning weapons and sharpening bayonets. He located his second lieutenant, Sam Grant.

"Grant!"

"Sir?" the lieutenant answered.

"I have my orders from General Taylor. Captain C. F. Smith and I are to pick one hundred fifty men each from our respective regiments and advance as skirmishers."

Grant's eyebrows rose, but he made no other expression. "Yes, sir . . ." he said, a question in his tone.

"You will assume command in my absence. Take good care of my company, Lieutenant."

Grant looked surprised, perhaps even apprehensive, but he drew himself to attention and saluted. "Yes, sir."

Amused at the protocol, McCall smiled and returned the salute. "I'll pick ten or twelve men from each company in the regiment until I have my hundred and fifty. That will leave you with about forty men to command.

"I will do my best, sir."

"See that you do."

He turned away and began to stroll through the troops gathered casually about the smoldering campfires. "Sergeant Johnson!"

The grizzled veteran of the Indian frontier snapped to attention. "Yes, sir."

"Come with me."

"Yes, sir."

He saw a stout Irish lad. "McFarlen! Come with me."

"Aye, sir."

McCall spotted a middle-aged private—a Dutchman who claimed he had served with General De Kock in the jungles of Java. "Rediker!"

"Coming, sir!"

He chose nine more men from his own company and ordered them to proceed to the Matamoras Road where it entered the tall timber that had given name to Palo Alto. He proceeded to the next nearest company, spoke to the unit commander, and chose ten men who looked serviceable. Then he went on to the next company, and the next, until he had gathered one hundred fifty soldiers.

Captain Charles F. Smith arrived on the Matamoras Road with his chosen troops from the Second Artillery just minutes after McCall arrived.

"Column of fours!" McCall shouted. "Fourth Infantry on the left. Second Artillery on the right!"

The men gathered from various companies milled about in confusion.

"You heard the captain!" Charles F. Smith yelled. "Form a column of fours facing down the road! If you are Second Artillery, you will fall into the two rows on the left. Fourth Infantry will form the two rows on the right! Move!"

Within a minute the column had come together.

"Attention!" McCall ordered. "Left face!"

He and Smith walked briskly among the ranks, inspecting the soldiers' muskets, bayonets, ammunition belts, and canteens.

McCall moved out in front of the formation to address the soldiers. "You are well aware that the enemy has withdrawn to the south on the Matamoras Road. You've been handpicked by Captain Smith and me to advance into the chaparral as skirmishers, by order of General Taylor. We fully expect to find and engage the Mexican Army between here and Fort Texas. Those of you from the Fourth Infantry will follow my orders. Those of you from the Second Artillery will follow the orders of Captain Smith." He turned to Smith. "Captain?"

Smith paused, listened to the distant bombardment of Fort Texas.

"Do you hear those guns? Think of your fellow Americans besieged at the garrison. They have sustained an almost continual bombardment for seven days now. They are no doubt running low on ammunition, food, and water. I'm sure if you were there, you would want someone leading the way with supplies and reinforcements. Remember them and do your duty. As skirmishers, we will harass the enemy ahead. We will not charge until the rest of the army comes up. And then . . . we will *all* charge!" He looked at McCall and nodded.

"Right face!" McCall shouted. "Forward, march!"

As the column entered the chaparral, McCall heard a cheer swell among the ranks of Taylor's army. Those men being left behind knew that they would soon march down this same road to do battle with an army superior in number to their own. The cheer stirred McCall's blood to the point that the hair stood on the back of his neck.

After marching two miles into the thick of the thorny forest, he halted his troops just short of a bend in the road around which he could not see.

"Sergeant Johnson," McCall said, "take three men and scout the road ahead. When you find the enemy, do not engage. Send two of the men back to report to me."

"Yes, sir!" Johnson pointed at three privates and trotted to the bend in the road ahead. Peering carefully around the bend, he watched for a moment, then passed out of view.

The sun bore fiercely down on the men in the open road.

"The rest of you find some shade and rest," McCall ordered.

It was almost a half hour later when two of the privates came trotting back to McCall's formation.

"Report," McCall said, quickly returning their salutes. Both young men had the same wild look in their eyes.

"Sir, we found 'em. They're throwing up breastworks in the place where the road crosses the ravine."

Resaca de la Palma, McCall thought. "Did they see you?"

"No, sir. We was careful to stay hid."

The other private chimed in, "Sir, the Sarge said they've got two companies of infantry on the road on this side of the *resaca*. Between the infantry units, they have a battery of guns—they look like twelve-pounders. The guns are deployed on both sides of the road. And there's more infantry down in the *resaca*, too. A couple of regiments, from the looks of it. We saw the colors for the Tampico Battalion."

"Well done," McCall said. He turned to Captain Smith. "Captain, let's gather the men around us."

"On your feet," Smith said. "Gather around."

When the men had crowded around the two officers, McCall gave his orders. "We will pass quietly down the road. When we reach Sergeant Johnson, we will deploy in the thick brush to either side of the road—the Fourth to the left and the Second to the right. We will spread out in line formation, facing the enemy. We will advance through the thicket until we see the enemy. After you hear my first volley, you may all fire at will. They will turn their cannon on us, so use the cover to your advantage. We are here to skirmish and harass the enemy at long range. We will not charge until the rest of the main army comes up behind us. Understood?"

The men mumbled and nodded.

"Do you have any words for the men, Captain?"

The fiery artillery officer glared at the enlisted men surrounding him. "The honor of your country and your fellow soldiers is at stake here. I expect you all to behave with honor and courage." He nodded at McCall.

McCall formed the men into a column of fours and led them down the road. Reaching Sergeant Johnson, he sent Captain Smith into the chaparral to the right then led the men from his own regiment into the thorns and cactus spines to the left. Immediately, he found the undergrowth almost impossible to penetrate. Every step caused a scratch or puncture wound to some part of his body. Still, he found that he could push through the mesquite limbs and stomp down the cactus in his path with his boots. His men followed him single file.

"Sir," Sergeant Johnson said under his breath, "allow me to go first for a while. You're getting all the best stickers."

McCall smiled and nodded. "Keep going in the same direction. When you hear me give a bobwhite call, stop and whistle the same call back to me. At that point, the men will advance in line to the south."

"Understood, sir."

He let Johnson lead the way into the thicket while he himself stayed in place. After some thirty men had filed past him, he whistled like a bobwhite quail and waited. Johnson returned the whistle.

"Pass the word down the line," he said to the soldiers on either side of him. "Turn south and press on toward the enemy."

The order was passed from man to man. McCall stepped over a prickly pear and plowed through a catclaw bush that ripped his trousers. Every man would now have to break his own trail. Sweat and blood trickled down his neck as thorns continued to poke through his woolen uniform. The acrid odor of weeds he trampled assaulted his nostrils. After some fifty or sixty excruciating yards, the dense brush began to open up somewhat and he found that he could weave his way around the thornbushes and cactus needles.

He began to hear the voices of men ahead, and the cadence of shovels digging trenches. He crept carefully forward until he saw the glint of bayonets and the white leather shoulder harnesses of Mexican infantrymen, or perhaps of the elite grenadiers from Matamoras.

"Halt," he said, keeping his voice low. Signaling the men closest to him to take aim through the veil of leaves and twigs, he began to give the orders in a hoarse whisper.

"Ready . . . Aim . . . Fire!"

The volley erupted and brought screams and shouts from the Mexican advance guard.

"Reload!" He heard more shots from all along the U.S. line and felt the Mexicans had been taken by surprise.

"Fire at will!" he shouted.

He planned to let the men near him get off two more volleys before ordering them to withdraw deeper into the brush for protection. But after just the second round, he saw the white smoke blast of a Mexican artillery piece, followed immediately by the loud report and a spray of grapeshot popping through the vegetation all around him. A private beside him fell over backwards and lay motionless. McCall went to look the man over and found a bloody hole in his forehead where a ball had penetrated his skull, killing him instantly.

"Damn it!" he yelled, dragging the dead man. "Fall back! Retire firing!"

Another cannon blast, and the chaparral around him whirred with projectiles and rattled with snapping wood. He took the ammunition belt from the slain private. The thought of the man's body being forgotten and lost in this thicket did not sit well with him.

"Soldier, carry this dead man to the rear and leave him on the road!"

"Yes, sir!" The private threw his dead comrade across his back and plowed through the thorns to the rear.

"Stay low and reload, men!" McCall scrambled forward to retrieve the musket the dead man had dropped and knelt behind a larger mesquite trunk to reload it. He took a paper cartridge from the ammunition box and tore the end off of it with his teeth. He poured the powder and ball, plus the three chunks of buckshot, from the paper tube into the muzzle of the musket. He used the ramrod to push the empty paper tube down the barrel as wadding.

"Take cover and fire at will!" he said, pushing aside his fear of another load of grapeshot.

He found a handy fork in a tree limb and took steady aim at the white X of an enemy soldier's leather chest belts, barely visible through the foliage. He fired. Gun smoke obscured his view, but when it cleared, his target had vanished.

"Continue firing!" he shouted as he returned to the protection of his mesquite trunk. He found himself out of breath but went about the reloading methodically, though his hands trembled with the excitement. All down the skirmish line he heard a ripple of firing from the U.S. troops. Then another cannon blast from the *resaca* and a scream from someone to his right.

Be steady, he thought. *Do your duty.* He hoped the rest of the army would not be long in arriving.

Captain
EPHRAIM KIRBY SMITH

Resaca de la Palma
May 9, 1846

Ephraim Smith left the open prairie, marching at the head of his regiment with his company of infantrymen. He felt the breeze die as he entered the thicket of sharp thorns and spiny leaves. Ahead, he found the dense chaparral broken only by the road upon which the Fifth Infantry treaded. He had his orders. Advance on the enemy. Engage the Mexican Army and break through its lines to open the Matamoras Road.

"Good luck," he had said to his brother, Edmund, just minutes ago, before Edmund had gone to lead his own company.

"I'll see you at Fort Texas for supper," Edmund had replied.

They marched until noon, covering five miles. Now Captain Kirby Smith could not only hear but also *feel* the artillery blasts. He knew they were Mexican guns, for no U.S. ordnance had yet advanced. Another mile and he could make out the crackle of the skirmishers' muskets over the incessant grind of boot soles on dirt. Shouts came from the rear.

"Halt!"

Looking back, he saw Captain Ridgely of the flying artillery leading his battery. A few Texas Rangers under Captain Sam Walker accompanied Ridgely.

"Step aside, men!" Smith shouted. "Off the road!"

His troops gladly scrambled off the trace to let the artillery lead the advance.

Ridgely nodded at Smith as he rode past. Smith lifted his chin in respect. The memory of how his regiment and Ridgely's battery had faced down the cavalry assault by General Torrejon's lancers was less than a day old. Behind the artillery captain came gunners mounted on the matching team of black horses pulling limbers hitched to six-pounders or caissons.

Good, Smith thought. *Let Ridgely's grapeshot and canister soften the enemy line before we charge.*

His men reclaimed the road after the passing of the six-pounders. "Forward, march!" a sergeant shouted.

The noise of the battle grew until stray chunks of grape or shrapnel began to pepper the chaparral ahead of him. He came to a bend in the road. Around the bend, he found the bodies of slain U.S. soldiers sprawled on the roadside—seven of them. A few wounded men sat with their backs against some tree trunks, bleeding. Captain Smith looked beyond these men to find smoke hanging thick in the air down the Matamoras Road.

"Form a skirmish line to the left of the road!" Smith yelled at the men in his company. "Fight your way through the thorns!" He drew his saber and hacked down a mesquite limb in his path. Just a few steps into the brush, he looked back and could see only a handful of his men. The rest were already hidden behind the veil of uninviting vegetation.

He let his ears guide him to the ground held by Captain McCall, who had led the skirmishers forward hours ago.

"McCall!" he shouted, catching sight of the captain, somewhat shocked to find the officer's uniform caked with dirt and blood.

McCall motioned for him to stay low. "Ephraim?"

"Yes."

"Is the whole army coming up?"

"The Fifth is moving into position by companies on both sides of the road."

"What about the Fourth?" McCall inquired of his own regiment.

"They were ordered to attack the Mexican left flank."

"Artillery?"

"Ridgely's battery is unlimbering now."

"Dragoons?"

"Captain May's company is coming up."

McCall frowned. "It's *Major* May now."

"He received a brevet from yesterday?" Smith asked, surprised.

"Yes."

"I hadn't heard."

"I just hope he gets closer than he did at Palo Alto."

"What's the situation here?" Smith asked, gesturing toward the enemy.

A round of grape tore through the woods all around him. Smith felt one projectile tick against his shako hat.

"*That's* the situation!" McCall shouted.

"Damnation!"

"The *resaca* is just ahead. The Mexicans have three or four companies of infantry on the near bank, guarding the road. They have one battery on this side of the ravine. More on the opposite bank, hidden in brush. I imagine they have a brigade of infantry down in the *resaca* itself, waiting for us."

Just then, Smith heard artillery orders being shouted—in English. Though he could not see through the chaparral, he knew Ridgely's battery was about to open up.

"Ridgely's going to take a pounding if we don't charge soon," he said to McCall.

McCall nodded. "We must move to the right, closer to the road. The brush there is more open. The men can weave among the bushes. We've got to charge their batteries, Kirby. If we take the big guns, we can clear the road!"

They heard Ridgely's first volley erupt.

"Let's move!" Smith said, yelling back over his shoulder to his troops. "Move to the right. Prepare to charge the enemy batteries!"

As they progressed, Smith found the open spaces McCall had described and began to see more men from his regiment. Ridgely let another volley loose. Smith was drawing a breath with which to order the charge when he heard the command come from his right.

"Charge, Fifth!"

"Charge, Fifth!" he echoed. He felt lightning coursing through his veins as he ran forward with his men, some releasing their tension in unintelligible shouts. They had sprinted only a few yards when he heard the great rumble of hundreds of hooves. Looking to the right, Smith saw Major May's company of the Second Dragoons charging at full gallop down the road toward the hell-storm of the *resaca*. May rode his magnificent warhorse, Black Tom, at the head of his company, saber drawn, long hair and beard streaming over his shoulder.

Ephraim Smith sensed that May now sought redemption for his

reluctance, yesterday at Palo Alto, to approach the enemy within close proximity.

At the sight of the mounted attack, the men of the Fifth released a concerted war yell and charged ahead with new swiftness. Smith found himself running with his saber over his head, weaving around thorny bushes and leaping cactus patches. A cannonball shattered a mesquite tree beside him, a flying limb knocking him down. Disoriented, he scrambled to his feet and found himself facing the wrong way. There, on the road, astride Old Whitey, he saw General Taylor watching the battle, enemy fire whistling all around him.

Smith turned and resumed his charge, now twenty yards or more behind his men. Beyond his infantrymen, he witnessed May's saber-wielding dragoons flushing Mexican gunners from the nearest enemy battery—eight guns situated on the road in front of the ravine. *May is definitely getting closer today.* But the battle-crazed mounts of the long-bearded, long-haired dragoons could not be checked at the captured battery. The horses, many of them half-trained mustangs, plunged into the *resaca*, fighting the bits in their mouths as their riders desperately fended off Mexican bayonets with sabers. Meanwhile, the Mexican gunners reclaimed their artillery pieces, the dragoons having scattered every which way.

A lull in the shooting resulted on both sides as men fought hand to hand or reloaded muskets and cannon. As he continued to charge, Smith could just hear the booming voice of an enraged General Taylor shouting behind him:

"Take those guns and, by God, keep them!"

The first soldiers of his company to arrive fired point blank at the Mexican artillerymen, bowling several of them over backwards. He saw a Mexican captain die with his hand on his cannon, refusing to retreat. The men of the Fifth continued to attack, some stabbing the remaining gunners with bayonets. The punctured men made horrible noises. As he charged between two captured twelve-pounders, Smith noticed his men turning one of them, preparing to fire upon the Mexicans, even though the enemy musket balls ricocheted strange songs of warning off the cannon tubes.

A regimental bugler whom Smith recognized as a German immigrant marched a captured Mexican general toward the rear. The look of pure pride on the bugler's face was almost comical. Now Captain Smith realized that the prisoner was General de la Vega, the noted Mexican artillerist.

Suddenly, the newly brevetted Major May dashed up and leaped from Black Tom, seizing the prisoner that the bugler had captured.

"Get back to the front line, Private Wonsell! I'll take this prisoner to General Taylor!"

Wonsell, the bugler, fumed but could only release his captive to May and turn back to the fray. Major May led General de la Vega and Black Tom to the rear.

Past the captured Mexican battery, Smith saw his screaming men now clashing with a superior number of enemy soldiers with bayonets, down in the brushy ravine. He jumped over the body of a dragoon who had been pulled from his horse and stabbed to death. Spotting a Mexican soldier trying to reload a musket behind an agarita bush, Captain Smith lunged, leading with the point of his saber. The soldier jumped aside and jabbed menacingly with his bayonet point.

"Run, you devil!" Smith yelled.

But the man did not run. He plowed mindlessly through the spiny leaves of the agarita bush, pushing his bayonet point ahead of him. Smith just managed to parry the sharp point aside with his saber, then desperately hacked at the man, his sword chopping halfway through the enemy soldier's neck.

He did not look back at the man he had slain. He squatted to catch his breath and gather his wits. All around him, semi-obscured by the wicked woods of the chaparral, men clashed in screaming, bloody knots. He saw one U.S. private beating in the head of a Mexican soldier with a rock. He knew his soldiers were outnumbered, yet he felt the Mexican line falling back, inch by inch.

"Captain . . ."

The voice had come from nearby, weakly. Smith looked about to find a man dragging himself out of the underbrush. The man had lost his hat, and shocks of gray hair stood out from his balding head. Remarkably, his distinctive spectacles were still in place on the bridge of his nose.

Smith recognized his regimental commander, Lieutenant Colonel James S. McIntosh. "Sir!" he said, stumbling toward his commander. He reached the sixty-year-old McIntosh and noticed the blood-soaked fabric of his tunic where a bayonet had run him through from his belly to his back. He found another wound, where a bayonet had entered his mouth and come out the back of his neck.

Smith knew that his colonel had been severely wounded more than thirty years ago in the War of 1812. He wondered if it had been this bad. He propped the old warrior up, fearing that he might well be dying.

"Sir, is there anything I can do?"

McIntosh spit out some blood and glared through the lenses of his spectacles. "Yes, Captain. Give me some water and show me my regiment."

As Smith clawed at the canteen on his belt, a wave of soldiers from the Eighth Infantry came pouring down into the brush-choked ravine, their battle cries stirring his blood. Then the first volley of the Mexican cannon—captured and turned upon their former masters—roared over the Resaca de la Palma and sent hailstorms of grapeshot denouncing Mexico's claim to this coveted, bloodstained soil.

Lieutenant
SAM GRANT

If anyone had asked him beforehand, he would have said that the chaparral was impenetrable. Yet here he was, penetrating it—albeit with great difficulty. He twisted and ducked through the thorn-infested shrubbery. Briars clawed his skin and ripped his uniform as he pressed forward with his company.

The Fourth Infantry had been ordered to attack the Mexicans' left and to flank them if possible. The battle for Resaca de la Palma had been raging for some time up ahead and to his left. He was doing his best to join the conflict, but the thicket was so dense that he could only keep a few of his men in view as they pressed forward.

His ominous responsibility as acting company commander weighed heavily upon him. He had seen only one battle—yesterday—and had scarcely taken part in it. Now he was expected to lead the company. With no landmarks to be seen in that forest of spines, thorns, and stinging thistles, he had only the sound of the battle to guide him. Was he leading his men in the right direction? The percussion of the artillery and the crackle of muskets seemed to be getting louder, so he pushed on through undergrowth that would discourage a javelina.

Suddenly, enemy projectiles hissed all around his ears, followed by a deluge of shattered branches raining from above.

"Get down!" he ordered. He did not have to give the order twice as he found himself staring at dirt. He noticed a trail of ants filing by as if this were just another ordinary day. He didn't like this position. He could see no enemy soldiers from here, so he could not engage. The brush was too thick to charge through. He would lead his company into a massacre if he tried.

Another volley of enemy artillery raked overhead.

"Stay low!" he shouted to his men. What was he supposed to do now? He waited for another round from the Mexican cannon. When it came, it did no damage to his little section of chaparral. It soon became evident to him that the artillery fire was not even intended for him but for some other unit. The enemy did not even know he was here.

He thought about withdrawing but knew he could not. He could never back up. Yet he could not go forward. He decided to go farther to the right. Perhaps he could lead his men around the enemy's flank.

"Right face!" he yelled. "We will look for more open ground to the right!"

Men picked up their arms and veered toward the extreme right wing of the U.S. advance. Here he found the brush less dense, yet still formidable. At last he saw an opening—a mere goat trail—that led forward to a section of the *resaca*. Through the chaparral that laced the ravine, he could see enemy soldiers milling about on the opposite bank.

He knew it was his duty to charge that position. "Halt!" he said, as his men came out of the brush into the small opening.

The soldiers stopped and looked his way, many of them wild-eyed with fear.

"Prepare to charge down that trail!"

The soldiers checked their bayonets and cocked their muskets. Then they stared at him, some trembling but all standing their ground. Grant pulled his single-shot percussion pistol from his belt and drew the hammer back until it clicked into place.

"Charge!"

His long, slender legs carried him forward toward the *resaca* as enlisted men vied to pace him. They swarmed down the trail around him and poured into the gully. He felt the spring tension of his trigger on his finger as he led the way with his pistol muzzle. Across the ravine, enemy uniforms caught his eye. The Mexicans quickly threw their hands into the air.

"Halt!" Grant shouted to his men. "Hold your fire! Keep a sharp lookout!"

Now he realized that most of the enemy soldiers were wounded. The captured men included a colonel. He also saw dead Mexican fighters sprawled here and there on the ground. The realization came to him: he had just charged a position that had already been overrun by other U.S. infantrymen before him.

He chose three privates near him. "Take these prisoners to the rear," he ordered. The men were happy to have the assignment.

"Lieutenant!" a private shouted. "Over here!"

He looked up to see the man pointing at something, so he strode quickly over. "What is it, Private?"

"Lookee there, Lieutenant Grant. I'll be damned if that ain't the top of a tent pokin' up above the mesquites!"

Grant saw the eagle-and-snake flag fluttering from a tent pole not more than a musket shot through the brush. "Let's head that way," he said.

General
MARIANO ARISTA

Resaca de la Palma
May 8, 1846

He had sat at his desk—writing reports and sipping tea—while he listened to the snipers and sharpshooters across the *resaca*.

Nothing more than a skirmish, he had thought. *Taylor will not attack in full force today. He will not.*

Of this he felt so confident that he had ordered all the pack mules unloaded and all the teams unhitched from the supply wagons. The beasts needed to graze along the prairies that opened up toward the Rio Grande. He knew his army would hold its ground today. Resaca de la Palma was simply impregnable.

He had granted the honor of commanding the defense of the *resaca* on this day to General Romulo Diaz de la Vega. A veteran of the war for independence from Spain, the war against the Texas revolutionaries, and the French invasion of Veracruz, de la Vega could be trusted to guard the Matamoras Road until the real battle began, tomorrow. He was a skilled artillery officer and one of the men whose loyalty General Arista did not question.

Arista took a last gulp of tea from his dainty, glazed cup and wondered at the incessant nature of the artillery fire. He could smell the smoke from burning powder wafting through his tent. He finished his regrettable letter to President Paredes, put his pen aside, and listened. Musket fire crackled sporadically. It didn't sound like an all-out attack. But the artillery fire had rumbled constantly for some time. Was de la

Vega wasting precious ammunition? Perhaps the Americans had brought up a battery to test the stronghold and harass de la Vega's entrenched position.

He set his concerns aside. No messenger had brought him news of a major assault. He felt certain that Taylor would only test his defenses today and attack in earnest tomorrow.

Mañana. *Si*, mañana.

But now he heard men yelling, screaming. He picked out words as the voices came closer.

"*Ay de mi!*"

"*Me ahorro, Dios!*"

Cries of desperation. Entreaties of abject horror.

Next came musket fire from *behind* his camp! His army had been flanked!

General Arista jumped up from his padded chair and leaped for the tent flap, dashing it aside. His soldiers were running, stumbling over one another, retreating in terror. Some of them stampeded through his very camp. Most of them had dropped their weapons.

"Stop!" he yelled. "Stop and hold this ground!"

The men just ran, some of them wounded and bloody.

"Cowards! Stop!"

Where was his aide-de-camp? What had happened? How could this be?

Now he saw enemy soldiers advancing methodically on his headquarters through the chaparral—each man firing his musket, reloading, advancing again.

Captain Berlandier came running to his tent, covered with blood.

"Where have you been?" the general demanded.

"At the field hospital, General! It happened so fast!"

"What has happened?"

"The Americans have taken the *resaca*!"

Arista felt his anger begin to boil. "Where is General de la Vega?"

"He was captured, sir! The men all say he was captured!"

Damn de la Vega's ego, he thought. *He would not ask for reinforcements?*

Now Arista thought of his reserves. He had placed Ampudia's brigade and the cavalry under Torrejon in reserve far to the rear. He was not ready to give up this ground so easily.

"Pedro!" he cried to his trusted servant. "Bring my horse!"

"*Si*, General!"

"Sergeant Major!" he shouted to the leader of his personal guard. "Hold my headquarters!"

"*Si*, General!"

"Capitan!"

"*Si*, General!" said the bloody Captain Berlandier.

"Order General Ampudia to advance on the Americans now. Go quickly!"

Berlandier ran for his horse, tethered nearby.

Arista went back into his tent for his tunic, his saber, and his shako. When he stepped back out, he found his guard barely holding the enemy infantrymen at bay with their muskets. Pedro stood with his horse. He mounted while Pedro held the reins at the silver bridle shanks. From the saddle he could see more Americans coming. Dozens, scores, hundreds . . . They swarmed around three sides of the camp, leaving only one escape—south down the Matamoras Road.

A musket round buzzed by and popped through the canvas of his tent, not far from his head. He glanced and saw four holes in the fabric from the standard-issue U.S. load—a bullet and three buckshot.

"Leave the tent!" he ordered. "Fall back to Ampudia's position!"

Reining his mount away from the attackers, he galloped to General Torrejon's brigade of lancers, situated beyond enemy artillery range, eight hundred *varas* to the rear. As he approached, he saw them mounting and forming up in a column of fours. He rode directly up to Torrejon.

"Why have you not advanced?" he demanded.

"We have been awaiting the orders of General de la Vega," Torrejon said calmly.

"De la Vega has been captured! The *resaca* has been overrun by the enemy." The general drew his saber. "We must charge now!"

Torrejon's eyes widened as he drew his own sword. "Forward!" he shouted.

The bugler blew the signal and the entire column moved ahead at a walk, with Arista leading the way up the Matamoras Road.

"Trot!"

The bugle signaled the quicker gait and the column responded.

Another hundred *varas* and Torrejon shouted, "Gallop!"

The bugle pealed and the rumble of hooves swelled.

They passed through Ampudia's reserve infantry marching toward the front line of the American assault. General Arista was now leading the charge through his retreating infantrymen who had been routed at the *resaca*.

"Turn around, you cowards!" he yelled. "Return to the line and fight!"

His mount lunged and snorted as he encountered the first surprised Americans. He swiped at the nearest enemy with his saber, but the man leaped into the chaparral. Over his shoulder, he saw a lancer probing the thicket with his spear point, hoping to find the American. Then a musket blast tore the cavalryman from his saddle.

Onward he charged into the *resaca*, toward the more open ground on the other side, where he hoped his lancers could hunt down the enemy with their ten-inch steel points. But enemy musket blasts tore into his mounted men from the brush on either side of the road. Across the ravine, he found his own cannon pointed at him. Beyond, the timber had been blown to flinders by the artillery of both armies. He rode right into what looked like two whole regiments of U.S. foot soldiers.

One of his own captured artillery pieces tore a dozen lancers out of the column. Others fell around him in a hail of musket fire. Horses whinnied their shuttering death rattles and men screamed in terror and pain. It was lost. The battle . . . lost . . .

"Retreat!" he ordered. The bugler was dead, but the riders needed no musical encouragement to withdraw. As the general fled, he knew he deserved a bullet in the back for this blunder, but somehow the enemy fire veered around him and struck soldiers ahead of him in the retreat. A corporal, hit in the shoulder, dropped his lance and listed to one side. Arista grabbed him and held him upright as their mounts galloped stirrup to stirrup out of the enemy phalanx.

Lieutenant
SAM GRANT

Resaca de la Palma
May 9, 1846

By the time Grant closed in on the tent his soldiers had spotted, his company had been joined by hundreds of troops from his regiment and others. He had approached from the west, having unknowingly flanked the enemy lines. The Mexican soldiers were now fleeing en masse toward the river. He had seen the battalion of Mexican lancers attack, led by generals Arista and Torrejon, only to be repulsed by a withering American fire.

Now he ran right up to what appeared to be General Arista's headquarters tent, the enemy resistance having melted away to the south. He still had not fired his pistol, so he used its barrel to pull the tent flap aside, half expecting to find the general-in-chief himself. Instead, he found a writing desk strewn with papers, an inkwell nearby. Beside it he saw a silver tea service on a folding camp table.

Rushing back outside, he located his company corporal. "Corporal Stewart!" he yelled. "Pick three men and guard this tent until General Taylor arrives. Disturb nothing!"

"Yes, sir!" the corporal said, seemingly honored by the assignment.

He was now down to about twenty men under his command. Some had been sent back with prisoners. Others had gotten lost in the chaparral. But, to his knowledge, none had been killed or wounded. "The rest of you, come with me. We will continue to pursue the enemy and clear the road for the supply train."

As he marched his company southward along the road, his men began to mingle with soldiers from other regiments. He came to the supply train that Arista had been forced to abandon. Wagons had been unhitched, packs removed from mules. Arms, ammunition, provender, all manner of supplies had been left behind.

"Sam!" He heard the familiar voice of Lieutenant Frederick Dent.

"Frederick! Thank God."

"Are you all right, Sam?"

"Yes."

Frederick Dent's young face looked unusually grim. "Did you draw the claret?"

Sam smirked. "Back home, I knew an old veteran of the 1812 war. I asked him once—a boyish question—if he had ever killed a man in the war. He said he charged the enemy once and cut a man's leg off. I asked why he had not cut his head off instead. The old man said, 'Because someone had done that before me.'"

Dent shook his head, but chuckled. "You talk in circles sometimes, Sam."

"I never fired a shot today. Every position I charged had already been overrun by some other company."

Dent nodded, then gestured at the abandoned equipage all around them. "Well, we completely surprised them. They left everything behind."

They continued to march along in the chaos, toward Fort Texas.

"Have you received any new orders?" Grant asked.

"None." He glanced back over his shoulder and grabbed Grant by the arm. "But look, Sam! There rides General Taylor down the road on Old Whitey!"

Grant felt somehow relieved to see Taylor coming up from the rear. He could not imagine the responsibility that must have weighed upon the general's shoulders on this day, yet Old Rough and Ready seemed to bear it with ease.

"I suppose we should continue to pursue the enemy unless we receive orders to the contrary," he said to Dent.

"I suppose so. Right down to the Rio Grande."

Then what? Grant wondered. If they drove the entire Mexican Army of the North out of Texas, would that satisfy General Taylor? President Polk? Congress? The American people? Today was Saturday, May 9. It was possible that the news of the Thornton debacle at Rancho de

Carricitos had reached Washington, DC, by now via steamship. By Monday or Tuesday, Congress could be debating full-fledged war against Mexico.

He spat on the ground to clear his mouth of grit and his mind of politics. *Forget all of that,* he thought to himself. *It is not within your purview. Tomorrow is Sunday. The day of the Lord. A day for worship. Thank God I am still alive.*

"I'm going to write to Julia tomorrow," he said to Lieutenant Dent.

"That's good, Sam."

SARAH BORGINNES

Sarah poured the last of her coffee into Captain Loud's tin cup and looked north over the parapets toward Resaca de la Palma.

"Thank you, Mrs. Borginnes," the captain said.

"I wish it could be stronger, Captain, but—"

Before she could finish her statement, an enemy cannonball announced its arrival with a hissing scream as it slammed into the earthen wall just below Loud's battery. Sarah threw herself to the dirt, which had been packed hard by wheels of guns and boots of men for so many days now that she had lost count. Loose dirt and dust rained down on her from the impact.

"Range that goddamned gun!" Loud yelled. He looked down on Sarah. "Are you injured?"

"Hell no, Captain!" she said, springing to her feet. "Just another near miss from those damned Irish deserters."

He smiled, his teeth looking like pearls next to the soot-blackened flesh of his face. He had remained on his feet. He held his hand over his cup to prevent dirt from falling into his coffee.

"Can you tell what's going on up the road?" she asked.

He shook his head. "My ears are ringing too loud to hear much. But I trust General Taylor will fight his way through with our supplies. Tell me, Mrs. Borginnes, how is Major Brown today?"

She frowned. "One step from heaven's fold, I'm afraid." She sprang aside to make way for two men lugging a crate of ammunition up the embankment. "I'd best tend to my boys," she said to Loud.

He bowed slightly and touched the grimy brim of his campaign hat.

From the ramparts of Fort Texas she had listened, when she could steal a moment, to the battle raging up the Point Isabel road. She had seen the clouds of dust and smoke rise from the chaparral. Yet it was impossible to know what was going on in that bramble-choked thicket. She had too much to do inside the walls of the garrison to stand for very long and watch the road for signs of one army or another.

Most of the Mexican soldiers surrounding the fort had left two days ago to meet General Taylor's army on the wagon road, but a regiment had been left behind to carry on the siege. A number of enemy batteries had also remained on the Rio Grande del Norte to harass the besieged defenders of Fort Texas. The past two days, however, had brought about a sharp decline in the artillery fire directed at the fort. Everything now depended upon what was happening in the chaparral up the road to the north.

As she hiked to her cook fires, she prayed silently, *Please, God Almighty, get General Taylor through them Mexicans with them supplies.*

She threw some more lumber from broken ammunition boxes under a cauldron and stirred its contents—gruel made of weevil-infested oats. Throwing a handful of roasted coffee beans into the only grinder in the fort, she cranked the handle furiously, anxious to return to the parapets. Having refilled the coffeepot, she hung it over the fire to heat. The next pot was now boiling over the embers, so she wrapped a dirty rag around its handle and marched away with it toward the gunners manning the east walls of the garrison.

Climbing the embankment on weary legs, she greeted Lieutenant Braxton Bragg, who was overseeing the battery of twelve-pounders on the east point of the star-shaped fort.

"Hot coffee, sir!" she sang. "Sorry it ain't stronger, but I'm having to ration the coffee beans. Supply's running low."

Bragg nodded without smiling. "Do not apologize, ma'am. It is you, not the coffee, that has kept the boys' spirits up these past few days."

She felt a bit stunned at his statement. Braxton Bragg was not usually one to hand out compliments. "Just doin' my part, sir." She poured his cup half full.

She had almost finished divvying up the coffee among the artillery-

men when a nearby private on watch with a telescope shouted, "Lieutenant Bragg! Something's happening downstream." He pointed.

Sarah followed the soldier's gaze and saw, a quarter mile away, men
streaming and stumbling from the timber, toward the river.

"Give me the glass!" Bragg ordered. Steadying the optics on a sandbag, he took a moment to find the action.

Sarah saw more and more men pour from the chaparral to the banks
of the Rio Grande. Dozens, scores. What did it mean?

"By God, they're Mexicans!" Bragg announced. "They're retreating!
Running for their goddamned lives!"

A cheer rose among the men and spread along the ramparts of the
beleaguered garrison. Sarah raised her coffeepot and added her voice to
the victory cry. All the worry that the bombardment had twisted up in
her came out in a tooth-rattling ululation. She watched now as fleeing
Mexican soldiers rushed to the river by the hundreds. They began to de-
scend the riverbanks and flounder into the swift current. They were clawing at one another, overcrowding the few boats to be found at the water's
edge.

*God bless General Taylor, that rough-and-ready old warhorse! He's coming
to save us! Thank you, God!*

"Fire!" a lieutenant shouted.

A volley from two guns sent exploding shells into the mass retreat.

"Cease firing, men!" Bragg ordered. "No need to waste powder and
shot. The river will kill them now."

Lieutenant
JOHN RILEY

Lieutenant John Riley sighted along the tube of the ancient brass cannon, eyeballing the trajectory for his next shot. His last attempt had fallen just short of Captain Loud's emplacement of eighteen-pounders. He would risk a bit more powder behind the next ball. His little battery of Irish gunners had been issued the most antiquated artillery in the Mexican Army of the North, yet he was determined to prove the mettle of his men. The touchhole to this brass six-pounder had been blown out to the diameter of his thumb from decades of firing. He wasn't sure how much more powder the tube could take, but he was willing to risk another fistful to lift the next round into the muzzle of one of those big eighteens.

His preferred target would have been Lieutenant Bragg, but Bragg was on the far side of the star fort and out of his range. For now, he would settle for Captain Loud's battery as his target, but he hoped to find that nativist bastard, Bragg, within range before this war was over.

Through the ringing in his ears, a peculiar sound caught his attention. It resembled a gust in the treetops, then the distant bellowing of beasts such as geese, jackasses, or cattle. When he saw the flailing of men's arms on the top of the earthen star fort, however, he knew he was hearing the rise of a battle cry from the enemy.

"John!" cried a private named Barney Hogan. "Look!"

Riley grabbed the private by the ear and twisted it. In the U.S. Army they had shared the same rank. "You'll refer to me as *Lieutenant Riley*, Private!"

"Yes, sir! But, Lieutenant . . . look!" He pointed up the Matamoras Road that ran between his battery and fort.

Riley lifted his eyes to see hundreds of Mexican soldiers running toward him. He released Private Hogan's ear. Far away, up the road to Point Isabel, he saw an American flag in the distance. "Faith and begorra," he grumbled. "It's a rout, to be sure."

"What'll we do?" Hogan asked, rubbing his ear.

"Get off one more shot, then join the retreat," Riley replied.

"Should we not stand and fight the bastards?"

"It's hard to fight, dangling from the end of a rope."

"What, then?" asked Private August Geary. "Do we run like cowards?"

"Better to be a coward for a minute than dead the rest of your life. Now get to the river and prepare yourselves to cross it. I won't have the whole of our company hanged or drowned on this day."

The men stared at him.

"Retreat! That's an order! Hurry, before your fellow soldiers come and pull you under. Take anything wooden that will hold you afloat."

The men emptied crates and gathered the pine poles of ramrods and bore sponges to use for flotation. They slipped down the riverbank toward the Rio Grande as Riley loaded the cannon with a double dose of powder. He kissed a six-pound brass cannonball before shoving it into the muzzle of the gun.

"Say hello to the bloody heretic nativist Protestants." He patted his cannon like a favored old horse.

"Are you coming, Lieutenant?" asked Private Barney Hogan.

"I'll be along after this parting shot. Go, now. This gun may blow itself to bits."

Private Hogan disappeared below the brink of the riverbank as Lieutenant Riley picked up a coil of fuse material. With a knife placed beside the coil, he hacked off a ten-inch section of the fuse known as "black match," a cotton string covered with a dried slurry of glue and black powder. It was old technology compared to the primers and lanyards the Americans used, but it was what he had been issued by the Mexican Army.

He jammed the black match into the touchhole of the old piece and

found a squib with a burning ember on the end. He blew on the ember
to enliven it and touched it to the end of the fuse. He watched a second
or two, to make sure it would burn, then calmly turned away to take cover
under the brink of the riverbank in case the little gun really did explode.

Sliding down the well-used trail, he threw himself down to bury his
face in the dirt. The explosion jarred the ground; its recoil sent the cannon rolling backwards down the riverbank, right past him, and crashing
through what was left of the timber in this war-torn valley. He sprang
quickly to his feet and looked over the brink to watch the path of his
shot. It sailed over Loud's eighteen-pounders and fell into the interior of
Fort Texas, probably harming no one.

"You lucky bastards," he said, disappointed.

Now the first of the fleeing Mexicans began to trot and stumble past
him to the riverbank. Before joining them, he emptied an ammunition
crate that looked like it would float. He paused to watch the crazed men
tumble down the riverbank, already exhausted from running for miles.
He stayed put for a while, instinctively feeling uneasy about joining the
mob. From his perch atop the bank, he could see that his own men had
made their way across the river, the current having carried them downstream. The retreating Mexicans were not so lucky.

The first men found a small boat hidden along the bank. They clambered aboard, crawling atop one another like ants. As the boat drifted
from the bank, others came splashing into the water to ride along, until
the weight of exhausted men swamped the boat. Men disappeared under-
water and did not return. Only two still held fast to the boat as it
bobbed up.

By now men at the river's edge were being pushed into the water by
many others behind them, and none seemed fit to swim. They trampled
and clawed one another down into the muddy water, creating a raft of
dead men floating, sinking, spinning in the current.

"By God, they're all going to die," he said under his breath. He knew
he had to distance himself from this throng to survive his own crossing.

Carrying his crate upstream, he tried to get some of the men to follow
him, but he only knew a few words of Spanish.

"*Alla!*" he said, pointing upstream. "*Venga!*"

Finally he grabbed a couple of soldiers much smaller than himself and
made them come along. "*No bueno aqui,*" he said, pointing down to the
river. Then he pointed upstream. "*Bueno alla!*"

A few other followers began to tag along, recognizing his insignia as an officer. Riley led them away from the retreating mob to a safer place along the bank. Finding a trail, they filed down to the water. Here, Riley gathered up an armload of driftwood and handed it to the nearest man. The others saw his reasoning and found their own makeshift rafts. Satisfied that he had given a few men a shot at survival, he took off his hat, his tunic, and his boots and latched them inside his handy crate. He waded into the water, feeling the muddy riverbed quickly drop away under his feet.

Now he was floating, the crate just buoyant enough to keep his mouth above the surface as he kicked for the opposite shore. The current caught him and he started moving swiftly downstream. He looked toward the Texas bank to watch hundreds of soldiers, who had survived whatever Taylor's army did to them at Resaca de la Palma only to trample one another into the Rio Grande mud. It felt like poison to his soul to see so many fellow Catholics die needlessly in one final baptism.

He turned his face away, sickened and demoralized. Downstream, he saw a boat crossing the river. Exhausted soldiers floundered toward it. So many desperate men clawed at the gunwales that the skiff began to take on water. From the middle of the vessel, a priest stood up and held his crucifix to the sky. Then everything went under—men, oars, the boat, and the cross.

President
JAMES K. POLK

Washington, DC
May 13, 1846

The president realized that he was no longer listening to the ramblings of the general-in-chief of the army, Winfield Scott. He was staring at Scott's jowly face as he spoke, but he had ceased to absorb the general's words. All around Scott, Polk's office on the second floor of the presidential mansion hummed with the excited conversations of cabinet members, though no cabinet meeting had been called.

Four days of unending anxiety and utter turmoil had robbed the president of many hours of sleep and more than a few meals. Last Saturday, the express mail had arrived from the Texas coast aboard a navy steamer. With the dispatches came General Taylor's latest missive, stating that "hostilities may now be considered as commenced."

A scouting party consisting of two companies of dragoons led by a Captain Seth Thornton had been attacked on the U.S. side of the Del Norte by an overwhelming force of Mexican cavalry. Eleven American soldiers had died. Captain Thornton had been rendered unconscious and his second-in-command, a Captain Hardee, had been forced to surrender. The survivors of the attack had been taken prisoner. American blood had been shed on American soil.

Even before this, Polk had been outraged that his envoy to Mexico, John Slidell, had been curtly rejected by the new president of Mexico, Mariano Paredes, who had overthrown the duly-elected president, José Joaquin de Herrera. Negotiations with Herrera had been promising, to the point that Polk thought a war might be avoided and much territory purchased from Mexico. But the new head of state, Paredes, hated everything American and had refused to even recognize Ambassador Slidell.

A diplomat rejected! The newspapers and much of the citizenry had been rightfully angered by the affront. And now the Mexican military assault Polk had long expected had finally occurred. Yes, he had expected, even hoped for, the Mexican attack. And yet he felt embarrassingly unprepared to react.

Since receiving the news, the President's Mansion had seethed with activity. An emergency cabinet meeting had been called Saturday evening. An address to Congress had been prepared and delivered, urging a declaration of war and executive authority to prosecute the conflict. On Monday, the House of Representatives had passed a bill to that effect by a vote of 173 for, 14 against. The next day, Tuesday, the Senate passed the same bill 42 to 2.

Now it was Wednesday, and preparations for war with Mexico were still developing. How many volunteers should be called upon and from which states? How many new regular army regiments should be formed? Who would lead them? How many millions must Congress allocate to fund it all?

Polk's office in the President's Mansion served as the hub of the chaos. For four days, visitors had come and gone in an unending procession of bombastic egos spewing wild opinions. Military leaders, senators, representatives, foreign ambassadors, cabinet members—all felt the need to weigh in, no matter how uninformed. Many of the politicians sought commands in the new regiments that would soon be created by Congress. To Polk's gratification, his cabinet had been united from the onset of the war news. Not even Secretary of State James Buchanan had proven truculent, as was often his nature.

Polk caught himself staring at one of Scott's war medals on the ostentatious uniform the general had chosen to wear. They didn't call him "Old Fuss and Feathers" for nothing. Scott was much taller than Polk, and the medals came to eye level on the president. He tried to concentrate on Scott's rambling diatribe.

". . . some time to sort out the logistical challenges . . . munitions and provisions . . . congressional funding . . ."

Polk looked past the braided silk epaulet on Scott's shoulder to see his secretary of state, James Buchanan, enter his office, a document of some kind in his hand. Weary of listening to the general, he was more anxious to see what Buchanan had up his sleeve, for that familiar, belligerent glint was back in Buchanan's eye.

"Very well, General," he said to Scott, interrupting whatever it was that he was saying, "you may return later today with a more complete report of a formal nature."

"I understand, Mr. President. I have just one other issue to discuss with you."

Someone in the office laughed at something, which annoyed Polk. Daylight streamed pleasantly in through the window, as if nothing were the matter. General Scott stood silent before Polk.

"Yes, General," Polk said, guessing what the issue might be, "I am prepared to tender to you the field command of the army to be raised. You are entitled to it, according to your rank as general-in-chief of the army."

Scott came to attention. "I accept."

Polk shook the general's hand as he retired, his ostrich-plumed chapeau tucked under his elbow. Yes, Scott was an old warhorse, hero of the War of 1812 and a frontier Indian fighter. Still, Polk lacked complete faith in him, finding him slow to action and overly scientific in his strategies. He had no choice, however. Scott's position entitled him to the command.

When General Scott vacated the office, Polk summoned Buchanan with a twitch of his index finger.

"Mr. President," Buchanan began, "I have prepared a draft of a dispatch to be sent to our ministers in London, Paris, and other foreign courts, announcing the declaration of war with Mexico. May I read it to the cabinet for approval?"

Polk nodded. "Gentlemen!" he shouted to the cabinet members lounging about his office in conversation. "Mr. Buchanan requests that you all lend an ear."

Polk walked around behind his desk and sank wearily into his stuffed leather chair as the men turned toward Buchanan. He had not yet thought of informing the foreign courts and was gratified that his secretary of state had seen to it. Yet he could not ignore the unexplained, mischievous expression on Buchanan's face. What was he up to now?

Buchanan began to read his draft, which proceeded logically enough to announce the declaration of war to the rest of the Western world and to explain the causes of the conflict. Then the secretary of state stopped, coughed, and shuffled a new sheaf of paper to the forefront.

"Furthermore, the object of the United States of America is not and shall not be to dismember Mexico or to make conquests upon her territory. The Rio Bravo del Norte is the boundary beyond which the United States will make no claim. The United States does not go to war with a view to acquire either New Mexico or California or any other portion of the Mexican territory."

"Stop there!" Polk said, sitting forward in his chair. "Making such an unnecessary declaration to foreign governments is improper and unwise. The causes for war set forth in my message to Congress and the accompanying documents will suffice for any dispatch sent abroad."

Buchanan appeared to be perplexed. "We must reassure the world that our motives are not of an imperialistic nature. This is not a war of acquisition."

Polk stood, astonished. He had often heard Buchanan speak in favor of expansion to the Pacific. Why would he now change his mind? "It remains to be seen what honorable acquisitions might be warranted and proper."

"We have no claim to any land beyond the Del Norte," Buchanan replied.

"In making peace with Mexico, we may obtain California or any other portion of Mexican territory sufficient to indemnify our claimants and defray the expense of war, which Mexico, by her long continued wrongs and injuries to our citizens, has forced us to wage."

Buchanan rolled his eyes and flailed his arms, rattling the sheaves he clenched in his fist. "These wrongs and injuries . . . exactly what *are* they, Mr. President?"

"The list is long," Polk answered, raising his voice. "I refer you to the attorney general." He gestured toward John Young Mason.

The dignified, clean-shaven John Mason stood and tugged at the sleeves of his coat. "We might begin with the American citizens slaughtered ten years ago at the Alamo."

"They should have surrendered," Buchanan blurted.

"That would not have helped them," Mason argued. "Colonel Fannin's men *did* surrender at Goliad, and they were all massacred in cold blood!"

"Santa Anna ordered them shot as pirates—foreign citizens invading a sovereign nation. The Americans were mercenaries."

"What about the American citizens captured at Mier, who were forced to draw lots for their lives?"

"The Black Bean Incident?" Buchanan said with a scoff. "More piracy!"

Mason stepped forward, shedding his coat, as if preparing to fight. "You dare to take Mexico's side?"

Secretary of Treasury Robert J. Walker held Attorney General Mason back.

Buchanan looked at Polk. "Mr. President, is it not my duty as secretary of state to predict how Mexico will argue her side in this conflict and how she will present her case to the foreign courts?"

Polk struggled to control his contempt. "Mexico's abuses against American citizens are legion!" he snapped. "Americans have been murdered and robbed for decades at the hands of Mexicans. May I remind you that France suffered the same indignities to her citizens living in Mexico and invaded Veracruz to extract reparations?"

"France settled for less than a million dollars. A far cry from a third of Mexico's territory!"

"Abuses against Americans far outweigh whatever France suffered! Our proximity to Mexico has made our citizens infinitely easier to victimize!"

Buchanan slapped his draft of the dispatch down on the president's desk. "Mr. President! We have obtained a declaration of war from Congress based solely on the issue of American blood spilled on American soil! This is a border dispute, nothing more."

"The attack on the Del Norte is only the most recent in a litany of abuses waged against our nation and our citizens. You must go back and read my message to Congress—of which you approved, I might remind you. The issue of indemnification is prominent."

"The message never stated that Mexico would pay with her territories."

"Mexico has no other means by which to pay, and yet pay she must! Our nation has attempted for many years to acquire legal compensation from Mexico, to no avail. Our citizens have been robbed and imprisoned without recourse, murdered without justice. Restitution is long overdue. Indeed, the issue of reparations *alone* is justification for war."

Secretary of War William L. Marcy stood. "The president is right on this. Mexico has forced us into what is sure to be an expensive war. She must be forced to make amends to make peace."

"Peace?" Buchanan railed, turning on Marcy. "We have scarcely begun to wage war and you speak of peace! Think practically, gentlemen! When England hears of our declaration of war, Lord Aberdeen will demand to know whether we intend to acquire California or any other Mexican territory. If we do not answer that question, I think it almost certain that England and France will join with Mexico in the war against us!"

Ah, so this was the real issue, Polk thought. *Fear of war with the powers of Europe.*

Secretary Mason took a step toward Buchanan. "And why would England or France do such a thing?" he demanded. "Perhaps because they also wish to acquire California? That, too, would justify war, according to President Monroe's doctrine, which states that no European power must ever again be allowed to colonize any portion of North America."

Polk listened to the room erupt with opinions on the matter, mostly in his favor and against Buchanan's views. He had been wondering when Buchanan would stir up trouble. The man seemed to see it as his duty to find ways in which to disagree with his administration.

Finally, Buchanan turned back to Polk. "Mr. President, will you not reconsider? If you make no claim on Mexico's territories, you may prevent an unnecessary war with England and France as well."

Polk walked around the desk to look up at the taller Buchanan. He resolved to speak slowly and plainly. "Neither as a citizen nor as president will I tolerate any meddling of European powers on this continent. Our war with Mexico is of no concern to any foreign government. Any inquiry from abroad about acquisitions of territory will be viewed as insulting to this administration. If any such inquiry is made, I will not answer it, even if the consequence should be war with all of them!"

Buchanan sagged as if the wind had been kicked out of him. "Then you will have war with England as well as Mexico, and probably with France also, for neither of these powers will ever stand by and see California annexed to the United States."

This cowardly statement disgusted Polk. "Before I would make the pledge you recommend in your dispatch, I would *embrace* the war which all the powers of Christendom might wage, and I would stand and fight until the last man among us fell in the conflict!"

Buchanan shook his head in warning. "This does not bode well for settlement of the Oregon question that we are so close to securing by treaty with England."

"I have said a hundred times," Polk replied, "that Mexico has nothing to do with Oregon and Oregon has nothing to do with Mexico. We will do what is honorable in both cases, each independent of the other."

Buchanan let out a huge sigh. "Then the members of this administration will have to live forever with the consequences of those decisions, Mr. President."

Polk suddenly understood his secretary of state's reluctance to pursue an offensive war. Buchanan intended to run for president! Should an offensive war prove unpopular in future months and years, he could rightfully claim that he had been against it.

"And you, Mr. Buchanan, must strike from your dispatch any mention of dismembering Mexico, of acquiring California, or of the Del Norte being the ultimate boundary beyond which we would not claim. I will not tie up my hands now as to the terms on which I would make peace with Mexico in the future."

Buchanan made no reply, but he snatched up his draft of the dispatch from the president's desk and stormed out of the office.

General
ANTONIO LÓPEZ
DE SANTA ANNA

Santa Anna swayed to the gentle roll of the *Arab* as the vessel steamed toward the harbor of Veracruz. Seated on a stuffed leather settee in the ship's saloon, he rubbed the stump of his amputated leg to help the blood circulate—a ritual he engaged in before strapping on the wooden peg.

"You know, Maria, my love," he said to his young wife, seated near him, "Napoleon was exiled to Saint Helena after having outraged all of Europe."

She smirked at him in a good-natured way. She was wearing her finest gown and had gotten over the seasickness of the open Gulf. He knew she was happy to be returning to Mexico, though exile in Cuba had not been as dreary as Napoleon's stay on Saint Helena.

"Of course, my exploits do not yet equal those of Napoleon's," he said with an air of modesty. "But I have the advantage over him in two respects. One, I will not die in exile as he did. And two, I can show by my mutilated body that I have suffered for Mexico."

Maria turned her pretty young face toward the open saloon door. "Juanito!" she yelled at her husband's manservant, her voice shrill and demanding. "Come help His Excellency with the peg!"

General Antonio López de Santa Anna winced. How could such a pretty young wife possess the voice of a caged parrot? He had married Maria Dolores Tosta four years ago, when she was only fifteen and he was almost fifty. It had caused a public uproar at the time. Not only because she had been such a young bride but also because Santa Anna had announced his plans to marry her a mere month after the death of his first wife, Doña Inez. But scandal seldom concerned the Napoleon of the West, as the general liked to think of himself.

Juanito burst nervously into the saloon. Like all the servants, he was terrified of Maria Dolores Tosta. Santa Anna was aware that they called her "Tostada" behind her back. It meant, he gathered, that her heart was toasted like a burned tortilla, unable to sympathize.

Juanito saw the prosthetic leg on a nearby chair. Though affectionately called "the peg," the fake limb was skillfully constructed of wood and cork and carved to resemble a real leg. It even wore a shoe.

"*Pronto!*" Maria ordered. "His Excellency wishes to stand on the deck to greet his admirers."

"*Si*, senora," Juanito replied as he fumbled with the leather straps and buckles of the prosthetic limb.

Santa Anna reached into the pocket of his coat for the letter signed by the president of the United States, James K. Polk. He took it out and unfolded it for one last look. He began to chuckle. Months ago, he had sent one of his more persuasive agents, Colonel A. J. Atocha, to Washington to make a deal with President Polk. As a result, Polk had sent a secret courier—a naval officer named MacKenzie—to Havana to deliver the letter that Santa Anna now held in his hands, along with secret orders allowing him passage through the American naval blockade of the Mexican coast.

Polk's letter was worded vaguely, so as not to be used against him should it become public. It invited Santa Anna to "explore peaceable and diplomatic solutions" to the "conflict between two neighboring nations," should Santa Anna somehow find himself "once again in control of the great and proud nation of his birth."

Blah, blah, blah, Santa Anna mused.

MacKenzie, the American who had delivered the letter, had explained precisely what Polk intended. He would allow Santa Anna through the U.S. blockade. Santa Anna would use his influence and political skills to return to power. Then His Excellency would sell Nueva Mexico and Alta California—and everything in between—to the United States.

But Antonio López de Santa Anna had absolutely no intention of selling so much as a grain of sand to the insufferable *Yanquis*. He had orchestrated his return to Mexico. Yes, he would become president again. Then he would raise an army that Napoleon Bonaparte would envy and drive the gringo hoards all the way back across the Sabine.

He felt a vulpine smile spread across his face like a bend in the Rio Bravo.

"You love that letter more than you love me," Maria said, watching him fondle the tattered edges of the paper.

"That is not possible, my dear. I am merely fond of this letter because it amuses me so much. Can you believe that the president of the United States would order his navy to allow my return to Mexico? Me! The Hero of Veracruz! The Conqueror of Tampico!" He laughed and slapped his good knee.

Earlier on this day, the *Arab*, a British mail packet with clearance to sail in and out of the blockade, had heaved to alongside the *St. Mary's*, a U.S. Navy vessel. An officer and two armed sailors from the *St. Mary's* had rowed over on a skiff to make inquiries as to the purpose of the *Arab*'s voyage.

"Maria, did you see the look of astonishment on the boarding officer's face when I showed him my letter?" He shook the parchment at her and laughed loudly.

She rolled her eyes. "Yes, of course I saw the fool. I was standing right behind you, like a good little wife."

"Can you believe the gullibility of President Polk? He thinks I'm going to sell California to him!"

Maria shook her head in disbelief. "*Esta loco!*"

"Wait until he sees the army I am going to lead northward, Maria! General Taylor will wish he had never crossed the Rio Bravo!"

Juanito finished buckling the straps of the peg leg.

"Lift me up, Juanito!"

The general rose to the strong helping hand of his manservant and tested his balance on the wooden limb. Taking a step, he leaned on Juanito's shoulder, wincing a little at the way the peg leg pinched the flesh of his stump. Hobbling out of the saloon, he beheld a beautiful view over the bow of the *Arab*. *México!* The sun fell lazily beyond the distant peaks of the Sierra Madre Oriental. A golden hue enveloped the Port of Veracruz, her city, her palace, her harbor. San Juan de Ulúa loomed off the starboard bow—the 240-year-old Spanish fortress built on a reef in the bay.

A single cannon shot roared from the parapets of San Juan de Ulúa, smoke billowing before the bow of the *Arab*.

A proper salute to the return of a hero, he thought. He waited for more cannon fire, but none came. But for the one volley, only seagulls and salt spray welcomed him home. Sunlight dazzled him, dancing upon the waves. As the steamer chugged ever nearer to the harbor, Santa Anna could just make out the pier where he had lost his leg to a French artillery shell eight years previous.

The memories of that day came flooding back into his mind. His military rivals had criticized him for remaining with his troops all day, behind the walls of the barracks, while the French marines looted the city and took General Mariano Arista prisoner. His rivals did not understand military and political strategy. He had waited until the French invaders began to row back to their ships. Then Santa Anna mounted a white charger and led his soldiers down to the docks in a dashing show of resistance. Drawing his sword, he raced his stallion up and down the street that paralleled the docks—and even out onto the pier itself—in full view of the French naval vessels, as if he had just chased the invaders away to save Veracruz and all of Mexico.

Then, in a historic moment both tragic and serendipitous, a lucky shot from a French cannon exploded just over his head. The shrapnel killed his horse and shattered his left leg below the knee. The memories faded then, until he woke up in the hospital, minus the leg.

"*Mira*, Maria! See the site of my sacrifice for my beloved Mexico! Just as I chased the invaders out to sea, a shot from a French ship—"

"I know the story," Maria said, grabbing his hand to steady him as the steamer rocked. "Come, now, to the bow, so your supporters can salute your return."

The peg leg's purchase on the rolling deck of the steamer proved precarious. But, by holding Maria's hand and Juanito's shoulder, the general slowly hobbled forward. At the forecastle, he found a flagman signaling the shore. Letters had been written, predicting the date for the return of the former president of Mexico. The *Arab* was well known here at Veracruz and had certainly been spotted out to sea by lookouts. Troops would be gathering on the pier, along with Santa Anna's most loyal political lieutenants. He prepared himself for a triumphant reunion.

"Juanito, I have an important mission for you."

"*Si*, General."

Santa Anna took a last look at his letter from President Polk and handed it to Juanito. "Destroy this letter. Go below and throw it into the boiler fire."

"Yes, Your Excellency."

"It is a pity that I cannot boast of how I outsmarted the president of the United States, but my enemies would accuse me of collusion if they saw this letter. Go now, and hurry back to help me onto the pier when we arrive."

Arriving at the docks, he found a handful of his trusted agents, a single platoon of infantrymen, a small brass band, and a gathering of curious citizens. Juanito returned from the boiler room in time to help him across a gangplank to the pier. Still feeling the sway of the open seas, Santa Anna felt obliged to hold his manservant's shoulder as he trudged toward his supporters.

The first to step forward was Manuel Escandon, a profiteer who had benefited from dictator Santa Anna's takeover of abandoned church properties, which he sold to chosen investors, including Escandon.

"*Viva México!*" Escandon shouted. "*Viva* Santa Anna!"

No one added the customary echoes.

"Manuel," Santa Anna said, shaking Escandon's hand, "just one cannon shot as a salute to my return? Only one?"

Escandon shrugged his apology. "The generals did not want the Americans to mistake your salute for an act of aggression."

"This fear of the *Yanquis* is disgusting," Santa Anna groused. Then he smiled and added, "But this will change."

"Ah, senora!" Escandon said, bowing before Maria.

Santa Anna looked past Escandon to the others who had come to greet him. He recognized the familiar faces of Haro y Tamariz, Tornel, Sierra y Rosso, Valencia, Canalizo . . . Generals, politicians, bureaucrats. All useful men, if closely supervised. He stepped forward, shook off his manservant's helping hand, and pointed at the soldiers on the jetty.

"Why are these soldiers not standing at attention? Where are their officers?"

"The officers all went to a tavern in the town," Escandon admitted. He turned to the men in uniform. "Fire a musket salute to Santa Anna's return!" he shouted.

A few of the men loosed random shots out over the Gulf.

"Strike up the band!" Escandon goaded. "The Hero of Veracruz has returned!"

As he listened to the band butcher a haphazard version of some march, General Antonio López de Santa Anna inhaled a breath of Mexican air and offered his elbow to Maria. With his comely wife, he hobbled up the pier toward sacred ground. Though he fumed inwardly at the disorganized welcome he had received, he forced himself to smile and swagger as if reviewing the troops. Soon, he told himself, there would be parades in his honor. There would be banquets, festivals, concerts, and celebrations. Just like old times.

"I have returned," he said to himself, under his breath. Just then, he noticed an old man standing in his path on the dock. As Santa Anna limped nearer, the graybeard shook his fist at the general.

"Santa Anna, you scoundrel!" the curmudgeon railed. "For more than twenty years you have endeavored to ruin our country! Why did you not stay in Cuba, where you could reign as king of the cockfights?"

Santa Anna drew himself up into a defensive posture, though the tirade had done little to ruffle him. He had been called worse than king of the cockfights.

"Sir, you stand with two good legs upon the very pier where I lost one of mine in defense of *Madre México*!" Now he looked the old man in the eyes and smiled at him. "There was a day, and my heart expands with the recollection, when leading forward the popular masses and the army to demand the rights of the nation, I was hailed by the enviable title Soldier of the People! Allow me again to assume that selfsame title— nevermore to be given up—and to devote myself until death to the defense of the liberty and independence of the republic!"

The words had come straight out of the speech he had been rehearsing for days, but the old man before him seemed to swallow them as impromptu and sincere.

The aged citizen's glare softened as he glanced down at the peg leg. "God save Mexico," he said, stepping aside to let Santa Anna and Doña Maria pass.

Captain
JOHN RILEY

Captain John Riley traced the pattern of a crucifix across his chest as he rose from the altar. His daily prayers attended to, he now turned back to his preparations for war. With a touch of sadness, he glanced around the unfinished interior of the chapel. Almost complete and ready for mass, its construction had been halted by the American invasion. Now it served as an ammunition depot for the earthen fort recently built around it. Where lines of new wooden pews had once stood in ranks, crates of powder, shot, shells, and fuses now crowded the floor. Riley wended his way among them as if navigating a maze, until he passed under the stone arch of the cathedral door.

Stepping out into the dazzling Mexican sunlight, he visually inspected the earthen walls of the fort that had been built around the Catholic temple. The intended churchyard was now surrounded by a rectangular rampart with arrowhead-shaped bastions projecting from all four corners. Eight heavy artillery pieces were in place, ready to hurl shot, shell, grapeshot, and canister at the American invaders coming from the north. These were modern eighteen-pounders of English manufacture, far superior to the ancient Spanish six-pounders he had fired at Fort Texas on the Rio Bravo.

Looking around, Riley's eyes fell upon the new pine pews that had been removed from the chapel, now piled haphazardly against the outer wall of the stone church. Nearby, he saw several women smoking cigarettes rolled with corn husks. The Mexicans called these women *soldaderas*. They traveled with the army to cook and clean, and sometimes to tend wounded men, reload muskets, or even fire upon the enemy themselves. It was rumored that some of them provided other services of a more intimate nature.

"*Buenos dias, mujeres!*" Riley sang, flashing a smile.

The women returned his greeting, some nodding or smiling.

Riley gestured toward the pews stacked against the church wall. "*Aqui es mucha lena para los fieros del campo.*" His Irish brogue tainted his limited vocabulary. *Here is much firewood for the camp.*

One of the *soldaderas* snuffed out her cigarette. She wore a tattered palmetto hat, a common cotton dress, and sandals. Around her trim waist she had tied her red-and-yellow rebozo as a colorful sash.

"*Si*, Capitan," she replied, grabbing a nearby ax and marching forward to bury the blade in a wooden pew.

The rest of the women searched for tools or began stacking the wood split from the lumber. They had learned to respect the big foreigner, not only for his size and his swagger but also for his obvious skills in leadership and knowledge of artillery.

In large strides, Riley now climbed the steep dirt slope to the northeast bastion and looked back at the beautiful, white-walled city of Monterrey, a thousand yards to the south. This small fortified churchyard, which the Mexicans called the Citadel, stood as the first line of defense for Monterrey, the capital city of the state of Nuevo León. It guarded the road to the town of Marin—General Taylor's most likely path to Monterrey. It was here—at the Citadel—that John Riley expected to exact his revenge on the sadistic nativist officers of the U.S. Army.

He walked among young Mexican enlisted men serving as gunners and returned their salutes. He approached privates Barney Hogan and August Geary—U.S. deserters like himself—who were watching the senoritas chop up the church pews. General Ampudia's plan, at least for now, was to mix the U.S. deserters with Mexican soldiers in these artillery units. But Riley had already spoken to his superiors about his dream of forming a mostly Irish battalion of gunners. The Irish and other immigrant soldiers in the U.S. ranks were still being abused by nativist officers and continued to come over to the Mexican ranks—the Catholic side of the conflict.

"Top of the day, lads," he said, greeting the two privates.

"Good day, sir!" Hogan replied.

"Top of the day, Captain!" Geary puffed on his clay dudeen.

Riley smiled and propped his fists on his hips. "Shouldn't you *scalpeens* be on the lookout for the enemy instead of gazing upon the *soldaderas*?"

"Begging the captain's pardon, sir. We couldn't help but wonder . . ."

"Speak your mind."

"Sir, is it right to chop up such furniture? Pews right out of the church?"

"The Lord provides in ways most mysterious and wonderful. You will thank the Almighty later when you fill your bellies with a hot meal cooked over the sacred fires fueled by that holy wood."

Geary smiled. "Amen, Captain. So I will."

Hogan nodded. "Aye, we both will, sir. Sure we will."

Riley leaned forward and towered over the privates. "This churchyard is now your fortress, men. It is your shield and your stronghold protecting from harm. Defend it well and by the glory of God we will prevail over the heretics from the north!"

"Aye, Captain!"

"Aye, sir!"

Riley turned away from the men and ambled toward fellow Irishman Patrick Dalton, who had deserted the U.S. ranks back at Camargo and had become a lieutenant in the Mexican Army. Dalton was peering northward through a telescope resting on freshly placed sandbags.

"What do you see, Lieutenant?"

Dalton's green eyes angled his way. "Some riders are approaching from the *bosque*."

Bosque de San Domingo, Riley thought—the Americans' camp. "Rangers? Engineers?"

Dalton shrugged. "Too far away yet to say, Captain."

"Keep your glass trained upon them, Patrick. Today could be the day."

"Yes, sir."

Riley's journey from Matamoros to Monterrey had begun four months ago with a hellish retreat through the desert to the town of Linares—two hundred miles of thirst, starvation, and exhaustion covered in just ten days. Many of the soldiers had lost their shoes crossing the Rio Bravo in that chaotic retreat from the Resaca de la Palma. Their feet suffered horribly from sharp rocks and cactus on the forced march. Countless men died of sickness and exposure on the trail. Many others used their muskets to end their own sufferings. The bedraggled survivors—including

Riley's band of deserters—stumbled into Linares to drink at the town's fountain, their uniforms in tatters. The local citizens gaped upon them in shock. What horror had reduced the Army of the North to this?

The same citizens rallied to feed the survivors and mend their uniforms. It was in Linares that General Arista faced court-martial and was dismissed as commander of the army for his losses at Palo Alto and Resaca de la Palma. General Mejia took his place. The rank and file loathed Mejia, who looked disdainfully down at them through his blue-tinted spectacles.

It soon became obvious that General Taylor intended to march upon Monterrey, so Mejia led his three thousand survivors northwest from Linares, over mountains and through canyons that reminded Riley of his time with the British Royal Army in Afghanistan. The march was a slow one along steep trails. One day he watched a hapless soldier slip and fall to his death in a remote gorge.

Finally Riley crossed a high pass to see the gleaming city of Monterrey below, a silver strand of clear mountain water—the Santa Catarina River—running past the southern limits of the capital city. Steep, treeless hills called *cerros* rose to the south and west of the little city of stone. Orchards and cornfields grew just outside the town walls. Cattle—mere dots on the landscape from this distant ridge—grazed in open pastures. From his vantage on the mountain pass, Riley could make out a large, ornate cathedral at the east end of town, an open plaza standing in front of it. North of town he saw the new cathedral that he would come to know as the Citadel. To the west, the fortresslike Bishop's Palace overlooked the town from a formidable hill.

"'Tis beautiful, is it not?" a fellow Irishman had said to him, as they gazed down on Monterrey after the arduous march.

"Aye," Riley said, thinking sadly of the wife and son he had left behind in Ireland. "It brings to mind the Glens of Antrim back on the auld sod."

At Monterrey, the army rested and ate well. Riley was promoted from lieutenant to captain for his bombardment of Fort Texas. Fresh Mexican recruits arrived on the southern road from Saltillo, along with artillery, ammunition, and even gold and silver coin to pay soldiers. Riley learned that the Mexican government had passed legislation that would award land grants and farming equipment to deserters from the U.S. ranks. As an officer, he would receive a league and a labor—some 1,200 acres—for his service to Mexico. The captain could not help but dream of bringing his wife and son to Mexico, after the war, where he would live out his life as a landed *patrón* and a celebrated veteran.

At night, Riley would stroll through the streets and plazas from the cathedral to the town fountain, his captain's uniform attracting shy glances from senoritas who smoked small cigars and wore dresses that bared their shoulders and ankles. He enjoyed the music and dancers, sampled intoxicating drinks like tequila, mescal, and pulque. His taste buds savored beef, pork, mutton, and poultry; potatoes, beans, squashes, and tomatoes—all enlivened with spices and herbs and aflame with peppers of varied volatility, ranging from tepid to explosive. These street victuals were almost always consumed without a plate or silverware, by wrapping them in the ubiquitous corn tortilla.

Before long, the foreign deserters from the U.S. Army became celebrities in Monterrey, especially the hulking and handsome Captain John Riley. For a few weeks, Riley enjoyed life in the city and practiced his Spanish. General Ampudia arrived to take over the army, much to Mejia's consternation. Mejia had made almost no preparations for Monterrey's defense. Ampudia, on the other hand, ordered every enlisted man to labor on entrenchments and fortifications. He hired civilian workers, too, and Monterrey quickly became a fortified city. Besides the Citadel, the army added two small earthen forts to protect the eastern edges of the capital city. One was dubbed La Teneria, after a nearby tannery. The other was called El Rincon del Diablo, the Devil's Corner. Each was shaped like a horseshoe, the open side facing back toward the town.

The Bishop's Palace—El Obispado—stood on a high slope west of town known as Independence Hill. The ornate palace, built long ago by Spaniards, had now been fitted with embrasures and artillery that had been dragged up the gentle eastern slope of the *cerro* by men and beasts. The bishop himself consented to Ampudia's plan to use the main cathedral in town for ammunition storage. More recruits and conscripts arrived, swelling the ranks of the Mexican Army of the North to 7,300.

In the city, citizens used sandbags to build snipers' nests on the flat rooftops of houses. Riley learned that most of the houses included roof access via ladders or stairs, either from the outside of the house or within. These ladders or steps facilitated access for maintaining the stucco roofs after rainstorms and for stargazing on pleasant nights. They also gave soldiers easy access to their parapets of sandbags.

And now, on this fine Saturday, the battle for Monterrey seemed poised to commence. General Torrejon's lancers had kept a close eye on General Taylor's approach from the north. Taylor's force, now numbering over six thousand men, had arrived at the patch of timber known as Bosque de San Domingo, a favored picnic site blessed with a strong spring of sweet water. Riley expected General Taylor to attack from his position in the timber, about three miles from the Citadel. He had requested and been granted the command of a battery of two guns on the northeast corner of the Citadel. He had organized his crates of shot, shell, and canister; his ramrods and sponges; his fuses and lanyards. He had drilled his mixed crew of Mexican and Irish gunners. He was ready for battle.

"Captain Riley!"

He turned to Lieutenant Patrick Dalton and found him peering through his telescope. "What is it, Lieutenant?"

"The riders continue to approach from the *bosque*. One rides a pale horse." He looked away from his lenses and smiled at Riley. "I'm damned if it's not Old Whitey. The rider wears a broad-brimmed panama."

Riley leaned over the parapet. With his naked eye he could just make out the distant shapes of the riders. "And almost in range."

"Aye, and that's not all. Another rider looks like your old friend Bragg."

He turned back to the interior of the Citadel. Glancing over the Mexican troops standing or strolling about, he located the plumed campaign hat of his superior officer, Colonel Francisco Rosendo Moreno, who spoke English.

"Colonel Moreno, sir!" he shouted.

The artillery veteran looked up at him.

Riley pointed in the direction of the *bosque*. "*Americanos*, sir! A dozen riders, *más o menos*. One looks like General Taylor himself! I ask permission to fire, Colonel!"

Moreno cocked his head sideways and stared up at Riley for a few seconds. "Prepare to fire, Capitan." The colonel began strolling casually toward Ridley's battery.

Riley smiled and turned to his men as he felt his pulse quicken. "To your posts! Turn this gun!" he ordered. "*Vuelva te!*" he said to the Mexican gunners under his command. "To the right. *Derecho!*"

Together, the men lifted the trail piece of the gun from the ground and muscled the big eighteen-pounder a few degrees to the right.

"There! *Alto!* Lieutenant Dalton! Range?"

"They're beyond the stake we drove for fifteen hundred yards, sir."

Riley felt his temper flare. "Give me the range to the target, Lieutenant, not the bloody stake!"

Dalton seemed shocked by the outburst but pulled his wits together and replied, "Nineteen hundred yards, sir."

Colonel Moreno had climbed to the bastion now and strolled to Dalton's position. "The glass," he said, holding out his hand.

Lieutenant Dalton gladly handed the telescope to the colonel.

Captain John Riley fetched the tangent scale from the gun's tool case. Cut from a flat sheet of steel, the scale's curve on the bottom matched the arch of the gun's breech. He placed the scale on top of the breech and looked down the long tube toward the muzzle. Eyeballing the stair-step notches cut in the top of the tangent scale, Riley chose the notch for 1,900 yards and sighted the target.

"Higher!" he ordered. "*Alto!*" He had become accustomed to giving orders in English and Spanish so all the men in his battery would understand.

Private Hogan stepped in to turn the elevating screw under the breech, raising the trajectory of the tube as Riley continued to sight along a line described by the tangent scale and the muzzle of the gun.

"*Alto!* Stop there!" He looked at Colonel Moreno, who was peering through the telescope at the distant riders. "This gun is ready to fire, Colonel. *Listos!*"

Moreno continued to peer through the scope as he replied in a conversational tone of voice. "They have halted to look over the ground. General Taylor has foolishly exposed himself. Remind him of the perils of such carelessness, Captain. You may fire at your discretion."

"Prime!" Riley barked. He watched impatiently as one of the Mexican gunners inserted the friction primer into the vent hole. The same man stretched the lanyard attached to the primer out to the left of the gun.

"*Listos!*" He checked the positions of the men around him as some covered their ears with their palms. "*Fuego!*"

The eighteen-pounder roared, lurched backwards, and belched an instant plume like a silk flower from the sleeve of a magician. The heavenly scent of scorched powder filled his nostrils. As wind pulled the smoke aside, Riley saw a faraway puff of dust kicked up by the solid cannonball, to the right and short of the target.

"Turn the gun left! *Izquierda!* Halt!" He took hold of the elevating screw with his own hands and gave the tube a touch more elevation.

"Sponge!" He watched and waited as men sponged the bore. "Load!"

A soldier pushed a cartridge containing a powder charge and an eighteen-pound cannonball into the muzzle of the weapon.

"Ram!"

As he continued issuing the orders, a gunner poured priming powder into the touchhole, inserted the primer, and stretched out the lanyard. He imagined his next shot taking Braxton Bragg's head off.

"*Listos!*" He checked his crew. "*Fuego!*"

His eyes blinked at the percussion, then strained to see. A spray of dirt obliterated the enemy riders, and his heart swelled to think that he might have accomplished a direct hit on Bragg or Taylor. Such a shot at this range would become legend! He looked at his commander.

Moreno chuckled as he peered through the telescope. "That one landed a few paces short and bounced right over Taylor's palmetto hat."

Riley sprang for the elevating screw to make the slight adjustment. "Sponge!" he shouted, desperate to get another shot. "Hurry!" His frustrated mind scrambled for the Spanish translation, but he couldn't conjure the word. "Load . . . Ram . . . Prime . . ."

"Cease fire, Capitan," said Colonel Moreno. "General Taylor has chosen to retire from the field."

Riley felt the old rage well up in his viscera. He wanted to bend the steel tangent scale in his hand but knew he needed it intact. He slammed the scale back into the tool kit and kicked toward an ammunition crate, but he stopped short lest he damage the loads. Still his anger swelled. Then he saw the sandbags. Making his hands into fists, he released his ire on a bag, hitting it again and again with his left fist and his right until the fabric ripped open and spilled sand onto the toes of his boots.

"God curse you bastard American heretics!" He saw his own saliva spray from his lips as he railed. "Spawn of the bloody British hordes!" He tore into the next sandbag stacked on the parapet, punching it until his knuckles bled. And still the lifelong ire stewed inside.

Forced out of Ireland! Chased from America! Treated like a dog. No more! No more! This is John Riley's last stand!

He stopped and stared at the sandbag he had beaten to tatters, his lungs heaving like a blacksmith's bellows. He felt his heart pounding furiously in his chest. His muscles strained against the seams of his uniform. Collecting himself, he turned and looked at the men around him, finding them gawking at him as if looking upon a madman. His breath came and went in huge gales.

Colonel Moreno stepped forward and put his hand on Riley's shoulder. "Save your fury for tomorrow, Captain. The enemy will return."

Major General
ZACHARY TAYLOR

The Mexicans called it Bosque de San Domingo—a pleasant picnic ground situated in the timber surrounding a clear creek. The Americans had dubbed the place Walnut Springs. Zachary Taylor—brevetted to major general after Palo Alto and Resaca de la Palma—figured some Yankee volunteer had misnamed the place. As he slipped through the hardwoods with his camp chair, his spare pair of boots, and his polishing kit, he easily identified the big trees towering over him as pecans, not walnuts.

Finding a relatively secluded place out of sight from his headquarters tent, he sat on his chair and opened the bootblack's kit. He was within shouting distance, should some emergency arise. Otherwise, he sought a few minutes' solace from the constant solicitudes of his subordinates— particularly the very thorough William "Perfect" Bliss, who had been brevetted to a major after the recent victories.

Taylor had a second reason for desiring a modicum of aloneness. Four days ago he had looked at his calendar to see the date September 15 taunting him like a haughty stare from the grim reaper. September 15 invariably caused the general great, lingering sorrow. His daughter, Sara, had died on that day, eleven years ago. Now, in his grief, he sought solitude, though solitude was difficult to find in an army camp of 6,600 men.

The boots were his excuse, but both pairs did need polishing. Taylor detested flashy uniforms—he dressed in common civilian clothes, think-

ing of himself more as a Louisiana planter than a general in the army—
but he insisted on keeping his clothing shipshape. This usually entailed
sewing on buttons, darning socks, and patching rips with his own hands.

"You know, General, sir," Bliss had told him two days ago, "we can
pay a laundress to patch that shirt for you. That woman the men call the
Great Western is said to be enamored with you, sir. I am certain she'd
be honored to serve as General Taylor's tailor."

"Nonsense," he had replied, ignoring Bliss's jest. "I'll have it patched
myself before a laundress could find her needle and thread. Besides, it
gives me something productive to do while listening to these blasted volunteers whine about who should have rank over who."

Opening his kit, he removed the stiff-bristled brush and vigorously
knocked the Mexican dust from one of his spare boots. Walnut Springs
was situated only a few miles north of the fortified city of Monterrey,
where the Mexican Army waited. The enemy might attack at any time,
and even if they did not, Taylor planned to begin his offensive against
them at dawn tomorrow. He had no qualms about dying with his boots
on, so long as they wore a proper military shine.

After brushing the boots, he removed his palm leaf hat and threw it
on the ground behind his chair. He was in the shade here, and there was
a nice breeze to cool the sweat on his brow. Now he opened his tin of
boot polish and grabbed a clean rag from the kit. He began at the toe of
the boot, smoothing the black paste over the leather. As he finished the
first boot and prepared to begin on the second, he sensed someone walking his way. Looking up from his task, he saw a man in uniform, wearing the insignia of a captain. Taylor knew all the West Pointers. This
captain was a stranger to him—an officer from one of the new volunteer
units.

"Good morning, old-timer," the captain said, stopping in front of his
chair.

"Mornin', Captain," Taylor drawled, a bit puzzled by the familiar tone.

"Say, you look like you've been marching along with this man's army
quite a spell. I'll bet you can tell me where I might find General Taylor's
headquarters tent. I've just arrived to join my regiment and I need to report."

Taylor smirked, realizing that the man did not recognize him as the
commander of the army in his civilian attire. "Wal, Captain, the general's tent is just over yonder a ways," he said, affecting a pronounced

drawl. He pointed, the rag dangling from his hand. "You can see Old Glory a-poppin' in the wind."

"I see. Thank you, old-timer." The volunteer took one step toward the headquarters tent, then stopped and turned back. "Say, what do you charge for a shine?"

Taylor looked at the captain's footwear. "Fifty cents a boot, but those look right shiny already."

"Not these; my others. I'll run get them."

Taylor chuckled as the captain trotted back the way he had come. He finished working on his spare boots and removed the pair he wore, to polish them next. He wondered if he would actually get away with tricking the captain into paying him fifty cents for bootblack services.

These volunteer officers included all sorts. Some were reliable leaders of men, but many had been elected to their commanding roles based on popularity or wealth, though they might possess scant military knowledge. As a rule, their volunteer units lacked the discipline of regular army men. Back at Matamoros, where the volunteers began to flood his ranks, Taylor had had to crack down on shenanigans ranging from needless gunfire to brawls to abuses of Mexican citizens. He was satisfied that his disciplinary actions had made an impression, but the question remained: Could the volunteers fight?

That uncertainty had dogged him on the hard road from Matamoros, through Camargo and to Cerralvo. Deeming the road too rough for wagons or heavy artillery, he had used pack mules and had brought only light field guns with him. The bull batteries that had served so well at Palo Alto had to be left behind.

At Cerralvo, however, things began to improve. The troops found freshwater in abundance, along with groves of trees and productive pastures. The inevitable illnesses—dysentery and fevers—that had buried more than 1,500 men back on the Rio Grande proved less lethal at Cerralvo.

Even so, new concerns of a political nature began to mount. President Polk and Secretary of War Marcy wrote to Taylor constantly, demanding a long-range strategy for the war. Taylor would commit only to the next objective: Monterrey, the capital city of Nuevo León. He hoped that the Mexicans would sue for peace, should he take Monterrey.

This seemed to infuriate Polk. The state capital of Nuevo León impressed the president very little. He insisted on a plan of war that would include the conquest of Mexico City—the national capital. General Taylor could read between the lines written to him by Polk. He knew, from the glowing newspaper accounts of his leadership at Palo Alto and Resaca de la Palma, that he had become a hero to the citizens of the United States.

Plain old homespun Zach Taylor had begun to receive eager missives from power brokers inside the Whig Party. There was talk of running him for president in 1848. If *he* knew this—here on the lonely Mexican frontier—certainly Polk and the Democrats had realized that he had become a political threat. Taylor was savvy to the ways of politicians. He considered it quite possible that Polk and his cabinet might rush him into an embarrassing defeat that would ruin his chances as a presidential candidate. Taylor did not intend to let this happen. He would not risk the lives of soldiers for the ambitious whims of politicians.

Old Rough and Ready understood that the enemy needed to feel fear and respect for the United States Army, but not hatred. He had seen hatred toward the Mexicans in the eyes of the Texas Rangers, in the words they used and in the way they fought. That ire was the result of the slaughter at the Alamo, the massacre at Goliad, the Black Bean Incident at Salado. Taylor knew that he could have ordered the killing of hundreds more Mexican soldiers as they fled from their defeat at the *resaca* and floundered across the Rio Grande. That would only have ignited a nationwide fury in Mexico. Even in war, there were rules of honor, and commonsense reasons to adhere to them.

The realization that he might actually become president of the United States in the next election would make him more cautious rather than more reckless. He owed more to his men and to the citizens of the United States than he owed to the president.

He glanced up for the captain he had just met, but he didn't yet see the man coming back with his boots. He did, however, recognize a familiar personage walking through the grove in the distance. Just catching sight of the man brought back the old familiar sorrow, touched with a morsel of anger that made him feel ashamed. It was Colonel Jefferson Davis, commander of the Mississippi Rifles. That he should have to share this camp with Jeff Davis almost exactly eleven years after his daughter's death seemed a cruel accident of fate.

He remembered how he had first met West Pointer Jeff Davis at Fort Crawford on the northwestern frontier, just after the Black Hawk War

in 1832. Taylor had taken command of the First Infantry, in which Davis
served as a second lieutenant, and had engaged in a skirmish with Black
Hawk's warriors.

Later, when Taylor's family moved to the fort, Lieutenant Davis would
meet his commander's daughter, Sara Knox Taylor, who was only eigh-
teen. A relationship developed between the two, despite Taylor's objec-
tions. He had no desire to see his daughter marry a soldier. Taylor himself
felt he scarcely knew his own children due to his military service. So
young Jeff Davis resigned his commission and became a civilian so he
could marry Knox, as she was usually called. Still Taylor objected, hoping the infatuation between the two would wane.

But three years passed and Sara Knox Taylor turned twenty-one—
old enough to make her own decisions about whom she should marry.
Still against the union, Zachary Taylor stubbornly refused to attend his
daughter's wedding, though the ceremony occurred at his own sister's
home in Louisville, Kentucky. Mr. and Mrs. Jefferson Davis moved to
Mississippi and began preparations to farm on eight hundred acres of
plantation land given to Jeff by his older brother.

Then the horrible news came, just three months after the wedding.
Jeff and Knox had decided to visit Jeff's sister and her husband at Locust
Grove, in Louisiana. There, both of them came down with malaria. Knox
did not survive. Remembering the reading of the letter that told of his
daughter's agonizing death still caused a withering melancholy to well
up in Old Rough and Ready's heart.

Jeff Davis had barely survived the disease himself. And then, what
did he do? Took off on a trip to Cuba. Cuba! Then New York! He had
gone on to become a successful planter in Mississippi, then a senator. A
few years after the tragedy, Taylor and Davis had accidentally crossed
paths in New Orleans. Over lunch, they talked and reconciled. But
still . . .

Rationally, Taylor knew that disease was to blame for Knox's death.
Emotionally, he could not shake the notion that Jeff Davis had taken his
daughter away from him and gotten her killed. His inability to forgive
made him feel terribly ashamed. Until the day came that he could embrace Jeff Davis as a son, he knew he was not fit to call himself a Christian.

Movement caught the corner of his eye to the right and he looked that
way to see his new acquaintance, the captain of volunteers, trotting toward

him with a pair of dirt-caked boots. He had finished shining his own boots, so he pulled them on as the volunteer approached.

"Here they are, old-timer," the captain said, slowing to a walk and dropping the boots on the grass. "I'll be at the general's headquarters if you care to bring them to me. I have your fifty cents in my pocket."

"Wal, they're a bit dirtier than you let on, but I guess a deal's a deal, Captain."

"I've an extra ten cents for a job well done."

"Fair enough, sir. By the way, the general sometimes wanders off from his headquarters, but he's never gone too long. Wait a spell and he'll wander back."

"Your advice is appreciated." The captain began to drift backwards toward the general's tent. "I will wait at least as long as it takes for you to finish those boots and bring them to me."

"He will surely be back by that time," Taylor said, with an air of authority in his tone.

The captain nodded and walked away.

Taylor knocked the dirty boots together to dislodge some of the dried-on mud. From his kit he produced a small knife that he used to scrape away the stubborn clods that clung to the soles. Meticulously, he brushed clean and then polished the boots to an enviable sheen.

Picking up his hat, his bootblack kit, and the two pairs of boots, he sauntered to his headquarters. He caught sight of the captain conversing with some other officers. He paused until the volunteer looked his way.

"Ah, there you are," the captain said, striding toward him. "Thank you, old-timer. The boots look brand new."

The general glanced about to see the astonished expressions on the faces of the officers within earshot. He gave the boots to the captain and held his hand out for his pay. The captain dropped sixty cents into his waiting palm.

Now Taylor drew himself to attention, jutted his chin, and threw his shoulders back. "Major Bliss! Where are you?"

Bliss appeared from the headquarters tent. "Yes, sir, General Taylor! I'm here!" He rushed to Taylor's side.

Taylor saw the color blanch from the captain's face. "Major Bliss, this officer of the volunteers wishes to report. See that he finds his regiment."

The mortified captain dropped his boots, came to attention, and saluted. "Begging the general's pardon, sir . . . I had no idea that you were . . . Sir, will you accept my most sincere apology?"

Taylor returned the salute and felt a good, hearty laugh roar up from his belly. "No apology needed, Captain. You caught me out of uniform. You are now the only captain in *this man's army* who can afford to pay a general to shine his boots!"

For a moment, as he listened to the nearby officers guffaw at the captain's expense, he felt no worry, no sorrow, no guilt. Then he saw Colonel Jefferson Davis approach the gathering and he remembered the anguish of his loss and the burdens of his overwhelming responsibilities.

Lieutenant Colonel
SAM WALKER

Rain-soaked and hungry, he watched dawn break across the valley. To the south, through the gray morning haze, he could just make out the road to Saltillo hugging the north bank of the Santa Catarina where the river and the road both sliced between two imposing peaks—Federation Hill on the south bank and Independence Hill on the north. His lips curled in a vengeful smirk as he remembered the last time he had passed between those two hills. Four years ago he had marched down the Saltillo road as a prisoner of war. Now he was back, and this valley looked much more appealing through the eyes of a conqueror than those of a captive.

Sam Walker had been elected lieutenant colonel by the men in his recently formed regiment called the First Texas Mounted Volunteers. Though officially volunteers in the U.S. Army, every one of Zach Taylor's soldiers knew them for what they truly were—Texas Rangers. He was second-in-command only to his friend John Coffee Hays. Jack Hays had missed the early battles at Palo Alto and Resaca de la Palma. He had been scouring the Texas settlements, handpicking his recruits and training them for war.

It felt good to be under Hays's command again. Hays was the bravest man Walker knew, though he didn't look like much at first glance. He was neither tall nor particularly muscular. Clean-shaven and wiry, he did not fit the gangling, bearded prototype of the Texas Ranger. But he possessed unaccountable toughness of body and spirit. Everything about

Hays bespoke a fluid grace of movement and certainty of mind and heart. Nobody could shoot straighter than Jack Hays, whether standing flat-footed with his rifle or at a full gallop with a Colt revolver. Horseback, he could throw himself all over his mount like the Comanche he had so often battled. Unhorsed, he could run for days afoot at a long trot—and sometimes did, with the Delaware and Apache scouts he employed.

Like Walker, Hays was now twenty-nine years old. He had come from Tennessee. Walker knew he was kin somehow to Andrew Jackson and had come to Texas after San Jacinto with letters of introduction from men in power. He had met President Sam Houston and presented himself for service to the new Republic of Texas. Houston sent him to join a company of Texas Rangers under Captain Erasmus "Deaf" Smith, Houston's famed spy and hero of the Battle of San Jacinto. By the time he turned twenty-one, Hays was captain of his own company of Rangers.

Walker did not meet Hays until he himself came to Texas, in forty-two. They did not get to know each other well right at first, for Walker found himself captured at Mier and marched to Mexico City as a prisoner. It was only after his escape and return to Texas that he began to ride with Hays's company of Rangers. By this time, Sam Walker was almost as famous as Jack Hays, for his exploits in Mexico had been published in the New Orleans *Picayune*.

When he joined Hays's company, his new commander presented him with two Colt five-shot revolvers manufactured in Patterson, New Jersey.

"Take care of these weapons, Sam," Hays had told him. "Now we will shoot bullets faster than the Comanches shoot arrows." Since that day, it was hard to keep count of all the battles with hostile Comanche, bandits, and regular Mexican troops, including the Sisters Creek fight, where the Comanche lance had run Walker clean through. In all of these engagements, Hays had led with one consistent intent: find the enemy and attack, regardless of the odds.

"When I joined Deaf Smith's Rangers," Hays had told him one night in camp, "there were about ninety boys like me who came to Texas after the Alamo. I can count on one hand those who are still alive."

Walker hadn't seen Hays much during his long convalescence from his lance wound and his return to action under General Taylor. But he was aware of the new development in Hays's life. Captain Jack had fallen in love. He was to marry Susan Calvert, whose family had moved to Texas from Alabama. She was a beautiful girl, Walker thought. But he had to wonder, would Hays's upcoming marriage to Miss Calvert temper his fearlessness? He would likely find out on this very day.

General Taylor had made the risky decision to divide his forces in order to attack Monterrey from the west and the east, simultaneously. The eastern assault was intended as a mere feint. The western division, under General William Worth, was expected to do the real bloody work of storming the city.

The great Jack Hays was now a colonel, and his Rangers were in the vanguard of a sweeping maneuver around the western edges of Monterrey to seize the Saltillo road, Federation Hill, and eventually Independence Hill, upon which the ancient Bishop's Palace perched, now fortified with Mexican infantry and artillery batteries. If they succeeded, they would cut off General Ampudia's line of communications, supplies, and reinforcements from the south, not to mention his ability to retreat. Once that was done—and Walker had no doubt of success—they would attack and take the walled city of Monterrey itself.

Yesterday at noon, he and Jack Hays had met with General William Worth, commander of the western division. Worth had requested that the Rangers lead his advance on western Monterrey.

"Gentlemen," Worth had said at the end of the briefing, "here at Monterrey, I intend to earn a grade or a grave."

Worth had missed the battles in the Rio Grande Valley because he had resigned his commission due to a dispute over who outranked whom in Taylor's chain of command. Worth, a brevet brigadier general, had refused to serve under Colonel David E. Twiggs. He had traveled all the way to Washington, DC, to plead his case. Then, when Worth read the news of Palo Alto, he withdrew his resignation and hurried back to Texas to get in on the fighting. Yes, General Worth was obsessed with promotion, but Walker considered that a good motivation to win the upcoming fight. Walker had his own obsessions and motives, mostly centered around revenge.

Yesterday afternoon they had ridden from Walnut Springs, circling far around the Mexican batteries on Federation Hill. In the distance, behind them, they had heard the cannonade begin between Taylor's batteries and the Black Fort—a fortified cathedral that the Mexicans called the Citadel. Here, on the western outskirts, the Rangers had skirmished with Mexican cavalry and dodged enemy artillery fire.

Last night, a hard rain had pelted them for hours. They had brought no tents or rations with them, and though they had found pigs and chickens to slaughter at an abandoned farmhouse, they discovered that if they lit cooking fires, the Mexican gunners lobbed shells at them in the dark. But cold and hungry was often the Rangers' way, and Walker didn't dwell on hardships. The damp chill only made his old wounds ache for new companions.

As for the hunger, he remembered something he had heard General David Twiggs say back at Walnut Springs, explaining why he always took a laxative the night before a battle: "A bullet striking the belly when the bowels are loose might pass through the intestines without cutting them."

If that were true, Walker thought, this would be as good a day as any for a belly wound, for he hadn't eaten a bite in almost twenty-four hours.

By the dark of the predawn hours, they had advanced to this point, until Colonel Hays called a halt to let his men catch some rest and await daybreak. Now the Rangers slowly woke by ones and twos and fumbled with their tack and weapons, readying themselves for another eventful day of rangering.

Peering through the mist across the Saltillo road, Walker suddenly caught signs of movement. Colors, rendered pastel by the light fog, nonetheless emerged. Reds, blues, greens. Tunics, pennons, plumes. Cavalry. Mexican lancers. They were already on the move, and some of the Rangers were still sleeping.

"Jack," he said, just loud enough that Hays could hear him, some thirty paces away.

"I see them," Hays replied. The colonel mounted his horse. He was hatless, having lost his sombrero somewhere in the dark. He had a red bandana tied on his head like some reckless pirate. "Get the men ready. I'll buy us some time."

"Wake up, boys!" Walker kicked a young recruit lying on the ground with his hat over his face. "Draw your cinches and prepare to mount. Check your loads, too. The Mexicans are just across the way, there."

Wondering what Hays had in mind, he mounted his horse for a higher vantage from which to watch the colonel lope his steed gracefully toward the lancers, a rifle shot away. Under the lifting fog, he could now make out an entire regiment of Mexican cavalrymen, led by a colonel wearing a red-plumed hat. They had obviously spotted the Rangers, for they had spread out in line formation in preparation to attack. The Rangers were outnumbered two or three to one, but this would matter little to "Devil Jack," as Hays was known among Mexicans and Indians.

Hays reined in his mount halfway between the two forces and made a grandiloquent bow from the saddle. The valley was quiet enough that Walker heard his commander's shout, aimed at the Mexican leader: "Colonel! *Desafiarte a un duelo en este terreno! Hombre a hombre!*"

A duel? Walker thought. *Man to man?* He held his breath, hoping to catch the Mexican colonel's reply. It came almost instantly, in a bold baritone: *"Acepto!"*

Walker shook his head as he smiled. This was Jack Hays's idea of buying a little time? "Rangers!" he shouted. "Mount up! You're gonna want to see this."

Hays rode back toward his men, turning his horse in tight circles, first to the right, then to the left, filling the mount with excitement for the charge. Meanwhile, the Mexican colonel threw down his hat, removed his coat, tossed aside his canteen and other accoutrement unnecessary for dueling. Finally, he drew his saber and waited, his fiery mount prancing most gracefully beneath him.

Walker squinted through the day's first ray of sunlight. He saw Colonel Hays draw his sword. Both combatants charged into the middle ground, their mounts kicking up mud as they built speed. Walker worried over Hays's inexperience with the saber but no longer had any questions about the amount of sand left in the craw of the groom-to-be.

At full gallop, the two duelists closed the distance between them quickly. Ten lengths shy of the clash, Hays suddenly threw his sword aside and veered slightly to his right. He drew a Colt five-shooter from his belt, threw his body down across the right side of his horse, reached under the neck of his mount with his revolver in hand, and fired a shot that hit the brave Mexican colonel in the chest. The vanquished leader rolled backwards over the rump of his horse and hit the ground, dead.

Hays wheeled his horse to return to the Rangers. "Dismount!" he shouted. "Sam! Dismount the men!"

Walker understood the strategy. "Dismount, boys! They'll be coming madder than hornets! Use your rifles first. Keep your mounts in front of you!"

A bugle sounded the charge on the Mexican side and some four hundred lancers sprang forward from the Saltillo road. He cocked his rifle and rested it over the seat of his saddle.

Hays returned to the line, leaped from his horse, and drew his carbine from his saddle scabbard. "Hold your fire!"

The horses of the Rangers, trained at this maneuver, behaved remarkably well with the enemy regiment rumbling down upon them.

"Hold your fire and don't forget to aim!" Hays shouted, as cool as ever.

As Walker watched the glorious menace of the Mexican assault, the steel lance points, jutting skyward, began to dip downward, the nine-inch blades threatening ghastly injury and vicious death. The leveling points made his heart pound, but he shoved aside thoughts of another lance wound and picked his target—the attacker advancing nearest to him. Over the iron sights of his rifle, he drew a deadly bead.

"Hold your fire!" Hays ordered. "Hold . . . *Aim* . . . Fire!"

The entire line of Rangers erupted in white smoke and rifle balls as enemy riders tumbled from their saddles. Walker saw his target drop dead from the back of his mount just a few steps away. Mexican horses plunged wildly through the Texas front, carrying empty saddles or riders, both untouched and wounded, some slamming into the mounts of Rangers and knocking men off their feet.

Walker held tightly to his reins as his warhorse pulled in alarm. The Mexicans fought to check their mounts, but their battle-crazed beasts charged fifty yards or more beyond the Rangers before the lancers could regroup for another assault. Walker was satisfied to see that, beyond them, though too far away to be of help anytime soon, the main body of General Worth's division was marching toward the Saltillo road.

Knowing there would be no time to reload their long arms, he returned his to his saddle scabbard, having settled his mount. "Boot your rifles, men! Grab your pistols! Keep your mounts in front of you!" Around him, he saw all his men standing, though a few held bleeding wounds from the lance blades.

"Get ready!" Hays yelled down the line. "We can whip them if we stand our ground!"

The second Mexican charge was on its way.

"Hold," Hays yelled. "Aim . . . Fire!"

Again, the deafening staccato of gunshots rang. Bullets tore into the gaudy uniforms of the lancers that charged courageously through the line of Rangers, though one in five were shot from their saddles. Walker had time to use two rounds from his Colt and emptied two more saddles as a result. And still the lancers turned and regrouped for yet another charge.

Smoke stung his nostrils as Walker looked to one side to see a young recruit throw his single-shot pistol down and draw his bowie knife.

"Private!" he yelled, handing his Colt revolver to the young man. "There are three live rounds left in there."

The wild-eyed private nodded appreciatively and took the gun. "Thanks, sir!"

"I want that back, you hear?"

"Yes, sir!"

Walker drew his second Colt revolver and pulled his horse in front of him, once again resting his firearm across his saddle seat. Amazed at the resilience of the Mexicans, he still sensed a lack of zeal in this third charge. The enemy mounts were winded, and the men had to be demoralized by their losses.

"Fire at will!" Hays hollered.

The next volley killed a score of enemy riders and halted the attack. The Mexican bugler was blowing the retreat from somewhere far down the line, but the bloody lancers were already falling back, some stopping to pick up their dead or wounded. Walker glanced about him and saw one young Ranger sprawled on the ground, apparently dead. Others had been slashed by lance blades, but none of those injuries appeared mortal.

Sergeant Buck Barry, an experienced Ranger, strode among the recruits, goading them up. "There's more to come today, boys! We've yet to secure the road or take a hill. Catch the loose horses. We'll need them. Reload your weapons."

The sergeant ambled toward Walker. "The boys done good," he said.

Walker nodded. "They made a hell of a thrust, but we stood our ground."

"We must have killed eighty of them."

"I'd say closer to a hundred," Walker replied.

"I'll never call a Mexican a coward again."

Walker took the borrowed revolver back from the young recruit. "We are on their ground now, Sergeant. They *will* fight."

Colonel
JOHN COFFEE HAYS

Hays stood on the battleground, holding the reins to his mount. He
watched a small party of his Rangers escorting his wounded men to the
rear, behind General Worth's line, where a surgeon's tent presumably
would be established. Most of the injured men could still ride, but one had
to be borne away on an improvised litter made from a tarpaulin stretched
between two Mexican cavalry lances, carried by four Rangers on foot.

Enemy round shot from Federation Hill, across the river, began to
thud into the prairie around the Rangers. Hays looked up the Saltillo
road, which led to the outskirts of Monterrey, where he saw Mexican infantry marching toward him. He knew more cavalry would be coming,
too, to avenge their slain riders.

Swinging his gaze back to the rear, he spotted a battery of flying
artillery speeding into position to shell the enemy foot soldiers. Behind
them, Worth's main column marched double-quick. He smiled, sensing
the odds shifting to favor the American assault.

He took a swig from his canteen and rinsed the dust and grit from
his mouth, spitting it into a shiny puddle of fresh blood on the ground
in front of him. He wondered what his fiancée, Susan, would have thought
about his duel with the Mexican colonel. He realized that this was the
first time in his life he had ever considered what a woman might think
of his martial exploits. He decided it was better not to ponder it.

He liked thinking of Susan, though. He remembered the picnics they had enjoyed, an easy buggy ride beyond the outskirts of San Antonio. They would find a shady spot with clear water running among live oaks or bald cypress trees and feast on the treats she had prepared. On the way back to town, he would hand the reins of the buggy horse over to Susan and jump out to run alongside the vehicle for a few miles to keep his legs and lungs strong. Susan would laugh at him and shake her head as he paced the horse's trot.

Hoofbeats snapped his mind back to the Saltillo road. He looked up to see Sam Walker approaching with the regiment's five captains. Good. Walker was always reliable, and frequently indispensable. The men rode up, pulled rein, and dismounted.

"Gentlemen, we have prodded the dragon," Hays began. "They will send many more to avenge those we have already slain. It's time for some Comanche strategy."

He looked at thirty-four-year-old Ben McCulloch, artillery veteran of San Jacinto, cavalry commander against the Comanche at the battle of Plum Creek, and hardened veteran of dozens of Ranger campaigns. "Ben, mount your company. You'll be the bait." Hays pointed to the road leading into Monterrey. "Wait there until the lancers come around that hill and see you. When they attack, you retreat."

McCulloch scowled.

"I know you don't like to retreat, Ben, but you'll get your chance to draw blood."

Now Hays addressed his other four captains. "The rest of you will dismount your companies. Order every fifth man to conceal the horses in the chaparral. We will place you in ambush along the road. When the enemy follows Captain McCulloch's retreat down the road, open fire."

He looked into the eyes of Captain Richard Addison Gillespie, a thirty-one-year-old Ranger veteran. Like McCulloch and Sam Walker, he had served at the Battle of Sisters Creek. He and Walker had both been run through by Comanche lances there. Though Hays had expected neither to survive that day, both stood before him now, ready for the next fight.

"Ad, conceal your men in that ravine across the road."

Gillespie nodded.

Next in the circle was Captain Kit Acklin, another survivor of Sisters Creek.

"Kit, hide your company in that cornfield to the left of the road."

"All right, Jack."

"Captain Green, place your company behind that stone wall. Major Chevaille, you take the next arroyo."

The men nodded and all turned away to take up their positions, save Walker, who stayed with Hays.

"What about you and me?" Walker said.

"We'll ride a furlong toward Saltillo," Hays replied. "When McCulloch's retreat reaches us, we'll order him to turn and attack the enemy."

"Very well, Jack. We'll attack with him, of course."

"Of course."

They galloped to their position down the road and turned to watch the Rangers slip into their hiding places. As the last men concealed themselves, a rattle of gunfire came from the direction of Monterrey. Captain McCulloch's company came at a gallop, retreating from a battalion of Mexican cavalry riding hot behind them. McCulloch led the pursuers into the jaws of a deadly cross fire as Gillespie and Acklin, then Green and Chevaille, ordered their companies to fire. The effect on the lancers was horrific. Men toppled from their saddles by the score.

Quickly, McCulloch was upon Hays and Walker, the pursuit of the Mexicans having faltered.

"About-face, Ben!" shouted Hays. "Charge them!"

He and Walker sprang forward on their rested mounts to lead the counterattack. Dismounted Rangers poured out from the gullies, cornfields, and chaparral, and from behind the rock walls, crowding the Mexicans so closely that their long lances became ineffective. The Texans dragged men from saddles and clubbed them with empty pistols, stabbed with swords and bowie knives.

Now Hays, Walker, and McCulloch's bloodthirsty company rode full speed into the melee, firing single-shot pistols, Paterson Colt revolvers, and sawed-off double-barreled shotguns, turning the Mexican attack into a crippled retreat back toward Monterrey.

Hays watched as a Mexican lancer swung the shaft of his weapon into the face of one of McCulloch's men, Jim Freaner—a former newspaper reporter with the New Orleans *Delta*—unhorsing Freaner. Fearing Freaner would get lanced, Hays was surprised to see the erstwhile journalist spring to his feet, draw his pistol, and shoot the Mexican lancer from the saddle. Then, quickly, he caught the reins of the slain enemy's mustang and leaped aboard the captured mount.

Now, beyond the feat he had just witnessed by Freaner, Hays noticed General Worth's column approaching—Worth himself at the head of his division.

"Let them go!" Hays shouted, as the enemy cavalry unit retreated back toward Monterrey. "We have the road! That's what we came for." He looked at the dead men scattered on the ground around him. He didn't see any of his own men dead, and only a few were nursing wounds.

"Colonel Hays!" shouted Worth as he cantered to the scene. "Well done. That was a splendid maneuver."

Hays nodded politely. "The road to Saltillo is now ours, General. My regiment is at your service for the next objective."

"Precisely what I came to talk to you about. I believe we must attack Federation Hill immediately." He pointed to the long, narrow hill across the river to the south, its ridge adorned with two fortified batteries— one on the east, the other on the west. "I have held a council of war with my officers. Half of them think the hill can be taken. The other half fear our losses would be too heavy, due to the steep incline. What say you, Colonel?"

Hays did not hesitate to answer. "It can be done, sir. In my opinion, the western division can take it."

"Then we'd better do so before enemy reinforcements arrive from Saltillo. Give me three hundred Rangers. I will send a like number of my infantry."

"Yes, sir."

"You have half an hour."

"We are ready now, General."

Worth smiled. "Then kindly grant *me* half an hour to secure this road before we attack that hill."

Hays nodded. "As you wish, sir."

Worth reined away and Colonel Jack Hays turned to look up at Federation Hill. His men would have to cross the swift Santa Catarina River in full view of Mexican gunners and musketeers. Then they would have to scale the steep, rocky slopes to storm the two fortified positions on either end of the hill. So be it. This was why he came to Mexico.

Captain
JOHN RILEY

From his vantage on the northeast bastion of the Citadel, Captain John Riley had watched the enemy battalion massing to the northeast, just out of artillery range.

Lieutenant Patrick Dalton stepped up to his side. "How many do you reckon now, Captain?"

"Not enough to take this fort," he said with sincere confidence. He estimated the American battalion at eight hundred men, but he saw no reason to alarm his gunners with such numbers.

For twenty-four hours, Taylor's army had been shelling the Citadel, with little effect on materiel or morale. The Mexican gunners occasionally fired back, but the commander of the Citadel, Colonel Francisco Moreno, wisely preferred to save ammunition to defend against an all-out infantry attack.

General Taylor's engineers had found a secure place from which to operate—a natural depression in the terrain, just deep enough to protect their gunners and supporting infantry from the Citadel's fire. Still, Taylor had not brought much heavy artillery with him. Riley knew from the reports of spies, scouts, and deserters that Taylor had just one ten-inch mortar and two twenty-four-pounder howitzers hidden down in the swale. These high-trajectory arms were difficult to fire with any accuracy. Riley felt quite secure in the Citadel.

Behind him, he heard hoofbeats. He turned to see the gates of the fort open to admit a courier from Monterrey. The rider jumped from his horse and ran to Colonel Moreno as he reached into his tunic to present the correspondence he carried.

Riley slapped Lieutenant Dalton on the shoulder. "Keep a sharp eye about you. I'm bound to see what this rider is about." He trotted down the slope from the battery. By the time he arrived at Moreno's side, the rider was already in the saddle and on his way back to Monterrey.

"Colonel Moreno, sir," Riley barked. "Captain Riley reporting to receive new orders." He presented a salute and looked at the wrinkled note, which Moreno was still reading.

Casually, Moreno returned the salute, seemingly amused by Riley's boldness. "Are you wondering about the courier's correspondence, Captain?"

"Only if it pleases the colonel to inform me, sir."

Moreno smiled. "Very well. The Americans have succeeded in securing the Saltillo road to the west of Monterrey. Do you know what this means, Captain?"

"Yes, sir. No supplies. No reinforcements. No communications with the government."

"And no retreat."

Riley nodded. "For my men, there must be no surrender. We are ready to fight to the death."

"Of course you are. If you surrender, you will be hanged as traitors. Why do you think I requested that your men join my company of gunners?" He gave Riley a self-satisfied smile.

"Colonel, my men are honored to serve with Mexico against this invasion of *hereticos*."

"You will get your chance, Captain. Very soon, if I am not mistaken." Moreno lifted an eyebrow in a fatherly kind of way. "Tell me, Captain Riley. Do you ever regret deserting the American Army?"

"Never. I was treated like a dog in that army. But here, among fellow Catholics, I enjoy the respect of my brothers in arms. Here, I am a *capitan*!" He knew he was telling the colonel what he wanted to hear, but in truth he meant every word.

Moreno nodded in approval. "*Bueno*, Capitan. I expect you and your men to teach the *Yanquis* about the perils of invading *Madre México*."

Riley drew himself up to his full height and saluted. Just as the colonel returned the salute, Lieutenant Dalton called out from Riley's battery. "Captain Riley! The drums! Taylor has ordered the long roll!"

"To your post!" Colonel Moreno said, his eyes flashing with defiance. "They are coming!"

Riley ascended the earthworks in great strides and found Dalton looking through the telescope over the sandbags.

"Report, Lieutenant."

"I can make out the colors of the First and Third infantries."

"Under General Twiggs," Riley said, more to himself than to his lieutenant.

"It would seem so, sir. I also recognize the new regiments from Tennessee, Mississippi, and Baltimore."

Riley chuckled. "So, Taylor wants to try out his volunteers. Any cavalry?"

"None, sir."

"Artillery?"

"I spotted but a single battery of the flying artillery, sir."

"Under whose command?"

Dalton handed the telescope to his superior with a grin. "It appears to be none other than the cursed lout Braxton Bragg, sir." He pointed. "You know he's a brevet captain now, sir."

"Is that a fact?"

"Aye, sir, according to the latest deserters from the American ranks."

Riley trained the glass on the broad American line now marching toward the Citadel. Through the lenses, he quickly spotted the horse-drawn limbers of the flying artillery. Then he recognized Braxton Bragg, the worst of the nativist officers, astride a tall sorrel.

"Come closer then, will you, you bloody bastard," Riley said in a growling voice.

"Not likely, sir. Twiggs won't march his men straight between the Citadel and La Teneria."

Riley looked toward the southeast, at the old tannery on the outskirts of town, about a mile away. Near the tannery building, General Ampudia had ordered the construction of a horseshoe-shaped earthen fort named for the adjacent hide works—La Teneria. Dalton had a point. Attacking one fort or the other made some military sense. But to march *between* the Citadel and La Teneria, within range of the guns of both forts, was unthinkable. Yet, on came the U.S. battalion.

Colonel Moreno stepped up behind Riley, having climbed the earthworks at his leisure. "Load canister," he said calmly.

"Load canister!" Riley echoed in a shout. He watched as his men moved like the gears of a Swiss clock, meticulously loading the fixed cartridges of powder and canister—tin cylinders filled with hundreds of lead balls. When fired, each flimsy tin can would rupture, releasing the .70-caliber projectiles in a deadly hailstorm.

"Ram!"

He looked at the enemy again, astonished to see them still marching on a course that would lead them between the two Mexican forts.

"Arrogant fools," Colonel Moreno said.

"Prime!"

"*Numero uno*," the colonel said.

"*Numero uno!*" Riley shouted to the artillerymen at their stations around cannon number one. *Listos!*"

He looked at the colonel. The colonel nodded.

"*Fuego!*" Riley ordered.

The Irish gunner who held the primer's lanyard against his hip leaned away from the cannon and twisted his hips, as he had been trained, to make a sharp and steady pull on the cord. The primer shot sparks down the touchhole and sent the load hurling toward the American line.

Through his field glass, Riley witnessed a swath of men in sky-blue uniforms drop from the ranks as others stepped over their bodies and continued to march. Cross fire from La Teneria raked the American front with another wave of lead, causing similar damage.

"*Dos*," the colonel said. "*Listos?*"

"*Numero dos!*" Riley shouted. "*Listos!*"

"*Fuego.*"

"*Fuego!*"

The mammoth siege gun roared and lurched back on its chocks.

"Now, Capitan," Moreno said, "you may fire at will. Prove to me that you know the skills of an artillery officer. Protect this fort and the city of Monterrey." The colonel turned toward the southeast bastion to direct more firing from that point.

"Reload!" Riley yelled, feeling a surge of power he had scarcely even dreamed of possessing. He handed the telescope to Lieutenant Dalton. "Patrick, you are my eyes."

"Aye, sir!"

As he waited for his gunners to ram home the loads in his two eighteen-pounders, he noticed that the American line had ceased to march. Through the ringing in his ears, he could tell that the U.S. drums had fallen silent. Riley figured the enemy had realized the folly of marching between the two Mexican forts.

"Hurry, you *scalpeens*," he said to his men, "before they sound the retreat!"

His lieutenant, Patrick Dalton, trained the spyglass on the invading battalion. "Holy Mother Mary," he said. "Captain, they're reforming their battle line. They don't aim to retreat. They mean to charge upon the city!"

"Bloody fools. Let them try. Number one! *Uno! Listos! Fuego!*"

As he spoke, he saw Captain Braxton Bragg's battery of flying artillery dash ahead of the American infantry.

"Number one, reload! Lieutenant, give me the glass and swing the number two gun to the right. Follow Bragg's advance! *Numero dos, derecho!*" Through the spyglass, he watched as Bragg's battery halted to unlimber his two guns in preparation to shell the city of Monterrey.

The U.S. bugles ordered the charge as the voices of some seven hundred invaders yelled a battle cry. Over one hundred of them were already dead or wounded by the enfilading fire from La Teneria and the Citadel.

"*Numero uno, listos! Fuego!*"

The first gun roared and rocked aft.

"Patrick, are you on Bragg yet?"

"Almost, sir!"

"Reload number one," Riley said to the gunner manning the lanyard.

Dalton was eyeballing the target down the tube of the eighteen-pounder. "I'm on him, Captain! I've got Bragg!"

"*Numero dos!*" Riley thought back to the day at Fort Texas when Bragg had thrown a bucket of dirt clods in his face. "*Listos!*" Earlier, at Corpus Christi, Bragg had slapped him for no good reason and had insulted his Irish ancestry. He waited, allowing the infantry charge to catch up to Bragg's battery, which was almost loaded and ready to fire at the city.

Here's a bushel of Irish retribution, he thought.

"*Fuego!*"

Dalton's aim proved true. Hunks of lead kicked up dust and peppered

Bragg's battery. A gunner went down, holding what was left of his leg. A horse stumbled in its rigging and fell sideways, kicking. Another volley of canister from La Teneria tore into the invaders from the other direction, dropping another gunner and some charging infantrymen passing by. A load from the Citadel's southeast bastion fell short, but the spherical projectiles bounced and reached Bragg's beleaguered battery, splintering ammunition crates and the bones of the gunners.

"Reload number two!" Riley shouted. He noticed that the Americans' charge was now too far advanced for his first gun to fire, as the second gun now blocked its shooting lane. "Number one, stand down!"

Now it was evident to Riley that the enemy assault was intended all along to capture La Teneria, not the Citadel. The Americans had fought their way so close to La Teneria that firing upon them from the Citadel at this point would endanger his fellow Mexican Army gunners at the redoubt. Why the Americans had approached La Teneria between the two forts was still a mystery to Riley. What a blunder Twiggs had made, to the tune of two hundred American casualties. He could have stayed out of range of the Citadel and assaulted La Teneria from the east or southeast. At any rate, the only target Riley still had in range was Braxton Bragg's crippled artillery battery.

Riley looked through his field glass. To his disappointment, Bragg stood untouched and unfazed. His fieldpieces had fired once each at the stone walls of Monterrey, the exploding shells causing scant demolition. Bragg was gesturing violently at his men to reload and continue firing.

"Sir?"

Riley tore his eye away from the glass and looked at Lieutenant Dalton, finding him ready to fire the reloaded cannon. Riley nodded. "Fire."

"*Fuego!*" Dalton yelled.

The giant scattergun slung another tin can of man-made hail through the ranks of the U.S. artillerymen, yet Bragg remained unscathed.

"Reload!"

Riley glanced beyond Bragg to see that the infantry charge had effectively been halted, though a few tough and lucky Americans had survived to reach the outskirts of Monterrey, where Mexican defenders now fired down on them with muskets, from sandbagged rooftops. Though the charge had moved beyond the range of the Citadel, La Teneria continued to hammer the invaders.

When he looked back at Bragg, he saw something he couldn't make sense of, so he trained his telescope on the flying artillery again. While Bragg's surviving men reloaded the field guns, Bragg himself hovered over a slain horse, busying himself by stripping the harnesses and rigging from the carcass of the beast. He seemed not to notice the salvo that ripped through his ranks from La Teneria.

"What the devil is he doing?" Lieutenant Dalton asked.

Riley shrugged. "I suppose he doesn't want the rigging to fall into the hands of his enemies. Is the gun ready?"

"So it will be in a flash, sir."

Riley panned across Bragg's battery with his scope. He made out several corpses strewn about. A horse with its guts protruding from a belly wound grazed as if mindless of its hopeless plight. Men too wounded to stand took refuge between two of the guns, which offered a modicum of protection from the cross fire.

"It's ready, sir! *Listos!*"

Riley looked into the black eyes of the Mexican corporal who manned the lanyard on the eighteen-pounder. He glanced back toward Bragg, then again at the corporal. "*Pobres pendejos,*" he said. *Poor assholes.*

The corporal nodded, pulled a bit of slack from the lanyard.

"*Fuego!*"

Captain
ELECTUS BACKUS

You are really in it now, Electus. What have you gotten yourself into?

He tried to gather his wits. He willed himself to think in spite of the screams of nearby men and the roar of distant cannon from two forts, to function through the odors of guts and smoke.

Stop! Think! Look at your surroundings!

He started with himself. By some miracle, he was unwounded. He found himself holding his saber and felt ridiculous because of it. As he sheathed the weapon, he saw a musket on the ground before him. He picked it up. Looking around now, he found a dead soldier missing part of his head. He took the belt with its ammunition pouch from the soldier's corpse.

A load of canister ripped through the men around him, taking two of them down. It was as if God had hurled a handful of thunderbolts at him to get his attention. He looked back at the American line and found that he was closer to the dwellings of Monterrey than any other U.S. soldier in sight. His instincts made him yearn for cover as a musket ball hummed by his ear. His eyes locked in on the nearest building—an adobe farmhouse in the middle of a cornfield on the outskirts of town.

"You, Private!" Captain Electus Backus said to the man nearest to him. "Get to that house! Get to cover!"

The man, dazed and bug-eyed, looked at the adobe and began

stumbling toward it. A couple of his comrades followed, absorbing the logic of utilizing the protective walls.

"Hey!" Backus yelled at a clot of infantrymen trying to reload. "Take that house! We need the cover!"

Now he had managed a small amount of movement on the stalled front line. He waved and yelled at others to follow, directing a burly sergeant to lead what was left of his company to the mud-brick home in the shot-ravaged cornfield.

He, too, ran toward the cover of the walls. As he leaped over the dead and dying, he thought about his father, whom he barely remembered. Electus Backus Sr. had died as a lieutenant colonel, defending Sackets Harbor in 1813. Young Electus Jr. was only nine years old then, but he would learn how his father had stood firm on the right flank until he fell to a British musket ball late in the day.

This might be my day, the forty-two-year-old West Pointer thought. He knew his father had lingered for eight anguished days before dying.

Storming the abandoned farmhouse and its surrounding stalks of corn, Captain Backus's new makeshift company grew to about a hundred souls who had instinctively joined the advance. The first soldiers had already stormed the house, finding it abandoned.

"Reload and catch your breath, men! Take cover in the tall corn." He saw a young soldier who had lost his weapon in the chaos. "Take this musket, Private, and don't lose this one!"

"Yes, sir," the boy said, gratefully accepting the weapon and ammunition.

Backus saw a ladder leading to the roof of the farmhouse. He knew it was risky, but he desired the elevation for a better look around. As he ascended, he wondered if the farmer and his family had been fond of climbing up on the roof to look at the stars at night. Standing on the flat dirt roof, he looked to the northeast and found that the rest of his battalion had retreated through the galling canister storm from the Black Fort and La Teneria. He must have missed the order to withdraw in the noise of the bombardment. He was alone here, on the outskirts of Monterrey.

Now he looked farther toward the east, at the nearest building—a larger two-story made of stone. *That's the distillery,* he thought, remembering the combat engineers' map of the Mexican defenses east of Monterrey. And beyond the distillery he could see the new earthen redoubt called La Teneria.

A bullet landed between his boots and he knew he had been spotted by some distant sniper. He clambered down the ladder and found the sergeant who had helped him rally the men. He didn't know this sergeant, as the men had been gathered haphazardly from the remnants of various companies from different regiments in the confusion of the cross fire.

"Sergeant, we're going to take the next building. It's the tequila distillery. On the other side of it is La Teneria—the fort that was blasting the hell out of us a minute ago."

The sergeant grinned. "Listen here, boys!"

Captain Backus was surprised to hear the man speak with a thick Irish brogue. It was rare for an immigrant to attain the rank of sergeant in this army.

"I said shut up and listen to your orders!" A bullet hit the adobe wall a foot from the Irishman's head. "The captain has ordered us to take the next building, and by God, we will take it!" He looked at Backus. "Captain?"

Backus saw no reason to hesitate, as the enemy musket fire grew on his current position, the bullets popping through the leaves and stalks of corn. "On your feet, men!" He drew his saber. "Charge!"

The captain and his new sergeant began running between rows of corn, toward the distillery no more than a hundred yards away. As his band of survivors trailed along behind, Backus heard the battle yell welling up from the desperate men. He, too, loosed a scream, which scarcely sounded as if it could have come from his own lungs.

When the Mexican defenders on the top of the distillery looked over the walled-in roof, they seemed astonished to see Americans charging their position from the west. They hastily opened fire. Backus heard screams and shouts behind him as men were hit, yet he charged on. He sprang over an irrigation ditch and took cover behind a rock wall enclosing the compound of the distillery.

"Halt here!" he ordered, gasping for breath. "They're reloading. Prepare to fire at the rooftop when they appear again!"

As the men took cover behind the wall, using it to steady their muskets and rifles against their heaving lungs, the heads of enemy soldiers began to appear again over the top of the tannery roof. The first Mexican soldiers to show themselves were killed almost instantly.

"Shoot through the windows! Make it hot for them in there!"

The men released a rough salvo at the few windows on the west side and soon saw Mexicans pouring out of the building and running toward the next earthen fort to the south—a smaller, horseshoe-shaped redoubt called El Diablo. One of the captain's American riflemen killed a fleeing Mexican as he ran.

Backus waited for a few men around him to reload, but could hesitate no longer. "Bayonets!" he yelled as he leaped the wall, waving his saber. "Charge, men, we've got them on the run!"

As he sprinted among strange vats and pine shipping crates, a long-legged private outran him to the nearest door. The young soldier jumped into the doorway and fired his musket as a Mexican bullet tore through his chest, sending him reeling backwards. Backus charged in, wielding his saber in the relative darkness of the room. He smelled the strong, sickening odor of fermenting agave as he felt his blade hit someone. As his eyes adjusted and scores of Americans swarmed in behind him, he focused on enemy soldiers crawling out of windows. Guns fired and bayonets rushed forward as the Americans overwhelmed the defenders, killing some and chasing others up the stairs.

The Irish sergeant led the charge up the stairway, followed by his enlivened troops. Falling in at the bottom of the stairwell, Backus could hear the hand-to-hand melee above him. He felt astonished at the bravery of his men, and even at his own courage, as the momentum swept him upward and he became oblivious to any thought of personal injury.

Bursting onto the second floor, he slipped in a pool of someone's blood but quickly recovered his balance. His men had killed the few enemy defenders on the upper floor. Captain Backus saw a ladder that led through a trapdoor to the rooftop. He sheathed his bloody saber so he could climb the ladder. Emerging into the daylight, he found only corpses of Mexican soldiers on the roof. He pulled himself up, gasping for breath. Taking his campaign hat from his head, he peeked over the two-foot rock wall that protected the roof.

Now Backus noticed something he had been unable to see from the roof of the farmhouse. There was another building, 120 yards away, that was closer still to La Teneria. He knew from briefings and councils of war that this was the tannery that had given name to the new fort—La Teneria. The old tannery, a large stone building, had been fortified by General Ampudia's soldiers. As he looked harder, he realized that the enemy soldiers on the tannery roof were firing north at the retreating Americans, over sandbags stacked on the roof. But on this side—the west—there were no sandbags. The Mexican musketeers were exposed and were unaware that the distillery had been taken.

Backus scrambled back to the trapdoor and shouted down to the floor below. "Sergeant! Where are you?"

"I am here, Captain!" the man yelled back.

"What is your name, Sergeant?"

"Maloney, sir."

"Sergeant Maloney, order half the men to defend the doors and windows downstairs. Order the other half to reload before they climb to the roof. Tell them to keep low and out of sight once on top."

Captain Backus heard Maloney barking orders below. Soon infantrymen began to climb to the roof, their bayonets leading the way through the trapdoor. He ordered the bloodstained soldiers to crawl and spread out along the inside of the east wall, facing the tannery. Sergeant Maloney now appeared at the top of the ladder, on the roof.

Backus pointed at the tannery. "That will be our target, Sergeant."

"Glory be," Maloney said, looking over the wall at the tannery. "They didn't expect anyone to get this far, did they, sir?"

"I want four ranks, Maloney. The first rank will fire, then fall back to reload, and so on. Understand?"

"Perfectly, sir!"

Maloney began dividing the men into four ranks of about ten men each. When they were in place, Backus gave his orders.

"First rank! On my order!"

"Wait!" Backus said. "Listen, men. You are sharpshooters now. Aim accordingly and don't waste a single ball. Go ahead, Sergeant."

"Prepare to fire!" Maloney ordered. "Ready . . . Aim . . . Fire!"

The musket salvo peppered the sandbags and uniforms atop the tannery.

"Fall back! Next rank, forward!"

The men in the second rank crawled forward and used the wall as their rifle rest. "Ready . . . Aim . . . Fire!"

The third rank fired, then the fourth. The first rank had reloaded by now, and the well-timed barrage had cleared the tannery roof of defenders.

Captain Electus Backus heard the strains of a bugle through the ringing in his ears. "Sergeant, can you make out that bugle call?"

Maloney cupped a bloody hand behind his ear. "It's the retreat, sir."

Backus saw the American battalion he had so recently been a part of drawing ever farther away, leaving him and his handful of men alone on the outskirts of Monterrey. He saw Braxton Bragg's battery of flying artillery stranded, its horses killed, wounded men huddled between the fieldpieces. He saw scores of dead lying on the battlefield between the two Mexican forts and knew that many more had been dragged along with the retreat.

"Retreat?" the captain said, scoffing. "Through the canister again? The hell we will. We've got a foothold here, Sergeant."

Maloney nodded his agreement.

"Old Rough and Ready never quits a fight once it's started. He'll order another bayonet charge."

"Sure but he will, sir. And when he does, we'll be in place to attack the old tannery building from the rear."

"Pick two riflemen to man opposite corners of the rooftop as lookouts. The rest of you men take cover downstairs. El Diablo is bound to start shelling us any second now. They know we're here. When Taylor orders the next charge, we will attack the tannery. Be sure you are reloaded, rested, and ready!"

Second Lieutenant
SAM GRANT

Monterrey
September 21, 1846

He twisted in the saddle and looked back at the supply wagons he was leaving behind at Walnut Springs. As regimental quartermaster for the Fourth Infantry, Sam Grant's orders were to remain behind to guard the supplies. But the morning's cannonade and musket fire had roused his curiosity, so he had mounted a horse to ride to the front.

A few minutes' canter brought him to the swale in the terrain where the foot soldiers of the Fourth guarded the two twenty-four-pounder howitzers and the ten-inch mortar that were attempting to shell the Black Fort, without much success. The mortar seemed especially ill-suited for the task, looking more like some witch's cauldron than a proper artillery piece.

The Black Fort. Grant knew the Mexicans called it La Ciudadela—the Citadel. Why not call it by that name to avoid confusion? The other fortifications east of Monterrey—La Teneria and El Diablo—were called by their Spanish names, so why not La Ciudadela? Second lieutenants did not enjoy the authority to make such decisions, so Grant kept his mouth shut and went along with "Black Fort."

As he rode past the artillery, he saw the men of his regiment standing in formation, fixing bayonets and buckling cartridge belts in apparent preparation for an advance. A flash of white fabric caught his eye, and Grant focused on one of the regimental surgeons spreading a sheet on the ground. Upon this sheet—in plain view of the infantry—the sawbones began casually tossing surgical implements with reckless de-light, all the while smiling and chuckling at the soldiers who were about to march into battle. At first glance, Grant thought this bit of theater cruelly unnecessary. Then he considered the possibility that the sur-geon might require such cavalier antics to prepare himself for the grue-some tasks of the day.

The drummers began the long roll and the men of the Fourth marched toward the battle raging east of Monterrey. Grant sat on his horse, feel-ing left out. He thought about his orders to remain behind. He knew he should follow his orders and return to the supply train. He tried to rein about and ride back over his mount's hoofprints, but he could not. The next thing he knew, he was spurring forward to join his regiment in the assault. The men were moving double-quick, but he caught up to them easily by trotting down the road that led from Walnut Springs into the city. Scanning left and right of the road—both ways up and down the line of advance—he saw bristling bayonets, the regimental colors, a line of drummer boys. But he saw no one mounted, other than himself.

A horrible whistling scream pealed through his ears as a round of can-ister from the Black Fort played the plains like a drumhead, then rico-cheted into the line, taking half a dozen shrieking men off their feet.

Oh, God, I should have obeyed my orders. He could not turn back now. He could never turn back.

The Black Fort seemed too far away to the right to reach the men, but another round of hellish projectiles proved that assumption lethally flawed. *This line of assault is madness! Had the combat engineers not ranged the big guns of the Black Fort?*

Now, La Teneria—dead ahead—also opened up on the Americans, with more canister. He had never dreamed of seeing human bodies ripped so casually into carrion. He saw things he could scarcely believe were real: shattered bones sticking out of writhing men; a man trying to hold his intestines inside his ruptured torso; a corpse without a face. Horrors as-saulted his senses: the smells of urine and feces, sulfur and smoke; the screams of men and flying projectiles; the sting of gravel peppering his hands and face from a near miss by an exploding shell; the taste of his own vomit, which he had coughed up and choked back down.

Minutes ticked by like hours as Grant kept a tight rein on his horse and watched the men stagger forward, splattered by the blood of their comrades, until fully one-third of them were dead or wounded. Finally he heard some officer shout an order to march left, to the east, away from the cursed Black Fort.

"Follow me!" Grant yelled at the nearby men, his voice cracking. "Move left!"

He rounded up some survivors and herded them east, out of range of the Black Fort. As he trotted to the new position, Grant saw Lieutenant Charles Hoskins waving at him. Grant knew Hoskins, the regimental adjutant, to be in rather poor health.

"Sam!" the adjutant yelled. He doubled over, coughing. His face was beet red and he seemed about to collapse.

"Are you all right, Hoskins?"

He wagged his head back and forth and drew a wheezing breath. "Your horse, Sam . . . May I? I can go . . . no farther . . . on foot."

"Of course." Grant got down and helped Hoskins up onto the Ring-gold saddle.

"Thank you, Sam. I must find Colonel Garland. I will return your mount later."

"Godspeed, Charles."

Looking around, he spotted a private on a horse. He ran toward the soldier. "Hey, Private! Dismount! I need your horse."

The private obeyed.

Grant found the new mount more skittish than his first, and more powerful as well. This he liked. He might find himself in need of mobility. He heard an order to march farther south and moved that way at a trot, encouraging stunned men to follow him. Though out of the Black Fort's range, La Teneria could still fire upon the Fourth as they pushed on. Canister once again tore into the ranks.

Noticing a cornfield ahead, Grant shouted at the enlisted men nearby. "March through the corn, boys!" As he cantered forward, looking for an officer in charge, he saw a horse galloping full speed to the rear, no rider in the saddle. It was the mount he had given to Lieutenant Hoskins. He loped on and recognized his regimental commander, Colonel John Garland.

"Sir," he said, saluting. "Lieutenant Grant reporting for duty."

The fifty-four-year-old colonel's gaunt face showed the strain of the awful morning. "Why are you here, Grant? Shouldn't you be with the supply train?"

"I got curious. Sir, have you seen Lieutenant Hoskins?"

"He's dead. You're my adjutant now. Stay close, Grant. We're going to charge that fort again."

Major General
ZACHARY TAYLOR

Walnut Springs
September 21, 1846

Angrily, the general wadded the note from Colonel John Garland's courier between his thick palms.

"Goddamned Twiggs and his laxatives!"

He had counted on General Twiggs to lead the assault on eastern Monterrey this morning. But Twiggs always took a laxative the night before a battle, to loosen his bowels in case he got gutshot, as if that would make the least bit of difference to a Mexican musket ball. Taylor had long believed that Twiggs, though a brave soldier, took the laxatives to avoid soiling his britches in battle. Unfortunately for some three hundred dead or wounded men, Twiggs had taken too much of the laxative and was so cramped this morning that he could not even stand, much less fight. So Taylor had called upon Colonel John Garland to lead the advance.

"It's Garland's fault, not yours, sir." Major William Bliss stood at Taylor's side, his pad of foolscap ready, his pencil sharpened.

"You heard my orders to Garland this morning, did you not, Bill?"

"Sir, you told him to lead his column off to the left, keeping well out of reach of the enemy's shot. Then you said, 'And, Colonel, if you find that you can take any of the little forts down there with the bayonet, you better do it. But consult with Major Mansfield first.'"

The general was amazed at his adjutant's recall. "You're damned right that's what I told him. And what the hell was Mansfield thinking? Why would Garland and Mansfield blunder in between the Black Fort and

La Teneria—the two biggest forts on this side of the city?" He said this with conviction, but he could not ignore his own guilt for failing to give Garland more specific orders.

The ghastly news from the front line held that hundreds of men had fallen to the canister and musket fire in the span of a few minutes. He could only hope that General Worth's division was making better headway on the west side of town.

"What are your orders, sir?"

Taylor tried to channel his anger toward something positive. "We must not let those brave men die in vain. Order General Quitman to prepare the Mississippi and Tennessee regiments to assault La Teneria." He thought suddenly of his former son-in-law, Colonel Jefferson Davis, who soon would be leading the Mississippi Rifles into battle.

Bliss scribbled. "Sir, is the assault still a diversion, or do you now intend to advance into the city from the east as well as the west?"

Taylor's hawk's-eye mind was peering down on the bloody battlefield. "Bill, I don't know that yet," he snapped. "But the men must have the satisfaction of running Old Glory up the flagpole at La Teneria. I won't have men slaughtered for naught."

Colonel

JEFFERSON DAVIS

"Commence firing!" he yelled, as a load of grapeshot from La Teneria sang through the rank and file, killing and wounding soldiers who had marched straight into it.

Musket balls kicked up dust almost at his toes, but the three cannon atop the enemy fort were reloading just now, causing a break in the cursed canister and grapeshot. His regiment's rifles played a staccato drum roll, but Colonel Jefferson Davis saw only one enemy fall, back behind the sandbags of La Teneria. The rest of the rifle bullets fell short.

He knew this was the third wave. Colonel Garland and his regulars had tried twice to assault the fort, taking heavy casualties in an ill-planned assault through the ripping cross fire of the Black Fort and La Teneria. Now Davis's Mississippi Rifles had been thrust into the fray and Davis was determined to show the regular army officers that his volunteers could fight.

Davis's commander, General John A. Quitman, had already shown himself wiser than Colonel Garland by staying out of the range of the Black Fort's canister, though the Black Fort had lobbed some solid shot into the ranks. The three guns of La Teneria, however, had taken their toll on the Mississippi and Tennessee regiments. Davis had personally seen several of his men fall, each time feeling as if pieces of his own flesh were torn away with them.

He looked with desperate pride at his men. Wearing slouch hats and red shirts, they stood apart from the regular army's uniformed men. They were standing their ground in the face of the enemy onslaught of lead. Turning his eyes back toward La Teneria, he estimated the distance to the fort at 180 yards—still too far away for effective rifle fire.

"Reload and hold your fire, men!" he shouted.

He searched for the nearest officer and found First Lieutenant Daniel Russell, commander of Company D. "Damn it, Lieutenant Russell! We must get closer! Why waste our ammunition at this distance? Move your men forward!" He turned and strode briskly toward the fort to lead the way.

Lieutenant Russell ordered his company forward, double-quick, and Davis joined them at a trot as they caught up to him. The companies to the left of Company D followed. Grapeshot ripped into the men who had stayed behind, but it howled over the heads of Colonel Davis's advance.

It's actually safer here, he thought. *Now we are under the trajectory of the artillery.*

At sixty yards he halted the men. Glancing over his left shoulder, he saw Lieutenant Colonel Alexander McClung, his second-in-command, running forward with his Tombigbee Volunteers to catch up. Davis did not always get along with McClung, but he never questioned the man's bravery.

"Halt and prepare to fire!" Davis ordered. "Ready . . . Aim . . . Fire!"

As the rifles of his men belched lead and smoke, he saw Mexican musketeers and artillerists fall away from the cannon on the parapets of La Teneria. For a moment, not a shot was fired from the fort.

A screaming sense of urgency overtook Jeff Davis. "Now is the time!" he yelled. "Great God, if I had thirty men with *knives* I could take that fort!" And the Mississippi Volunteers indeed carried knives, with ten-inch blades, in lieu of bayonets.

Davis heard Lieutenant Colonel McClung's booming voice: "Follow me, boys!"

He looked left and saw McClung careering headlong toward the fort, followed by his men from Tombigbee. The Mississippi Rifles had no explicit orders to rush La Teneria at this time, but Davis would not be left out of this assault.

"Charge!" he yelled, drawing his sword and sprinting to catch up to his subordinate. Immediately, the entire Mississippi regiment surged forward, and a great rallying battle cry arose. Davis could also hear the Tennessee Volunteers, to the left of his own regiment, joining the assault. A tingle shot up his spine and made hair stand on the back of his neck.

If I am to die, I will die running into it, not away from it.

Colonel McClung now charged up the parapet to an open embrasure through which one of the artillery pieces had just fired. Pausing at the top, he waved his sword and urged the men forward. Davis, along with some of his enlisted men, passed through the next embrasure, followed closely by a throng of volunteers.

Now atop the battlement, he noticed a fortified stone building—the tannery—guarding the rear sally port of La Teneria. To his surprise, he found the tannery under heavy fire from some U.S. troops who had somehow gotten behind the Mexican defenses and captured the nearby distillery. For the first time today, the Mexicans were the ones in the cross fire. The effect was electric. The defenders panicked and fled both the dirt redoubt and the tannery building. A man in a Mexican officer's uniform ran from his post, stumbling through the creek coursing behind the tannery. Enemy soldiers threw down their muskets and sprinted away toward the smaller fort to the south—El Diablo.

Volunteers from Mississippi and Tennessee now poured over the walls of the earthen lunette and pursued the Mexicans. Davis found himself plunging down to the floor of La Teneria, past dead and wounded Mexican defenders and scores of weapons that had been dropped during the rout. He saw two of his men taking down the Mexican flag from the fort's flagstaff. With his soldiers, he chased some Mexican gunners to the stone tannery. The fleeing men tried to shut the gate in the high rock wall that surrounded the place, but the Mississippians were too close behind and kicked the gate in before it could be barred. The Mexican soldiers hid behind the pilasters of the front portico of the building, dropping their weapons and throwing their hands up in the air.

An enemy officer stepped forward to offer his sword to Davis. A round of shot from El Diablo whistled by, but Davis ignored it and took the Mexican officer's sword as a token of surrender.

"Lieutenant Townsend!" he shouted, catching sight of the commander of Company K. "Take charge of these prisoners and receive their arms!"

"Yes, sir!" Townsend said.

Now a group of regular army infantrymen trotted around the tannery from the back side, led by a captain. The blood on the men's uniforms suggested they had seen close combat this morning.

"Captain! What is your name?"

"Electus Backus, First Infantry, at your service, sir!" He saluted.

"Was it your men who fired on the fort from the rear?"

"Yes, sir. We took the distillery building earlier and waited there to support the next charge. Your charge, sir. It was a welcome sight."

Davis shook the man's bloodstained hand. "I'm Colonel Jefferson Davis, Mississippi Volunteers. Your cross fire was crucial to our taking this fort. Well done, Captain."

A cheer rose, and Davis looked over his shoulder to see the Stars and Stripes running up the flagpole over La Teneria. Pride welled up in his chest, only to be smothered instantly by the sight of four men carrying a body on a colorful Mexican blanket with knots tied at each corner to help the bearers keep a tight hold on the makeshift litter. He could see blood dripping through the blanket, having soaked all the way through the fabric.

"Sir," one of the soldiers said, catching Davis's eye. "It's Colonel McClung."

Davis dashed to the side of the men lugging the blanket. He found McClung unconscious and moaning. Two fingers were missing from his left hand and blood ran from a wound to his left hip. "Go quickly," he said. "See that you get him to the surgeon's tent."

The American flag over La Teneria now attracted the attention of El Diablo's artillerymen a quarter mile away. An exploding shell showered shrapnel down on the Americans.

"Mississippi Rifles!" Davis shouted. "Prepare to advance on El Diablo!"

Their spirits buoyed by the capture of La Teneria, the men raised their weapons over their heads and cheered their commander.

Major
LUTHER GIDDINGS

The lane led his mount between a sugarcane field and an orange orchard, past sheds and adobe farmhouses, until it opened upon a view of the objective of his regiment. As he reined to a stop, twenty-three-year-old Major Luther Giddings heard hoofbeats behind him and turned to see the regimental adjutant, Second Lieutenant Andrew Armstrong, loping up to his side.

"Is that it?" Armstrong asked.

"Yes," Giddings replied. "His satanic majesty, El Diablo." He glanced back to see his Ohio Volunteers coming up behind him, double-quick.

Two exploding shells erupted overhead at once, causing pieces of shrapnel from each to crack menacingly together in midair as others rained down on his position. A private screamed and fell in the lane to his rear. A corporal dragged the wounded man into a toolshed for some protection.

Giddings remained exposed at the point where the farm lane ended at a shallow irrigation canal. On the other side of the canal ran a well-traveled street. Along the far side of the street, a solid rock wall extended a good one hundred yards to the left and to the right.

Giddings pointed. "That wall could afford cover and bring us within rifle range of Diablo," he said to the adjutant.

"Yes, I see. But, look now . . ."

Giddings turned back to the open ground to see dozens of Mexican skirmishers—some of them dressed in white cotton peasant garb—charging forward to secure the other side of the rock wall themselves.

"Damn, they've taken it before us," he said.

A battery hidden behind a rude abatis of felled trees suddenly blasted a load of grapeshot down the lane where he straddled his mount. Giddings heard the balls whistle past his ears and thud into men behind him. A sergeant in the color guard fell dead, and the flagstaff he had been holding was shattered.

"By God, we are in for it now," Giddings said to himself.

"I'll advise the colonel of the wall," Armstrong said, reining his horse toward the rear of the column.

Giddings turned back to study the open ground between him and the objective. Straight ahead, two hundred yards away, stood the crescent-shaped earthen redoubt, its cannon steadily belching grape, shell, and canister in various directions, including his. Down the canal and street that ran away to his left, he could make out the American flag flying over La Teneria. He knew from dispatches that Captain Ridgely had taken over the captured Mexican artillery pieces there and was now using them to fire upon the Mexicans' Fort Diablo.

Looking right, up the canal and the street that ran alongside it, he found his view obscured by smoke from musket fire.

Mexican foot soldiers intimately acquainted with the streets and defenses of Monterrey had harassed his men relentlessly for the past hour, killing a few and wounding several. His regiment's first objective had been the Purisima Bridge, but they had found it too well fortified by a *tête de pont* at the bridgehead. So General William Orlando Butler had ordered Major Giddings and the First Ohio Volunteers to swing east and assist in the assault on El Diablo.

He decided now that he would make the charge on foot with his men. He dismounted and tied his nervous horse to a pomegranate hedge.

"Major!"

He looked down the lane to see the adjutant, Armstrong, coming back with General Butler himself—the "poet general," as he was called. Butler sat ramrod straight on the horse he rode—a handsome man, clean-shaven, with a thick shock of hair parted on the side. His eyes forever looked concerned and intelligently engaged.

"Advance to the rock wall!" General Butler shouted, an exploding shell punctuating his order. "Take that wall!"

Giddings now found the din of the growing artillery battle so great that he could not hear his own voice. He began waving his men into position along the canal, sending the first company to the left, the next to the right, and so on, as musket balls and grape continued to ravage his volunteers.

General Butler now galloped to the front. He drew his saber. "Fire!" he yelled at the men nearest to him—the only ones who could make out his order over the din of battle.

The Ohio Volunteers, anxious to burn their first cartridges in the battle, began firing at the Mexican skirmishers behind the wall.

"Charge!" Butler yelled, spurring his horse forward.

"Come on, boys!" Giddings shouted, sprinting toward the canal.

Young men with wide eyes and teeth set for the wildest work of war leaped forward, ran across open ground, and plunged into the shallow canal. Some fell, soaking the powder in their ammunition pouches. A private at Giddings's side stopped to fill his canteen and was shot down. Adjutant Armstrong rode his mount into the canal, where a grapeshot tore through his leg and into the side of his horse. The lieutenant fell into the water, his wound gushing blood, his horse floundering and stumbling away from him. Enlisted men dragged Armstrong back toward some farm huts, so Giddings continued to charge on foot, thankful that he had left his horse behind. Up the other side of the shallow ditch he scrambled, trying to stay ahead of his men.

Climbing out of the canal to the street, he was astonished to see the Mexican defenders along the other side of the wall fleeing back to the houses of Monterrey. A few of his men still had loaded rifles and used them to shoot down some fleeing enemy soldiers.

Giddings trotted across the street with musket balls peppering the dirt around him and grapeshot whistling overhead. He collapsed behind the wall, his heart pounding and his lungs heaving. He was relieved to have gained the protection of the wall, but he was also perplexed over how readily the Mexicans had been ousted from it.

Why would they give up this wall so easily?

"Stay down and reload!" he ordered, during a brief lull in the shelling.

A corporal beside him pulled the ramrod from his rifle and used it to seat the powder and bullet he had poured down his muzzle. "We'll give 'em hell now, Major!"

Giddings nodded and patted the boy on the shoulder. Still, he felt strangely uneasy about having taken the wall. He looked to the right, where the smoke down the street was beginning to clear. Some four hundred yards away, he could now make out a bridge. *The Purisima Bridge?* He remembered the big guns behind the *tête de pont.*

God, no, he thought. *Have we been baited to the slaughter here at this wall?*

The private beside him rose to rest his loaded rifle along the top of the wall. A flash of fire appeared at the bridge. Giddings tried to pull the private down in time, but the load of grape tore into the ranks to his right, one of the balls causing the head of the young rifleman beside him to burst like a dropped melon. Exploding shells drowned out the screams of men, and Giddings knew he could not hold this wall without a great loss of life from the guns at Purisima Bridge.

He looked for the poet general and saw soldiers carrying the unhorsed Butler away, wounded, through a hail of musket fire. He happened to spot Lieutenant Colonel Weller across the irrigation ditch, waving for the troops to perform a retrograde maneuver.

Thank God!

"Fall back!" he yelled. He stood and motioned his men to the rear. Across the canal, he saw the regimental standard, the broken flagstaff having been splinted by the guard. "To the colors! Fall back! Take cover!"

Crossing back over the canal, he grabbed a wounded man and dragged him toward safety. In the water, he saw the rippled reflection of a shell detonating overhead. The water—rather clear, the first time he crossed—was now stirred with silt and streaked with curving tendrils of blood.

Major General
ZACHARY TAYLOR

Sitting atop Old Whitey, just beyond the range of the Black Fort's big guns, he peered through the twilight at the distant city of Monterrey. Plumes of smoke trailed from the eastern and western extremities of the town, looking like the scorched wings of some battered angel. Major William Bliss straddled a bay horse to his left.

"General Taylor, sir. Looks like rain coming from the northwest."

Taylor nodded. "The artillery shakes it from the sky."

Never in his military career had he imagined such a dreadful day. More than 120 brave men slaughtered like quail before the scatterguns of bird hunters. Almost four hundred wounded or missing. A peculiar and burdensome thought struck him. He was in the habit of writing letters to the families of men killed in action. But after this day . . . how could he? There was so much to think about. So much to worry over. When would he find time to write to 120 parents and widows?

He took some solace in the knowledge that La Teneria had been captured. The reports said that the volunteers under his former son-in-law, Jeff Davis, had taken down the Mexican banner and hoisted the American flag up the pole. But the hold on La Teneria was tenuous, and the Black Fort remained unconquered.

The Ohioans had assaulted the Purisima Bridge—gateway to the north side of Monterrey—only to be repulsed by entrenched Mexican defenders. They had veered east to join Jeff Davis's attack on El Diablo.

They fell under the command of Major General William O. Butler, leader of all the volunteer regiments. And there the Mexicans opened an enfilading fire from Purisima Bridge, wounding the old poet warrior, Butler, Taylor's second-in-command. His troops had been forced to retreat.

He looked away to the east, only to see some three hundred men digging a mass grave for soldiers who woke up alive this morning.

He shifted his gaze to the far-off western end of the city. There, under General William Worth, things had gone as planned, if not better. The missives carried by hard-riding couriers glowed with accounts of the Texas mounted rifles—Hay's Rangers—and their fantastic exploits. After securing the Saltillo road, the Rangers and the Fifth Infantry had mounted a bold attack on Federation Hill, which rose to the south of the road and the Santa Catarina River. While wading the swift stream, they had taken heavy cannon and musket fire from the two small forts atop the hill. And yet they refused to falter in their advance.

From that point, Taylor had been able to watch the attack through his spyglass as five hundred U.S. soldiers bravely scaled the steep, barren slopes of Federation Hill. So far away was the hill that the men themselves could not be seen, even through the glass. But the puffs of smoke from their muskets revealed their line of assault as they climbed with remarkable rapidity to the summit. They captured both artillery emplacements and chased the surviving enemy soldiers from the hill.

Yet there was another prominence that had to be taken, west of town and north of the Saltillo road: Independence Hill. On the slope that faced the town stood the Bishop's Palace—a veritable castle that looked as if it had been built long ago. Taylor feared that it would not be as easily conquered as the little redoubts on Federation Hill. He knew from the reports of the couriers that General Worth planned to assault Independence Hill at dawn.

As he fretted over all of this, he realized that Bliss had begun to speak. ". . . so I've come up with a solution if you'd like to hear it."

Taylor blinked as a large raindrop hit the back of his hand, which rested on the pommel. "I'm sorry, Bill. Solution to what?"

"The letters. All of the letters that must be written to the families of the men killed today."

"Yes, I'd like to hear your solution. I've been dreading it."

"I'll write an appropriate letter and submit it to you for your approval.

Then I'll recruit a dozen lieutenants to pen ten copies each. All you will need to do is to sign each letter."

Taylor nodded. "I suppose you will have your scribes leave a blank space for the name of each man killed?"

"Exactly, sir. I will fill in those names myself."

He frowned. "I don't like the impersonal nature of it, but we have no alternative. We must not dwell on death when the battle has yet to be won by the living."

Just then a lonely bugle began to play taps at the mass grave for the men slain on this bloody day. Taylor reined his mount to the east. He touched his fingers to his hat brim in a salute that he held to the end of the familiar dirge.

Raindrops peppered the riders now.

"Sir, you should retire to your tent before the deluge begins."

Taylor spurred Old Whitey toward Walnut Springs. "Nonsense, Major. I will visit the hospital tents and all of my wounded officers before I retire."

"As you wish, General."

"Bill," the commander said, softening his voice, "do you know the nature of General Butler's injury?"

"No, sir, but I gather from the reports that it was not deadly."

Taylor grunted, thankful. "Did you know he's a poet?"

"Yes, I had heard that, sir."

"He gave me his book once. *The Boatman's Horn.* The poem of the same name is not bad. Not bad at all."

"Do you remember it, sir?"

"It's a long poem. I only remember one part. The part about the music of the horn. That bugle back there reminded me." Taylor coughed and prepared to recite from memory.

"Music, the master-spirit that can move
Its waves to war, or lull them into love—
Can cheer the dying sailor on the wave
And shed bright halos round the soldier's grave."

Major
LUTHER GIDDINGS

He woke from an unintended nap, aching and hungry. All was dark. The events of the bloody day flooded his thoughts like an explosion of canister. *My men*, he thought. Major Luther Giddings crawled out of his tent, his muscles racked with cramps from the exertions of the battle.

Outside, a cold drizzle caused rainwater to stream down a wrinkle in his tent canvas and patter upon the sodden ground. He could not see it in the dark, but he could hear it. It laughed at him and mocked his thirst. He felt for it, found it gushing cold on his palm, then fell to his knees and drank from the little cascade, opening his mouth like a baby bird in a nest.

Struggling to rise to his feet, he thought once again of his men and his hunger. He might have trudged to the officers' mess but decided instead to take his meal with the enlisted troops. He felt he owed them. They had followed his orders and performed bravely under heavy fire. His Ohio Volunteers had lost fifteen dead and forty wounded.

Dragging along through the camp at Walnut Springs, he spotted a fire among the rows of tents. A cook served soldiers standing in line. As he approached, one of the enlisted men waiting for a meal saluted.

"Good evening, Major Giddings."

Others turned to salute.

"At ease, men." Giddings returned the salutes. He stood there for an awkward moment.

"Would you like a plate, sir?" the cook asked.

"If there's any left after the men eat," Giddings replied.

"There's plenty, sir."

The soldier at the head of the line handed his plate and cup to Giddings.

"Well, if you're sure there's enough. Thank you, Private." He stepped up to the warmth of the fire. The cook ladled out chunks of boiled beef from a cauldron suspended over the fire as another soldier placed a hard biscuit on his plate. A third took his tin cup and filled it with coffee from a nearby pot.

"I want to thank you, gentlemen. Not just for the food, but for your composure and bravery under fire today."

"It was a hot little skirmish, wasn't it, sir?"

"You might say so."

"This way, sir," said a man who had already filled his plate. "We've a table of sorts under that canvas, yonder."

Giddings followed the men a short distance to a wide board, ten or twelve feet long, propped up on sawhorses at either end.

"Pull up a chair, sir, and set your plate down."

In the dim light, Giddings could barely see the table, but he did as the soldier suggested.

"Major, them lancers," a rifleman began, pausing to chew, "did you ever think you'd see such a thing?"

The memory cut like his own knife stabbing the chunk of beef that he raised to his mouth. Lancers, one hundred strong, had ridden out of Monterrey to harass his regiment as it withdrew from El Diablo. His Ohio Volunteers didn't know how to form a hollow square—the traditional defensive formation against a cavalry attack—but Giddings had ordered them to form up behind a chaparral fence and level their muskets and rifles on the attackers.

"It was lucky for us you noticed that brush fence, Major. But I wish to God them lancers would've rode closer."

Giddings said nothing, but he remembered the Mexicans viciously spearing helpless American soldiers wounded by the artillery barrage earlier in the day.

"Yes, they were brave enough to attack the wounded men, but lacking in moral courage to get within range of our sights."

"That *one* did," a corporal recalled. "Brave man. An officer. Rode right up to us and was shot dead."

"Which one of our boys was it that went out and fetched his boots?"

Giddings stabbed another piece of the tough beef. "That was Lieutenant Hughes, of Company A," he said. "Hughes had lost his shoes crossing the canal ditch at El Diablo and was left barefooted as the day he was born. It was he who pulled the dead lancer's boots off and said there was never a better fit."

Some men chuckled, briefly.

"Say, who was that boy climbing that tree during all the shelling?"

"Oh, that was some kid from Company D."

"What the hell was he doing?"

"It was an orange tree. He climbed up there to pick an orange."

"With all that lead and shrapnel flying around?"

"It was for his pal. A boy named Joe Lombeck. Shot clean through and dying. Begging for water, but all the canteens were empty. So that kid brought his pal Lombeck an orange."

Utensils clacked against tin plates for a while.

Giddings swallowed and reached for his cup. "The damnedest thing I saw was Private Myers, of the rifle company, getting shot in the mouth." He slurped at the strong coffee.

"In the mouth?" a soldier said. "Did it kill him?"

"The musket ball that hit him must have flown a long way, or was fired with a poor powder charge. It shattered some teeth and then lodged in the back of his throat, but he was able to cough it up. Then, spitting out his broken teeth and some blood, he said, 'That was a pill too bitter to swallow, but damned if it hasn't salivated me for revenge!'"

The men laughed as the light from an approaching lantern began to illuminate the table. Giddings looked up to see the regimental surgeon lumbering toward the table with his plate and the lantern. Blood covered the surgeon's apron.

As the surgeon placed the lantern on the table, one of the soldiers leaped back from the board, knocking his chair over backwards.

"That's a finger! That's somebody's cut-off finger on the table!"

Now Giddings focused on the board between the plates and cups. To his disgust, he saw thin strips of human flesh and globs of clotted blood. He, too, pulled his chair back and stepped away, as the surgeon began to laugh.

"Oh, for Pete's sake, boys!" cried the doctor. "We had to borrow your table in the surgery tent for a while when business was booming. We only cut off some legs and arms upon it. And that finger." He resumed laughing.

Giddings realized that his men were looking at him for a solution. So this was war. He decided it was time to toughen up.

"Lift your plates and flip the board over," he ordered. "Is it not better to dine around this table now than to have lain upon it today?"

The men solemnly followed his order. One by one they reclaimed their places around the grisly plank. They ate in silence, for the surgeon had ceased to chuckle.

SAM WALKER

Independence Hill
September 22, 1846

He jammed the cold, wet toe of his boot into a crevice and stuck his skinned knuckles into another crack in the rocks above his head. He knew that if he slipped, he would fall twenty feet from the sheer cliff, then tumble hundreds more down the muddy slope of Independence Hill. Pulling himself laboriously upward, he hooked an elbow over the rim rock, then a knee. He dragged himself up and over the stony ledge and rolled over onto his back to catch his breath and rest his aching muscles.

Staring upward, Lieutenant Colonel Sam Walker noticed that the cloudy sky had turned from charcoal to slate. He could now see it silhouetting the sandbags atop the hill that he had been climbing for the past three hours in the rain and dark. Mexican defenders would be waiting behind the sandbagged walls of the little redoubt they called Fort Libertad, still some one hundred yards up a steep slope, on the summit of Independence Hill. Dawn was fast approaching, and with it mortal combat would commence.

Walker had eaten nothing but a couple of roasted ears of corn for the past day and a half. In the same time, he had caught only a few fleeting minutes of sleep in the mud and rain, without a blanket. But when he touched the grip of his Colt revolver, he knew he would rally for the imminent attack.

A few hours had passed since Colonel Jack Hays had wakened Walker by touching his shoulder—from a distance, with a stick. Walker tended to wake up fighting.

"We're going to collect some Mexican sentries," Hays had said.

Walker had risen willingly. His old wounds ached when he slept in the mud. He much preferred sneaking behind enemy lines in the dark. He and Hays, with a few picked Rangers, had found the first sentry asleep—an easy catch. Prodding the surprised soldier with the tip of a bowie knife, they had forced him to lead them to the next sentry along the base of Independence Hill. Then to the next, and the next. Within two hours, all the sentries on the west side of the hill had been captured and sent back to General Worth's camp as prisoners of war.

It was all part of Hays's plan, which General Worth had approved. Storming Federation Hill in the daylight yesterday was one thing. But Independence Hill was higher, steeper, and fortified with a castle—the Bishop's Palace, or El Obispado. So Hays had proposed a nighttime ascent of the steepest slope for a surprise attack at dawn. He and Walker had led some three hundred Rangers, U.S. regulars, and volunteers in the three-hour climb.

Now, as he rested atop the rim rock, he felt a pebble hit him in the face. He looked back toward the precipice in time to see a grimy hand tossing a second pebble at him. He recognized Captain Ad Gillespie reaching out to him for assistance. Yesterday, the same Captain Gillespie had distinguished himself by being the first U.S. soldier to breach the walls of the gun emplacement atop Federation Hill. Walker rolled toward him, grabbed his wrist, and helped his fellow Ranger scramble atop the cliff. Soon, Colonel Jack Hays appeared on the brink nearby as other Rangers and soldiers came up from below. Walker and Gillespie helped pull some of them up, and he signaled to them to spread silently along the slope for the final ascent.

The sky continued to brighten as they moved among boulders large enough to provide some cover. Walker, in the lead, had climbed to within thirty yards of Fort Libertad. As he paused to look back on the progress of the men, he heard the crack of a musket from above and the hum of a bullet careering off of rock. Shouts and more shots followed.

"Save your loads and charge that wall!" he ordered.

He felt his legs churning up the slope as the few Mexican defenders at the sandbag parapets reloaded. The assault had obviously surprised them. They had never dreamed the Americans would scale the steepest

flank of Independence Hill on such a cold, wet night. But he knew reinforcements would be coming fast from the palace if he didn't rout the
enemy at the sandbags of Fort Libertad.

"Charge, boys!"

The reloaded Mexican muskets began to pepper his ranks again, but
his men ducked and darted behind rocks as they ascended. Walker
grabbed the branch of some sort of low-growing scrub to aid in his mad
scramble upward.

He heard Hays's voice far to the right. "Give them hell, boys!"

Closer, to his left, Walker heard the infantry leader, Major Vinton.
"Fire!"

Walker drew his Colt revolver as he took his first look over the sandbags. He shot the nearest Mexican soldier dead. The man next to him
charged with a bayonet, probably thinking Walker held a single-shot
horse pistol. He shot this defender in the face as he felt his fighting spirit
lifting him over the rampart. He shot a third Mexican infantryman
caught reloading at the wrong time.

Ad Gillespie leaped over the battlements near him. Walker heard the
familiar slap of a bullet against human flesh and saw Gillespie stagger
back a step. Doing his best to ignore his obvious wound, Gillespie waved
his men onward over the battlement. A pair of Rangers from Gillespie's
company stopped to render aid to their commander.

"Boys, stand me up behind that ledge," Gillespie said. "I will do some
execution on them yet before I die."

Walker clearly heard the words, then saw Ad cough a spray of blood.
His ire flared as he wished to hell he had seen which Mexican had shot
his friend. He fired his last two shots from his Colt, clearing the way for
more Rangers and soldiers from Major Vinton's "Red-Legged Infantry"
to vault over the sandbagged wall. A young U.S. Army private fell dead
at Gillespie's feet, but Gillespie was still standing, leaning against the
sandbags, using a boulder for cover, firing his Colt methodically.

The stunned Mexicans were now on the run down the gentle eastern
slope of Independence Hill, back to the fortified Bishop's Palace five hundred yards away. With them, they took three pieces of artillery that
Walker wished he could have captured.

Now he rushed to Ad Gillespie and reached his friend about the time
the Ranger slid down the wall to sit on the rocky summit, leaving a trail
of his blood on the sandbags.

"That's naught but a scratch," Walker said, taking a knee beside Gillespie.

Another Ranger brought an open canteen and trickled some water into Gillespie's mouth. Other Texans crowded around as Gillespie's eyes locked on to Walker's.

"The Comanche give us worse than that at Sisters Creek, Ad. You and me, both run through with spears. You hear me?"

Gillespie smiled and nodded a time or two.

"This don't hardly liken to that none at all, Ad. You rest now and we'll patch you up."

Gillespie's eyes rolled as he coughed a final spray of blood and slumped, his body quivering, so that it put Walker in mind of a sleeping dog dreaming of some chase.

Some U.S. soldiers had clawed Fort Libertad's Mexican flag down from its staff. A cheer rose among them as the Stars and Stripes replaced the Eagle and the Snake. But the men from Texas remained silent, gathered around Captain Ad Gillespie, as Walker gently eased his eyelids closed.

Shouts down the hill caught Walker's attention. He stood and looked over the sandbags to find four infantrymen using ropes to laboriously drag the heavy bronze tube of a twelve-pound howitzer up among the boulders. Farther below, he could see pieces of the dissembled gun carriage being lugged upward, along with crates filled with ammunition and fuses.

"Help those men drag that cannon up here," he said to the Rangers who had gathered around their fallen comrade, "and we'll fire a fittin' salute to Captain Ad Gillespie. If some Mexican happens to get in the way of it, I don't think Ad will mind."

Walker himself scrambled back over the sandbag to help Lieutenant Roland of Duncan's battery heave on one of the ropes tied to the tube. He found Roland and his men completely covered with mud and almost too exhausted to accomplish the final few yards of the climb with their heavy burden.

As regulars hastened to reassemble the howitzer, the first Mexican round of solid shot fired from the Bishop's Palace hit the hilltop short of the Americans, bounced, and flew over their heads.

"There's your warning shot, Lieutenant," Walker said to Roland. "Best get that piece put together before they range this ground." He turned to his men. "Boys, take them sandbags and build some cover in front of this howitzer!"

With impressive rapidity, the U.S. troops slapped the howitzer pieces together and rammed a load down its muzzle. Walker witnessed the first round fired at the palace—the salute to Ad Gillespie. Its shell exploded over the high stone walls of El Obispado, blasting an enemy sharpshooter from the rampart. The unfortunate defender fell to his death and landed in front of the large wooden palace gates.

At this moment, Walker saw the double gates open wide. Scores of foot soldiers streamed out. Lancers came swarming around the outside walls of the castle. They began forming up by companies, then by regiments. They were going to use their superior numbers to counterattack.

He heard Colonel Hays shout and found Jack waving for him to join a council of war with Major Vinton of the regular army and Captain Blanchard of the Louisiana Volunteers. Walker sprinted in that direction as more artillery fire flew from the palace.

"Sam, we're going to show these boys some Injun strategy." With a dried yucca stalk he held in his hand, Hays gestured toward a crude battle map he had traced in the mud with the same stalk. "You'll sneak your company around the left flank, staying below the rim rock, out of sight of the enemy. I'll take the rest of the Rangers to the right flank, also hidden over the edge. Captain Blanchard's company will advance in full view of the enemy and fire, then retreat. You know the lancers will pursue him. Infantry, too. When they do, your men and mine will close behind them, with Major Vinton and Captain Blanchard in front of them."

Walker nodded. "We'll cut a fair number of them down and storm the castle before they can get the gates closed."

"That's the idea," Hays said, a wry smile flashing across his face. "We must go quickly, before they form up. Meanwhile, Lieutenant Roland will harass them with that howitzer."

Within minutes, Walker had his men in position on the left flank. Alone, he peered between two boulders, watching the enemy battalions move into position. He had ordered his men to stay behind him, out of sight.

Walker marveled at Jack Hays's strategies and wondered why the American officers didn't have the good sense to employ similar tactics.

The West Pointers liked to march large bodies of men directly at enemy emplacements, over open ground. Hays, on the other hand, had learned from renegades and bandits how to feint and retreat, ambush and counterattack.

Now, before the Mexican defenders could advance up the slope toward the Americans, Captain Albert Gallatin Blanchard led his so-called Phoenix Company, of the Second Louisiana Infantry, double-quick toward the palace. Walker frowned as he watched them halt out of effective musket range, but he couldn't say that he blamed Captain Blanchard for not getting too close. Blanchard's job was to provoke a counterattack. His foot soldiers would have to outrun the Mexican cavalry and would need a good head start.

Blanchard's fifty men raised their rifles. Blanchard yelled, "Fire!" Fifty musket balls hit the dirt in front of the Mexicans, and Blanchard's men turned to run back up the slope, where Major Vinton waited with the rest of the regulars and volunteers.

The affront created the desired result. A Mexican cavalry officer harangued his lancers and advanced at a trot, followed by the infantrymen who had streamed out of the castle. Walker studied El Obispado as the Mexicans marched past his hiding place. He saw a few sentries atop the palace walls, but he would be beyond their musket range when he led his men out into the open atop the hill.

When the rear of the enemy formation had marched by, Walker looked down at his Rangers and tossed his head toward the sloping summit in a subtle invitation for his men to follow him. His company climbed to the open ground and quietly walked into position behind the Mexicans. Across the slanted mountain slope, he saw Jack Hays and his men coming from the right flank to cut off the enemy's escape route back to the castle. Hays strode nonchalantly toward Walker, until they met in the middle. Their Rangers had spread out across the battleground, their numbers far inferior to the Mexicans but with superior rifles, Colt revolvers, and the element of surprise in their favor.

"When the shooting starts, let's watch a spell," Hays suggested.

Walker nodded. "Time comes, we'll know to cock our hammers."

Like spectators, they looked on as Major Vinton's infantrymen fired a deadly volley into the lancers. Blanchard's troops, having reloaded, added a second hailstorm of lead that ripped into the enemy riders. Horses screamed and fell; others galloped, riderless, through the enemy infantry, back toward the palace. Walker wished, briefly, that he might catch one to ride. The Mexican foot soldiers tried valiantly to advance through the melee that the cavalry had become, until the U.S. howitzer fired a round of grapeshot into the middle of the enemy line.

Hays elbowed Walker. "That ought to do it."

Walker nodded. "Cock your hammers, boys!" he shouted.

"Don't fire until I do!" Hays added.

A shout went up among the regular army troops on the summit, and Walker knew the U.S. charge had begun, though he could no longer see the maneuvering through the smoke. There was so much smoke, in fact, that Independence Hill now resembled a volcano. The Mexican brigade faltered and surged to the rear, back toward the supposed refuge of the Bishop's Palace, only to find a hundred or more Rangers standing in their way.

Walker drew both Colts and looked at Hays. Jack would wait until the Mexican bayonets were just paces away. On came the lancers, charging back through their own infantry. Seeing that they would have to fight their way back into their castle, the riders lowered their lance tips and galloped headlong down the slope.

Hays touched off a shot, followed by a hundred well-aimed bullets. The mountaintop shook as tons of men and horseflesh slammed into the rocky earth. Walker fired four more rounds from his right-hand Colt.

"Let us part ways, Sam, and let them pass between us on their way back to their castle. We'll catch them in our cross fire."

Hays turned to lead his men in a sprint toward his original position on the right flank as Walker, too, withdrew to the left, waving his men back toward the rim rock. The two wings of Rangers served to funnel the enemy riders and foot soldiers into a stream that flowed between them. Then the Texans opened fire again.

Walker used his five rounds from his left-hand Colt and began to remove the barrel from the revolver to insert a new cylinder loaded with five more rounds. His Rangers had withdrawn to the edge of the mountainside, where they could use the rim rock for cover as they methodically reloaded and fired. Lancers dropped from their saddles by the dozens. Infantrymen tripped over their own dead and wounded. And now the U.S. regulars and volunteers raised a yell that would almost rival that of a Comanche raiding party, as they pressed hard upon the rear of the Mexicans' chaotic retreat.

"Hold your fire and reload, boys," Walker ordered as he replaced the barrel on his left-hand Colt and reached for the matching weapon. He could disassemble a revolver without looking at it, so he kept his eyes trained on the Mexican retreat as he worked. "Let the army chaw their tail till they pass us by."

He remembered watching military parades march down city streets, between throngs of onlookers. Well, this was one hell of a parade, all right, complete with screaming men and horses, gushing blood, shattered bones, and spilled guts. The surviving Mexicans were so focused on getting back into El Obispado that they had wildly fired only a handful of bullets toward the Rangers.

When Vinton and Blanchard had pushed the enemy past Walker's position, Walker turned to his men. "You boys ever storm a castle before? Well, here's your chance. Fall in with the regulars and push the enemy hard before they can barricade their gates." He cocked his Colt and took off at a trot toward the palace. "Charge, Rangers!"

Ahead of him, Vinton's men had trundled the howitzer down the slope to the formidable old palace. As the Mexicans tried to shut the rear gates of the palace, the sole American artillery piece fired a solid ball into the heavy wooden doors, blasting one of them to splinters. Blue-coated soldiers surged inside.

As he approached, Walker heard weird echoes ringing from inside the high stone palace walls. Gunshots, bayonets clashing with sabers, and screams of dying men raised a hellish din from within. Still Walker rushed ahead, pushing his way through the volunteers to get inside. Under the high, vaulted ceiling, the howls of war rang with an even more wicked timbre as horses whinnied crazily, bullets whirred off of marble arches, and a bugle attempted to rally the defenders. Smoke hung so heavy in the air that it stung Walker's eyes and nostrils. He could taste it on his tongue and it whetted his appetite for blood. Yet he could not get beyond the army troops pressing ahead of him to join the battle.

Looking around, he saw a towering portrait of a saint, or some such personage, wearing a scarlet cape. The portrait must have been twelve feet tall. Next to it stood an arching passageway supported by carved columns. It occurred to him that he could climb the square base of the column—a solid block of stone three feet high. He ran to it and leaped upon its corner. Now he could see over the heads of the combatants. He saw dismounted lancers hacking at U.S. soldiers with sabers; a teenage

American boy holding a Mexican sergeant to the floor by his throat as he used his bare fist to bloody the sergeant's face; a Louisiana Volunteer using a piece of the splintered palace door as a club to beat back the hard-pressed Mexican defenders.

Walker aimed his Colt into the second rank of the Mexicans, shooting over the American fighters. His five rounds dropped five uniforms but drew attention. By the time he pulled the second Colt from his belt, he had musket balls chipping stone masonry all around his head. Still, he held his high ground and aimed with purpose. A distant *escopeta* fired a weak blast of shot at him, peppering his face. His eyes were spared, but one of the small projectiles lodged in his lower lip.

He dropped from the stone block and belted his Colt. He drew his sword from its scabbard and tried to push forward.

"Let me through!" he yelled. "Step aside, damn it!"

But the Mexican defense faltered at that moment and surged backwards. Soon, every able-bodied defender was on the run, out through the front door of the palace and down Independence Hill to the city of Monterrey. A cheer rose up among the Americans as they pursued the retreating throng through the palace.

Walker stepped over dead men he had shot down with his Colt just minutes before. He held his sword over his head and loosed a Comanche howl that startled even the hardened men around him. He passed among more paintings of saints, ornate arches, and gold crosses encrusted with jewels. Soon he was breathing the fresh mountain air outside the front of the palace. He looked down the slope and watched the Mexicans sprint to the houses of Monterrey, some of them tumbling head over heels in their haste to escape alive.

Colonel Hays stepped up to his side. "Those devils fight hard, but they've got no leadership."

Walker grinned. "They got leaders. They just ain't got no Jack Hays."

Hays looked at him. "What happened to your lip?"

"Buckshot."

"Let me see." Hays grabbed him by the chin and prodded his lower lip with grimy fingers. "It's not deep. I'll squeeze it out of there. Brace up. It might smart."

Walker dared not wince as the colonel manipulated a large pebble from his bloody lip.

Hays caught it in his hand and studied it. "That ain't buckshot, Sam!

That's a little bitty rock." He laughed. "They must be low on shot. They're loading their blunderbusses with pea gravel!" He tossed the pebble aside and wiped his bloody hand on Walker's sleeve.

Another wave of cheering arose as the colors of the Louisiana Volunteers ran up the flagpole in front of the palace. A few miles away, across the Black Fort, General Taylor's artillery fired a salute to Old Glory flying over El Obispado.

Walker slipped his sword into its scabbard. He looked to the south and gazed down upon the Saltillo road, where he had marched in chains four years before, on his way to a Mexico City prison. It felt good to be free, to conquer, to avenge. He thought about Ad Gillespie lying dead upon the hilltop.

He looked down on the city of Monterrey. He knew they would fight there next. This was not finished. Not even close.

"There is much more to do," Hays said, as if reading his thoughts.

Lieutenant
SAM GRANT

East Monterrey, Mexico
September 23, 1846

Sam Grant crouched on the roof behind a parapet of sandbags, his eyes
darting constantly, searching for enemy snipers atop the houses of Monterrey. A hundred yards away he caught a brief glimpse of a ramrod that
appeared above the enemy battlements for a mere second. A Mexican
defender was reloading.

"Look, Sarge," he said to Sergeant Amos Abbot, the best marksman
in his company. "On a line that runs just left of the cathedral, about a
hundred yards away."

"Yessir?" The sergeant swung his muzzle in the direction described.

"On the corner of that house that stands a little higher than the rest.
Give him a moment. He's tamping his load about now."

"Sir, I'll watch that corner," Abbot said. "If you would kindly watch
everywhere else, my gumption will hold."

"You may rely upon me, Sergeant."

Musket and rifle shots cracked away nearby and in the distance; then
an artillery piece roared, as the two men on the roof waited.

Lieutenant Sam Grant had awakened before dawn in the camp General Twiggs had established to protect La Teneria, the captured Mexican redoubt on the east side of town. A council of war before breakfast
had informed him that, during the night, the Mexicans had withdrawn
farther into the city. Grant thought about how that order must have demoralized the brave Mexican defenders who had fought so hard to hold

El Diablo and the Purisima Bridge two days ago. Still, he understood General Ampudia's reasoning. He would concentrate his forces around the town plaza and the cathedral, which, according to captured informants, had been filled with ammunition with the bishop's blessing.

Ten companies of the Third and Fourth infantries—including Grant's company—had advanced to test the Mexicans' stronghold around the plaza. The fighting had been hard and bloody, but the Americans had advanced slowly, house by house, street by street, to within one or two blocks of the plaza.

Grant had seen enough of this strange, foreign land to know the layout of the typical Mexican town. Each city revolved around a centrally located plaza. Here in Monterrey, all the streets that led straight to the city's main plaza were now protected by barricades and artillery. Any man who stepped into one of those through-streets risked eating a round of grapeshot from a twelve-pounder.

The cross streets were not perfectly safe, either. Mexican shooters lurked on the rooftops, behind sandbags, and sometimes shot from windows in the stone or adobe houses. But here the Americans had some advantage. Most of the defenders used ancient muskets. The U.S. invaders carried more modern muskets or rifled long arms.

Grant had been told that, of the dozen or so U.S. officers involved in this morning's assault, five were already dead. He knew he might be next. He felt lucky that he had found time to write to Julia yesterday. For all he knew, that letter might be his last.

"There," Abbot whispered.

Grant glanced back at the sandbagged corner a hundred yards away. The enemy sniper he and Abbott had taken this roof to locate was leaning over the sandbags, aiming downward toward some hapless U.S. soldier on the cobblestoned street.

Quickly, Grant thought, fearing for the unknown American infantryman in the sniper's sights. Before he could finish the thought, Abbot's rifle fired. Grant crouched so near that he could feel the percussion of the shot in his face. The Mexican sniper jerked grotesquely, slumped, and slid out of view.

"Let's move!" Grant ordered.

He crab-walked across the packed-clay roof, through the trapdoor, and down the ladder into the adobe house. He passed the sneering inhabitants of the home—citizens who had been too poor to evacuate the

town. Quickly, he ran out through the shattered wooden door that Abbot had kicked in a few minutes earlier.

"*Hasta luego!*" Abbot said to the home owners in a singsong voice as
he vacated their beleaguered abode.

Grant ran to the corner but stopped short of the street leading to the
plaza. Abbot slid to a halt behind him.

"We'll draw a volley," Grant said. "You run across first. I'll go after
you."

Abbot smirked. "Sir, you needn't *always* take the most dangerous job."

"I'm giving you an order. Go!"

Abbot backed up a few steps to get a running start and ran across the
street guarded by the cannon a few blocks away. The sergeant made the
crossing without drawing cannon fire. Grant waited a few seconds,
then sprinted into the shooting lane. Just before he reached the safety of
the other side, the inspiration struck him to look over his shoulder and
wave the next soldier on behind him, though he had no other men under
his command at this intersection.

"Nice acting, sir," Abbot said.

"When they fire, we've got to run directly at the cannon for one block,
then take a right."

"I don't think they're going to buy your theatrical—"

The last words of the sergeant's sentence were obliterated by the blast
from the Mexican twelve-pounder as hailstones of lead screamed by down
the street.

"Run!" Grant led the way into the cloud of smoke that he hoped would
hide him and Abbot for the hundred-yard race. He hoped the enemy
would reload slowly. He hoped they didn't have a second gun ready to
fire. He hoped and hoped until he hurtled around the corner to the safer
cross street. Here, he found six Americans from the Third Infantry who
had apparently been pinned down by the sniper Sergeant Abbot had
killed just minutes ago.

Beyond them he saw dead men laid out in the street and wounded
soldiers sitting on the cobblestones, leaning against the walls.

"Sir, what do we do?" a corporal said. "Our officers are all shot or
dead."

Grant looked at the weary fighters, their hands, faces, and uniforms
stained with blood and powder burns. Except for the corporal, they were
all privates.

"How are you boys fixed for ammunition?" Grant asked.

"Sir, we're all down to a few rounds." The corporal opened his near-empty ammunition pouch to bolster his claim.

Grant knew the scattered men of his own company were in the same fix, one or two blocks farther back. He turned to Sergeant Abbot and pointed to the sandbags above, where the sniper had died. "Sarge, take these men and hold that rooftop, but do not advance closer to the plaza. I'll do my best to get you some more ammunition. In the meantime, choose your targets well and don't miss."

Abbot nodded and kicked in the door to the house. As the privates streamed in behind Abbot, Grant caught the corporal by the sleeve.

"Do you have any idea where Colonel Garland is?"

The corporal pointed down the side street, to the south. "Sir, you'd have to cross that goddamned street again, with them cannons waiting for you."

"Where is the general?" he demanded.

"If you make the crossing alive, there's an alley to the left. It will lead you to the general's headquarters in an abandoned store. But there's snipers everywhere, sir."

Grant nodded. "Hold that rooftop!" he ordered, pointing to the door Abbot had kicked in.

The corporal swallowed hard and charged into the house.

"Sir, look out below," Sergeant Abbot's voice warned from above.

Grant looked up to see his first sergeant at the sandbagged corner formerly held by the enemy sniper. Abbot held a fistful of the dead sniper's uniform as he muscled the corpse over the parapet. Grant leaped aside as the dead man's body slammed into cobblestones and lay in a twisted heap. Half the man's head had been blown away by Abbot's rifle ball. The horrific spectacle made Grant yearn to put some distance between himself and the corpse, even if it meant sprinting again into the path of Mexican ordnance.

Grant turned south, took a breath, and ran across the street as fast as he could. The Mexicans were becoming more vigilant, and they loosed a round that just missed his heels. He found the alley to the left and trotted to the next block, where he located General Garland's field headquarters in a haberdashery guarded by a handful of enlisted men. Half a dozen horses were tied nearby. Grant ordered the guards aside and entered the store.

"Lieutenant Grant reporting, sir," he said with a salute.

Two captains and a major turned to scowl at Grant, as if he had upset their tea party or something. His regimental commander, Colonel John Garland, looked up from the chair where he sat. A map of Monterrey lay spread on a table in front of him. He threw himself back in his chair and sighed.

"Report, Grant." Garland brushed his fingers against his brow in an irritated salute that seemed more like a swat at a mosquito.

"Sir, my company is two blocks from the plaza, with one advance platoon at one block away and holding a rooftop there. Sir, we need ammunition."

Garland stood and paced across the store, rubbing his brow. His long, thin strands of dark hair snaking over his pale scalp made him look quite mad to Lieutenant Grant. He seemed beleaguered by the stress and losses of the past two days. He looked back at his staff.

"Gentlemen, we must find a volunteer to ride back to General Twiggs. We need ammunition soon or we will have to withdraw."

Grant stepped forward. "I volunteer, sir."

Garland returned to his map on the table and tapped it with his index finger. "You'll have to ride past several streets guarded by enemy artillery."

Grant nodded. "Yes, sir. I'll need a mount."

"Take Major Barbour's horse. Barbour's dead."

Grant thought about Major Phillip Barbour, killed in the prime of his life. "Yes, sir. Which horse might that be, sir?"

"It's the sorrel, Sam," said Captain Ben Alvord, of the Fourth. "Come on, I'll show you." ·

Grant walked outside with Alvord.

"This was Barbour's mount," Alvord said.

Grant looked at the lean sorrel with approval. "What happened to Major Barbour?" he asked as he pulled the cinch tight on the saddle.

"Musket ball got him. Just around the corner there, in the street."

Grant grabbed the pommel and threw a long right leg over the cantle without using the stirrup.

"You'll get through, Sam. You can ride."

"I've been watching the Texans. Learning."

Alvord smiled. "I know. I've seen you training."

Colonel Garland stepped out with a note, which he handed up to

Grant. "If General Twiggs can't help with the ammunition, ride all the way back to General Taylor's headquarters."

"Yes, sir," Grant said, saluting.

"Godspeed," Alvord said.

Grant looked north and thought about the Texas Rangers he had witnessed. From watching them, he had learned to position himself on the side of a mount—to use the horse as a shield. He spurred and turned the sorrel several times in the street, first to the left, then to the right. This horse would have to know who was in charge from the get-go.

Grant spurred to a full gallop and slid to the right side of the running beast. His right hand held mane and reins. His left elbow hooked the pommel. His right foot was in the stirrup, but his left leg bent at the knee around the cantle. By the time he crossed the first street guarded by Mexican guns, only his left shin and forearm were exposed to enemy fire.

The gun fired at him after he was two full lengths onto safe ground. Now, on came the next intersection. The cobblestones passed under him in a blur as horseshoes clacked a staccato rhythm. Again, the cannon shot was far too late to cause him harm. He crossed a third street, then pulled himself up onto the saddle and reined the sorrel to a stop. Ahead, he saw American gunners reloading a six-pounder that had two ropes tied to its trail. This reloading was taking place in the safety of the cross street, in Grant's pathway.

What the devil are they doing? Grant thought.

He rode closer, letting the sorrel gelding catch some wind. He recognized Captain Samuel French giving the orders to reload. One of the ropes tied to the cannon's trail ran across the street to three gunners, who waited at the other end of the rope. A sergeant used a linstock to light a fuse at the breech of the cannon.

"Heave!" Captain French yelled to the men across the street.

The artillerymen pulled their rope, causing the loaded howitzer, fuse burning, to trail into the street, but its muzzle turned back toward Grant as it lumbered into the intersection. Grant quickly dismounted and stood behind his horse. Once in place in the middle of the street, French ordered the men on his side of the intersection to pull their rope, which turned the muzzle of the gun toward its intended target—a Mexican barricade a few blocks away.

The six-pounder and a Mexican gun fired at each other simultaneously, filling the street with deafening blasts, clattering projectiles, and blinding smoke. Grant quickly mounted and rode forward to speak to Captain French.

"Where's the rest of your crew?" Grant asked, as the men pulled the cannon back into the side street for reloading.

French looked up at him, his face blackened, his eyes wide and white. "Dead or wounded. Where are you going?"

"I'm riding to request ammunition."

"Good. We're running out fast."

"Smart thinking with the ropes," Grant said. He glanced at the gunners as they rammed the next load of grape down the tube, and he knew the Mexicans would be almost reloaded by now as well. "I'd better ride."

French nodded and turned to his crew. "Sergeant! The fuse!"

Grant rode back the way he had come for a few yards, then turned about, spurred his mount, and slid to the right side of the horse, clinging to cantle and pommel. The enemy did not bother to fire after he cleared the intersection. He figured they were probably awaiting another chance to disable French's gun.

He galloped on past the next crossing, and the next, blasts whirring behind his sorrel's flaxen tail. Now he pulled himself up onto the saddle again, knowing that he was beyond the streets guarded by Mexican ordnance. He let his pony slow to a trot and noticed a sentry standing guard in front of a captured house.

"What's this, Private?" he asked.

"Wounded men, sir."

Grant dismounted and tied his horse to an iron ring embedded in the stone wall for just that purpose. He loosened the saddle cinch to let the animal breathe deeply. He entered the makeshift hospital. Immediately the odors of urine, feces, and vomit assailed his nostrils, yet he forced himself to take stock so he could report the situation to his superiors.

Looking across the room, he saw men lying about on the floor with all manner of injuries to their limbs, heads, and torsos.

"Sam," a voice said.

He looked and found the familiar face of Lieutenant John C. Territt. As his eyes swept down the man's body, he saw Territt's hands trying to hold in his bowels, which were protruding from a belly wound. Grant's legs grew weak and he dropped to one knee beside Territt, his head swimming and his stomach turning.

"I'm riding to report to General Twiggs, John." He focused on Territt's eyes so he wouldn't faint from the sight of the ghastly wound. "I will tell him you're here."

Territt nodded. "Is it bad, Sam?"

Grant wasn't sure if Territt even knew what he was saying. "I will send help, John." He forced himself to stand on shaking legs. "I must go quickly."

Outside, Grant tightened his cinch, mounted, and left at a lope for General Twiggs's headquarters.

Shall I report that place as a makeshift hospital or a morgue? Why am I riding high, unscratched, while men like Territt writhe in their pain and delirium? Why did we come here? Why did we not stop at the Rio Bravo?

Questions haunted him as he searched the rooftops for snipers, the streets for artillery, and the cornfields for lancers.

JOHN COFFEE HAYS

Colonel Jack Hays walked out of the Bishop's Palace and pulled his captured sombrero down low over his eyes. His second-in-command, Lieutenant Colonel Sam Walker, strode through the stone archway beside him. From this vantage, they could look down over the streets of Monterrey from a perspective usually reserved for things with feathers.

Colonel Jack Hays grabbed Walker's sleeve and swept his hand across the urban terrain below. "Sam, this is better than looking at General Worth's map. You know this town better than I do. How would you lead this attack?"

With his stubbled chin, Walker pointed southwest. "You see the Saltillo road?"

"Clearly."

"Once inside the city, its name changes to Calle de Monterrey. If you look close, you'll see that it forks a couple of blocks into town. That left fork is Iturbide Street."

Hays squinted at the buildings and thoroughfares a few hundred feet below and a half mile away. "Iturbide leads to the north end of the plaza, and Calle de Monterrey leads to the south end."

"Right," Walker said. "The houses on those streets don't stand alone. They all run together, each house sharing a wall with the neighbor."

"That will make them harder to take."

"We'll have to go through those walls inside the houses."

Hays could tell Walker had been thinking hard about this. More than just a border warrior now, Walker had stepped into his role as Lieutenant Colonel of the Texas Mounted Volunteers.

"I don't reckon it'll be easy, Sam, but those are our orders. We clear those city blocks between those two streets and we'll carve a path to Ampudia's headquarters at the plaza." He waited for Walker's reply, but none came. "You take Calle de Monterrey and I'll take Iturbide."

"Colonel Hays, if you please . . ."

Walker's tone surprised Hays, for his friend rarely spoke to him with such military formality. "What is it, Sam?"

"I request Iturbide Street."

"Why's that?"

"They marched me down that street in leg irons four years ago. I aim to return with shootin' irons today."

Hays smiled. "You may have your choice of streets, Colonel. You take Iturbide. I will take Calle de Monterrey."

This morning, they had heard faraway gunfire and knew that General Taylor had renewed the attack on the eastern end of Monterrey. About noon, Hays had received orders from General Worth to report to the Bishop's Palace, where Worth had established his new headquarters. He and Walker had ridden immediately up Independence Hill to the palace, where they found General Worth strutting about like a king in his new castle. Worth had ordered them to dismount four hundred Rangers and advance into western Monterrey on foot. The fighting would be house to house, hand to hand.

Now he and Walker mounted their horses for the ride back to the Ranger camp to assemble their storming parties. They would be supported by Worth's artillery battalion and troops from the Seventh and Eighth infantries. But the Rangers would serve as the tip of the bayonet for the thrust toward the plaza.

"I wasn't at Mier, Sam, but today's fight will be a lot like the rooftop battle there."

The two Rangers let their horses walk down the slope.

"I was in the advance guard that got captured the day before Mier. I could only listen to the fight from the calaboose."

"Well, there are a few other boys in the outfit who were there. Bigfoot Wallace, for one. I've heard him tell the story so many times that I feel like I was almost there."

"That and a thousand other stories," Walker said.

Hays chuckled. "Bigfoot's been known to spin a yarn."

"And stretch the blanket."

Their mounts plodded down the grade.

"We have one advantage here that they didn't have at Mier," Walker said.

"What's that?"

"Artillery."

"Well, yeah, Sam, but it won't do us much good today in those narrow streets."

"I'm not talking about the guns. I'm talking about the shells."

Hays looked at his second-in-command and narrowed his gaze. "I don't follow you, Sam."

"I have an idea."

"Well, do tell."

Lieutenant Colonel
SAM WALKER

He ran forward in the darkened house and slammed his shoulder against a wooden door to the next room. The door cracked and flew open. Lieutenant Colonel Sam Walker charged in and noticed light streaming in from the trapdoor to the roof. A musket fired from behind an overturned table, its bullet creasing Walker's scalp. The Mexican foot soldier leaped over the table and advanced with a bayonet, but Walker fired with his Colt revolver until the enemy defender fell dead in the middle of the room.

Another fighter, dressed in the white cotton clothes of a peasant, tried to climb the ladder to the roof, until Walker's bullets brought him tumbling down.

"Take the roof, Jake," he ordered the Ranger behind him. "Take three men with you."

The Ranger named Jake climbed the ladder. "Come on, Henry! You, too, Lem, and bring that kid, Cooper."

Outside, small arms cracked in an irregular cadence, punctuated by the boom of a Mexican twelve-pounder. For hours, now, Walker had led his two hundred men up Iturbide Street. He had storming parties in the houses, in the streets, on the roofs, and in the small backyards behind the houses along Iturbide Street. The progress had been slow, for the stubborn Mexicans would not retreat until hard pressed. But, by signaling back and forth to Hays's battalion on Calle de Monterrey, the two spearheads could support each other with cross fire or flanking maneuvers. They had now advanced to within a few blocks of the plaza.

Shoving his spent revolver under his belt, he yelled back into the room behind him. "Bring the crowbars, boys! We're going through the wall to the next house!"

Two young Rangers entered with pry bars and a pickax. They tore into the wall with their tools, sending dust and rock shards flying across the once neatly kept room. Walker spotted a chair lying sideways on the floor. He righted it, sat down, and removed the barrel from his Colt. He reached into his ammunition pouch for a spare cylinder already loaded with five shots. This he switched with the spent cylinder as he listened to the gunfire from the roof.

Just as he put his reloaded Colt back together, Jake yelled down from the trapdoor.

"Sir, Colonel Hays is signaling from the next street!"

"What's he want?"

"He wants us to flank the Mexican battery on Calle de Monterrey and roust 'em out of there while he attacks from the other flank."

"I need five minutes to get through this wall, then we'll flank that barricade."

"Yes, sir, I'll signal back."

The men with the pickaxes and crowbar tired and handed their tools to other Rangers who had been waiting to take over with fresh muscle. Walker watched them tear through stone and mortar as he fought off memories of men hurt or killed in the assault today.

"We're gettin' close, Colonel Walker," one of the Rangers said.

Walker stood. He yelled through the door he had broken down. "Where's that shell?" he demanded. "Bring the candle, too."

A Ranger came into the room carrying a spherical mountain howitzer shell with a paper fuse inserted into the fuse plug. The fuse had been trimmed to three seconds. Another man brought a lighted candle, his palm shielding the flame as he moved swiftly into position.

"One more whack ought to do it, sir," said the Ranger with the pick.

"Against the wall!" Walker ordered.

The men hugged the wall on either side of the hole being gouged by the tools. This maneuver had become routine, after hours of breaking into one house after another on this bloody day. This was Walker's idea of which Hays had approved. All day his warriors had used the exploding artillery shells in their dangerous game of breaking and entering from house to house.

Now Walker drew his Colt and took his place beside the damaged wall. He nodded to the man with the pick. "Hit it hard," he said.

The Ranger made a mighty swing that caused a large stone to fall away from the hole, creating the opening to the next house. A musket barrel jutted through from the other side and fired, but missed the Rangers who had wisely positioned themselves against the wall. Walker forced the barrel of his revolver through the hole, firing three times. He waited a few seconds, but no other shots came from the other side.

He belted his Colt. "Shell!" he said, holding out his hand.

The Ranger with the howitzer load handed it to Walker.

"Flame!" Walker took the candle handed to him. "You boys best hunker down now." He touched the fire to the fuse on the shell and watched it burn for a second, then dropped it through the hole in the wall and dove for the corner.

"Fire in the hole!"

The blast hurled large stones into the room and deafened Walker. He nonetheless sprang to his feet and leaped blindly through the gaping hole clouded by dust and smoke. Muzzle blasts appeared as orange flashes through the smoke in front of him. Walker fired his Colt, heard screams through the ringing in his ears.

Suddenly someone was upon him, and he felt something sharp slash through his shirt and past his ribs. In the dark and choking dust, he grabbed his attacker's wrist, prodded around with the muzzle of the Colt until he felt the body mass he sought, and pulled the trigger.

Now the candle was in the room and men in Mexican uniforms could be seen withdrawing to the next room, slamming a door behind them. Walker looked down at the dead man he had shot through the heart. He pulled his own shirt up to see a flesh wound bleeding, one of his rib bones exposed.

"You hurt, Colonel?" a Ranger asked.

He shook his head. "Missed my vitals. You men clear this house. I'm going back out in the street to rush that barricade for Jack." As he turned, he tripped over a body and found a young Ranger who had caught a musket ball upon entering the room. He knelt and found the boy conscious, a grimace on his face. He knew this kid. A hard case, and brave: Corporal John Fullerton, from Company K.

"We'll get you out of here," Walker said to Fullerton.

"I can still fight," the corporal said. "Put me in the doorway and I'll guard the rooftop across the street."

Walker nodded. The dust was settling, and light from the trapdoor revealed a large pool of blood spreading around Fullerton's resting place. "I'll get somebody to help you out there. Till then, you just rest, and know you did one hell of a job."

"Yes, sir."

"I'll mention you to the generals. You're liable to get a medal or some-thin'."

Fullerton grinned through his pain. "I don't need no goddamn medal, sir. I served with Sam Walker."

Walker squeezed the young man's shoulder and nodded. He rose. Coughing up some dust, he passed back through the hole blasted by the shell and returned to the doorway on Iturbide Street.

That kid's probably already dead, he thought. *That's what serving with Sam Walker will get you.*

He remembered that Jack Hays was expecting him to flank an artil-lery barricade about now. "Buck!" he shouted, spotting Sergeant Buck Barry guarding the street. "Get a dozen men and come with me!"

"Yes, sir! Where we goin'?"

The enemy twelve-pounder around the next corner hurled another round.

Walker pointed toward the source of the blast. "We're gonna flank that piece and get some revenge for John Fullerton!"

Colonel
JOHN COFFEE HAYS

West Monterrey, Mexico
September 23, 1846

Hays removed his hat to peek around the corner with one eye. The Mexican gunners were still unaware of his presence, two blocks away, busy reloading their twelve-pounder following the last shot.

This would have been the perfect moment to attack. Where the devil is Walker?

"Mike!" he hissed in a hoarse whisper.

Major Mike Chevaille, his third-in-command, looked down from the rooftop. He had taken up a well-sandbagged position recently abandoned by Mexican sharpshooters.

Hays made a demanding shrug with his shoulders.

"Still no sign of them, Jack."

"We can't stay here forever without being spotted. I'm of a mind to charge without Walker!"

A barrage of rifle fire drew Hays back to the corner for another peek.

"That's them!" Chevaille said. "I see Walker and Buck Barry with a herd of Texans!"

"Fire!" Hays cried, showing his vitals now around the corner as he took aim with a rifle. He saw a Mexican gunner drop as the white smoke cleared. Some half dozen Rangers fired from rooftops, having stealthily slipped around the left flank of the Mexican barricade. Now Sam Walker and his men were attacking the right flank.

"Give 'em hell, boys!"

Hays left his rifle and led his men down the street at a sprint, as others on the rooftops rose into view to cover the ground assault. He felt the familiar rush of danger charge his legs with power as he pulled two Colt five-shooters from his belt. Hugging the right side of the street so that his bullets wouldn't fly straight down the middle, toward Walker's men, he aimed at a slant at the defenders of the barricade. A brave gunner trying to ram a shell down the muzzle of the cannon caught his first round. His following nine bullets, and the storm of lead from the other Rangers, killed seven gunners and sent the survivors running for their last refuge at the main plaza.

He heard U.S. soldiers cheering, down Calle de Monterrey, as the Texans captured the cannon and began to turn it toward the plaza. Hays waved the regulars on from the barricade, urging them forward to hold the position. Throughout the day, the army troops had gotten more aggressive about following close behind the Texans' advances.

"Guard these streets!" Hays shouted to his men as he watched Walker trot his way from Iturbide Street. "These buildings may still be occupied by shooters."

Walker arrived, a toughened sneer on his powder-burned face. A cake of bloody dust covered his clothes and flesh.

"Sam, if you had any more soil on you, you'd be real estate."

Walker did not reply.

Hays now felt that old creeping sense of someone staring—probably across the irons of a rifle. He looked upward and toward the plaza and saw the belfry of the central cathedral, visible over the rooftops. A silhouette moved in the open top of the old stone bell tower.

Pulling Walker by his elbow, around the corner to safety, he said, "Watch that bell tower, Sam. There's a sharpshooter up there."

Walker had his hand up and yanked his arm free of Hays's grasp. "This is a hell of a time to worry about Mexican marksmanship."

"I didn't say I was worried."

Hays looked up at Major Chevaille, who had run across the rooftops to reach the corner over the barricade. "Mike, watch that belfry on the plaza for snipers!"

"I've got my sights on it, Jack."

A lull in the gunfire allowed human sounds to be heard. A man screamed in pain somewhere. A Mexican officer shouted an order. Then . . .

"Did you hear that, Sam?"

"Can't hear much over the ringing." Walker pointed at his ears.

"There it is again! An order to reload. In English! I can hear Americans on the east side of the plaza. We've got them all but corralled, Colonel!"

One side of Walker's scowl curled up to form a half grin. "I aim to sleep in the post office on the plaza tonight."

Hays felt his eyebrows gather. "The post office?"

"That's where they chained us Mier prisoners four years ago. And there I will return, with shootin' irons instead of leg irons."

Colonel Hays nodded and flashed a smile at Walker.

A shot from Major Chevaille's rifle made a chime ring from the cathedral tower.

From the roof, Chevaille laughed. "Ha! Blood on the church bell, boys!"

ZACHARY TAYLOR

Old Rough and Ready stood over his map of Monterrey, peering down at it. Pebbles marked the locations of various U.S. units closing in on the main plaza of the capital city. Worth and the Rangers were clawing closer, inch by inch, to the west. Elements of Quitman's brigade had pushed equally close to the cathedral, on the east side of the plaza.

Pebbles on a map.

With his next breath, Taylor somehow found himself soaring over real terra firma adorned with beleaguered buildings and bloody streets. He could hear men shouting, screaming, crying. Gunfire rattled and cannon roared. He glided through the rising smoke, hawk-like, to gaze down upon the enemy troops crammed into the plaza. They stood ready to die, rank upon rank, file upon file, their bayonets fixed, their swords sharpened. He knew his men could whip them in a final bloodbath at close quarters, but he feared hundreds would perish on both sides.

Far away, he heard the tapping of Major Bliss's West Point ring on his tent pole. Like lightning, General Zachary Taylor came flashing back into his bodily vessel, back into his headquarters tent.

"Sir, there are new dispatches from Worth and Quitman," Bliss said.

Taylor blinked away the impossible sights, sounds, and smells he had just witnessed. "Come in and tell me what they say, Bill. My eyes have grown weary from staring at this damned map."

"Sir, an officer waved a white flag on the west side and handed over a letter from Pablo Morales, the governor of Nuevo León, who is trapped in the city. He requests that the noncombatants be allowed to leave the town."

Taylor frowned. He didn't like to think of civilians getting caught up in battles. This was his first taste of leading an assault in an urban environment, and the idea of families getting trapped in their own homes did not sit well with him. On the other hand, they had had weeks to vacate the city and should have done so if they were not prepared to risk their own lives.

"Bill, what would you do?" Taylor asked.

"I would deny the request," Bliss said.

"Why?"

"We would have to suspend our attack. They are trying to buy time, that's all. Also, with the civilians gone, the Mexican Army would have more rations and they could hold out longer."

Taylor nodded. "I agree. We will deny the request. What else?"

Bliss shuffled through some papers. "Generals Quitman and Worth both request a coordinated attack on the plaza before dark. They believe the Mexican Army of the North can be crushed by nightfall."

Taylor stared at the map without really seeing it. He knew President Polk would favor the final attack. If it succeeded, Polk could take credit. If it failed, he could blame the field commander. Oh, how James K. Polk would love to see Old Rough and Ready dash his own chances to become the Whig candidate for the presidency.

"Sir?" Bliss said. "What are your orders, sir? Do you authorize the coordinated attack?"

"No."

"No? Sir?"

He glared at Bliss and raised his voice a notch. "No, I do not authorize the attack. On the contrary, I order all units engaged to withdraw for the night."

Bliss, looking stunned, held the dispatches in his hand, offered them up to Taylor. "Sir, the Texas Rangers are begging for orders to attack the plaza. The Mexicans are all but whipped."

Taylor felt his temper flare, and he dashed the dispatches from his adjutant's grasp with a swipe of his meaty palm. "I will not provide the Mexicans with their own version of the Alamo to avenge!" he shouted.

Bliss staggered back a step.

Taylor took a deep breath. "I know we could crush them tonight, Bill. But the toll on our own ranks would be insupportable. They are superior to us in number. Our men—especially the Texas Rangers—are exhausted and near starved. If our men must fight again tomorrow, they will fight rested and with food in their bellies. General Ampudia can ponder his own fate overnight. Order the men to withdraw a safe distance from the plaza."

"Yes, sir." Bliss stooped to pick up the papers from the ground.

Taylor dropped to one knee to gather a few himself. "I lost my temper, Bill."

"It's understandable, sir."

Taylor struggled to rise, his knees stiff and aching. As he handed over the sheaves, he placed a hand on Bliss's shoulder. "We are deep inside a foreign and hostile nation, Bill. Our supply line is tenuous. Ampudia may counterattack in the dark on streets he knows infinitely better than we do. That old war dog, General Santa Anna, is raising a new army down south. We cannot afford to lose two or three hundred of our best soldiers, and I fear that would be the toll for storming the plaza tonight."

"I understand, sir."

"Has the ten-inch mortar been moved into place at the cemetery in Monterrey?"

"Yes, sir. The gunners await your orders to fire upon the plaza."

"They must not fire until the infantry units withdraw. I don't want an errant mortar falling on our own men that close to the plaza."

"Yes, sir."

"Once our men are clear, we will bomb the hell out of them overnight. General Ampudia can ponder his chances with shells falling about that cathedral full of ammunition."

"I will prepare the written orders for your approval, sir."

"Very well. Do it quick, before those Texas Rangers lose their patience and attack on their own accord."

"Yes, sir," Bliss said, hustling out of the commander's tent.

Taylor decided he should try to rest while Bliss executed the orders. He lay on his cot and listened to the distant cannon fire. He closed his eyes, but thoughts of supply lines, troop movements, and battle strategies swam in his head like schools of fish. He tried to conjure a vision of his plantation in Louisiana but could not for the life of him visualize it for more than a few seconds before the war dragged his worries back to

Mexico. He could not even remember what his own wife's face looked like.

So he decided to direct his thoughts elsewhere. Lately, he had found that he could escape his burdens for a while by losing himself in a new form of reverie. Years ago, such musings would never have occurred to him. Only recently had he begun to picture himself in a new and lofty role.

Though he rarely wore a uniform, in this new fantasy he imagined himself in full dress plumage, with sashes, epaulets, and medals. He stood in front of a great crowd outside the President's Mansion in Washington. A judge—probably a Supreme Court justice—presented a Bible. In his fantasy, he solemnly placed his old soldier's hand on the Good Book, to be sworn in as president of the United States of America.

Captain
JOHN RILEY

It was a darling little bomb. Embroidered in golden thread, the insignia on the lapel of his tunic depicted a bursting sphere with a sparkling fuse. The *soldaderas* had done an impossible job of cleaning the soot and grime of the three-day battle from his artillery uniform—right down to the bomb-burst insignia that identified him as an artillerist. Captain John Riley was a gunnery officer, by God. In this he took great pride.

Standing alone in the makeshift tent the *soldaderas* had fashioned for him from a square of canvas, he donned the jacket, the seams straining about his muscular shoulders. He had washed his face and hands in a bucket of water but had not had a proper bath in a week. No matter. If he survived this day he would find a clear mountain stream and cleanse his body, if not his soul.

The battle for Monterrey was over. The Americans had not dared to attack the Citadel—which he now knew they called the Black Fort—but they had managed to capture every other fortification manned by Mexican defenders. General Ampudia had not had the stomach for mortar fire falling upon the plaza so near the crates of ammunition stacked in the main cathedral in town. Ampudia had waved the white flag and asked General Taylor for terms of surrender.

Ampudia's surrender disgusted Riley and his men. Many other Mexican officers agreed, some labeling their general a coward. As for the exact terms of the surrender, Riley had heard only rumors, and those tidbits of information had come to him in Spanish, a language still mostly mysterious to him. But now he had been summoned by his commander, Colonel Francisco Moreno. Moreno, because he spoke English, had been chosen by Ampudia to negotiate terms with the Americans. He would know the details of the agreement with Taylor.

Riley placed his kepi on his head, left his tent, and marched to the cathedral-turned-ammunition-depot in the middle of the Citadel. All around him soldiers rushed about like ants, preparing to leave the Citadel and march south under armistice terms that were still unclear to him. Men loaded wagons, hitched mules, and shouted at one another in Spanish.

Through this chaos, Riley strode into the cathedral, down the nave, to a little stone room behind the chancel, which Colonel Moreno had chosen for his headquarters. His profound worry made him plod more slowly as he approached the room. Since hearing of the surrender, two questions had haunted him: Had Taylor demanded that all U.S. deserters in the Mexican ranks be handed over? If so, had Ampudia agreed to give them up?

An affirmative answer to both questions meant almost certain execution for him and his men. Hanging? Firing squad? The dread weighed heavily upon his heart and mind. Yet there was hope. There was always hope. Perhaps the colonel had good news.

He found the doorway open and saw Moreno at his desk, writing. He knocked on the pine door.

"Begging your pardon, Colonel, sir. Captain Riley, reporting as ordered."

Moreno pointed at a chair but did not look up from the report he penned furiously, like a mad composer finishing his opus.

Riley sat and waited and worried. Finally the colonel completed his chore and swiveled in his chair to face his subordinate.

"Captain Riley," he began, "I wish to brief you in English on the details of the surrender and the resulting armistice so that you may inform your men what awaits them on this less-than-proud day."

Riley nodded. "A gesture most appreciated, sir."

"As you probably know, I was chosen as one of the officers to negotiate with the Americans."

"An honor to your professionalism, sir."

Moreno chuckled. "And to the fact that I happen to speak English, no?" He rose and paced the small room. "It was an experience not without intrigue, I assure you. Across the table, the American negotiators included General William Worth himself. Also a colonel named Jefferson Davis—a former senator from Mississippi and commander of a volunteer regiment. He was among the first to breach the defenses of La Teneria. And finally, Major General James P. Henderson, the governor of Texas and commander of a regiment of Texan volunteers."

"General Taylor was not present?" Riley asked.

"Only at the end, when the negotiations had been completed. The Americans provided a translator. I am satisfied that they were not aware of my fluency in the English language. This gave our committee a slight advantage over theirs. I spoke only Spanish during the negotiations."

"Canny."

"It was General Ampudia's idea. I will confide in you, Captain Riley, that I did not approve of the general's decision to surrender. But that sly old war dog . . . As a negotiator of terms . . . Well, let us just say that Ampudia got quite a bargain from Taylor."

"A bargain?" Riley hoped the deal did not include deserters from the U.S. ranks.

"The Army of the North will withdraw honorably from Monterrey— southward to San Luis Potosi. Our men will retain their personal arms and ammunition. But, alas, we are allowed to keep only one battery of six cannon. We must leave the big guns of the Citadel behind."

Riley groaned. "A tribute to our marksmanship, sir."

Moreno nodded. "*Claro.* There will be an armistice of eight weeks."

Riley's eyebrows raised. "Very generous. How did General Ampudia manage this?" He was still hoping that he and his men had not been made pawns in this exchange.

Colonel Moreno leaned forward with a wry grin. "Ampudia told Taylor that an American envoy has been welcomed into the city of Mexico to negotiate peace with the government!"

"Is it true?"

"No, it is a complete fabrication!" Moreno laughed. "While we took our coffee, I overheard Colonel Davis say to General Worth that the war was over! The fool!"

Riley tried to smile, but the worry over his fate, and that of his men, would not allow the expression. "About my men, sir. What is to become of us?" He saw Moreno look him in the eye. The colonel's grin melted away, and he seemed to read on Riley's face the dread he felt in his guts.

"You will surrender the Citadel with the rest of the defenders. In fact, it is almost time."

"And then, sir? What then?"

The realization seemed to slap Moreno in the face. "*Dios*, Capitan! You don't think we would hand you over to the Americans! *Nunca!* You fought bravely for three days with little food and sleep. You engaged and killed the enemy with great skill. You are Mexican soldiers now."

"And General Taylor agreed to this?"

"To be honest, the topic did not even arise. You are safe, Capitan. Your men will not be molested."

Riley bolted to his feet, the great weight lifting from his shoulders. "I must inform my men, sir." He felt an unexpected tear well up in one eye.

"Wait, Riley. There is another matter. Mexico's most cursed blessing, Santa Anna—or perhaps he is a blessed curse—has somehow returned to power to the south. He is raising an army to meet the American invaders." Moreno turned to gesture toward his desk. "I have just written a letter to General Santa Anna, extolling the skill and professional behavior of your men. I have recommended to him that you be placed in command of a battalion of immigrants recruited from the American ranks. This is what you wanted, was it not?"

Riley came to attention, pride forcing the last of the dread from his heart and soul. "That it is, Colonel, sir! That has been my fondest hope for myself and my men since I left the bloody heretics of the north!"

Moreno chuckled at his enthusiasm. "Steady, Capitan. General Santa Anna will have to approve. And, he is Santa Anna. One never knows what the old cripple might be thinking. We will see. For now, you are dismissed. Prepare your men to evacuate the Citadel and repair to the main plaza of Monterrey."

Riley saluted. "Thank you, Colonel! You will never regret your recommendation!" He made an about-face and strode from the room feeling more buoyant than he could have imagined upon entering. A tingling sensation shot up his neck and formed his lips into a fierce and menacing smile.

* * *

The exodus from the Citadel had gone smoothly yesterday. A regiment of American regulars had swept into the fort as soon as Moreno's men had vacated it. They had run the American flag up the pole to the tune of a twenty-eight-gun salute—one shot for each state in the United States.

Now, a day later, Riley stood shoulder to shoulder with his fellow defenders—the better part of Ampudia's Army of the North, formed up by regiments in the public square of Monterrey. The plaza still smelled of corpses and carrion, though most of the dead bodies had been removed and the carcasses burned. The stench did nothing to ease his nerves. He had begun to feel uncomfortable again about his safety, and that of his men.

Riley looked up at cheering American soldiers lining the rooftops of buildings all around the plaza. Some brandished weapons and screamed oaths at the conquered army below them. He turned his back to the cathedral towers and looked west. There, on top of the post office, stood the legendary Texas Ranger Sam Walker, with several of his hard-bitten men. Riley had been told that Walker had refused General Taylor's order to withdraw from the plaza the last night of the battle. He had spent the night in the post office—a place that had once served as his jail.

The Rangers looked menacing, but he feared the soldiers of the Fifth Infantry more than the Texans. He had not only deserted them but also fired upon them from the Citadel. He hoped General Taylor could control his victorious troops. Riley believed what he had been told—that Taylor had made no demand for deserters. Still, he felt uneasy. He knew his men stood out among the Mexicans. The former U.S. deserters were one hundred strong. Some sported blazing red hair. All were fair-skinned and sunburned. For these reasons, the Mexicans had begun to call them *los colorados*—the red ones.

How many American soldiers would love to take a shot at a deserter who had hurled bushels of grape and canister into their ranks?

Stand firm, Captain. Show neither weakness nor fear.

At length, drums rolled and bugles blared. Captain Riley took a seat on a caisson hitched to a limber behind a team of half-starved horses. The cavalry filed out of the plaza first, followed by infantry units. Finally, the artillery regiments began to roll.

He hadn't been shot yet. Maybe his luck would hold.

Lieutenant Patrick Dalton stepped up to Riley's side and marched along as Riley rode.

"Have you seen the men of your former regiment, sir?"

"Do not speak of it, Lieutenant. Think of camping this evening along a clear mountain brook."

Dalton took several steps, his eyes glancing nervously up at the Americans on the rooftops. "Aye," he said at length. "As a lad I once traveled up the River Slaney into the Wicklow Mountains. Did you ever see the Wicklows, Captain?"

"I ne'er did," Riley admitted. "I was a Galway lad with no means to wander."

"There are trout to catch in the River Slaney. Would that I could camp there this evening."

As the limber he rode bumped along over the cobblestones of the Calle de Monterrey, he began to feel more at ease. The bill of his kepi hid the color of his face from the Americans on the rooftops above him. He remembered strolling along this tree-lined thoroughfare before the battle. How beautiful and shady the street had seemed. Now the trees were all blasted to splinters and the homes and shops scarred by cannon fire aimed down the street at the Americans. So much grape had been hurled down Calle de Monterrey that the fronts of the houses looked as if plows had been pulled across them.

He trundled slowly onward until Calle de Monterrey became the Saltillo road. The homes and shops of the town gave way to fields and farmhouses—most of them also ravaged by artillery fire. Here, Riley found both sides of the road lined four deep with American soldiers. The dread began to sink into his stomach again as a psalm echoed, from somewhere long ago and far away, in his head: *Who rises up for me against the wicked? Who stands up for me against evil-doers? If the Lord had not been my help, my soul would soon have dwelt in the land of silence.*

This he needed to hear just now, for he began to pass by the men of the Fifth Infantry, to his right. The very regiment he had joined on Mackinac Island and deserted on the Rio Grande. The men were no longer on rooftops but alongside the road, at eye level. There was no hiding under his brim now.

Help me, Lord.

"Hey! By God, if that ain't Riley!" yelled some soldier among the Americans.

Riley kept his eyes trained forward as he felt his jaw tighten.

"The dastard!"

"You turncoat!"

"Traitor!"

"Treason! Hang him!"

"Hang them all! The whole sorry Irish lot!"

The din of angry voices grew around him, melding hisses, huzzahs, and howls.

Though I walk through the valley of the shadow of death . . .

Riley's heart pounded furiously to the rhythm of clopping hooves.

"May God help us," said Lieutenant Dalton.

"Keep your eyes straight ahead, Patrick!" Riley replied.

At length, the Fifth Infantry fell behind the procession, but then along came the ranks of the Third Artillery. These men also jeered at the deserters, for Riley and his men had poured heavy fire into their ranks from the Citadel. His nerve now bolstered by surviving the wrath of the Fifth Infantry, Riley allowed his eyes to dart among the men of the Third Artillery. He searched out and found Braxton Bragg, for the immigrant-hater sat ahorse that lifted him high above the rank and file.

Staring now at Captain Bragg, Riley waited until the sadistic nativist officer locked eyes with him. Each man glared at the other as Riley rolled past. From Bragg, Riley expected to hear all manner of curses and threats, but the American only scowled and remained silent. His lips formed an angry snarl, but Riley thought he could actually make out a hint of respect—perhaps even a modicum of fear—in Bragg's eyes.

He broke the staredown and looked forward through the dust of the marchers ahead of him. Up the road, he saw mountains looming. He thought now only of that clear mountain stream that awaited him.

Beside him, he heard Lieutenant Patrick Dalton heave a great sigh. "'Tis our own little flight of the wild geese, Captain."

"Aye. And lucky we are to have survived it."

"To fight another day."

Riley nodded. "And with the luck of the Irish and the blessing of General Santa Anna, we will fight again under our own banner. The flag of Saint Patrick!" He smiled, the weight of Monterrey now rolling from his shoulders like cannonballs down a hillside.

JAMES K. POLK

What a pleasant surprise, Polk thought. Finally, a man of culture, intelligence, and propriety sat across from him at his desk. The gentleman had only been sitting there a minute or two, engaging in polite small talk, but it didn't take James K. Polk long to measure the quality of a man.

This visitor, the honorable Francis M. Dimond, had been summoned from his home in Bristol, Rhode Island, for this most important meeting. Dimond had served as U.S. consul in the city of Veracruz for some time in the past. He was about Polk's age, maybe a few years older. He had dressed quite appropriately, in black trousers and waistcoat, a white shirt, and a black silk scarf. His wavy brown-and-silver hair seemed to cascade into striking sideburns in the shape of muttonchops. He was quite a handsome man—regal nose, strong chin, high forehead.

"I explored the Caribbean as a restless youth," Dimond was saying, a hint of a smile curling his lips. "My first post abroad was as consul at Port-au-Prince."

"I was not aware of that," Polk admitted. "And from there?"

"I took the position in the consulate at Veracruz, which I found a much more important and intriguing post."

Polk nodded. "And how long did you serve in Veracruz, Ambassador Dimond?"

"Ten years, Mr. President."

"Excellent." Polk placed his fingertips on the desk in front of him, almost as if preparing to play a piano. "Mr. Dimond . . ." He stared earnestly at the ambassador. "At this point I must impress upon you the most delicate nature of our discussion today. I am obligated to insist that every detail spoken between the two of us must remain absolutely confidential, as a matter of national security."

Dimond leaned forward in his chair, a most serious air emanating from his dark eyes. "You may rely upon my utmost discretion, Mr. President. I am well acquainted with the protocols involving the security of our nation."

Polk nodded. "Very well." He kicked his chair backwards and rose to pace behind his desk. "Describe to me, if you can do so from memory, the Mexicans' military defenses at the port of Veracruz."

Dimond interlocked his fingertips like timbers on a log house. "My memory is very clear, Mr. President. You may rely upon its veracity." He seemed to stare up at the curtain rod behind the president. "Since the French Navy invaded in 1838, some improvements have been made on the defenses protecting the harbor. Hundreds of modern guns are mounted in the city, and more inside the fort of San Juan de Ulúa, situated on the reef in the harbor. Large guns, sir. Up to twenty-four-pounders. And some heavy mortars as well."

Polk paused in the steady cadence of his slow pace behind the desk. "Yes, so I've gathered. I have been advised against attacking the harbor itself. But what about a landing somewhere along the coast, near Veracruz, yet out of range of the guns in the city?"

Dimond nodded. "I believe there exists just such a chink in the armor, Mr. President. A few miles south, off the coast, there is a tiny uninhabited island called Sacrificios. Vessels sometimes anchor in the lee of the island during storms. Across from Sacrificios, on the mainland, stretches Collado Beach. I have visited this beach on picnics and such. It is ample enough to land a large army out of range of all the big guns of Veracruz."

Polk was looking out through the window now. It appeared to be a beautiful autumn day in Washington, DC. Most of the leaves had already changed colors. He had promised Sarah that they would take a carriage ride to enjoy the fall foliage, but now it was too late. He tore his gaze away from the pane, wheeled, and looked directly at Ambassador Dimond. "And what of the defenses around the *rear* of the city?"

"As you know, Mr. President, Veracruz is a walled city in the old Spanish style. The wall and its fortifications begin on the coast to the south of the city, extend all the way around the western limits of the city, and end at the coast to the north of the city. But the old wall is in poor repair. It is mounted with older guns, and many of them are unserviceable."

"Do you believe the city could be invested from the rear and forced to surrender?"

"Because of the strained relations between Mexico and America, I have studied the possibility of such an attack for years. I believe it can be done, Mr. President. However . . ."

"Yes?"

"I have two concerns."

Polk sat back down in his chair, in case he should need to take notes. "What are they?"

"The first is the yellow fever season. The Mexicans call it *el vomito*. Veracruz must be secured before the annual return of this disease in the spring, and our army moved inland, away from the coast. Otherwise, the yellow fever will kill many more men than Mexican bullets would."

"I am aware of the *vomito*. The name somewhat amuses me in its horrific simplicity. I understand the necessity for haste, Ambassador Dimond. Now, what is your other concern?"

"The possibility of enemy reinforcements arriving from Mexico City. Especially with Santa Anna back in power."

The name rankled Polk as he remembered how he had been duped into letting Santa Anna return to Mexico. "And according to the papers, he is back in control in Mexico because of *my* gullibility!"

Dimond laughed. "Those fanciful stories in the Whig journals? I don't believe a word of it!"

Polk nodded his approval. "I wouldn't expect that a man of your abilities and experiences would believe it. Now, about Santa Anna. Do you know him well?"

"We have met, of course, but no one truly knows the enigmatic Santa Anna. He has always been a disaster for Mexico. He cares about himself more than his country. As a military leader, he has been known to spend more money on ostentatious uniforms and medals for his officers than on ammunition and food for his men. He will steal from anyone, any way he can, anywhere, anytime. He taxes everything under the sun, right down to the wheels of the peasants' oxcarts. He forces the tiniest businesses to loan him money that, of course, will never be repaid. He even seizes properties from the Catholic Church and sells them cheap to his cronies and henchmen. It is said in Mexico that Santa Anna only wants three things: money, money, money."

Polk allowed himself a rare chuckle. "His history suggests that he excels at building large armies. How does he manage to recruit so many soldiers?"

"He sends parties of ruffians galloping across the countryside, conscripting peasants and Indians like slavers preying on the tribes of Africa. But he also plays upon the patriotism of the wealthy class for money and leadership. As a propagandist, he knows no equal. He plays the press like a cheap violin. He blames everyone from Congress to his fellow generals for his defeats and takes credit for winning battles in which he barely participated. If he had not lost his leg on that pier in Veracruz, he would have been executed by now. And yet . . ."

"Yes?"

"He is capable of moments of absolute fearlessness in battle. He has a knack for seizing attention at the right moment to bolster his ambitions. He is unpredictable and dangerous."

Polk leaned back and folded his arms across his chest. He had heard enough about Santa Anna. "This landing south of Veracruz . . . the following bombardment and investment of the city . . . how many men do you think would be required for its success?"

Dimond shook his head carefully. "Sir, I served in the diplomatic corps. I have no martial experience."

"I understand this. Any recommendation you might make will be carefully scrutinized by military experts. But, Mr. Dimond, you have *lived* there. They have not."

Dimond seemed uncomfortable, yet he set his jaw and leaned forward. "No fewer than ten thousand men with ample artillery. And . . . Mr. President . . . were I in your shoes, I would prefer twice that number."

Polk rose to show Dimond to the door, very satisfied with the meeting and the information. "Your troop recommendations are quite similar to those of my top generals. Now . . ." He stopped at the door. "If you will consider one more favor."

"Of course, Mr. President. I am at your service."

"Can you remain in Washington a while longer? I would like for you to meet with my cabinet. I'm sure they will have more questions for you."

"I will be at my inn. And, Mr. President . . ." Dimond shuffled his feet and reached for the door handle.

"Yes, Ambassador?"

"Sir, my intentions upon returning to Rhode Island were to run for state legislature . . . perhaps governor someday."

"If I can do anything . . ."

Dimond looked embarrassed and waved off the suggestion. "No, sir, it's not that. I believe my plans may change. That is, if I can be of any service to my country. As an aide-de-camp, a guide, a translator. I daresay, after ten years in Mexico, I speak and write Spanish better than English. I know Veracruz and the road to Mexico City."

As a politician, Polk understood. There was scarcely a governor in the United States who could not claim some military experience. Dimond wanted his. He did not want to miss the coming fray, with all of its violence and possibilities of glory. But in spite of his political cynicism, the president could not have been more pleased with Francis Dimond. He beamed back at the ambassador.

"Your offer is deeply appreciated, sir, and will be considered very seriously."

Part III

MOUNTAIN, PLATEAU, AND BARRANCA

The Bloody Ground
of Buena Vista

Major
WILLIAM BLISS

Perfect Bliss rode a bay gelding down the cobblestoned street, past white-washed buildings and under the budding branches of apple and cherry trees that lined the thoroughfare. He admired the beauty of the city of Saltillo, situated on an open plain, flanked by peaks of the Sierra Madre. He glanced at his traveling companion, General Zachary Taylor.

"This Saltillo is a pretty little town, sir."

Taylor nodded. "I reckon the folks here didn't care for it to end up like Monterrey."

A group of Mexican children ran out onto the street to wave at the American general and his adjutant.

"Yes, sir, they have been quite hospitable." Bliss smiled and waved back at the barefoot urchins.

He liked the high desert air here at Saltillo. Since arriving, he had learned that the town boasted the nickname "La Ciudad del Clima Ideal." City of the Ideal Climate. Another moniker, "La Tierra del Serape"— Land of the Serape—laid claim to Saltillo as the birthplace of the garment now worn all over northern Mexico.

They passed a grand stone church with a bell tower and rode to the hitching rail in front of the American House, the unofficial meeting place for U.S. soldiers in Saltillo. From the outside, the American House looked like most other buildings along the street—a whitewashed stone structure with a flat roof, two small windows, and a carved pine door.

Bliss heard Taylor groan as he dismounted. He winced for the old general. He knew his commander suffered various aches, but Taylor never complained. Both men wrapped their reins around the slick rail and entered the American House.

Stepping inside, Bliss paused to allow his eyes to adjust from the brilliant blue sky to the darker interior of the combination hotel, saloon, and eatery. He saw several groups of soldiers enjoying drinks and conversation.

From behind the bar, the proprietress of the establishment looked at the door to see who had entered. Her name was Mrs. Sarah Borginnes, but she was known as the Great Western and "the Heroine of Fort Brown." The former army laundress's second husband—a Sergeant Borginnes—had died of illness back at Matamoras. Single ladies were not allowed to work as washerwomen for the army, so she had shifted careers. She had opened her first American House in Matamoras, where she served drinks and food to the troops and rented out rooms. She had later moved her establishment to battle-ravaged Monterrey, and now to Saltillo.

Here, Bliss had learned, Mrs. Borginnes allowed some of the local prostitutes to operate out of the American House. Indeed, he looked across the room and spotted no fewer than three senoritas sitting with men in uniform. It was rumored that the Great Western herself could be had for a price. Bliss didn't know that this was true, and his moral sensibilities forbade him from finding out for himself, but the prospect was not completely uninteresting, for she was a fine-looking woman.

Borginnes rushed to the door when she recognized General Taylor, her wavy auburn hair and her royal-blue skirt flying like the mane and tail of a beautiful filly.

"Oh, my, General, what an honor to host your return to the American House," she gushed loudly in a southern drawl.

Taylor smiled broadly. "The pleasure is all mine, Mrs. Borginnes."

She glanced briefly at Bliss, then trained her admiring gaze back on the general. "Would you like a private table? There's a nice one in the back."

"That would suit well, my dear."

Borginnes executed a pirouette that seemed too graceful for a woman her size, for she was taller than Bliss or Taylor. Looking beyond his commander as they followed their hostess to the back corner of the establishment, Bliss could not help admiring the woman's hourglass figure and graceful carriage.

"General Wool will be joining us this morning," Taylor said as he sat. "When he arrives, please show him to our table."

"Oh, my! It's a two-general mornin' here at the American House! May I offer you gentlemen a drink on the house?"

"Tea for me, ma'am," Bliss said.

Borginnes nodded and looked lovingly at Taylor.

"Do you have any sarsaparilla, dear?"

"I stashed a few bottles away just for you, General Taylor." She winked.

"Dear, this is your establishment. You are the commander here. Let us dispense with the formalities. Please call me Zachary inside these walls."

Borginnes gasped, then collected herself and smiled, revealing a gleaming row of straight teeth. "And you will kindly call me by my given name as well. It's Sarah."

"Thank you, Sarah."

"I'll bring the beverages, Zach."

Bliss chuckled as the hostess hurried away. "She skipped 'Zachary' and went straight to 'Zach.'"

"It's all the same, Bill." The general pulled a stack of envelopes from his coat pocket. He tossed about half of them at his adjutant. "Help me sort through the mail."

"I'll prioritize the envelopes for you, sir."

As Bliss combed through the correspondences from Washington and elsewhere, he was reminded of everything his commander had accomplished and endured since the victory at Monterrey. The best of it was the meteoric growth of Taylor's popularity in the newspapers—especially the Whig periodicals. The worst of it came from Washington, DC—particularly from President Polk and Secretary of War Marcy.

Polk and Marcy had sent scathing missives scolding General Taylor for not completely destroying Mexico's Army of the North at Monterrey and for allowing them to withdraw with their arms. They had ordered him to end the armistice immediately and to continue to prosecute the war. Then, curiously, they had directed him not to advance any farther south than Monterrey. Taylor boldly disobeyed this order and marched to Saltillo, taking the city without bloodshed, as there were no Mexican troops garrisoned there. He marched southeast to Victoria, also taking that town without firing a shot. Learning that Tampico had been captured by the U.S. Navy without resistance, he marched back to Saltillo, leaving a small force to hold Victoria.

Now he had established a line of defense stretching from Tampico to Saltillo and beyond, to Parras. It became known as "Old Zach's Line" in the newspapers. Then came the next assault from the rear—from the President's Mansion. Polk ordered Taylor to give up his best troops— General William Worth's division—for an invasion somewhere along the Gulf Coast—probably Veracruz. A painfully cordial letter from General Winfield Scott made it clear that Old Fuss and Feathers was assuming the command of the U.S. Army over Old Rough and Ready. Taylor was reprimanded for advancing to Saltillo and was told to go back to Monterrey with his depleted army, now made up mostly of newly arrived volunteers.

The insult was more than Taylor could bear. He had virtually broken off communications with Washington and had begun to conduct the war as he saw fit. Hence the meeting with General Wool today. Scouts and spies had discovered that Santa Anna was on his way from San Luis Potosi with some twenty thousand troops. Even with his ravaged army of six thousand, Taylor intended to stop Santa Anna and hold Old Zach's Line, whether the president wanted him to do so or not.

Thinking over all of this as he sorted through the mail, Bliss came across an envelope from the secretary of war. "Sir, here's one from Marcy," he said, handing it to Taylor.

Taylor took the envelope and scowled at it for a moment. "I'll prioritize this one myself," he said. Then he leaned sideways in his chair and slipped the letter under his rear end.

Bliss could not hold back his laughter. It became contagious, and he and the general had a long overdue chortle over the disrespectful gesture.

When Sarah Borginnes brought the drinks, she also brought an unexpected guest. Bliss knew the man—a legendary Texas Ranger, Ben McCulloch, veteran of San Jacinto, Plum Creek, and countless other battles under John Coffee Hays. He had served with distinction at Monterrey. Because of McCulloch's uncanny aptitude for tracking, trailing, and slipping behind enemy lines, General Taylor had brevetted the thirty-six-year-old to major and had appointed him chief of scouts.

"I thought I might find you here, General." The Texan removed his felt hat, unveiling a pale brow. His receding hairline revealed the shape of his regal crown. A short but thick beard, a straight mouth, and a wild, glaring pair of eyeballs rounded out his features. Like Taylor, he wore common civilian clothes.

"Sit down, Ben," Taylor ordered. "You look a might spent."

"I've come to report, General. I stayed the night before last in Santa Anna's camp."

Taylor let the letter in his hand slip from his fingers to the tabletop. He stared for a moment with his mouth open. "How close is he?"

"He's at Encarnación. Sixty miles south. Probably moving this way right now."

"Tell me about your visit." Taylor sat back in his chair and laced his fingers together across his belly.

"After dark, I posed as a laborer, slipped into the enemy camp, and climbed a hill. Come dawn, I got a good look at Santa Anna's army. He's got at least ten thousand foot soldiers, about four thousand lancers, and sixteen guns, ranging all the way up to twenty-four-pounders."

Bliss's brain added the numbers without effort. Fifteen thousand troops, give or take. What was left of Taylor's army amounted to six thousand men scattered from Saltillo to Agua Nueva. He thought he saw a hint of surprise in General Taylor's eyes.

"How did you get out of the enemy camp in broad daylight?" Taylor asked.

"They were burning green wood in their cook fires. I slipped out on a wisp of smoke."

"Very well, Major," the general said. "That's all I wanted to know. I am glad they did not catch you."

McCulloch stood and grabbed his hat. "Now, if you'll excuse me, General, I haven't et or slept in three days."

Taylor nodded and shook the major's hand. McCulloch did not so much as look at Bliss as he turned away.

The general nonchalantly went about sorting through his mail again, but Bliss knew he had to be a touch worried. He had not thought Santa Anna so near to Saltillo. Bliss kept his mouth shut and let his commander think things through. After a few minutes, he felt an imposing presence approaching from the front door and looked up to see General John E. Wool, who had ridden up from the south for the meeting.

Wool wore a smart uniform and a riding cape. His officers' forage cap was tucked under his elbow. When Taylor stood to greet Wool, Bliss grabbed the letter from Secretary Marcy and returned it to the table. It would not do for Wool to see Taylor plopping his ass on a letter from a member of Polk's cabinet. Bliss did not yet know where Wool's political sympathies resided.

The three men exchanged salutes and handshakes. Sarah Borginnes brought a mug of black coffee for Wool. She placed it on the table and turned dutifully away.

"I hope I haven't kept you waiting long," Wool said, taking his seat.

"Not at all," Taylor replied. "Any trouble?"

Wool shrugged casually. "Some guerillas took a few shots at us coming up Angostura Pass, but drew no blood."

"Have you talked to Ben McCulloch?"

"Yes, he reported to me this morning on his way here."

Bliss studied the old New Yorker as he and Taylor talked over the situation to the south. Bliss knew that both generals had been born the same year—1784. Like Taylor, Wool had fought the British in the War of 1812. He had rapidly made rank, due to his courage and organizational abilities. Recently, Wool had recruited 2,400 volunteer troops in San Antonio, Texas, and marched them south through Piedras Negras and Monclova to join Taylor in Saltillo. Wool's brigade was now at a place called Agua Nueva, waiting for Santa Anna's army to emerge from the vast desert to the south.

This was the first opportunity Bliss had had to study Wool's features up close. He was a lean man of average height, clean-shaven, and balding over the top of his head. What hair he did have on the side of his head swept forward toward his temples, as if he stood with his back to a stiff wind. His eyes gave the impression of haughtiness. Bliss had never seen Wool's mouth smile.

Taylor savored another sip of his sarsaparilla. "Major McCulloch believes Santa Anna is marching north now. You know the ground, John. Would you make a stand at Agua Nueva?"

Bliss pictured the village of Agua Nueva in his head. Several miles to the south, Taylor had established a supply depot, guarded by the Arkansas Volunteers, who called themselves Rackensackers.

Wool frowned. "I don't like the ground there. It's wide open. We will be outnumbered almost three to one, Zach. I fear we'd be flanked by their lancers, surrounded and destroyed by their artillery. We need ground we can defend."

"Where, then?"

"Hacienda Buena Vista, just above Angostura Pass."

"When I rode through there with my staff, I did not study it as a potential battleground. What is our advantage there?"

Wool leaned closer to his commander. "It is as if God has built a rampart for us at that place."

"You've studied the ground," Taylor said, more as a statement than a question.

"I know it like the back of my hand."

Bliss watched as Wool dramatically slapped his left hand onto the table, palm down, fingers slightly spread. His middle finger extended almost to the very edge of the table.

"The ground is something like this," he said, pointing to his left hand. "Let my old, weathered paw be our map. North is toward me. South is your side of the table. The Saltillo road runs northward past the ends of these spurs of high ground." He touched each of the digits on his left hand. "Angostura Pass is very narrow, between the tip of this longest finger and the rim of the deep canyon to the west."

Wool showed where the road ran between the end of his finger and the edge of the table.

"We can hold the road easily with a battery supported by two regiments of infantry. On the right flank, the ground drops off into this deep canyon that the enemy can ascend only with great difficulty."

Wool indicated the edge of the table dropping away into oblivion.

General Wool has rehearsed this presentation, Bliss thought. It was quite theatrical.

Wool continued. "This dried-up hide across my knuckles represents the plateau. It is tolerably level and open. On the left flank is a steep mountain." He indicated his wrist rising up to his forearm. "As you see, there are several fingers of high ground—spurs of the plateau that extend toward the road and Angostura Pass. The plateau is not a perfect five-fingered hand like God gave me, of course. Some of the fingers are longer than others, or wider, or even split, but you get the idea."

"So noted," Taylor replied.

"Between the fingers are ravines—rocky, brushy, and treacherous. If we hold the road at Angostura Pass—and we will—Santa Anna will be

forced to send his troops up the ravines between the fingers. We will have
the advantage of the high ground on the fingers of the plateau. His cavalry and ordnance will be hampered by terrain and vegetation. Our dragoons and flying artillery will be able to move swiftly on the high plateau
to block any advance that appears from the ravines."

Taylor nodded slowly and stared down at the relief map that Wool
had made of his left hand. "So, Hacienda Buena Vista stands right about
here." He tapped the tabletop off the end of General Wool's thumb.

"Your memory serves you well," Wool replied.

"I remember strong springs of good water there."

"Yes."

Major Bliss also remembered these springs at Buena Vista. They had
been channeled into a large, circular water tank of stone. The tank was
low enough that livestock could drink from it. By the nod of General
Taylor's head and a puckering of his lips, Bliss could tell that his commander approved of Wool's plan. Now Taylor nudged Bliss's elbow.

"Bill, write an order to the Rackensackers down south. Tell them to
remove our supply train from Agua Nueva and pull back, northward,
through Angostura Pass, to the springs at Hacienda Buena Vista."

Bliss watched Taylor trace the route around the plateau fingertips of
the human-hand map that Wool still held pressed to the tabletop.

"Yes, sir," Bliss said, clawing at his coat pocket for his notebook and
pencil.

"Then prepare orders for Captain John Washington's battery to occupy
and fortify the road at the narrows of Angostura Pass. Send an engineer
to design the fortifications."

"Right away, sir."

Taylor turned to General Wool. "When we withdraw our supplies,
Santa Anna will think we are retreating and he will press ahead even
harder. The enemy will be exhausted when they reach Buena Vista."

Wool nodded. "You know what tomorrow is?"

"Monday?" Taylor replied.

Wool's gaze drilled Bliss's eyes for the first time since entering the
American House. "Do *you* know, Major?"

"George Washington's birthday," the adjutant answered, risking a
slight smile.

"Ah, yes!" Taylor said. "A good day for Americans to fight!"

Captain
JOHN RILEY

Captain John Riley strode briskly toward General Antonio López de Santa Anna's headquarters, all the while sizing up the spectacle surrounding him. His battalion commander, Colonel Francisco Moreno, walked silently at his side.

The day had broken sunny and quite cool—a good day for fighting. He passed by Santa Anna's personal guard—an elite light cavalry unit bedecked with scarlet coats and known as the "Hussars of the Guard of the Supreme Powers"—the "supreme powers" being those of Santa Anna. Next, he passed the wagon carrying some twenty caged roosters brought along to entertain the commander and his officers in makeshift cockfighting rings. Passing by the crowing contenders, he came to the tent occupied by Santa Anna's courtesans—eight of them, by Riley's count, and all strikingly beautiful.

One of the senoritas stood in front of the tent, tossing water from a washbasin. She looked at him and smiled. "*Buenos dias*, Capitan Riley," she purred.

He nodded. "*Buenos dias*, senorita."

Colonel Moreno grunted his disapproval. "You have become quite popular in this army," he said, "but do not get too familiar with His Excellency's playthings."

"*Si*, Colonel," Riley replied. "I am a married man, though I haven't

seen my wife and son in over three years." Saying this made him wonder, sadly, how tall his boy had grown.

"All the more reason for caution. Find a young *soldadera* if you must,
but stay away from the president's property. He did not bring enough
women to share with junior officers. He has only one for every day of the
week and two for Saturday."

Moreno burst into laughter, and Riley joined him.

They walked on past the exquisite coach that transported Santa Anna.
It was pulled by six of the finest mules in Mexico and was large enough
to carry his staff or his courtesans, as his needs dictated.

Marching on around a bend in the barranca that had become Santa
Anna's camp only two hours ago, Riley caught sight of the opulent tent
that housed the supreme commander in the field. The red-and-green
canvas matched the colors of the Mexican flag that snapped in the north
wind above it. He and Moreno approached the hussar on guard at the
entrance. The enlisted man came to attention and saluted.

"Colonel Moreno and Capitan Riley reporting to His Excellency as
ordered," Moreno said, returning the hussar's salute.

The man ducked into the tent. After only a few seconds he returned.
"El Presidente invites you inside." He held the tent flap back for the
visitors.

Riley entered behind Moreno but could easily see over the colonel's
head and shoulders. Fine woven rugs carpeted the floor. Hand-carved
furniture made the place look more like a parlor than a camp tent. Silver
dishes and utensils awaited the president's next meal.

Now Riley spotted Santa Anna seated on a plush chair. His manservant, Juanito, knelt before him, attaching the famous peg leg to the president's stump.

"That's good, Juanito. Help me stand, then get out." The president
looked at Riley. "Capitan, hand me my staff." He pointed toward his portable writing desk with a nod of his head.

Riley saw the oak cane with the silver grip in the shape of an eagle's
head. The eagle's eyes were made of rubies. He handed the walking stick
to Santa Anna.

"Do you see, my fellow artillerymen, the sacrifices I have made for
Mexico? The years of privation and penury? Even the loss of my own leg!
But such is the life of a soldier for the people. *Sí?*

"*Sí*, Presidente," Riley said, in concert with the colonel.

"Soon, the legs of my charger will carry me with the speed of a raptor!" He brandished the silver eagle's head dramatically. "But for now I beg you to suffer my hobbling. Come outside with me."

Riley rushed forward to hold the tent flap aside.

Stepping into a ray of sun that had just cleared the mountain peak to the east, the supreme commander pointed to the north. "Do you see the crest of that hill ahead?"

"Yes, sir."

"Ride there. My chief engineer, General Mora y Villamil, awaits you at the foot of that hill. You are to determine if the hilltop is suitable for your artillery. If so, your San Patricios will place your battery there and wreak your vengeance on the barbaric heretics from the north who so mistreated you and your fellow immigrants in America."

Riley smiled and came to attention. He saluted and said, "With pleasure, Your Excellency!"

"You are a credit to the Catholic faith, Captain Riley. *Vaya con Dios.*"

Riley and Moreno turned back toward their camp, up the barranca, marching quickly along.

"Did you ever hear what became of Santa Anna's leg, Captain? I mean after it was shot off."

"By faith, I have not, sir."

"He had it buried with full military honors. There was a parade in la Ciudad de México."

"Sure, but that's a bit eccentric, Colonel."

"That's nothing. There's more. After Santa Anna was exiled to Cuba, the beggars and lepers of the city dug up the skeleton of his leg and dragged it through the streets! They pulled down the statue that he had commissioned in his own likeness and to his own honor!" Moreno threw back his head and laughed. "It is a miracle to see him back in power as president and commander on the battlefield. God help us all!"

Riley chuckled and thought back to his first meeting with Santa Anna. After the long retreat from Monterrey, he had been summoned for an audience with the president at San Luis Potosi. There, he had learned that his dream of forming his own battalion of Irish and other immigrant deserters would be granted, with Santa Anna's blessing.

He had named the battalion after Saint Patrick, the patron saint of Ireland. Saint Patrick's Battalion would become known to the soldiers and the citizenry of Mexico as the San Patricios. Next, Riley had set about designing a banner for his artillery unit. Upon a silken field of emerald green he imagined a golden harp flanked by shamrocks. Under the harp the familiar blessing *"Erin go Bragh"*—Ireland Forever—would declare allegiance to the Ould Sod.

Riley had taken his ideas and sketches to the sisters at the convent in San Luis Potosi. The nuns sewed and embroidered the banner expertly. Such had his fame spread in Mexico that the sisters considered it a holy honor to produce the flag.

As he began to drill his new gunners, Riley enjoyed almost daily reinforcements. Deserters from the American ranks continued to drift into San Luis Potosi by the score. Some had been lured away from the U.S. regiments by priests; others were guided south by rancheros. In time, they all became expert artillerists under the leadership of Captain Riley.

Finally, after months in San Luis Potosi, the orders came to march. The citizens of San Luis Potosi turned out to cheer the army on. General Santa Anna granted the San Patricios the honor of leading the twenty-thousand-man army northward to find and crush Zachary Taylor's forces. Bands played and senoritas blew kisses. But the march northward across arid lands quickly became brutal. Provisions dwindled. Water became scarce. Howling winter storms pelted the soldiers. As Santa Anna pushed them relentlessly onward, men died of thirst, exposure, exhaustion. And they began to desert the Mexican Army of the North as surely as Riley himself had deserted the American Army of Occupation.

Now, here at Angostura, Santa Anna's force had shrunk to some fourteen thousand, but they still outnumbered the Americans by more than two to one. Yes, the troops were tired and hungry, but Riley believed the marching bands and the oratory of General Santa Anna would stir the fighting spirit of the men.

As he and Colonel Moreno strode briskly toward their battalion's camp, Captain John Riley hoped he might soon witness the defeat of the American invaders. He had begun to dream of sailing his wife and son from Ireland. They could live as long as they wished to in Mexico, as landed celebrities. Eventually, when prospects improved in Ireland, he would return with his family to the Emerald Isle as a heralded defender of Catholicism.

Arriving at the camp of the Saint Patrick's Battalion, Riley and Moreno mounted their steeds. They rode toward the hill Santa Anna had pointed out to them. At the base of the hill, Riley found General Mora y Villamil waiting for them.

The chief of engineers pointed to the crest of the hundred-foot-high hill. *"Arriba!"* he said.

During his months with the Mexican Army, Riley had honed his horsemanship skills beyond his wildest expectations by observing and riding with his fellow officers. Though, to him, this hill looked too steep to ascend on horseback, the general and colonel charged up the slope without hesitation, and Riley followed, his mustang kicking rocks and dirt downhill in his efforts to keep up with the two riders.

Atop the hill, Riley could see Taylor's forces arrayed upon spurs of a plateau that slashed across the ground between the two armies. To the left, on the road that passed up Angostura Pass, he saw a battery of U.S. guns guarding the narrows. Two regiments of infantry supported the battery. As his eyes swept to the right, he saw infantry, dragoons, and flying artillery moving into position to guard the Saltillo road, the plateau, and the Hacienda Buena Vista, where Taylor had located his supply train.

The Americans, mostly volunteers, looked disorganized from this distance. They stood grouped in random clusters instead of regimented columns. They wore all manner of dull-colored and soiled uniforms. He saw only a few regular army units dressed in sky blue. He looked for his nemesis, Braxton Bragg, the immigrant-abuser. He had heard from fresh deserters that Bragg had won yet another promotion after Monterrey and was now a major. He could not identify Major Bragg from this distance. Not yet, but soon enough . . .

As his pony heaved for air and walked closer to the north rim of the little mesa he had climbed, Riley looked down at the slope of the hill that stood between him and the enemy. There, below, he found an eroded chasm, deep and narrow. He smiled.

"Colonel Moreno, sir," he said to his commander. He pointed down the steep slope to the hidden chasm. "God has given us a moat on this side of the hill. It puts a man in mind of the one that protects the old town of Athenry in County Galway, back on the Ould Sod."

His colonel smirked at him, then had to go about translating what Riley had said to the general.

Wheeling his horse about to view Santa Anna's army, Riley saw the brilliant red coats of the hussars, the crossed white shoulder belts of the infantry, the green-and-blue tunics of the lancers. It was a fine-looking army from a furlong, as Santa Anna had intended. Riley admired the way each regiment of cavalry, by Santa Anna's order, rode horses of matching color—grays, bays, sorrels, duns. All the regiments were grouped in their respective camps and were recognizable at a distance not only because of their regimental colors but also for their assigned shades of horseflesh.

Riley realized that General Mora y Villamil and Colonel Moreno were speaking too rapidly in Spanish for him to understand, but he could sense the conversation coming to an end. After a nod and a salute, the general charged back down the hill.

Moreno smiled. "You will place your battalion here, Capitan."

Riley looked down the severe declivity. "Yes, sir. We must break the guns down and haul them up piecemeal by ropes and manpower."

Moreno nodded. "The general will dispatch two companies of *zapadores* to support you."

"I'll order my men level the crest and reassemble the cannon."

"See that you do, Riley, and be quick about it. The Americans will be ranging this hill before you are finished."

The colonel reined away and plummeted down the descent. Riley followed, leaning precariously back to maintain his balance in the saddle and keep his mustang's weight on its hind legs. Reveling in his newfound equestrian skills, he spit dust from his mouth.

This is glorious, he thought. *What a day for battle!"*

Private
SAMUEL CHAMBERLAIN

Hacienda Buena Vista, Mexico
February 22, 1847

Private Samuel Chamberlain looked up to gauge the lay of the land, then returned his pencil to his sketch. It was just a study. He wouldn't have time to create a proper painting of Hacienda Buena Vista until after the coming battle—assuming he survived it. But this sketch would help him remember the lay of the land when he did have time, later, to deploy his watercolors and depict the landscape and the violence he expected to witness soon.

He sat on the ground as he drew, facing south, his back leaning against a boulder, his legs drawn up, his sketch pad on his knees. With the rounded tip of his pencil, he made a ragged, slanting slash on the left edge of the paper, depicting the steep, barren slope of the mountain to the east. Intuitively, he drew a fluid line across the page to the right, representing the rim of the plateau that stretched all the way to Angostura Pass. He began using the side of his pencil point, lightly shading in the shadows of a ravine beyond the plateau rim. Hastily he sketched in patches of prickly pear and cholla, a few scrawny pines, some magnificent yuccas, and a battery of artillery pieces to the far right. Finally, he made craggy lines approximating the crests of the distant mountains on the horizon.

He stopped to look at his rough rendering, swept up in the addictive lure of creating art from a blank page and a blunt pencil. With a few breaths, he had captured the rugged landscape—the battleground before the battle.

His messmate, a Texan named Boss Hastings, looked over his shoulder. "You ain't no Michelangelo, Chamberlain."

He frowned. "It's just a sketch, Boss."

"Well, draw some dead greasers in there for good luck."

"I'm sure plenty will be willing to pose later."

Hastings ambled away to josh with the other dragoons.

Private Samuel Chamberlain glanced at his cavalry mount—a tired sorrel now grazing on scant grass atop the plateau. After smiling with approval at his drawing, he got up and strode to his horse to stuff the sketch pad into his saddlebag. He then withdrew his notebook from the same leather pocket. The notes within would help him remember details after the war. He intended to write a lively account of his wartime exploits, once he returned to America, illustrated by his watercolors. Again, assuming he survived. He had already chosen the name for his book: *My Confession—The Recollections of a Rogue*.

Many of his messmates sat on the ground around him, writing letters to the folks back home, as men facing battle often felt compelled to do. He returned to his boulder and prepared to catch up on his note taking. As a dragoon, he had spent the past few days riding day and night and had not had time to sleep, much less to write in his makeshift diary.

He opened the bound booklet and flipped through the first few pages. Reading a few of his own passages, he was reminded of his travels since leaving Boston. Now just sixteen years old, Samuel Chamberlain had nonetheless done quite a bit of living in his time. Even as a child he had prowled the darker streets and back alleys of Boston. He had worked for a time sweeping up in a theater, where he had learned the rudiments of drawing and watercolor from the artist who painted the theatrical backdrops on stage.

By fifteen, young Sam Chamberlain had grown weary of the same old street scenes in the city of his childhood. He decided to visit an uncle in Illinois—without his parents' permission—taking his notebook, a sketch pad, and his watercolors with him. This visit had only ignited a powder keg of wanderlust that led him to lie about his age and enlist in the Second Illinois Volunteers.

Marching south to San Antonio, Texas, he fell ill and was given a medical discharge, against his wishes. The discharge came with enough money to get back to Illinois, but he had no intention of missing the war. Recovering from his fever, he hung around San Antonio, gambling his money away, until he enlisted in the First U.S. Army Dragoons in San Antonio, under General John Wool.

As he rode south into Mexico, he habitually slipped out of camp, and he tended to gravitate toward the same kinds of places and events that had lured him in at Boston and San Antonio: taverns, fandangos, gambling dens, brawls, brothels, and duels. All the while, he painted lively action scenes and tranquil landscapes and jotted down in his journal exaggerated accounts of his exploits with senoritas and Mexican gamblers.

Arriving at Monterrey after the battle, he had spoken to many of the men who had fought it and had painted gory renderings of the three-day fight, though he had not witnessed it himself. He decided that, when he got around to writing his book, he would try his hand at fiction by claiming to have taken part in the battle. He would insist that he had fought shoulder to shoulder with the renowned Texas Ranger Sam Walker, down Iturbide Street!

This would amount to a shameless fabrication, but he doubted anyone would ever read his bawdy memoir anyway. *Hell, I probably won't even survive to write it*, he thought. Since leaving Monterrey, he had come close to some skirmishes with the Mexican cavalry but had yet to participate in a true battle. It appeared to him now, on the ranges of the Hacienda Buena Vista, that he would finally get his chance to see the elephant, whether he was ready for it or not.

A cheer rose up from the rear. Chamberlain looked back toward the infantry tents and saw General Zachary Taylor ride onto the field to confer with General Wool. Taylor had been up at Saltillo all morning, securing his army's rear. Chamberlain returned to his mount and slipped the notebook back into his saddlebag. He doubted there would be time for writing now, and he felt he'd better check his tack and his weapons and keep his wits about him.

Looking toward Angostura Pass, he saw three six-pounders from Colonel John Washington's artillery battery and Captain John Washington's First Illinois Infantry guarding the narrows. It struck him that two officers named Washington held the pass on George Washington's birthday. If this was an omen, he couldn't be sure if it was good or bad.

Two regiments of volunteer foot soldiers from Illinois and Indiana, and his own regiment of dragoons, held the high ground on the plateau, along with Braxton Bragg's battery of flying artillery. Along the mountain slope to the east, the Kentucky Cavalry had been dismounted to serve as riflemen on the left flank.

Sweeping his gaze southward, toward the enemy camp, he saw that a battery of Mexican cannon had been painstakingly disassembled, dragged up a steep slope, reassembled, and mounted on a singular hill a half mile away across alternating spurs and barrancas. He had heard that the Irishman John Riley commanded those guns with his deserters from the U.S. ranks. From this distance, he could just make out a bright green flag—the banner of the infamous Saint Patrick's Battalion.

As he shook his head at the lunacy of deserting the United States to fight for Mexico, he saw his company's first sergeant striding his way.

"Stand to horse!" the noncom yelled.

Men rose to catch their mounts, which had been unbridled to graze. Chamberlain took his headstall from a saddle ring and slipped it over the ears of his little sorrel mustang, which he had given the exotic Arab name of Soldan. The pony tried to twist away, but the private held fast to his mane.

"Now, Soldan, I know you don't like your ears touched. Easy, now, and I'll do it quick."

With his bit and bridle in place, he decided to meander over closer to General Taylor's position. He might overhear something he could put in his book someday. As he approached, he noticed that Lieutenant Colonel May's dragoons had accompanied Taylor from Saltillo. May's men had been battle tested at Palo Duro, Resaca de la Palma, and Monterrey. A couple of them looked disdainfully down at Chamberlain as he approached, leading his mount. He didn't give a rat's ass for the bastards. May himself was a known blowhard who claimed to have captured General Romulo Diaz de la Vega back at the *resaca*, when witnesses all agreed that the Mexican general had presented his sword and surrendered to a regimental bugler. To this day, there wasn't a bugler in the army who would toot a note for Lieutenant Colonel May.

Ambling nearer, Chamberlain realized that officers from several regiments had gathered around generals Taylor and Wool for a council of war. Taylor had given Wool command for the day, so Wool was haranguing the officer corps as Private Chamberlain shuffled within earshot.

". . . and certainly you are all aware that today is the anniversary of the birth of the father of our country! I call upon each and every one of you, as soldiers and patriotic Americans, to celebrate this anniversary in a way that will confer an additional honor on the day!"

The officers raised their fists, applauded, and cheered their commander.

Chamberlain heard General Taylor give verbal orders to the commanders of the Second Kentucky and Third Indiana volunteer infantries. "You gentlemen find a way around that canyon yonder to the west and position yourselves on the other side of it." He pointed vaguely to the area he wanted occupied, a mile or so away. "If Santa Anna tries to slip around our right flank over there, you do your damnedest to turn him!"

After the officers had returned to their regiments, Chamberlain hung around Wool's headquarters, waiting for the battle to begin. Loitering ever closer to the generals' position, he overheard a courier report to General Taylor.

"Sir, the advance guard of the Mexican infantry is on the move with cavalry and artillery support." The rider pointed south.

Chamberlain turned and watched until he saw the colorful tunics and pennons of the enemy winding in and out of the ravines a couple of miles away. They came in column formation, like a great viper slithering down into the barrancas and up over the fingers of the plateau. Fluttering pennons and glinting steel made the beast seem to quiver and writhe as it moved his way. When the wind was right, he could hear a brass band belting out a military march, but in the distinctive Mexican style, with beautifully slurred notes that spoke of both joy and sorrow all in the same breath. As the minutes ticked by, the enemy came closer. His dust cloud arose. The band played louder. The columns dispersed right and left like segments of the snake splitting off, until they covered the whole country in front of the U.S. line.

"Shit a brick," Chamberlain said to Soldan. "There's a mess of them, ain't there?"

Now he saw a puff of smoke emerge from the muzzle of one of the guns under the emerald standard of the Saint Patrick's Battalion. The sound of the cannon shot made Soldan flinch, as a solid ball came screaming toward the U.S. line, landing in a spray of dirt a furlong short of Braxton Bragg's battery. A cheer rose up among the Americans and rippled all the way across the front.

Smiling, Private Chamberlain added his voice to the battle cry. Then he saw the surgeons setting up their tables near the hospital tent and laying out their bone saws. The smile slipped from his face.

After a while, he noticed that the Second Kentucky and the Third Indiana had found a trail to their position across the canyon. They were now so far away from action that they might as well have been camped on the Brazos. He wondered why Taylor had made the fool decision to send those men so far out of harm's way.

Chamberlain suddenly noticed Taylor, Wool, and Perfect Bliss monitoring the left flank with spyglasses. He followed the trajectory of the optics and saw what looked like a battalion of Mexican infantrymen—maybe three thousand strong—ascending the mountain slope to the east, to test the Americans' left. To flank the U.S. forces, they would have to cross a precarious gorge that slashed down the mountainside. But the dismounted horse soldiers of the Kentucky Cavalry were waiting with their rifles on this side of the gorge.

He leaned closer to Soldan's ear. "I wouldn't want to be a greaser in the iron sights of them squirrel-huntin' Kaintucks."

"Sir, there's a white flag approaching!"

It was Perfect Bliss's voice that Chamberlain had heard. He saw the rider galloping across the high ground, carrying the banner of truce. The rider dismounted in front of General Taylor. To Chamberlain, the rider looked decidedly paler than the rank-and-file Mexican soldier.

"Who the hell are you?" Taylor said, rather irritably.

The man saluted. "I am Major Liegenburg. I am a surgeon in the employ of the Mexican Army. General Santa Anna sends his regards, along with this missive." He pulled a folded sheet of parchment from his coat. It was sealed with a wax stamp.

Taylor snatched the message from the major's hand. "Are you Dutch, Major?"

"I am German born, General."

Taylor pulled the wax seal off and tossed it over his shoulder. He unfolded the paper and looked at the ink handwriting at arm's length. He handed it to William Bliss. "Bill, read this out loud and clear."

Private Chamberlain cupped his hand behind his ear and leaned closer. "'To His Excellency, General Z. Taylor,' et cetera," Bliss began.

"Illustrious Sir. You are surrounded by twenty thousand men and cannot in any human probability avoid suffering a rout and being cut to pieces with your troops. But, as you deserve consideration and particular esteem, I wish to save you from a catastrophe, and for that purpose give you this notice in order that you may surrender at discretion under the assurance that you will be treated with the consideration belonging to the Mexican character, to which end you will be granted an hour's time to make up your mind, to commence from the moment when my flag of truce arrives in your camp. With this view, I assure you of my particular consideration."

Zachary Taylor jutted his chin forward and glared at Major Liegenburg. "Tell Santa Anna to go to hell!" He turned to his adjutant. "Major Bliss, write that in Spanish and send it back by this damned Dutchman!"

Chamberlain chuckled and elbowed Soldan. A moment later, a rattle of musket and rifle fire began from the left flank. The private turned about to view the conflict. The Mexican infantry was attempting to get around the very head of the steep gorge so that they wouldn't have to cross the gorge to attack. But the Kaintucks had better weapons and held the high ground.

A Mexican soldier, shot by an American, tumbled down the mountain slope, apparently dead. A cheer rose from the U.S. ranks. A second enemy attacker slid down into the gorge; a third cartwheeled. More hurrahs arose, but soon the men grew wary of cheering death and settled in to watch silently.

"John," Taylor said to General Wool, "you have the field. I will return to Saltillo to see to the defenses in the rear."

After Taylor mounted Old Whitey and left with Bliss and May's dragoons, Chamberlain overheard General Wool issue a directive to his adjutant, Captain George Lincoln: "Dispatch orders for those two regiments across the canyon to return to the field of battle. Tell them not to leave until after dark, so Santa Anna will assume they will still be there in the morning. We are going to need every man available here tomorrow."

Chamberlain nodded approvingly. He was happy to have Wool commanding. He liked Old Rough and Ready as much as any soldier but considered Wool the better strategist.

The battle on the left flank continued sporadically until dusk, and news came back to headquarters saying that the Kentucky Cavalry had suffered seven men wounded while inflicting multiple kills upon the enemy. Private Samuel Chamberlain began to think he might actually get some sleep tonight, for a change. Then he saw his friend Boss Hastings trotting his way.

"Sam, we've received orders," Hastings said.

Chamberlain gave a weary sigh. "What the hell for?"

"Our squadron is to stand picket duty at the heads of all the ravines, all night."

Chamberlain spit on the ground. "Why us? The infantry is rested. They ought to go."

"Hell, don't blame me, Sam. I didn't give the order. Come on!"

A couple of hours later, Chamberlain found himself standing guard as a vedette in the dark, his greatcoat doing little to beat back the cold mountain air and the freezing drizzle that had begun to fall. He shivered as he fought off the seduction of sleep, and he wondered why he had ever enlisted in the first place.

A half hour ago, Boss Hastings had wandered away in the dark, though the men were supposed to stand guard in pairs. Chamberlain figured he had gone to take a crap or something, but he had been missing a long time now.

Since Hastings left, something had begun to stir across the ravines in the Mexican camp. He could hear large groups of men shouting, cheering.

"*Viva México!*"

"*Libertad o muerte!*"

"*Viva* Santa Anna!"

He imagined that General Santa Anna was rallying his troops with oratory. Perhaps planning a nighttime attack? They might be sneaking up the ravine below him right now. He could also hear some commotion at the base of the mountain. Were they building a new artillery emplacement? What the hell had happened to Boss Hastings?

A hoofbeat on gravel made him lift his carbine. "Who's there?" he demanded.

"Just me, Sam."

"Boss! What the hell? You near scared the shit out of me."

Hastings chuckled. "Now, don't soil your tongs. Lookee what I got ahold of." He rode up next to Chamberlain at the head of the barranca and pressed a glass bottle into his hand.

Chamberlain pulled the cork stopper and smelled. "By God, brandy!"

"French brandy."

"Where the hell did you get this?" Chamberlain took a welcome swig.

"I went to see Dr. Hitchcock at the hospital tent. I told him Captain Steen requested a stimulant against the cold. Damned if he didn't give me the whole bottle, with his compliments. Save some for the boys holding the horses and I'll bet we can get them to spell us awhile so we can sleep."

Chamberlain took a bigger gulp and felt the burning liquid plunge past his gullet, warming him from within. "You're a real chum to share it with me, Boss." He handed the bottle back to his messmate and smiled into the dark night, feeling much restored at the sudden turn of his fortunes.

General
ANTONIO LÓPEZ
DE SANTA ANNA

Buena Vista
February 23, 1847

She called herself Consuela. She was his favorite of the eight, though he was happy enough to have the other seven along as well. He could never feel satisfied by the touch of just one woman—not even the most talented and wanton Consuela.

He had stayed awake until two o'clock in the morning, haranguing his various regiments and overseeing a new artillery emplacement that would surprise the enemy at dawn. He had then summoned Consuela to his tent and had slept a few hours after coupling with her. Now he lay awake, listening to her familiar kitten-purr snores and feeling grateful for the warmth of her body against the cold of this night.

What will I say at dawn? How will I address the officers, the regulars, the conscripts? The usual rhetoric, of course. Invading heretics . . . Honor of Mother Mexico . . . Glory forever . . . Liberty or death . . .

He decided his delivery would matter more than his words. First of all, feign passion! It wouldn't be difficult today. His career—and perhaps even his life—depended upon the coming battle.

Second, choose the right uniform. The hat was especially important. No parade plumes today. That would be seen by his men as ostentatious and would make him a target to the enemy. He would don a common campaign hat and a drab cavalry duster. But under the duster, he would wear an infantry officer's blue tunic and white pants to appeal to the foot soldiers as well as the cavaliers.

Third, choose the right horse. Yes, the chestnut gelding. The little mustang possessed heart and unaccountable endurance. And his mount's smaller size would make him appear larger by contrast as he harangued his army from the saddle.

For months he had worked toward this day. Since that lukewarm reception on the pier, back in August, his task of regaining power had challenged and almost daunted him. After coming ashore at Veracruz, he had withdrawn to his Hacienda Encero, claiming that his leg gave him too much pain to travel to Mexico City. In reality, he thought it better to wait until the people demanded his return to lead the army against the greedy, bloodthirsty invaders from the north.

The public mandate came sooner than he expected, and he returned to the capital in triumph.

"I have but one request before I answer the call to arms for my beloved country," he had told the welcoming committee on the outskirts of Mexico City.

"What is it, General?" the leader of the delegation replied cautiously.

"Erect my statue again!"

The committee had conferred briefly and agreed to the demand.

"*Bueno!*" Santa Anna had said, cajoling the functionaries sent to woo him. "Now you must urge the government to take action! Gather troops and supplies at San Luis Potosi, where I will train the new army! Every day that passes without fighting at the north is a century of disgrace for Mexico!"

And so new troops arrived at San Luis Potosi, but the commissary did not. Nevertheless, he set his officers to work, drilling the starving recruits, who survived only through the kindness and patriotism of the citizens of San Luis Potosi who fed them and patched their tattered uniforms. Dry firing their muskets, they practiced marksmanship without gunpowder or bullets.

Worse yet, the newspapers had learned of his secret deal with President Polk to slip through the naval blockade. His political opposition now claimed that Santa Anna was a traitor who had conspired with the enemy to regain power. When asked about it by journalists, he laughed it off.

"My partisan opponents invent the most ridiculous scenarios! They will stop at nothing to vilify me! Next they will claim that President Polk came to a cockfight in Havana to purchase my loyalty. The people of

Mexico will soon see by my actions that my loyalties forever lie with Mexico!"

Somehow, he toiled on. The federal government sent little in the way of funds for the army. The state governments sent even less. The church made a loan of two million pesos, but Santa Anna chose to spend most of this on uniforms and medals while his soldiers grumbled for meat and bread.

Finally, he made the ultimate sacrifice. He mortgaged his own estate to obtain a loan for half a million pesos and made sure the government and the newspapers knew about it. In November, he received news that a congress had come together and selected him as the new president of Mexico. His vice president, Gomez Farias, would serve as acting leader of the nation while President Santa Anna led in the field.

President once again! His hopes swelled along with his ego. Then, another stroke of luck. He learned of the existence of ninety-eight bars of silver hidden in a mine near San Luis Potosi. He seized these for the public defense and had them minted into silver coins, some of which purchased long-awaited gunpowder and hardtack.

By January the public was demanding that he march against Taylor in the north. But Santa Anna was now aware of a pending invasion of Veracruz. The new U.S. commander, General Winfield Scott, had foolishly bragged about the plans to the press. Veracruz was closer than Saltillo, but Santa Anna chose to attack Taylor instead of defending Veracruz. He felt safer in the north, away from the seat of government, where hotheads might conspire with his army to overthrow him. He knew Taylor's army had been stripped of its best fighters so that they might serve under Scott. Almost all of Taylor's troops were now untested volunteers—amateur soldiers.

Santa Anna knew he needed a victory. Taylor's army was his obvious target. A U.S. courier had been killed and useful intelligence acquired regarding Taylor's plans. General Minon's lancers had captured two careless companies of volunteer U.S. cavalry, further weakening Taylor's force. It was time to march.

He left San Luis Potosi on a sunny day in early January. A band played "Adios" as senoritas blew kisses and citizens cheered the parade out of town. But the music and adulation soon faded as the march became a grueling three-week trek across 250 miles of hell. The high deserts of northern Mexico did not beckon travelers in the winter. Days could be scalding hot, only to release cloudbursts of driving sleet and snow. Nocturnal sandstorms chewed tents into useless netting. Icy nights killed starving men, who huddled together and shivered to death in their tattered clothes.

Then began the desertions. By the hundreds—then the thousands—hungry, frostbitten recruits melted into the mountains by dark of night. By the time he dragged his exhausted army out of the desert, he had lost thousands of men to death or desertion. This decreased his numbers to some fourteen thousand fighters, but he still outnumbered Taylor's force of about six thousand men. Even this force was divided. Taylor held La Angostura with just 4,500 men. The other 1,500 guarded his rear, nine miles away, in Saltillo.

Now the time had come to rise from his bed and attack. Militarily, he had prepared well and had confidence in his strategy. He had sent General José Minon on a road looping far around to the east to surround Taylor's reserves in Saltillo and cut off Taylor's retreat. The rest of Minon's cavalry, infantry, and artillery had already taken up strategic positions in order of battle, facing the American front here at La Angostura. He knew this battle meant everything to his future. To retain power he had to achieve a victory. He *had* to.

He relished a last, warm whiff of Consuela's ambergris perfume. He wondered if he should pray. If God even existed, would He listen to a man praying in bed with a whore?

Bastante! He threw the blankets aside and sat up on the edge of his bed.

"Juanito!" he shouted.

"*Si*, General?" came the groggy reply from his manservant, sleeping outside.

"Come light the lantern and get this whore out of my tent! Where in devil is my leg?"

"Coming, General!"

By dawn, he was mounted on the chestnut, attired as he had planned. He rode before regiments of cavalry and infantry, the mustang prancing under him.

"This horde of heretics from the north has invaded the sacred soil of *Madre México*," he railed, "and must be punished with vengeance, swift and merciless!"

Bands played up and down the front line but would fall silent when His Excellency came near so that the men could hear him.

"They have raped and murdered their way from Matamoros to Monterrey!" He scowled fiercely at his fighters and could see their ire begin to boil at the red-hot rhetoric he spewed.

"They have brazenly torched our cathedrals, clothed themselves in the ornaments of the altars, and thrown upon the ground the body of *Jesús Cristo*! They have made themselves drunk by drinking from sacred vessels and washed the blood of your brothers from their hands in holy water!"

Priests followed him with incense and crucifixes to absolve the warriors of their sins should they die on this day. They strode methodically, swinging ornate copper censers that streamed with the smoke of burning incense. The general caught a whiff of acrid smoke that seemed to fill him with a sudden reverence for everything sacred.

God, give us victory, he thought.

As the priests passed in front of the massed regiments, the infantry soldiers would kneel. The cavalrymen would doff their shakos and lower their lances. The lancers looked particularly formidable on this day. By the general's order, the men of each regiment rode horses of the same color. This gave each corps a uniform appearance and also would help Santa Anna identify the regiments from a distance so he would know whom to reward and whom to blame.

Thinking over all of this, he had not ceased in his diatribe. The words came to him without effort. The rhetoric was part of his very being and lived in his brain, even in his dreams.

"Today we will rid our country of this scourge of vermin and pestilence. Follow me, brave citizens of Mexico! Take up your arms and slaughter these foreigners who come to take what is rightfully ours!"

He had reached the east end of the line and found himself in front of General Santiago Blanco's division of infantry.

"General Blanco! Prepare to attack up the road and through La Angostura!" He drew his saber and held it above his head. "Bugler! Sound the advance!"

The clarion notes converted the entire line into a throng of cheering men who, at this moment, had forgotten about hunger and exhaustion and only desired revenge.

"Forward!"

He watched as General Blanco's men surged bravely into what Santa Anna knew would be almost certain death. But this attack on the American right was necessary to divert attention away from the real assault on the U.S. left.

Now General Antonio López de Santa Anna spurred his mount to the east and galloped before the advancing thousands all along the line. He smelled campfire smoke on the cool wind in his face, felt the power of the noble steed beneath him.

"Take up your arms! Advance!"

He pulled rein behind the hill upon which the San Patricio battalion awaited orders to commence firing.

"Fellow Catholics!" he yelled up to the hilltop. "Your moment has arrived to retaliate against the Protestant usurpers who have violated your honor with their oppression!"

Peering up at them, the general chuckled at the peculiar howls and gesticulations of the pale-skinned foreigners, many of them red-haired and ruddy-faced.

"Rain hell down upon the bastards! *Fuego!*"

The Irish commander, Captain John Riley, echoed the command, and the entire battery of big guns roared in unison. The whistling shells filled Santa Anna's charger with new spirit as he continued his gallop eastward. He sensed the beginning of his finest day as he plunged through the barrancas and up toward the higher ground of his right flank.

He galloped in front of General Julian Juvera's cavalry, who saluted him by dipping their lance points as he passed. General Anastasio Torrejon's lancers did the same, cheering him as he sliced the wind with his saber.

At the center of his line, he reined left and spurred his chestnut warhorse up onto a finger of the plateau, where he knew both his army and the enemy's would see him. Vaulting up onto the prominence, he waved his sword and let his mustang walk in circles, catching some wind. The battle cries that arose from his men made his heart swell.

"*Viva* Santa Anna! *Viva México!*"

Looking north, he took note of the American batteries and located the headquarters tent of General Wool. He remained exposed long

enough that American rifle balls began to hum past him and pepper the
ground around him. He waved his blade defiantly. A U.S. six-pounder
sent a shell crashing into the brush near him. He plunged his horse back
into the ravine and continued east, encouraging the brigade of infantrymen marching under General Francisco Pacheco.

"The Lord Almighty commands you to kill these damned heathens
without hesitation!"

He veered to ride in front of the line of march of General Manuel
Lombardini's hard-bitten foot soldiers.

"To spare any one of the enemy is to condemn a hundred of our women
and children to degradation and brutal death!"

Now he heard the cannon on the American right flank open up and
knew that General Blanco's elite regiment of engineers and the famous
Guarda Costa de Tampico was catching hell from grapeshot and canister. At the same time, he heard the old Brown Bess muskets of his infantry under General Ampudia taking shots at the Americans' left flank
on the steep mountainside. Because of Ampudia's disgraceful surrender
at Monterrey, Santa Anna had cast his command out on the flank, where
he was leading a rabble of raw recruits.

He came to the head of a ravine and rode up to high ground where
he could watch the battle commence. As planned, the Hussars of the
Guard awaited him here. From this chosen spot, Santa Anna would
watch the battle commence. The captain of the guard, Jesus Paniagua,
would pen orders dictated by His Excellency. The hussars would ride as
couriers, delivering his directives to the appropriate commanders.

"Help me down!" he ordered to the nearest hussar. "Walk my horse!"

As he shifted to test his balance on his wooden leg, he glanced over
the broad American line. He saw the U.S. ranks spread thin across the
spurs of the plateau, from the mountain on his right to the narrow pass
far to his left. It was easy to locate the inexperienced volunteer units of
the enemy army. They did not wear the sky-blue uniforms of the U.S.
regulars. The amateur regiments all invented their own silly-looking cos-
tumes. These were the targets he intended to attack with the brunt of
his army—the untested volunteers.

One of the hussars brought his jeweled walking stick to him. He
gripped the solid silver eagle's head and stabbed the tip of the cane into
the rocky soil, as if planting a battle flag. He loved the way his fingers

wrapped around the beak of that sculpted raptor's head. It felt like a talisman that conjured curses to his enemies.

He heard another thundering volley from the whole San Patricio battery firing in unison. The deadly loads of canister sailed into the front lines of one of those hapless volunteer units near the American left flank. Men withered beneath the well-timed explosions.

Santa Anna laughed. "A perfect volley by *los colorados*! Captain, what regiment is that the San Patricios just hit?"

"The Indiana Volunteers, Your Excellency."

"They are already falling back! Send a hussar to tell generals Lombardi and Pacheco to charge at once!" He pointed his staff down into the ravine to his left, where he could see the 7,500 men under Lombardi and Pacheco advancing slowly toward the Americans.

Another volley from Captain John Riley's band of deserters killed or crippled a dozen more American volunteers.

"Hurry, Captain! Now is the time!"

The blue sky, the roar of ordnance, the odor of burned gunpowder on the bracing wind . . . it all stirred his soul. It had been a long while since he had presided over a proper battle. He could feel the soft center of the enemy line recoiling. He would hurl his thousands at their few!

"Never mind, Captain! Bring my mount! I will ride there and tell them myself!"

Lieutenant
JOHN PAUL
JONES O'BRIEN

Buena Vista
September 23, 1846

He knew they were coming. He had watched thousands of enemy soldiers disappear into the barrancas, heading his way. Lieutenant John Paul Jones O'Brien fully expected to see at least a battalion of enemy infantry emerge from some stretch of ravine any minute now.

Proudly, he watched his men ram shells down the muzzles of his three guns—a twelve-, a six-, and a captured Mexican four-pounder. His artillerymen called any guns they manned "O'Brien's Bulldogs," and the name had caught on with the rest of Taylor's army.

Another blistering volley came from the Irish deserters across the way—the so-called Saint Patrick's Battalion.

"Take cover!" he ordered.

His men threw themselves on the ground, as did the green Indiana Volunteers supporting his battery. The exploding shells ripped into the volunteers, shrapnel flying everywhere, whirring off of cannon tubes, pulverizing human flesh. Men screamed in pain. Others died instantly and were now pain free.

Lieutenant O'Brien felt even more disgusted with the deserters than most soldiers in the U.S. Army. His name celebrated his own Irish blood, and he hated the damage the deserters had done to his heritage. But right now he had other concerns on his mind.

"On your feet! Man those guns! Make ready!"

He looked around at the Indiana Volunteers who were there to defend his battery. This was their first battle and they looked absolutely stunned.

He turned back to his gunners. "Fire!" he said, covering his ears.

The volley sailed toward his assigned target—a distant regiment of Mexican musketeers attacking the American left flank. His shots fell short. He wanted to get closer, yet his orders were to fire from this position in support of the Kentucky Volunteers, who had been holding that left flank on the mountain since yesterday.

"Load spherical case shot!" he shouted to his men. He turned to the Hoosiers. "You men stand your ground! You'll have your chance to fight any minute now!"

In this claim, he had no doubt. He knew from his West Point training why the Saint Pats were targeting his battery and its supporting infantry. They were softening up this part of the American line for the main enemy assault. O'Brien knew the gray trousers and matching gray frock coats of the Indiana Volunteers set them apart from the sky-blue uniforms of the U.S. regulars. Sly Santa Anna wanted to pit his troops against inexperienced volunteers.

He looked at his target again on the left flank. *It's too far away! Damn it, we have to get closer!*

"Bring the horses up!" he shouted. "Limber the Bulldogs!"

His men sprang to obey the new order. Anything was better than waiting for the next artillery barrage from John Riley's deserters.

"Where are we headed, Lieutenant?" asked his first sergeant, Tom Moore, who was sitting on the ground, binding a leg wound with a strip of cloth used as a bandage.

"Head that way!" O'Brien pointed toward the head of a ravine that would put him well within range of his assigned target on the left flank.

"You heard the lieutenant!" the noncom shouted, springing to his feet and limping into action. "Bring those horses, double-quick!"

Colonel Bowles, commander of the Indiana Volunteers, came stalking toward him, leading his horse.

"Are you daft, Lieutenant? You want to get *closer*? We must fall back, out of range of those big guns!"

O'Brien covered his sneer. As a West Pointer, he held respect for only a few of the volunteer officers, and Bowles was not one of them. The man had no military experience whatsoever. He had simply been elected colonel by his volunteers.

"Colonel," he shouted, "I am under orders to support the Kentucky Volunteers and I cannot do so without getting closer to the enemy! I would appreciate the support of your regiment in this maneuver. You may follow us as closely as you choose."

"We have no orders to advance!" Bowles complained.

The clamor of wheels on the rocky ground and the snorting of the artillery horses ended the conversation.

First Sergeant Moore trotted to him, leading O'Brien's horse. "Sir, we're ready to move, but what about our dead and wounded?"

O'Brien glanced at Colonel Bowles as he took the reins of his mount from the sergeant. "Colonel, I request your support in getting my wounded and dead moved to the rear."

Bowles sighed. "Very well!" He turned and stomped back to his regiment.

O'Brien slipped his boot into the stirrup of the Ringgold saddle and mounted. "Move the battery, Sergeant Moore. Quickly!"

O'Brien's gunners mounted the draft horses or rode on the limbers and caisson boxes. As the guns trundled closer to the enemy line, another barrage from the Saint Pats exploded just over the heads of the Indianans. Poor bastards. He hoped they would follow him closely and get out from under the trajectory of the big Mexican artillery pieces, at least for a while.

Within five minutes, he had established his new position and targeted the enemy musketeers on the mountain slope above him. The rifles of the Kentuckians were still holding tenuously to the head of the gully that slashed down the mountain and defined the left flank. But new waves of Mexican musketeers had inched closer and now threatened to break the resolve of the volunteers from Kentucky.

"We will fire in battery, gentlemen," he said, as his men tamped the loads in the guns. "Prime . . . Ready . . . Fire!"

This time, his three rounds of spherical case shot sailed directly into the front lines of the Mexican assault, relieving the beleaguered Kentucky riflemen.

"Reload!"

Now, from here, he could do some damage to the enemy until the Mexican batteries once again ranged his new position and drove him from this ground. His men hustled and loosed a second volley, then a third. O'Brien drew a breath of pride. His little battery had succeeded in stalling the Mexican advance on the flank. All his life he had endeavored to live up to his namesake, John Paul Jones. Now, finally, he thought he might be getting his chance to prove himself.

"Lieutenant O'Brien!" his first sergeant shouted. "The Hoosiers are not coming to support us!"

Looking back, he saw the Indiana Volunteers milling about in confusion. He spit on the ground. "Damned Bowles!"

"It looks like the whole regiment has volunteered to take the dead and wounded to the rear!" Moore said sarcastically.

"We will stay here and fire as long as we are able, Sergeant. Keep the horses close at hand in case we have to withdraw."

"Yes, sir."

"Are the Bulldogs primed?"

"They are, sir."

"Ready! Fire!"

The cannon roared. Again and again, with machined precision, his men sponged the tubes, rammed cartridges down the muzzles, timed fuses on the exploding shells. Because of their deadly fire, the left flank held.

But how long can we hold this ground before some enemy battery ranges us? And what of the Mexican infantry? The cavalry? When will they emerge from the ravines wrapped around our little peninsula of the plateau?

O'Brien's eyes swept the edges of the barranca. He saw nothing at first glance. Then . . . Wait . . . *What the hell?*

"Sergeant Moore! Do you see what I see? There! Patches of white on the ground, moving. Coming up from the ravine."

"By God, that's their white shoulder belts, sir! They're crawling into position to fire on us. There are hundreds of them!"

Dread plummeted into O'Brien's guts. "No. Thousands."

The first volley of musket fire swarmed through his battery, splintering crates and wheel spokes. A horse squealed and fell, kicking. A gunner howled as a ball hit his hip.

"Load grape! Grapeshot!"

In the hailstorm of bullets, the gunners loaded cartridges packed with powder and .70-caliber spheres of lead.

"Hurry! Turn the guns! Man the elevating screw! Lower the tubes!"

The musket fire only increased. Two more men fell. The blood of horses gushed into pools of human blood.

"Prime! Ready!"

The private nearest to him dropped his lanyard and fell dead. O'Brien rushed forward to grab the cord.

"Fire!" He pulled the lanyard, setting off the charge of the twelve-pounder. The six-pounder followed. The four-pounder, on a crippled carriage with busted wheels, also fired. Grape-size hunks of lead spewed into the enemy, wreaking horrible damage on human bodies. But, to O'Brien's alarm, another throng of Mexicans charged up from the ravine, more numerous than the first. Musket fire rained sideways through his battery. O'Brien heard his men screaming, cursing, moaning.

Then the first round of enemy artillery fire hit them, exploding just overhead.

"Reload! Double-shot the guns!"

"Hell, throw in some stones to boot!" Sergeant Moore added.

"Hurry! They're coming! Fire at will!"

The trio of field guns sprayed the enemy with double blasts of grapeshot, mowing down part of the charge. But more attackers came to replace the fallen ones. Artillery shells continued to explode all around the Bulldogs.

O'Brien was now manning the primers and lanyard himself, as most of his men were dead or wounded.

"One more time, boys! Give 'em hell!"

As the men loaded and the Mexicans charged, he took stock. Three horses and several men were down. O'Brien seemed to be the only man not wounded, and at least six men were killed.

"Sergeant, bring the horses! We will leave the four-pounder behind. After this volley, pull the six and the twelve back by the prolonges!"

"Yes, sir!" Moore sang.

"Fire, damn it!"

The volley blasted the nearest Mexicans backwards with its terrible force. And still, more came, stunning him with their unaccountable courage. At the tailpiece of the twelve-pounder, he uncoiled the prolonge—a rope with an iron hook tied to the end. He tossed it out to its full length, toward the rear.

"Here is the prolonge, Sergeant! Hurry!"

O'Brien now feared he might lose his guns to the enemy, though his men were frantically leading the horses to the guns. He put his hand on the wheel of the twelve-pounder and drew his saber. The first brave man to reach him ran at him with his bayonet. O'Brien sidestepped and hacked at the man, fairly cutting his arm off. He made a thrust for the heart as the man screamed and died.

Another volley came. He felt a bullet tear through the flesh of his calf, another through his thigh, and a third across his cheek and through his earlobe. He fought off the next attacker, crippling the man with a slash to the knee.

"We're ready, Lieutenant! Let's move! Mount the wheel horse! Your saddle horse is dead!"

O'Brien turned, ran past the cannon and the prolonge, and leaped aboard the only vacant saddle on the team of horses. The two guns began to roll at the end of the prolonges. He looked to both sides, saw dead or wounded soldiers draped over the thighs of other riders. Still other wounded men rode the limbers and a caisson someone had managed to hitch up. The limping horses struggled to pull. They left a trail of blood behind them as they narrowly escaped the oncoming hoard of Mexican patriots.

The attackers fell upon the four-pounder and cheered over its capture. Stray musket shots still hummed through O'Brien's bedraggled escape party, but the distance widened between his battery and the enemy. The Indiana Volunteers were nowhere in view. It seems they had broken ranks and run for Hacienda Buena Vista.

This was a disaster. He wondered if he would face court-martial for moving forward without orders. Every man in his unit was either dead or wounded, including himself. Was it his fault? No! By God, he had orders to support the left flank, and he could only fulfill those orders by getting closer.

He set his jaw and vowed silently to redeem himself yet on this day. This was not over. He had kept the two best guns out of the hands of the Mexicans. He had fought the enemy face-to-face and survived. But now he looked back at them through the chunks of mud kicked up by the splintered wheels. They were still coming. Thousands upon thousands of them. They had punched a gaping hole in the American line. The left flank was swinging back like a huge gate along the base of the mountain.

Is this battle lost? We are outnumbered! Where are the reserves? The dragoons? More artillery? Where the hell is everybody? I need more gunners, and sound fieldpieces to replace these crippled carriages.

He remembered the immortal words of his namesake: *I have not yet begun to fight!*

"Sergeant Moore!" he yelled. "We must find an ambulance wagon for the men. Then you and I will ride to Captain Washington to get a couple of six-pounders. Sergeant? Do you hear me, damn it?"

A private's voice spoke meekly over the rattle of the carriages. "Sergeant Moore is dead, Lieutenant."

O'Brien looked over his shoulder and found the wounded private holding on to the body of Moore—clinging to him to prevent his tumbling off of an ammunition box. Blood had poured out of a bullet hole in Moore's chest and was now dripping down the caisson and onto foreign soil.

SAMUEL E. CHAMBERLAIN

Buena Vista
February 23, 1847

With his heart pounding like some wild animal trying to escape a cage, he pushed the lever on the side of his Hall carbine. Smoke from the last shot trailed out as the block pivoted upward, revealing the cylindrical tunnel of the breech. Tearing open a paper package with his teeth, he poured the gunpowder from the paper tube into the open breech, trying to concentrate as musket bullets hummed past his ears. Now he reached into his ammunition pouch for a musket ball, which he pushed in on top of the powder. He closed the breech. Hands shaking with excitement, he managed to secure a percussion cap on the nipple under the hammer.

Now he looked up for a target, coughing at the bank of smoke that obscured his view.

"Get down, Sam!" Boss Hastings yelled. "You can see under the smoke!"

Private Samuel Chamberlain dropped to his belly beside Hastings and aimed at the X of a Mexican soldier's white cross-belts. It was an easy shot. The man was only forty yards away. He pulled the trigger and watched the soldier tumble forward. It was his second kill in the past few minutes of terrifying chaos.

Five minutes ago, he had been sitting on the ground, resting, holding the reins of his mount, watching Lieutenant O'Brien hurl shells from an advanced position to the left of his regiment of dragoons. Then came the attack. Santa Anna had sent an entire division of infantry, under

General Lombardi, up the barranca. The enemy first appeared to him just fifty yards from where he sat.

"Look there!" Boss Hastings had yelled.

The white cross-belts of the Mexican foot soldiers had popped up over the brink of the ravine by the hundreds. The sun had risen over the mountain and its rays struck the polished barrels of the Mexican muskets.

A forest of glistening tubes, he thought. *That will ring true in my book, should I survive this.*

"To horse!" an officer had screamed.

Smoke and musket balls had belched forth from the rim of the gully. As O'Brien vaulted into his saddle, he had noticed the way the Mexicans fired. Some took careful aim, with the butts of their weapons held against their shoulders. But many of them held the old Brown Bess muskets against their hips to absorb the mule-kick recoil of the weapons launching the .71-caliber balls.

His company commander, Captain Steen, had drawn his saber and waved it at the men. "Fall back and rally on me!"

The entire regiment had charged at a gallop to safer ground, a furlong back.

"Halt! Fours hold the horses!" Steen had ordered. Chamberlain was a three, so he had handed his reins to a messmate numbered four. Every fourth man took the reins of four horses to hold, farther back, while the bulk of the dragoons prepared to fire. Captain Steen had ridden back and forth behind his company, shouting orders.

"Cock your weapons and hold your fire. Do not fire until I order it!"

When that order came, Private Chamberlain made his first kill. Now he had killed his second enemy soldier and was reloading for a third shot, hoping he and his fellow dragoons could hold off the massive wave of attackers.

Somewhere behind him, he heard a bugle call for a charge and knew the order had come from General Joseph Lane, the brigade commander along this stretch of the front line. But, just as quickly, he heard the voice of Colonel Bowles, commander of the Second Indiana Volunteers, to his left. "Cease firing and retreat!"

The Indianans wasted no time obeying, even though Bowles immediately tried to countermand his own order. "No, not retreat. I meant retire. Retire firing! Halt! Do not retreat!"

It was too late.

The bulk of the Hoosiers reminded Chamberlain of a fleeing herd of deer as he watched them sprint for the rear, many of them dropping their weapons. Almost the entire regiment disintegrated in seconds. Only a dozen or so stood their ground with Colonel Bowles. The Mexicans saw the gaping breach the retreat created in the American line and veered toward it, streaming into the void, cutting off the extreme U.S. left— the Rackensackers and the Kaintucks—from the rest of the army.

To his horror, Chamberlain saw Captain Sherman's battery of artillery limber its guns to join the retreat. Now, noticing that they would have no artillery support, some panicked soldiers from the Illinois Volunteers also went the way of the Hoosiers, running for the rear.

Chamberlain saw a rider on a huge bay horse charging to the gap in the front line as canister and musket balls rained all around him. He recognized the man as Major Roger Dix. As the army paymaster, he was a popular officer. Dix seized the regimental colors from the Illinois standard-bearer and rode back and forth across the breach in the line to rally the men. As Chamberlain watched in admiration, a bullet hit Dix in the stomach and a second projectile penetrated his skull, killing him instantly. He dropped the battle flag and fell from the horse, but his brave act had emboldened the Illinois Volunteers, and they returned to the line to lift the regimental banner.

Still, Mexican foot and horse soldiers continued to charge the gap left by the Second Indiana, and Chamberlain wondered if this battle was not already lost. What remained of the left flank was melting away to the north, curving toward the rear in the face of the Mexican onslaught. The Arkansas and Kentucky skirmishers were left isolated and abandoned on the mountain slopes.

He finished reloading his carbine and looked for a target. Before he could fire, General Wool's adjutant, Captain Lincoln, galloped to the First Dragoons' position with orders.

"Captain Steen! Mount your dragoons and round up those damned cowards! Drive them back to the front!"

"To horse!" Steen shouted.

With musket balls and shrapnel humming around him, Sam Chamberlain was more than happy to fetch his mount.

"Catch those retreating men!" Steen ordered. "Run them down if you must!"

As he galloped toward the outbuildings of Hacienda Buena Vista, he

saw General Wool leading the Second Illinois Volunteers from the right
in an attempt to shore up the hole in the line left by the Indianans. Within
a minute, Private Chamberlain's fleet sorrel, Soldan, had overtaken the
fleeing men on the outskirts of the *rancheria*.

"Halt, there, you cowards!" he yelled.

The men ignored him, so he rode swiftly in front of the leading fugitives, took his right foot out of the stirrup, and kicked a couple of the
men down. Boss Hastings and others troopers did the same, slowing the
rout.

"Stop or you'll all have *C* for 'coward' branded on your cheeks!"

Chamberlain cut off about half of the leaders, like a vaquero turning
a cattle stampede.

"Turn around and march back! Pick up your damned weapons!"

Many of the men, winded from their headlong sprint, obeyed the
orders and stopped running. Others, however, charged into the regiment
protecting the supply wagons at Buena Vista or disappeared into the
barns, sheds, and adobe houses that made up the little village surrounding the ranch.

Chamberlain saw five men continuing toward the buildings and rode
into their path. Two of the soldiers were helping a third to the rear.

"Halt, there!" Chamberlain shouted. "Your orders are to go back to
the front line!"

"Damn you!" a private said. "You ain't no officer! Anyway, this man
is wounded in the foot!"

"Well, it only takes two men to carry him. What are you other two
boys tagging along for?"

"I'm carrying his weapon," a private said, brandishing two muskets.

"What about you?" Sam asked the last man in the procession.

"I'm carrying his hat. And I'm a corporal. *I* outrank *you*!"

"Aw, hell, Sam," Hastings said, having ridden up. "Let 'em go. They
might do some good yet, if the damned greasers attack the supply wagon."

Chamberlain frowned and turned back toward the battle line. Small
arms continued to crack all along the front and cannon shook the very
air. He and Hastings rode up behind the volunteers who had been rallied to return to the fighting.

"Come on, soldier!" Chamberlain shouted down at the Hoosier nearest to him. "March back to the front. The Mexicans are still coming.

You'd best pick up a musket on the way. You boys dropped plenty of them when you turned tail!"

Hastings rode up beside him. "We done good, Sam. There's probably a hundred here that we rallied."

Chamberlain nodded at his friend and looked around for his company commander, Captain Steen. He saw that Steen had overtaken Sherman's battery and had shamed the gunners into returning to the front. Chamberlain began to hope his army might survive, even though hordes of enemy infantry had broken through and were still pushing toward the supply train at Buena Vista. If they got there, they could capture the supplies and flank the entire U.S. force, surrounding it with superior numbers.

"Gentlemen!" Captain Steen shouted, returning to his dragoons at a lope. "We have new orders from General Lane. Our skirmishers on the far left flank have been cut off by the enemy advance. Look there, on the mountainside." He pointed southeast.

Chamberlain gazed over the spearhead of the oncoming Mexican assault that had penetrated the U.S. line. Through the musket smoke, he saw the stranded skirmishers fighting for their lives as a regiment of lancers approached them on the steep mountainside.

"Our orders are to ride through the Mexican ranks and bring the Kentucky and Arkansas skirmishers back to guard the supply train."

"Let's go save them Kaintucks' and Rackensackers' asses!" Boss Hastings blurted.

"First Sergeant!" Steen yelled. "Form a column of fours!"

Within a minute, Chamberlain found himself galloping toward the musket-toting Mexican infantry advance, Soldan's mane whipping in the wind like the crimson pennons on the enemy lance shafts.

"Draw sabers!" Captain Steen ordered.

Chamberlain drew his blade as he sped onward. *By God, if the boys back in Boston could see me now, they wouldn't believe this shit!*

A canister shell burst in Captain Steen's path, sending a ball through his thigh and into his mount's lung. The beast stumbled, throwing the captain to the ground before he reached the Mexican line. The charge faltered as Steen's dragoons milled about in confusion. Chamberlain pulled rein and looked down to see Steen put his palm over the bullet hole in his leg to stanch the flow of blood.

"Lieutenant Rucker, you are in command! Carry on!" Steen ordered, grimacing in pain.

Lieutenant D. H. Rucker wheeled to address the dragoons. "Form up in a column of platoons!"

The moment the men had fallen back into their places, the lieutenant shouted the order: "Charge!"

Within a few leaps, Soldan plunged in among the Mexican soldiers and Private Chamberlain brandished his saber. Many of the attackers were reloading their Brown Bess muskets as they steadily pressed on toward Buena Vista, but a few shot into the galloping dragoons. Most reeled aside to avoid the sabers and let the Americans pass through. Chamberlain got close enough to one enemy soldier to take a swipe at his head, but he only sliced the top of his hat off as the man ducked.

As quickly as he had entered the Mexican column, he was out of it, continuing to gallop up the slope toward the Arkansas and Kentucky skirmishers. The skirmishers now saw the dragoons coming to their rescue and gave up their position, running down the mountain on foot, toward their picket line of mounts. But they could not outrun the Mexican lancers, who pursued them, harassing their flanks, swerving in to skewer a few of the unfortunate volunteers with their glinting lance blades.

As he galloped forward, Chamberlain felt his anger begin to boil as he saw Americans taken out by the spears, again and again. One volunteer had stumbled and fallen, perhaps wounded, and was now on his knees, begging for mercy. The lancer nearest to him tendered none, driving the razor-sharp steel point into the fallen man's chest and pinning him to the ground, where he writhed in the throes of death.

But now the surviving Arkansas and Kentucky cavalrymen, who had been fighting on foot for almost twenty-four hours, reached their mounts, tucked away at the head of a gully. Private Chamberlain and the Second Dragoons dashed past them as they mounted, continuing the charge upon the hated lancers.

Too late to save, but soon enough to avenge, Chamberlain thought, thinking of his book.

"Use your carbines first," Lieutenant Rucker ordered. "Then your pistols and sabers!"

Private Chamberlain sheathed his saber and unhooked his Hall carbine from the ring on his saddle. Now in range of the lancers, he took aim as best he could from his galloping sorrel.

"Fire at will!"

He pulled the trigger and saw the horse stumble under the man at whom he had aimed. He rehooked his carbine to the saddle and drew his pistol from the pommel holster. The Mexican lancers had not faltered in their charge, though several in their front ranks had fallen to the Americans' carbines. The two bodies of horse soldiers galloped closer together, rumbling the mountain slope with a thousand hooves.

Chamberlain aimed his pistol. The lance tips were almost in his face when he fired. He saw the lancer in his sights roll backwards over the cantle of his saddle. Soldan dodged the next spear point, and Chamberlain used his pistol as a club, hitting the enemy rider in the face as Soldan carried him forward. He heard his own voice unexpectedly wailing a battle yell as shouts and gunshots rang out all around him.

He dropped his pistol and drew his saber. To his astonishment, Soldan continued charging headlong into the Mexicans, dodging spear thrusts as if he did this sort of thing all the time. Chamberlain witnessed a lancer bearing down on one of his fellow dragoons and swept in to catch the enemy rider off guard. With the power of Soldan's weight pushing him forward, he made a slash with his saber under the right arm of the lancer. He felt the resistance of flesh and bone through his hilt as human blood splattered his horse, his uniform, and his face.

Screams of horses and men—wounded and dying—filled the air, along with the ringing of saber blades and a few latent pistol shots. The lancers, staggered by the furious onslaught of the U.S. dragoons, reeled back, their bugler sounding a retreat.

"Halt!" Lieutenant Drucker yelled. "Let them go! Our orders are to escort the skirmishers. Pick up our wounded! About-face! Retire and rally at the supply train!"

Chamberlain felt his lungs heaving with excitement as he glanced around the battlefield. Blood ran in rivulets down the slope. Smoke drifted. The stench of some poor horse's ruptured paunch made Chamberlain gag, and he feared he would vomit. To his surprise, he found that no dragoons had been killed, though a handful of wounded men were mounted double behind messmates.

The Mexicans had carried away at least a dozen dead men.

As he bounced back toward the bloody battle, overtaking the skirmishers he had helped to rescue, he thought about the soldier he had
killed with his saber. Private Chamberlain himself was only sixteen,
and he judged the man he had sliced open like a melon at no more
than twenty. The tough-looking, brown-faced kid had never seen him
coming.

He thought about whether he should relate the horrible deed he had
done in his book. But no. He did not care to relive it. It was better off
forgotten, though he knew he would never shake the memory of that sinister moment and the sickening feel of his blade slicing through the
body of a living man.

He cleared his head and took stock of his situation. Below, the battle
raged all along the line. In the ravines, thousands upon thousands of
brightly uniformed enemy attackers crept toward the plateau held tenuously by the Americans. The U.S. left flank had swung back half a mile,
almost to Hacienda Buena Vista, where the supply train waited like bait
for Santa Anna's army. He knew that left flank was weak, though U.S.
troops were swarming toward it to prevent disaster.

From his vantage high on the mountain slope, he saw Lieutenant John
Paul Jones O'Brien returning to the front with two new six-pounders and
a fresh crew of gunners. He had already been overrun by Mexican
infantry once but had not had enough.

"You'd better toughen up, Sam Chamberlain," he muttered to himself.

Glancing to his right, along the mountain ridge, he saw a new regiment of lancers sweeping far around to the east, out of artillery range.
He knew their objective had to be the supply train.

Where the hell are the reserves? We are outnumbered! Overwhelmed!

Looking back downhill, he happened to catch sight of a white horse
ridden by a man in a broad palmetto hat. Taylor was coming from Saltillo
on Old Whitey! The general had brought May's company of dragoons
with him. Next came the red shirts of Colonel Jefferson Davis's battle-
tested Mississippi Rifles—heroes of Monterrey.

Chamberlain thought it odd how the presence of that old Indian
fighter, Taylor, bolstered his courage. He felt hopeful. This battle could
be won yet. This is why he had enlisted, was it not? He felt an urge now
to get back into position. Soldan sensed it, tossed his head, and released
a defiant snort.

SARAH BORGINNES

Saltillo, Mexico
February 23, 1847

Even from within the thick adobe walls of the American House, Sarah Borginnes could faintly hear the artillery, six miles away to the south. She expected she would listen to it rumble all day.

General Zachary Taylor had come in for breakfast early this morning. He had sat at his favorite table in the back with Major Bliss, Lieutenant Colonel May of the dragoons, and Colonel Jefferson Davis of the Mississippi Rifles. Other officers—those tasked with holding the city of Saltillo—had come and gone through the morning to consult with Taylor and receive their orders. Finally, Taylor and his men had decided to ride south and join the battle.

"Godspeed to you, Zach," she had said when he left. "I know the men fighting at Buena Vista will be glad to see you and Old Whitey."

He had smiled and taken her hand in his. "Sarah, they will be much happier to see you than me, once this battle is won." He had winked and walked out.

Now, some thirty minutes later, Borginnes felt sure that Taylor would have arrived at the battlefield by this time. If she knew Old Rough and Ready—and she did—he would use Santa Anna's hind end for a bootjack before this day was over.

Business was understandably slow at the American House today. Still, a few off-duty soldiers and officers seeking lunch were scattered around the saloon. Five ladies of easy virtue were laughing at the far end of the bar. Sarah Borginnes stood at the opposite end, near the door, so she could greet customers as they walked in. She was taking advantage of the lull in business by sorting through her stock of dishes, cups, and bowls to determine how many new vessels needed to be commissioned with the local potter. Breakage was common here at the American House.

The door flew open and a private from one of the volunteer regiments burst in, hatless.

"General Taylor is whipped!" he screamed. "The whole army is cut to pieces! The Mexicans are coming!"

She was only a few steps from the door, and by the time the private got to "Mexicans," she had made a fist of her right hand. She punched the private between the eyes hard enough to stagger him back to the door.

"You damned son of a bitch!" she yelled. "There ain't enough Mexicans from here to Veracruz to whip old Taylor! Now get your sorry jack-rabbit ass back to the front lines and fight like a man or I will see you branded a coward!"

The man pointed south. "But—"

She raised her fist.

"All right, I'll go back," he said timidly, now looking at the scowls of the soldiers in the bar. He turned to leave, his head held low.

Sarah pushed him out through the doorway and watched him mount a lathered horse he had ridden from the front. She made sure he pointed that horse south before she shut the door.

"Angelina!" she shouted to her most trusted employee. "Have one of the boys saddle my horse. I'm going to the front!"

Major
WILLIAM BLISS

Buena Vista
February 23, 1847

Approaching the battleground from the north, it had become obvious to Major William Bliss that General John Wool's defense plans had gone awry. He had encountered scores of demoralized soldiers drifting toward Saltillo, telling tales of the left wing collapsing under a huge wave of Mexican infantry and cavalry. General Taylor had ordered all such fugitives to return to the battle and had hastened forward at a canter.

Now Bliss could see a regiment of Mexican cavalry on the mountain ridge to the east, threatening to flank or encircle the U.S. Army. He could hear and sense great confusion on the left: the rattle of muskets, the screams and shouts of men, the squealing of wounded horses.

"It doesn't sound good, does it, Major?" General Taylor asked.

"No, sir."

"Let's ride up to high ground on the plateau and look things over."

Bliss spurred forward at Taylor's side, angling off the road to the southeast. Behind them, Lieutenant Colonel Charles May and Colonel Jefferson Davis followed. They rode up a steep, eroded slope to the plateau and reined to a stop on an elevated roll that afforded a view of the entire battlefield.

"Well, the right flank looks solid," Taylor said, "but what the hell has happened on the left?"

"The left has collapsed back almost to the supply trains, sir." Bliss struggled to emulate the calm demeanor of his commander. He looked on in horror as Mexican lancers speared wounded American men unable to flee and Mexican infantry soldiers bayoneted every fallen enemy in their path.

"Colonel Davis!" the general called out over his shoulder.

Taylor's former son-in-law spurred forward. "At your service, General."

"Look across the plateau between those two ravines, Jeff." Taylor pointed. "Do you see?"

"I see it clearly, sir. Looks like a battalion of infantry forming up there, flanked by cavalry. They intend to crush our left flank."

"Those damned muskets and spears are no match for your Whitney rifles. March your men double-quick to that point. Use the ravine on the left for cover until you are within rifle range. I will send artillery and the Third Indiana to support you. Stop that advance! Do it for Old Mississippi!"

"Yes, sir!" Davis wheeled away to fulfill his orders.

"Bill, where is Wool? Do you see General Wool?"

Bliss had already located Wool, dashing back and forth on a tall bay horse. "There!" He pointed back toward Buena Vista. "With the Second Illinois."

Taylor spurred Old Whitey to a canter, and Bliss stayed a neck behind. May followed, waving for his company of dragoons to catch up, apparently eager for orders. General Wool saw them coming and spun his horse to report.

"General!" Wool blurted. "We are whipped!"

Bliss was shocked at the outburst.

"That is for me to determine!" Taylor snapped. "Pull your wits together, John. The volunteers do not know that they are whipped. Let them alone. We'll see what they can do." Taylor turned to Wool's adjutant, Captain Lincoln. "Make yourself useful, Captain, and order the Third Indiana to support the Mississippi Rifles on the plateau." He pointed.

"Yes, sir!" Lincoln shouted, charging away on his mount.

"Colonel May!"

"Here, sir!" May spurred forward on his battle horse, Black Tom.

"Get on the other side of Buena Vista ranch and cut off those damned lancers trying to gain our rear. Secure our commissary and keep it secure. Ride like the devil, Captain, and give them hell!"

"Fours right-about wheel!" May's high-pitched voice sang.

Bliss watched the dragoons' snakelike column canter away toward Buena Vista.

"Come now, Bill," Taylor said to Bliss. "Let us have a word with Major Bragg."

Old Whitey bounded to an instant gallop as Bliss spurred to catch up. Bliss noticed Major Braxton Bragg's flying artillery rolling northwest toward Buena Vista. Taylor veered left to cut Bragg off.

"Halt, Bragg!" the general ordered. "Where are you going?"

"To support the commissary, sir. I was told the volunteers buckled."

"I need you elsewhere—"

A shell shrieked into the path of Bragg's halted advance and exploded, sending shrapnel whistling in every direction.

"By God, General," Bragg yelled, "that one would have hit us square if you hadn't halted us! Those damned Irish deserters have got a grudge on me!"

"I wonder why, Major. Now, listen. Can you hear me?"

Bragg nodded and cupped a hand behind his ear.

Taylor pointed. "You see the red shirts of the Mississippi Rifles?"

Bragg glanced. "Yes, sir."

"Advance and unlimber near enough to support their line!"

"Yes, sir. Who will support me, sir?"

Taylor scowled at the artillerist. "Major Bliss and I will support you! Advance!"

Bragg led his gunnery crew toward his new position.

"Let's move, Bill! I feel another round coming from the deserters!"

Bliss cantered along beside the general, back toward General Wool's position on the collapsed left. As they departed, a shell fell on the ground they had recently occupied with Bragg.

"Son of a bitch!" Taylor yelled as projectiles hummed past him. "Are you hit yet, Major?"

"By the grace of God, no, sir! Not yet!"

Returning to General Wool's position on the buckled left flank, Bliss looked northward to Buena Vista and the supply train. He saw that waves of Mexican infantry and swarms of lancers had been stalled by U.S. defenders using the supply wagons and the buildings of the *rancheria* for cover.

"The boys who bolted from the Second Indiana have found some sand left in their craws," Wool said. "They are holding the commissary."

"I'm more interested in the Mississippi Rifles right now," Taylor said calmly, his spyglass to his eye.

Bliss shifted his gaze southward. Through the smoke he could make out Jefferson Davis's red-shirted riflemen rushing out of the ravine to form a skirmish line in a precariously advanced position. Only 368 men strong, the Mississippians prepared to take on a brigade of infantry and a battalion of cavalry marching to finish off the American left. Bliss saw the Illinois Volunteers moving double-quick to support Davis, but they were not yet close enough to help. Fortunately, Major Bragg's flying artillery had pulled within range. His gunners were preparing to open fire on the Mexican position opposite Davis's red shirts.

"Steady, boys," General Taylor said, watching Jeff Davis through his telescope. "Steady for the honor of Old Mississippi!"

Seemingly innocent little puffs of smoke erupted all along the Mississippi line, and the leading ranks of Mexican infantry collapsed under the heavy fire of the Whitney rifles. The Mexican advance faltered. By the time the smoke cleared, the red shirts had reloaded. Bliss watched in awe as the Mississippi Rifles charged the overwhelming numbers of the enemy ranks.

"Well done, Jeff!" General Taylor shouted. "Hurrah for Mississippi!"

Bliss and the troops nearby raised a cheer. The Third Indiana Volunteers continued to advance toward the red shirts while Major Braxton Bragg released his first salvo of spherical case shot into the Mexican front.

"Zach!" General Wool cried. "May is riding out to attack the lancers at Buena Vista."

Bliss watched May on his big black horse leading a saber charge into the flank of the Mexican cavalry column. The furious onslaught, aided by musket fire from Buena Vista, routed the lancers and sent them curling back up the mountain.

More cheers arose from the men clustered around Taylor and Wool.

Then a volley of canister from the Saint Patrick's Battalion fell nearby, wounding horses, dragoons, and foot soldiers.

"Lieutenant Rucker!" Taylor roared at the dragoon officer. The old fighter drew his saber and pointed it southwestward, toward the Saint Pats. "Take that damned battery!"

Colonel
JEFFERSON DAVIS

"Fire advancing!" he yelled. The Mississippi Rifles, having reloaded their weapons after their first volley, marched toward an enemy force that outnumbered them ten to one. In spite of the odds, he felt pleased to see that his men did not hesitate.

Now a spray of musket and *escopeta* bullets tore through his ranks from three angles. As he marched in the middle of the skirmish line with Company K, he saw Private Garrot go down, then Private Donovent and Corporal Butler.

In the next instant, something yanked his right foot out from under him, throwing him to the ground. Colonel Jefferson Davis felt a searing heat tear through his heel. Rifle shots and the screams of his men drowned out his involuntary cry of pain. He sat up and looked at his foot. A big musket ball from a Brown Bess had clipped the top of his spur, torn through flesh, and shattered the bone of his heel.

Get up!

He stood and tried to take a step, but the grinding of bone on nerves racked his whole leg with excruciating pain.

"Sergeant Hagomy!" he yelled. "I need my horse. Go back to the ravine where I tied my horse and bring him here!"

"Yes, sir!" Hagomy said.

Davis looked ahead at his men, still marching steadily into a fire even hotter than he had experienced at La Teneria. They dropped by ones and twos all along the line. But the survivors kept marching. Even wounded men continued to reload and shoot from the places where they had fallen on the open ground.

Sergeant Hagomy brought Davis his horse and helped him mount. Just slipping his right foot into the stirrup racked him with a pain that made him dizzy and nauseated. He could feel his own hot blood rising inside his boot.

He saw Sergeant Hagomy running to catch up to his unit—Company F—pausing only to take an ammunition pouch off of a dead comrade.

"Advance!" Davis said to himself.

Spurring the horse hurt like hell. He squeezed his knees together and used his reins to urge the mount into the fray. A shell burst overhead. Another musket volley flew from the enemy ranks. More of his riflemen fell. And still the red shirts continued to march into the face of the enemy.

Now is the time! If we fail to turn this enemy advance, the day is lost, the Army of Occupation flanked, surrounded and vanquished!

He drew his saber and dashed behind his advancing line of battle-hardened volunteers. "March on, riflemen! To the glory Old Mississippi!"

Balls buzzed past his head like swarms of bumblebees, and another shell burst over his regiment. More men fell, but the rest kept advancing, reloading, firing. He looked through the smoke and saw a shell from Bragg's battery explode into the Mexican infantry, now just fifty yards away. He saw the center of their line wither. The sure aim of his Mississippi Rifles dropped enemy fighters at a rate of one per second. Another shell burst over the Mexicans and they began to reel back.

"Halt!" Davis ordered. "Select your targets and aim as sharpshooters! Fire at will."

Rifles cracked. The steel nerves of the red shirts and the accuracy of the Whitney rifles forced the enemy to retreat into the reserves behind them.

Victory! But only for now.

He looked behind him for support and saw the Third Indiana approaching, but still too far away to help. He knew he had to fall back, help the wounded, rally his men, prepare for the next wave of Santa Anna's thousands, and hope for the quick arrival of the Hoosiers.

"Retire firing! Rally on me to the rear! Steady, men! Withdraw firing!"

He prayed to God and General Taylor to send him some support.

By God, we stopped them! We may have saved the battle. If only we can hold them back one more time.

Colonel Davis turned back to the rear to lead his men in the controlled retrograde movement. On the plateau between the two ravines, he now saw the bodies of his soldiers scattered haphazardly. He guessed three dozen men dead, an equal or higher number wounded. He rode past one bloodied corpse and recognized the lifeless face of Sergeant Hagomy, who only a few minutes ago had fetched his horse for him.

A stabbing pain roared up his leg from his wound, making his head swim. Blood had risen above his ankle in his boot.

"Colonel!"

He turned to see his adjutant, Captain Richard Griffith, running toward him.

"What is it, Captain?"

"Sir, the lancers have gone down into the ravine to the southwest. They intend to flank us and charge us from the rear!"

"I will find them, Captain. Lead the men in a steady withdrawal. Dispatch two men from each company to help the wounded to the rear."

Davis trotted to the edge of the ravine and peered into it as he rode. The banks looked too steep and choked with brush to facilitate a cavalry charge, even for the legendary Mexican riders. Half a furlong on, he came to a gentler slope with less vegetation. Below, he heard branches snapping, horses snorting. He reined to a halt and looked. There! Tunics of blue, green, and red. Lance tips glinting in the sun. The lancers were forming up for an assault.

He turned and galloped to his troops. "To the ravine, this way! Double-quick, men! We must ambush their cavalry!"

The men near enough to hear him came careering to his call as he led them to the place where he had seen the lancers gathering in the gully.

"Form a line on the bank of the ravine," he said, riding among his men. He took care not to shout too loudly, so as not to alert the enemy to his presence. "Do not fire until I give the order."

Now he saw the advantage of the ground he held. Here the barranca bulged into the plateau, creating a curve where his men could wrap around the coming attack and pour an enfilading fire down upon the enemy. More Mississippi Rifles took up positions on the brink of the bank as the lancers approached from below.

A Mexican bugle signaled an advance down in the ravine, and the enemy horsemen began to ascend toward the plateau. On they came, weaving among tall yuccas, scrubby oaks, and stunted pines. They seemed unaware that they were being watched closely over the iron sights of a hundred rifled barrels. At the head rode an officer with a red plume on his tall shako campaign hat. This officer picked the ground ahead of him, his gaze gradually angling upward. At twenty yards he looked up and saw Davis mounted at the rim of the ravine. The officer reined in and drew a breath—a gasp—as his eyes met those of Colonel Davis.

"Fire!" Davis shouted.

The officer was the first to die. Scores of others fell dead and wounded from the sheet of bullets fired from the Whitney rifles. The survivors wheeled back into the barranca and disappeared the way they had come.

"*Los Diablos!*" they shouted. "*Camisas Colorados!*"

"Reload!" Davis ordered.

The victory over the lancers made the pain in his heel lessen for a moment. He looked back toward his own army and saw a single piece of light artillery rolling his way. Good. The gun would add to Braxton Bragg's battery. His spirits soared. Beyond the fieldpiece, he saw the gray uniforms of the long-awaited Third Indiana, also known as the Indiana Grays, finally arriving within range of the enemy.

He ordered his regiment to retire to the place where their first charge had begun. Here, his survivors formed a line across the finger of the plateau, from the ravine on the left to the ravine on the right. The dead and severely wounded were carried down into the relative safety of the ravine on the left. Like Davis, many of his men were wounded but still able and willing to fight. He rode back to meet the artillery, which was bouncing to the battlefront at a canter. A lieutenant ordered his gunners to halt as he approached Davis.

"Lieutenant Kilburn reporting, sir!"

"What are your orders, Lieutenant?" Davis winced through the throbbing in his foot.

"I have none, sir. I saw you needed support and came forward on my own accord."

"Very well, Lieutenant. I am glad that you did. Take up a position in the center of my line and commence firing at the enemy."

"It is an honor, sir!"

Davis watched the artillerymen roll into place, unlimber, and prepare to fire. By this time, he knew he had been formed up in one place long enough for the enemy artillery to train their guns on him. A shell screamed toward him and burst in the ravine to his left. He knew it was only a matter of time until the Mexican artillerists corrected their aim.

Lieutenant Kilburn's six-pounder hurled its first shell into the Mexican reserves, provoking a cheer from the Mississippi Rifles. Smiling through his pain, Colonel Jefferson Davis now beheld a sight that wiped the grin right off his face. Around a bend in the ravine, ahead, came a huge column of Mexican cavalry, perhaps a thousand riders strong. Their lance tips, waving skyward, looked like the undulating hairs of an enormous stinging caterpillar of many bright colors, crawling menacingly toward him.

Looking back, he saw the winded Third Indiana Volunteers trotting to the front.

Kilburn's field gun fired.

A Mexican artillery shell fell in front of the red shirts and exploded, killing or wounding three men with shrapnel.

"Colonel Davis!" Adjutant Griffith shouted. "Here come the lancers!"

Davis heard the ground rumbling as he watched the great caterpillar charge, four hundred yards away and coming fast.

The Indiana Grays neared, under Colonel James Lane, four hundred men strong.

Davis's mind whirred. His West Point training told him that a hollow square was the recognized formation to combat a cavalry charge, with bayonets bristling outward from all four sides. But these volunteers had not been drilled in the complicated marching maneuvers required to create the square, and the Mississippians' Whitney rifles did not come equipped with bayonets.

Colonel Lane was almost upon him with his regiment and would expect orders.

He reined his horse to the front and looked at the ground ahead. His riflemen still held their line across the plateau, from ravine to ravine. He saw that if he ordered the Hoosiers to form a line in advance of his regiment's right, along the edge of the ravine, they would create a giant V formation that opened up toward the approaching Mexican riders.

"Colonel Lane!" he shouted, before Lane could report. "Follow me with your regiment!"

He angled to the right to lead the Hoosiers to their leg of the V formation.

We will be the V in Buena Vista. Let them charge into our cross fire!

With the Third Indiana in place along the edge of the ravine, he now turned back and saw about twenty gray uniforms milling around behind his red-shirted Mississippi Rifles on the left leg of the V. He galloped his way to investigate. Colonel William Bowles of the Second Indiana approached him on a gray horse. Davis was stunned to see Bowles almost in tears.

"Colonel Davis, my regiment has run away! This is all I have left!" He gestured toward the handful of volunteers who had stuck with him. "I wish permission to fight with your regiment."

Davis nodded. "Granted. Order your men to fill in where my riflemen have fallen."

"Colonel Davis!" Adjutant Griffith shouted. "Here come the lancers at a gallop!"

He felt the plateau tremble under him. Another shell burst overhead, wounding too many men to count. He saw a few of his red shirts easing backwards. Before he could say anything, he heard Captain William Haddon exhort the men, "Hold your ground, riflemen! The lines are the safest place to stand!"

"Well said!" Davis added, "The place of *duty* is the place of safety!"

Davis now charged behind his line of red shirts forming the left leg of the V. He saw the Indiana Grays in a perfectly straight file that formed the right leg.

"Hold your fire, men, until they get close! And then give it to them!" He rode behind his entire line, repeating the order.

"Do not fire until I order it! Let them get close! Our cross fire will repel them!"

Now he arrived at the angle of the V. To his right, the untested Indianans maintained their leg admirably, perhaps because they sensed the cover of the ravine behind them, should they have to fall back. His Mississippians were exposed on the open plateau, but each man stood as motionless as a rock, as silent as death, as eager as a greyhound.

"They're slowing down," Griffith said, watching the approach of the lancers.

"Yes, I see," Davis said. He had expected them to gallop headlong into his lines, but they had slowed to a trot. The strange V must have confused them.

"They're slowing to a walk!" Griffith said. "Almost in range."

Davis watched as the front rank of riders stalled, causing others behind them to swarm haphazardly around them at a trot. The lancers approached cautiously, their charge having slowed to a crawl.

"They are inside of one hundred yards," Griffith said. "Now ninety . . . Eighty . . ."

Davis drew a breath with which to shout the order.

Somewhere down the Indiana line, a nervous volunteer fingered his trigger a little too hard and fired. A split second later, the entire V erupted in a rolling volley that mowed down enemy men and horses like a giant's scythe. The Mexican cavalry rolled back on itself and fled, trampling infantrymen behind them, and disappearing into barrancas, around bends, and over ridges.

A mighty cheer arose along the V formation.

"Reload!" Davis shouted. The combination of his painful foot wound and the relief of his success almost made him faint, but he shook his head and sucked in a breath. Looking toward the rear, he was even more elated to see Captain Thomas Sherman unlimbering yet another field-piece to help drive the Mexican assault back farther.

"Look!" Griffith said, pointing beyond Sherman's gun.

Davis saw Bragg's artillery and a long column of cavalry, under Lieutenant Colonel Charles May, riding Black Tom, all coming to take the fight to the Mexicans.

"Tell the men to retire to the protection of the ravine," the colonel ordered. "Recover our dead and take care of the wounded. We will retire and await further orders."

"Yes, sir!" Griffith loped away to spread the order to the company commanders.

Now that the intense excitement had waned, Davis's pain almost overwhelmed him. He found sorrow over his casualties and fears of amputation or gangrene mingling with pride in his regiment and the glory of his battlefield stand. He would retire for now. He had saved the day. But then he heard a shell whistle nearby as the battle raged louder to the right and he knew the day might well be in need of saving again. This was not over.

Private
SAMUEL CHAMBERLAIN

As he trotted toward the Saint Patrick's Battalion, his carbine forever pivoted on its saddle ring, slamming hard against his kneecap. Jolting along in the column of fours beside his messmate, Boss Hastings, Private Samuel Chamberlain heard a rousing shout up ahead. He saw grimy gunners cheering the dragoons as they passed in front of Sherman's battery of flying artillery. The Irish deserters had pummeled Sherman all day long.

Down into the ravine he plunged, leaning back in the saddle and ducking thorny branches and the sharp points of Spanish daggers.

"Goddamn, there's dead greasers everywhere," Boss Hastings declared.

Soldan stumbled across corpses and wounded men. Chamberlain was sure some injured Mexicans were going to be trampled to death. That did not sit well with his conscience, but he reminded himself that he had seen many a helpless wounded American lanced or bayoneted to death on this day.

The stench in the gully turned his stomach. It smelled worse than a hundred dance hall outhouses, as scores of dying wretches had released all manner of bodily substances from their battered vessels. Not to mention the carcasses and corpses ripped open by shot and shell.

"We'll take that hill, sure 'nuff," Hastings said. "The muzzles of them big twenty-four pounders are aimed high. We'll slip in under them and chop us up some Irish turncoats."

Chamberlain followed the riders ahead of him as his company of dragoons rounded a bend that led up another branch of the barranca. He saw men ahead of him in the column pointing upward at something. Peering through the branches, the dust, and the gunpowder smoke, he saw the huge emerald banner of the Saint Patrick's Battalion lifted by restless breezes.

"Now's the time, Sam."

Up the right bank of the ravine he rode, raking Soldan's flanks with his spurs as he reached for the hilt of his saber. He felt his heartbeat quicken as he charged with his comrades onto a spur of the plateau that lay before the hilltop battery of the deserters. He looked up at the muzzles of the heavy artillery of the Saint Pats.

Suddenly, the regimental bugler sounded "to the right," and Chamberlain saw the men in front of him dashing desperately in that direction. Following the flow of the column, he saw that his company had almost plunged into a deep chasm with sheer banks that protected the hill like a castle moat. They were just beyond carbine range.

Lieutenant Rucker led the storming party along the chasm and around the hill to the right. Chamberlain could see that the only path up to the top of the hill led through Santa Anna's reserve infantry, which must have numbered a thousand men. Brown Bess musket balls hissed past them as they plunged back into a protective barranca and continued west. Soon the Saltillo road came under the hooves of the dragoon horses as Lieutenant Rucker abandoned his assault and led his troops up toward Angostura Pass.

"Well, shit!" Boss Hastings said, "I was all het up to kill me some of them redheaded peckerwood Irish bastards."

"Yeah, me too," Chamberlain said, sliding his saber back into the scabbard. "I hope Captain Washington recognizes us as friends and don't blow the hell out of us coming up the narrows."

His mount slipped, and he looked below to see rivulets of blood running down the rutted road. Next he rode among the bodies of courageous Mexican soldiers who had charged, wave upon wave, into the muzzles of Washington's artillery. The dozens of bodies turned to scores, then hundreds, as the riders approached the battery anchoring the U.S.

right flank. The corpses lay in heaps, along with the carcasses of horses. In places they blocked the road and had to be trampled upon by the dragoon mounts.

I'm getting used to looking at piles of dead men.

Washington's gunners were hailed, and the dragoons returned to the American side without having fired a shot or bloodied a blade on the Saint Pats. As Rucker led the men back toward their former position, a lightning bolt flashed and cracked. Thunder rumbled, mocking the lowly man-made ordnance. A northerly gust whipped through Soldan's mane as Chamberlain rode into a wall of icy rain. It refreshed him at first, but quickly began to chill him. He had thrown aside his greatcoat at the onset of the attack on the Irish battery and now wished he had it to wear.

"The Lord is on our side!" Hastings proclaimed. "That cold rain is drivin' right into the face of the enemy!"

The firing of small arms and cannon soon ceased on both sides as dragoon horses plodded through the downpour and flinched at the occasional thunderbolt. By the time the drenched cavaliers reached General Taylor's position, the rainstorm had blown south, revealing the most beautiful rainbow Chamberlain had ever seen. It rose beyond the Sierra Madre, arched across the clearing sky in a riot of colorful ribbons, and plunged into the canyon to the southwest.

"I'll take that as a good omen," Chamberlain said.

"I told you the Lord was on our side."

Tell that to the dead and wounded men in American uniforms.

At that moment, the Mexican artillery opened up on the American line again, and U.S. gunners returned the compliments.

Taylor noticed that Lieutenant Rucker had returned with his dragoons.

"Well, Lieutenant, it seems the deserters are still shelling us. Report!"

"We found the ground in front of the hill impassable, sir. I searched for better ground around to the rear of the hill, but ran into a division of infantry. They opened fire on us and we retired through the narrows."

"Very well, Rucker. Report to Colonel May's command. Perhaps he can find some ground more to your liking."

"Yes, sir!" Rucker replied, with just a touch of insolence in his voice.

Chamberlain rode with his dragoon company back toward Hacienda Buena Vista, where May's command awaited orders from General Wool.

Throughout the chaos of this day, May had collected regular army and volunteer troopers that now numbered close to five hundred sabers.

Boss Hastings leaned in close to speak to Chamberlain. "What an honor to serve under the hero of Resaca de la Palma," he said sarcastically.

"The great captor of General de la Vega," Chamberlain added.

Soldan had rested for a few minutes, when May's dragoons spotted a brigade of lancers riding along the base of the mountain around the U.S. left flank.

"They're going to attack Buena Vista!" Lieutenant Rucker said. "Our supplies."

"The Arkansas and Kentucky cavalries are there," May said.

"They are outnumbered," Rucker snapped.

"Here comes a courier from General Wool," May replied. "We'll see what he says."

Chamberlain watched as May wasted time conversing with the courier. He could see that, by now, the lancers were closer to the Rackensackers and the Kaintucks than May's dragoons were.

"We done lost our chance to save those boys' asses again," Hastings muttered.

Finally, May ordered a charge on the attacking lancers. For the sake of the volunteer cavalries, the bugler condescended to blow the signal. Soldan cantered toward the village, the supplies, and the volunteer horse soldiers soon to fall under attack. As he rode headlong, Chamberlain saw confusion among the volunteers from Arkansas and Kentucky. They failed to form a skirmish line as the lancers bore down on them.

"They look like sittin' ducks!" he yelled at Hastings.

Sporadic gunfire sputtered from the volunteers, but it wasn't enough to slow the lancers. The hard-riding Mexicans lowered their lance tips and thundered into the helpless Arkansans and Kentuckians.

Chamberlain was near enough now—as he galloped onward with May's five hundred—to see the horrors of the Mexican assault. In the confusion and lack of leadership, he witnessed most of the Rackensackers and Kaintucks turning tail for Buena Vista under the onslaught. General Archibald Yell—a former governor of Arkansas whom Chamberlain knew as an old dueler, a smooth-talking politician, and a hard drinker—drew his saber and charged the Mexicans. His blade hacked down or drove aside several lancers until one grizzled veteran ran his spear point into Yell's mouth and through the back of his head, unhorsing him most violently in a spray of blood, while another lancer stabbed the general through the chest.

Captain Porter of Arkansas and Adjutant Vaughn of Kentucky also died charging with Yell.

May's command was just seconds away from clashing with the flank of the Mexican cavalry brigade. Chamberlain drew his saber and joined the rolling "Hurrah!" of the dragoons, taking the lancers almost completely by surprise. Soldan used his body to slam into the first horse and rider he came to, knocking them down to be trampled underfoot by hundreds of American mounts. He swiped his saber downward onto the next lancer, hacking through the man's hand, where it held the lance shaft. All around him, hundreds of cavaliers wrought similar barbarities as voices screamed and blood spewed.

The Mexican column was cut in two, the front half circling around behind Buena Vista, toward the valley, as the trailing half curled back up toward the mountain. Sharpshooters from the supply train poured musket and rifle balls into the scattered lancers, unhorsing many of them. Thomas Sherman's flying artillery unlimbered two six-pounders and slung canister and spherical case shot into the group of lancers in the valley, driving them toward a distant mesa.

Along with the rest of May's men, Private Samuel Chamberlain pursued the back half of the divided column into the mountains. The emboldened dragoons chased the demoralized lancers into a canyon, where the Mexicans suddenly blundered into another regiment of Mexican cavalry, which had been riding to their aid.

Reining in Soldan to look over the edge of the canyon rim, Chamberlain saw the two groups of lancers milling in a state of chaos. He also noticed a large number of Mexican infantry in the canyon—probably driven there earlier by the Mississippi Rifles.

"Now who's the sittin' ducks?" Boss Hastings said, unhooking his carbine.

Orders came for number twos to hold the horses while the rest of the men dismounted and lined the bluffs overlooking the box canyon, or blocked off its access trails. Chamberlain and Hastings carried their Hall carbines and found a rocky crag that would protect their vitals while they fired down on the lancers. They nestled into position and awaited the order to fire.

Instead, an American artillery piece dropped a shell perfectly into the canyon, raining shrapnel among the trapped lancers. Another followed, and the Mexicans—seeing that they were surrounded and trapped—began waving white flags of surrender.

"Hold your fire!" Lieutenant Rucker yelled.

One of the Mexican cavaliers was allowed to ride out of the canyon and wave a white flag tied to the end of his lance pole, so that the U.S. artillerymen would see it and cease firing while negotiations were made for their surrender.

"Hot damn!" Hastings railed. "I thought we was gonna shoot some fish in a barrel!"

Chamberlain leaned back against the rim rock, where he could look over the entire field of battle. From his lofty perch on the extreme left flank, he gazed down upon the opposing lines stretched out to the west. The battlefront seemed feathered with plumes of gunpowder smoke that drifted toward the enemy side. The sun hung two fists above the horizon.

"We've ridden all over this bloody ground today, Boss." He pointed down at the landmarks below. "From the middle, to the left, then across to the deserters' battery, up through the narrows on the far right, and now we're back on the left again."

Hastings spat over the rim of the canyon. "It's been a dandy little trot."

"We've saved the left flank, Boss. We did it. And captured a few hundred lancers, to boot."

"Yeah, well, they're still fightin' like hell in the middle. Look down at all them greasers massed on the Mex side."

"You reckon they'll trot us back down there next?"

"Hell, I hope so. I ain't had my fill of killin' yet."

Chamberlain had had his fill for the day, but he wouldn't say so to Boss Hastings. Still, he was proud to have helped in the capture of the lancers and relieved that he didn't have to shoot any more of them from the rim rock of this canyon. What he had earlier feared was a hopeless situation on the left flank had now been repaired. But the capture of a few hundred lancers hardly took a drop from Santa Anna's bucket of soldiery. Taylor's army was still profoundly outnumbered and lacking in the heavy artillery of the Mexicans. From this vantage point, above the battleground, even a sixteen-year-old private could see that the next big Mexican assault would soon hit the center of the U.S. line. Would it hold? Or would he be among the next to be captured or killed?

Lord, let the sun set on this bloody day.

General
ANTONIO LÓPEZ
DE SANTA ANNA

General Santa Anna's chestnut warhorse stumbled while leaping off a small ledge but got his front legs back under him without tumbling. The rider felt the sting of branches whipping his cheeks as he dropped down into a barranca leading him eastward. Sweat now frothed the mustang's fur as the general continued to spur his mount. He knew it was time to retire this horse for the day and straddle a fresh pony. But first he intended to enjoy the spectacle of Pacheco's cavalry and Lombardini's division of infantry crushing the American volunteers.

All day he had dashed back and forth along the entire front line, urging his troops to repel the vainglorious invaders. Now he neared his right flank, expecting to find Pacheco and Lombardini advancing. Instead he arrived to see his soldiers falling back in disarray before a smaller enemy force led by the red-shirted Mississippi Rifles and supported by U.S. cavalry and artillery. He pulled rein and looked on in disgust as the chestnut heaved under him. His adjutant, Captain Jesus Paniagua, stopped beside him.

Santa Anna knew that the red shirts had recently arrived from Saltillo. But how was this possible? General José Vicente Minon's regiment of cavalry was supposed to have surrounded Saltillo to prevent the American reserves from reaching the battlefield.

"What has happened to General Minon?" he snapped, glaring at Adjutant Paniagua.

"Minon?" the captain said, reining in a prancing mustang.

"I ordered him to invest Saltillo!"

"Saltillo?"

"Never mind! He has failed somehow! Come, Paniagua! We must rally the infantry!"

"*Si*, General!"

The president of Mexico charged to the east to get closer to the troops and goad his foot soldiers into a counterattack on the *Camisas Colorados*. As he approached the colors of General Lombardini's division, he heard an artillery shell singing a familiar tune as it whistled its way from the American lines. He remembered that day on the pier at Veracruz.

Not again, he thought. *Not now.*

The percussion of the blast stunned him, and he instantly saw his noble mustang's head explode, splattering him with equine blood as he hurtled toward a hard, rising patch of ground.

From a black field of nothingness, he regained consciousness and found himself propped against the warm rump of his dead horse. Captain Paniagua knelt beside him. A sound like that of a waterfall roared in his head. The stump of his left leg pained him terribly. When he looked at it, he found his peg missing.

"Where is my leg?" he asked groggily.

"The straps broke, Your Excellency. Are you hurt?"

"What do you think, *bufon*? Of course I am hurt." He felt as if his ribs were broken and his skull cracked. "Has Lombardini begun the counterattack?"

"No, Presidente. There is problem. A battalion of lancers has retreated into the head of a canyon and they are now trapped there by the enemy. They have waved a white flag. They will be captured by the *Yanquis* if we don't do something."

Santa Anna blinked through the throbbing in his head as a load of canister exploded not far behind him, sending one of the lead balls slamming into the belly of his dead horse. It sounded like a drumbeat when it hit. His eyes began to focus and he saw a number of officers gathered around him. He recognized the face of General Manuel Lombardini, a brave warrior of many conflicts.

"General Lombardini, order three of your most clever officers to carry a flag of truce out onto the mesa." His head throbbed and his own voice sounded like an echo to him. "Ask the Americans for a cease-fire. While negotiations are being arranged, the trapped lancers can slip out of that canyon. Then the negotiations will be terminated and we can get back to killing these unholy bastards who are trying to steal our country!"

"*Si*, General!" Lombardini sang, a grin on his face.

"Also, order General Perez to bring his reserves up from the rear and prepare to attack the center of the enemy line."

"Yes, Your Excellency!"

"You are now in command of the battlefield until I order otherwise."

"It is my honor, sir!"

"It is only an honor if you succeed. If you fail, it is a disgrace. Those are my orders! See to it!"

Lombardini saluted, turned, and marched away. His junior officers went back to their regiments.

Santa Anna winced through the pain in his leg, his ribs, his head. Captain Paniagua looked blurry.

"Paniagua, find a horse for me and take me back to my headquarters tent. I must lick my wounds and get my manservant to repair the peg before I return to the battlefield."

"Yes, El Presidente!"

Paniagua trotted away to secure a mount from the cavalry, leaving the president alone for the moment. Santa Anna patted the sweaty rump of his dead horse.

"I am glad you died quickly. You were a good warhorse and served your country well."

He reached into the pocket of his tunic and found a ball of chicle. He tossed it into his mouth and began to chew it. It made him think of his Hacienda Encero, in the state of Veracruz, where the evergreen sapo-dilla trees grew naturally. There, he employed a *chiclero* to slash the bark on the sapodilla trees and collect the sap—chicle—that oozed from the wounds. Like many Mexicans, he felt that chewing chicle helped him relax and see things more clearly.

When one slashes a tree, it oozes sap. When a soldier slashes an enemy, he oozes blood. The sap can be useful. One can chew it. The spilt blood? Useless.

He knew he was not thinking straight. Everything around him seemed peculiar.

As he chewed his chicle, he sat on the rocky ground in the barranca and listened to the battle grind humans to sausage meat around him. This horrible thing he had brought to life now ravaged the mountains and mesas, beyond his control.

He needed rest, a pull from a jug of fine *añejo* tequila, and a chaser of laudanum. Juanito would fix the peg. Perhaps Consuela could tend to his other needs. The battle was not over. He would be back in the saddle after siesta.

Major General
ZACHARY TAYLOR

General Taylor stood over a map of Angostura Pass, huddled there with Major Bliss and other members of his staff. The industrious Adjutant Bliss had established a battlefield headquarters complete with a tent, a picket line for the horses, and a desk made of stacked ammunition crates. The map was spread across the desk, four fist-size rocks holding down its corners. Small stones placed on the map represented horse, foot, and artillery units from both armies. Bliss had dabbed all the rocks representing the enemy regiments with ink from his quill pen.

Minutes ago, a Mexican officer with a small escort had ridden out onto the plateau under a flag of truce. A courier had galloped to headquarters with a request from the Mexicans for a cease-fire to arrange for the surrender of some lancers trapped in a canyon by U.S. dragoons. Taylor had granted the cease-fire, sending riders galloping all along the front lines with the news. He had then sent Lieutenant Colonel Thomas Crittenden—a reliable Kentucky volunteer who served on his staff—to meet with Mexican representatives under white banners.

For the moment, Taylor enjoyed the absence of gunfire. He hoped the Mexicans had endured enough carnage and desired some kind of honorable cessation of hostilities. Meanwhile, he listened to Perfect Bliss report to the staff.

"We have received positive news from all along the front lines," Bliss was saying. "The right flank remains solid. The left has been reclaimed. The commissary is now secure back at Hacienda Buena Vista."

"What about the middle?" Taylor asked.

"Looks like trouble brewing there, sir. Messengers report a large body of Mexican infantry with cavalry support massing on the center of our line."

"How large?"

"A brigade, or larger."

"Is that tricky bastard Santa Anna using this cease-fire to gain the advantage on us?" the general demanded.

"I'm not sure, sir. A single eyewitness claimed that he saw General Santa Anna unhorsed by an artillery shell—perhaps injured or even killed."

Taylor shook his head and stared down at the pebbles on the map. "I don't trust that damned tyrant to honor a flag of truce," he growled.

A rumble of hooves approached. The staff looked south to see Lieutenant Thomas Crittenden and his escort returning at a gallop, having discarded their white flag. This did not look good to Taylor. The truce party drew rein and slid to a stop, kicking up mud that spattered Taylor's coat and face.

"What the devil happened, Colonel?" General Taylor demanded, wiping spots of mud away from his cheek.

"It was a ruse, sir. While we were negotiating on the plateau, the enemy regiment that we had trapped in that canyon slipped out under the protection of the white flag and formed up to surrender. A Mexican courier rode up to them, and suddenly they all bolted for their camp. Then the Mexican negotiators threw down their white flag and disappeared at a gallop into a ravine, leaving us there like a bunch of fools."

General Taylor took the palm leaf hat from his head and threw it angrily onto the muddy ground. Major Bliss swooped in to pick it up. He used his sleeve to wipe some grime from it.

"That goddamned old lying dog Santa Anna!" Taylor railed. "From here forward, Major Bliss, let it be known that no flag of truce from the Mexican side will be honored!"

"Yes, sir," Bliss said, handing the general's hat back to him.

A shell from the Saint Patrick's Battalion exploded dangerously nearby. The U.S. batteries of flying artillery answered immediately, and the battle resumed.

"Bill!" Taylor shouted.

"Here, sir."

"Order Hardin's First Illinois to the main spur of the plateau in the middle of our line. Send the Second Illinois and the Second Kentucky in right after them. Then get word to Jeff Davis to move his men to the main plateau as well."

"Yes, sir," Bliss said as he scribbled on his pad of foolscap with his stub of a pencil.

"Where's the nearest artillery, Bill?"

"Lieutenant O'Brien's battery, sir." Bliss pointed to a pebble.

Taylor shot a puzzled glare at Bliss. "I heard he got the hell pounded out of him this morning."

"Yes, sir, but he acquired two serviceable six-pounders from Captain Washington at the narrows. He put together a new crew of gunners and went back to the front. He's been shelling the Mexican right all afternoon."

Taylor nodded. That was the kind of fighter he needed now in the middle of his line. "Send in O'Brien's Bulldogs to support the First Illinois."

General Taylor looked far to the east and saw Lieutenant Rucker's dragoons riding back from the left flank, where they had trapped the lancers in the canyon for a spell.

"When Rucker's dragoons get here, I will order him to support O'Brien and the infantry. Then, Major Bliss, you and I and our staff will shift our headquarters to that locale ourselves. By the grace of God, we can finish this little game of checkers by sundown."

Lieutenant
JOHN PAUL
JONES O'BRIEN

Astride a fresh mount, Lieutenant John Paul Jones O'Brien trundled his new battery of Bulldogs—two six-pounders—up onto the fingertip of the main spur of the plateau. Ahead, he saw Colonel John J. Hardin's First Illinois Volunteers emerging from the barranca on the left to meet the oncoming assault of General Francisco Perez's rested reserves. Colonel Hardin led the men forward on his chestnut warhorse.

"Halt!" O'Brien yelled, arriving out in front of the First Illinois's line of march. The Illinoisans nearest to him saluted or nodded in respect. They had witnessed his heroic stand on the left flank earlier in the day. He looked around at his new crew. His old familiar gunners were all dead or in the surgeon's tent, but these soldiers knew how to man a gun equally well.

O'Brien dismounted. "Unlimber and load grapeshot! Take the horses down into the ravine!"

Looking to the northwest, he noticed that this long spur of the plateau pointed directly toward the narrows, in view of Washington's batteries. He felt sure that he could count on his company commander, Captain John M. Washington, for supporting fire if he and the First Illinois needed it.

By the time O'Brien's Bulldogs were loaded and ready to fire, Colonel Hardin's Illinois command had marched halfway to the next ravine. Hardin dashed all along the front of the line on his sleek chestnut mount, shouting encouragement to his men. Then the Saint Patrick's Battalion dropped an exploding round in their path. Immediately after the blast, a shout arose from the gully in front of the First Illinois and a host of fresh Mexican foot soldiers sprang from the arroyo. Musket fire ripped into the volunteers.

"Fire!" Colonel Hardin yelled, and the Illinois Volunteers returned the deadly salute.

The firing became general and men dropped along both lines, some screaming, some silent as oblivion.

O'Brien checked the trajectory of his guns, nodding in approval. "Prime . . . Ready . . . Fire!"

The Bulldogs tore two holes into the enemy line, but more defenders of Mexico kept coming. O'Brien now recognized the colors of Mexico's Eleventh Regiment and the Battalion of León—both seasoned units attacking green American volunteers.

"With canister, load!"

Behind him, in the brushy ravine, he could faintly hear the bugles of the Second Illinois and the Second Kentucky signaling the advance. He hoped they'd hurry.

"*Viva México!*"

The cry, to his left, surprised him. He looked that way to see a wave of Lombardini's hard-bitten veterans clambering over the brink of the ravine, bayonets gleaming in the evening sun. He felt his eyes widen and his mouth drop open.

"Oh, Holy Christ!" his sergeant shouted.

"Shut up, Sergeant, and turn that gun to the left!"

O'Brien watched as Lombardini's column swung across the plateau to effect an enfilading fire on the Illinois Volunteers—and on his battery of Bulldogs.

"Prime! Ready! Fire!"

The Bulldogs bucked backwards and a dozen of Lombardini's men crumpled. But now the Saint Pats dropped a round of canister in front of O'Brien. The invisible balls of lead from the explosion rattled against metal, wood, and skulls. He lost two men from his new crew and had to take up a lanyard from one of the fallen men.

"With double-shot grape, load!"

As his gunners endured near misses and flesh wounds from muskets, he glanced behind him. The Illinoisans were falling back, but steadily, firing as they retired toward the ravine to the rear. Colonel Hardin rode behind them as they methodically withdrew, warning them not to turn tail.

"God Almighty, Lieutenant!" his new sergeant yelled. "There's no end to the bastards!"

O'Brien looked left to find Lombardini's entire division marching down on him. His instinct told him to limber and retire, but his guts told him the entire day's struggle would be lost if he did so. He had to cover the First Illinois until they reached the cover of the ravine behind them. He had to hold generals Lombardini and Perez back as long as he could or else, he feared, the American center would collapse.

"Fire at will, men! Give them hell!"

Canister from the Saint Pats roared through his battery again, taking three men down. In the midst of such chaos, he could not tell whether Captain Washington was firing into the Mexicans from his battery at the narrows.

"Sergeant, get some boys from the infantry to serve these guns!" he said as he rammed a load of canister down the hot muzzle of a bronze six-pounder.

"Yes, sir!"

The sergeant brought a few infantry soldiers to man the Bulldogs, but musket balls and shrapnel continued to decimate his crew. The injuries to the bodies, heads, and limbs were ghastly, but he had no time to aid the wounded or mourn the dead. The Mexicans continued to shoot, load, and march his way, though his Bulldogs blasted hellish breaches in their lines.

"Lieutenant," his sergeant shouted, "they're going to capture our guns if we don't limber and fall back!"

"Not until the volunteers make it to the cover of the ravine!" He glanced toward the Illinois line and saw them almost to the gully. But they had left many bodies behind on the plateau. To his anguish, he watched Mexicans bayoneting numerous wounded Americans, some of whom were pleading for their lives.

A projectile ripped through the neck of his first sergeant, almost decapitating him. He could see now that he had neither the time nor the manpower to prevent his guns from falling into enemy hands.

I have not yet begun to fight . . . I have not yet begun to fight . . . I have not yet begun—

"One more volley, men! Double up on the powder and the grape! We'll blow the Bulldogs up in their faces!"

He served one of the guns himself as the nearest Mexican foot soldiers sprinted toward him in a deadly race to capture the artillery before he could fire one last volley.

"Give me the lanyards and run for the ravine!"

His men obeyed the order as he yanked both lanyards at once, ripping his attackers to pieces just steps away from the muzzles. To his astonishment, the bronze tubes of the Bulldogs failed to burst. He turned to run, but a ball hit his left thigh, spinning him to the ground. He stood and hopped away on his right leg, knowing that he could not outdistance the enemy. He decided to turn and face the Mexicans rather than take a bayonet in his back.

Spinning back toward his battery, he witnessed the sickening sight of enemy soldiers swarming all around his precious Bulldogs. Suddenly he felt arms grabbing him, dragging him to the brink of the ravine. Two of his men had come back to spirit him away through a fusillade of lead.

"We'll get you to the doctor, Lieutenant," one of the men said.

They lugged him down into the temporary shelter of the barranca, over rocks and through ocotillo cacti. Numerous cactus needles lodged in his thigh. He thought how he would have cussed on any other day, but today it was nothing.

He glanced left and right and saw both men bleeding. "Looks like we could all use a doctor, boys."

"Scratches don't count, sir."

"Where are our horses?"

"I don't know, sir. Run off or rode off."

He helped by using his good leg as they rushed him to the rear. He saw the Second Kentucky Volunteers streaming into the ravine, coming to the aid of the First Illinois. They streamed through a gap in the rim rock on the opposite side of the gorge. The gap appeared to be the only place to get into or out of the ravine from that side. O'Brien's rescuers dragged him toward the gap, but they had to wait for the Kentucky regiment to file in and vacate the narrow fissure in the bluff before they could climb out. When the gap cleared, O'Brien limped up and out of the ravine, his arms across the shoulders of his two stout gunners.

Emerging onto the next spur of the plateau, he found the Second Illinois marching to join the battle, now sounding like roaring, screaming hell down in the ravine he had just escaped. He hobbled onward toward the rear and the gruesome specter of the hospital tent, wondering if the volunteers could hold back the professional Mexican fighters.

Strangely, his wounded leg did not hurt much. Yet . . .

He had lost his guns and most of his men but had prevented the annihilation or capture of an entire regiment of infantry. He didn't know whether he would get court-martialed or promoted. That depended on which army won this battle. And right now, it might go either way.

Captain
SPEED SMITH FRY

He was a small-town lawyer and a mercantile operator. What the hell had he gotten himself into? He didn't belong here. No human being ought to witness such carnage. This was the valley of death he had read about in the Bible.

Captain Speed Smith Fry, commander of Company D, Second Kentucky Volunteers, stood in the ravine and watched his men fall around him. Privates Hamilton, Montgomery, and Vanfleet—dead. Their bodies interlaced with others, limb upon limb, on the blood-soaked ground.

A few minutes earlier they had stormed into this ravine through a narrow gap in the rim rock, but the Mexicans had spotted them from the opposite brink and were now firing relentlessly down into the volunteers from the plateau. They could not charge forward into the overwhelming numbers of the enemy. They could not retreat because the bank behind them was rimmed with a vertical bluff, except for the one gap, and that had already been swarmed by flanking Mexican infantry.

Suddenly he realized—with bullets humming and snapping branches all around him—that standing and doing nothing meant death.

"Move down the ravine!" he shouted to the men of his company. "Retire to the road and rally under the guns of Washington's battery!"

Now he at least had his men moving, but the fire from the old Brown Bess muskets continued from the rim of the plateau on his left.

"I'm going ahead to get orders from Colonel McKee! Follow as quickly as you are able!"

Musket balls ricocheted off rocks near him as he dodged boulders and yuccas, leaping over the bodies of the dead and wounded. He ran until he saw his regiment's commander, Colonel William R. McKee. He hoped the thirty-nine-year-old West Pointer would know what to do, as he ran up to him.

"Colonel! Captain Fry reporting!"

Colonel McKee, saber in hand, looked at him as if he were daft. A second later, a host of balls ripped bloody holes in the commander's tunic and he fell onto his back, his eyes staring vapidly upward, his hilt still in his hand.

An anguished yell erupted from Fry's lungs. He looked for second-in-command Lieutenant Colonel Henry Clay Jr., the son of Henry Clay, who was the founder of the Whig Party and the most famous politician in America. That didn't count for much now, in this hollow of death. But Colonel Henry Clay Jr. was a West Point graduate, too, and ought to know what to do.

Fry turned around, searching, until he saw Colonel Clay near the brink of the ravine, reloading his single-shot pistol. As Fry sprinted his way, the lieutenant colonel rammed home the charge, set the percussion cap, and cocked his hammer. Musket balls tore into him, knocking him backwards and sending him sliding down the steep ravine bank toward Fry.

Fry watched on in horror as the bloody Clay raised his pistol and fired one last round into the Mexicans. Fry ran to him, pulled him behind a boulder.

"Captain Fry . . ." the lieutenant colonel said, spitting out a mouthful of blood, "take my pistol home to my father." The weapon fell from Clay's grasp as his eyes turned to lifeless orbs.

"Oh, dear God!" Fry screamed. He picked up the pistol, stood, and waved his men toward the opening of the ravine below—toward the Saltillo road, toward Washington's battery, toward hope.

"Follow me! Down the ravine!"

He stormed through the bed of the gully and ran into the beleaguered Second Illinois Volunteers. There, he couldn't help noticing their commander, the dashing Colonel John J. Hardin—clean-shaven, handsome, mounted on his beautiful chestnut charger. He was a former regular army general, veteran of frontier campaigns. As Fry looked on, he saw Hardin rallying his men for a charge into the Mexican lines.

"Now is the moment!" Hardin yelled. "Let us seize the colors of the Hidalgo Regiment!"

Hardin turned to lead his men up the ravine bank, when a .71-caliber sphere of lead slammed into his chest.

Fry screamed like a tortured soul in limbo as he watched blood gush from Hardin's torso, onto his white trousers. The colonel dropped his sword and fell dead from the chestnut.

All the commanders are dead. I am now among the ranking officers in this pit of agony.

"To the road! Down the ravine! Rally on me!"

Men stumbled along behind him, tripping over their fallen friends. Ahead, through the undergrowth, he finally saw the open ground beyond the mouth of the ravine. From there, what was left of his regiment could run for Washington's battery and make a stand. But then, to his terror, he saw the bright tunics—red, green, and blue—of the hated lancers. The damned lancers were blocking the mouth of the gully! There was no escape from this cursed ravine!

Where is Taylor? Where is the flying artillery? Where are the reserves?

"Take cover!" he screamed, though he knew not enough cover existed for the survivors. "Reload! Make a stand!"

A shell screamed toward him and fell among the lancers at the mouth of the draw, exploding with deadly results for men and horses. *Thank God!* Washington had spotted the lancers!

"Rally on me, boys! Take aim and fight!"

Captain Washington's accurate artillery fire pummeled the lancers into a retreat, then turned on the Mexican infantry that was still firing down on the remnants of Fry's regiment. Canister, shell, and spherical case shot ripped through the ranks of Perez's and Lombardini's men on the mesa above. Captain Speed Smith Fry took hope for the first time since descending into this hellish gulch of death.

As the Mexicans reeled back from Washington's hail of steel and lead, the blistering fire from the plateau finally abated.

"Advance to the rim of the plateau!" he ordered. "Use the cover of the bank and fire on the enemy!"

Stunned soldiers crept upward with their weapons.

"Move!" Fry yelled. "This is your chance to avenge your slain comrades!"

He looked around and saw a man of the Illinois regiment, wearing sergeant's stripes.

"Sergeant, detail a platoon to take the wounded to the rear! Take only those that can be saved. The slightly wounded must stay here and fight."

"Yes, sir. What about the dead?"

"Leave them for now. And get your platoon back here as soon as possible. The enemy will rally and attack us again. We need every man!"

The sergeant began shouting the names of privates and ordering them to lift men bloodied by grievous injuries.

Fry picked up a musket and took an ammunition pouch from a dead soldier. He climbed to the brink of the ravine as he watched the survivors of the bloodbath fire into the retiring Mexicans. He was amazed that this part of the line had held. If the Mexicans had only ordered a bayonet charge into the barranca, if Washington had waited a minute longer to train his guns on the enemy, this battle would have been lost.

Captain Fry was no West Pointer. He was a simple country lawyer and a small-town mercantile owner. But he knew he had almost witnessed one of the biggest military blunders in American history. And it wasn't over yet.

General
ZACHARY TAYLOR

He galloped Old Whitey down the Saltillo road, then veered left toward the fingertip end of the main plateau. His adjutant, Major William Bliss, rode at his side. Other staff members followed closely behind.

Nearing the ravine where the Illinois and Kentucky volunteers had been trapped and decimated, he saw a wagon and team standing idle at the mouth of the barranca and cantered up to it to investigate. He found a bloody man lying, unconscious, in the wagon. The man's shirt had been opened. The wound to his belly revealed his intestines and pieces of broken ribs.

"I'll be damned," Bliss said.

"Not as damned as this poor soldier," Taylor replied.

"No, look, General. In the trees up in the gully."

Taylor tore his eyes away from the wounded man and saw a familiar figure in a royal-blue skirt, still wearing her barroom apron. Sarah Borginnes carried a bullet-riddled man in her arms as a mother would cradle a baby. The man, who was quite a bit smaller than her, was conscious but seemed unaware of what was happening.

"Stand aside, gentlemen!" she ordered as she approached the wagon.

Taylor and Bliss backed their mounts away from the dropped tailgate of the rig.

A shell whistled through the air, hit the rim of the plateau, exploded, and sent a shower of gravel clattering onto the wagon.

"Mrs. Borginnes," Taylor said, "you are in danger here."

She gently placed the wounded man on the wagon bed. Behind her, a sergeant and a few privates trailed out of the ravine, all carrying wounded men.

"This sergeant needed help with the wounded, and I can drive a team with the best of 'em," she said, wiping her bloody hands on her apron.

"You are a true patriot and brave woman, Mrs. Borginnes."

"Thank you, General. Open the gates of hell on 'em for doing these things to our boys."

He nodded and reined away. His spurs coaxed every morsel of speed from Old Whitey as he climbed up the rocky grade to the northern point of the main plateau. Emerging over the crest, he saw, ahead on the mesa, Major Braxton Bragg's battery of three six-pounders taking a pounding from enemy muskets and artillery but firing methodically into three advancing columns of Mexican infantry.

The First Illinois and the Second Kentucky had been almost destroyed in the ravine to his left, but for the artillery skills of Lieutenant O'Brien and Captain Washington. Bragg had rushed forward to shore up the weak spot in the line, and Taylor had ordered the Second Illinois and Jeff Davis's red shirts to move in as well.

But the Mexicans had rallied, sounded bugles, and begun yet another assault. In the face of this new onslaught, Major Bragg remained exposed, under fire, without infantry support. For now, his three guns were all that held back the next wave of hardened Mexican veterans who were advancing in three columns toward the untrained regiments of raw volunteers.

Galloping up to the little battery, Taylor drew rein on Old Whitey and shouted down at Bragg, "Did I not promise you that Major Bliss and I would support you, Bragg?"

Bragg's face, weary and grimy, looked up, his eyes wild. "That you did, General."

Taylor felt shrapnel tear through the sleeve of his duster as a shell from the Saint Patrick's Battalion exploded overhead. A bullet ticked his hat brim. He threw his right leg over his saddle pommel and gazed out toward the approaching enemy phalanx, coming in three huge columns. A bullet from the ravine to his right tore a button off of the general's duster.

"What are you using, Major? Grape or canister?"

"Canister, General!"

"Single or double?"

"Single," Bragg replied.

"Well, double-shot your guns and give 'em hell, Bragg!"

"Double-shot canister! Load!" Bragg ordered.

As gunners loaded their six-pounders, Taylor noted that the embattled volunteers from Kentucky and Illinois were now managing a respectable musket fire from the left-hand ravine.

"General Taylor," Bliss said. "Look to the rear! Sherman is coming with his flying battery!"

Taylor slipped his right foot back into his stirrup and turned his mount to the rear as projectiles continued to tug at his clothing.

A Saint Pat's shell fell nearby and burst, shattering the knee of one of Bragg's gunners.

Through the smoke, Taylor caught sight of Sherman wheeling from column into battery. "That's the spot, Sherman!" he yelled, though he knew the captain would not hear him.

All at once, he felt lifted above the fray to a place in the sky. Looking down, he saw the three enemy columns plodding onward, Sherman and Bragg hurling lead into them, the muskets of volunteers firing from the ravine. It was not enough to hold back the Mexicans. He needed more. He blinked and found himself astride his warhorse.

"Where the hell is Jeff Davis?" he said to Bliss.

"Colonel Crittenden rode to find him with your orders to move to the right."

"I pray the good colonel gets through. We need those Mississippi Rifles!"

Colonel
JEFFERSON DAVIS

He lay on his belly, peering over the brink of the ravine. His mount stood tied nearby, should his command receive orders to move.

For a couple of hours he had held this spur of high ground that had now become known as the Northern Plateau. His red-shirted Mississippi Rifles had spread along the ravine's edge as skirmishers and held off repeated probes by Mexican soldiers. The bloodiest part of the battle had now shifted to the middle of the U.S. line, on his right. There, on the main plateau, musket and rifle fire and booming artillery punctuated the screams of men and horses.

"Colonel Davis!" The shout came through the underbrush from across the ravine he held. "Are you there?"

"Yes, I am here! Who are you?" He could not see a thing through the brush and lingering rifle smoke.

"It's me, Colonel Crittenden. General Taylor orders your command to the right! March west and attack the enemy's flank at once!"

"Very well! I am on the way!"

He rolled over and grabbed the long, straight limb his adjutant had found for him to use as a crutch.

"Captain Griffith!" he shouted as he laboriously drew himself to a standing position, feeling the blood squish about in his right boot. "Bring my horse and help me mount."

Within minutes his Mississippi Rifles, along with the Third Indiana

Volunteers, had begun a double-quick trot to the west. They crossed the Northern Plateau and plunged into the next ravine. They climbed out of that gully and onto a narrow, uninhabited finger of the plateau.

"We are close now!" Davis shouted to his men as they filed past his mount. "We will meet the enemy on the next branch of the mesa."

Down he rode, leading his battalion into the last barranca between him and the enemy. The din of battle now rattled his teeth and battered his eardrums. Spurring his mount up the rock-strewn bank, through small trees stripped of foliage and limbs by artillery blasts, he arrived on the main plateau.

Assessing the situation, he saw General Taylor several hundred yards to the west, sitting on Old Whitey, watching Bragg's artillerymen work their guns like madmen. Nearer to him—three hundred yards away— he witnessed a column of Mexican infantry marching toward Taylor and Bragg. Beyond them, through drifting smoke, he thought he could make out a second and even a third enemy column, also bearing down on Bragg's position. Now he saw a muzzle flash from another battery be- yond Bragg's. Probably Sherman's.

"Captain Griffith," he said, seeing his adjutant emerge from the gully on foot. "Lead the men out onto the plateau. Form a skirmish line. We will charge that column's flank and commence firing. Quickly, before they reach our batteries!"

The red shirts led the way onto the mesa, followed by the Third Indiana Volunteers and Colonel Bowles's handful of Second Indianans.

"Forward!" Davis yelled. "Guide center! March!"

His men started forward in an almost perfectly straight line. He rode behind them, gauging their progress, reining in his mount to match their speed. The grand scope of the scene before him suddenly struck him with such awe that for a moment he could not feel the roaring knife points of pain stabbing his wounded heel. The odors of smoke, horse sweat, and damp earth; the din of ordnance and musket fire; the spectacle of flash- ing muzzles, glinting blades, men marching toward danger . . .

At this speed, he could see that he would not arrive within range of the Mexican flank before it overwhelmed Bragg's battery.

"Double-quick! March!"

Yes! His men leaned forward with eagerness, mounting a long trot, like wolves on the prowl. The Mexican column had now moved to his right to the point that he could see the rear of the column. The enemy seemed unaware of his approach. The timing would be dangerously close, but he felt he could get within rifle range and fire into the Mexicans before they bugled their three columns to charge Bragg's and Sherman's guns.

"Company . . . Halt!" he ordered.

The men stopped some 120 yards from the enemy flank.

"Prepare to fire . . . Take aim . . . Fire!"

A staccato ripple of smoke plumes licked the air in the direction of the enemy column. The effect on the Mexican flank and rear stunned Colonel Jefferson Davis with its military effectiveness and mortal inhumanity. Dark blue tunics dropped in waves as survivors stared down at their comrades, wondering what evil had wrought such death.

"Reload!" Davis yelled. Sensing a fleeting advantage, he watched his men ram loads and fix percussion caps. He ordered another double-quick advance, another halt, and another volley, this time even closer to the enemy column, hard upon its damaged right flank.

When the barrage flew, the Mexican infantrymen broke and stampeded into the column to their left, creating a shock wave of fear that spread through the middle column and into the left column. Within a minute, all three prongs of the Mexican advance had fled in a terror-stricken retreat, against all the urgings of their officers to stop and fight.

"Advance firing!" Davis yelled. "Rally on Bragg's battery!"

As he rode along slowly behind his men, he pulled his slouch hat down low to shade his eyes. Ahead, the sun approached the horizon, signaling a coming end to this hideously glorious day. Though the Americans had not yet won, they had been spared defeat—at least for the day. What would tomorrow bring? How long could this battle go on? Could he remain conscious to lead his men another day?

Davis shrugged off the unending throb of misery down in his boot. It now seemed like a natural part of him, like breathing or blinking. As he rode across the plateau toward Taylor's position, he looked at the dead and wounded men strewn over the sanguine ground. So many had met their maker. Even more would carry scars for a lifetime. He knew he was one of them, though his scars from today would not show. One was in his boot. The other was carved through the center of his soul.

Captain
JOHN RILEY

Thrice today Captain John Riley had thought he had witnessed the defeat of Zach Taylor's cursed army. This morning, from his vantage point on this hill, he had seen the American left flank collapse, only to be reclaimed. More recently he had seen the middle of the U.S. line retreat into a perfect trap down in a bloody barranca, where he pounded the hell out of them with shell and shot. But Santa Anna's infantry had been driven back by Yankee twelve-pounders. And just now he had watched in screaming denial as red shirts and flying artillery somehow scattered three columns of veteran Mexican foot soldiers into a rearward rout.

"Has God Almighty forsaken Mexico!" he had railed. "What more can we hurl at the bloody bastards?"

What would come next was obvious to an experienced artillerist like Riley. Now that the Mexican infantry had retired in disgrace, the U.S. guns would have one target left to fire upon: the hilltop battery of the Saint Patrick's Battalion.

All day he had followed the orders of Colonel Francisco Moreno and slung loads at targets all over the battlefield. But at times when Moreno left him to his own devices, he had sought out his own targets: Bragg and Sherman. Now Moreno had left the hill to confer with Santa Anna about the devastating turn of events on the largest spur of the mesa. Captain John Riley had just two targets in mind. The two most abusive nativist officers in the U.S. Army. Braxton Bragg and Thomas Sherman. And they were within range of his twenty-four-pounders on the big mesa.

"What are your orders, sir?"

Riley turned to look at the soot-blackened face of Lieutenant Patrick Dalton. "We're about to take a pounding, Lieutenant. You take command of the three guns on the left and destroy Sherman's battery on the mesa. I'll train the right half of the battery on that bastard Bragg."

"Load canister!" Dalton shouted.

Riley grabbed him by the sleeve to hold him back. "I heard a story from a priest who slipped among the Americans at Monterrey. He said when they were camped at Bosque de San Domingo—the stupid Americans called it Walnut Springs—some of Bragg's own men, immigrants no doubt, tried to kill him. They rolled a howitzer shell with a short fuse into his tent in the dark of night. He somehow avoided a journey to hell from the explosion."

Dalton brandished his fist toward the U.S. line. "I wish they had killed the bloody fucker."

"I offer a hundred thousand prayers of thanks to God that they *didn't* kill him. I desire that pleasure for my own."

"Faith," Dalton said, "may your aim hold true."

"Man your guns, Patrick. They are lifting their muzzles as we speak. We will promptly find ourselves in a true and deadly artillery duel."

His warning was punctuated by a howitzer shell that exploded in the gully in front of his hill. Seeing his men ready, with lanyards in hand, he ordered the eighteen-pounder nearest to him to fire on Bragg's battery. Looking through his spyglass, he could see that the shot fell short.

"Turn the screw one time and load!"

He stepped over to the next cannon, a twenty-four-pounder. But before he could order a round fired, he heard the shriek of an incoming shell. It hit the hill at the base of his sandbagged parapets and exploded on impact, tossing a spray of sand into his eyes.

"Private!" he roared. "Pull the lanyard and destroy that goddamned trifling sixer!"

The twenty-four-pounder thundered and shook the hill beneath his feet.

"Did you strike home, lad?" he asked, still trying to blink sand from his eyes.

"I shot long, sir! I'll adjust!"

"See that you do! Next! Ready! Fire!"

His guns, and Dalton's, kept up a steady barrage, until they began to land shots dangerously close to Bragg and Sherman. But Bragg, Sherman, and Washington were now striking equally near to the hilltop.

"Lieutenant! We will fire in battery at our targets. Are you loaded and ready?"

"Ready, sir!"

"Make ready! Fire!"

Six mighty weapons simultaneously spewed smoke, spark, and projectiles toward Bragg and Sherman. But before Riley could judge his accuracy, a volley from one of his sworn enemies hit the carriage of a twenty-four-pounder, killing two of his crew and disabling the gun. Knocked onto his back by the blast, he looked up at the silken banner of the Saint Patrick's Battalion, now riddled by shrapnel.

"Fight!" he screamed, springing to his feet. "Load, fire, and fight for the glory of the Auld Sod!"

As the sun sank, his men continued to hurl insults and ammunition at the American batteries, damaging but not destroying the flying artillery units under Bragg and Sherman. He lost another man, dead, and three more wounded. Finally, after dark, Colonel Francisco Moreno rode up onto the hill and ordered the Irishmen to cease firing.

"Captain Riley, I suggest you come with me. His Excellency Santa Anna has called for council of war. Plans for tomorrow will be formed."

"What plans, sir? We fight to the death! We fight until the enemy limps back to his slave plantations and his filthy city slums!"

"Careful, Riley. I suggest you hold your tongue and listen to El Presidente. He will decide the course for the morrow. And you will follow orders."

Riley spat on the ground but did not argue.

"Lieutenant Dalton, you are in command in my absence. I am going to receive our orders from the president."

We will crush them at dawn, he thought. *They have been battered to a pulp all day long. One last assault will baptize this ground with their blood!*

General
ZACHARY TAYLOR

He had made up his mind to go to the hospital and find out for himself. Rumor had it that Jefferson Davis was among the officers killed.

"I'll never believe it," he had said to Major Bliss. He heard himself repeat it over and over, as if he couldn't stop saying it. "I'll never believe it . . . I'll never believe it . . ."

"I'm trying to determine whether or not it's true, sir. I don't yet know exactly where Colonel Davis is."

"I am going to find him myself."

With a troubled mind, he had ridden Old Whitey through the dark to Santiago Cathedral, which now served as a hospital for the wounded soldiers. Stepping down from the saddle, he noticed a wagon in front of the old Spanish church. It looked like the one Sarah Borginnes had used to transport wounded soldiers. He walked to it, curious, and peered over the sideboards. To his surprise he found a man lying in the wagon bed, missing a boot, his foot propped up on a folded piece of tent canvas. Not just any man, but his former son-in-law, Colonel Jefferson Davis.

"Hello, General," Davis said.

"Oh, thank God, Jeff. I had heard you were killed."

Davis chuckled. "I heard that myself."

"How bad is it?"

"Just my foot, sir. Shot in the heel this morning."

"My poor boy. I wish you were shot in the body. You would have a better chance of recovering soon. I do not like wounds in the hands or feet. They cripple a soldier awfully."

He immediately regretted saying it. What was he thinking? Exhaustion must have addled his mind. But Davis only chuckled at him.

"It hurts like hell, but the surgeon said I'll probably keep my foot. The bullet carried some pieces of iron from my spur into my heel, so he's a bit concerned about blood poisoning."

"You look pale. Maybe it's just the moonlight." He glanced up to see clouds slicing wildly in front of a bright moon, two-thirds full.

"I lost a boot-full of blood."

Taylor leaned his elbow on the sideboard of the wagon. He felt weary.

"General, I've heard that Henry Clay was killed. Please tell me it's not true."

"I am sorry, Jeff, but it is true. I know the two of you graduated West Point together. I am told he died gallantly."

Davis groaned and shifted in the wagon bed.

Taylor sighed, half in relief and half in regret. "I have come to rely upon you and your Mississippi Rifles, Jeff. I saw with my own eyes how you saved the battle for us twice today."

Davis shrugged and winced. "I did my duty. Nothing more."

Taylor patted him on the shoulder. "I'll go find someone to get you out of this wagon and into a bed."

"No, I asked to sleep here," Davis said.

"Why the devil would you do that, Jeff?"

"So they can haul me back to the battleground before dawn. I will mount my horse and continue to lead my regiment."

Taylor shook his head. "It's getting cold out here."

"My friend, Captain Eustus, is in the cathedral right now, looking for a blanket. He will sit up with me tonight."

Taylor smiled. "Very well, Jeff. You have a good view of the towers of Santiago in the moonlight."

"General, have all the regiments called roll?"

"Yes. They have all reported."

"What were our losses today, sir?"

"Six hundred and fifty-nine casualties." It sounded like someone else's voice when he heard himself speak.

"How many killed?"

"Two hundred seventy-two. There will be more, of course." He heard a scream of pain inside the chapel.

"No word from Santa Anna?"

"None. But his casualties must have been twice that of ours."

"What do you expect he'll do, General?"

"I imagine he will attack us in mass at dawn."

The two men fell silent for a long moment as soldiers moaned inside the cathedral.

"Jeff . . ." Taylor began. "I have regrets . . . There are things I should have . . . I know you did not cause my daughter's death, Colonel. I should have said so long ago. It was not your fault."

His forearm rested on the sideboard.

Jefferson Davis placed his cool palm over the back of Taylor's wrist and gripped it firmly. "We both lost someone. It was hard to handle."

Taylor placed his weathered palm over the back of Davis's hand. "Yes. Even harder than this day."

"I didn't know what to do, so I just ran away from it. To Cuba, New York. I should have visited you and Mrs. Taylor to explain what had happened, but I lacked the courage to face you."

Taylor pulled his palm away from Davis's hand and placed it on his shoulder. "Your courage is now forevermore unquestionable. My daughter was a better judge of a man than I."

Captain Abram Eustus bolted from the cathedral doors and trotted to the wagon with a blanket. "All right, Davis, you lazy slacker," he joshed. "I've come to tuck you in!" He stopped when he recognized the commander of the army. "General! My apologies. I did not see you there." He saluted.

"As you were, Captain. I'm going in to see the wounded men. Take good care of Colonel Davis." He patted Davis's shoulder.

"Yes, sir."

Taylor plodded toward the huge, carved double doors of the sanctuary. He stopped short and took a few breaths of fresh mountain air. He then set his jaw and entered the cathedral.

Private
SAMUEL CHAMBERLAIN

He woke with a start, feeling himself about to fall from the saddle. Pulling himself upright on Soldan, he blinked at the moon-washed landscape and shook his head like a hound flapping its ears, as if that would help him stay awake. He had never felt so weary in his life.

His company had once again, unfairly, been ordered to stand guard as vedettes through the night. Within ten minutes he had fallen asleep in the saddle. Now he had awakened to realize that he was no longer at his guard post on the plateau. Looking around, he found himself back at the Hacienda Buena Vista, where Soldan was drinking from the water trough fed by natural springs. He had slept right through his mount's walk to the trough.

"Shit!" he hissed. "Damn you, Soldan!"

He was more than a mile from his assigned duty station. This was the sort of thing that could get a sentry bucked and gagged for leaving his post. Returning to the front, he had passed numerous corpses, many of which had been stripped by the Mexicans. In the moonlight he saw wolves and coyotes dashing through the killing zone and heard them fighting over the human meat.

He reached the ravine he had been ordered to guard to find his messmate, Boss Hastings, asleep on his horse. The Texans had mastered the art of sleeping in the saddle without falling off. He reckoned he was getting pretty good at it himself. No one had even missed him. He noticed a picket line of lancers mounted on white horses, about two hundred yards away. He could hear them humming. One of their songs sounded like a mournful version of "Love Not."

He dozed off and on through the night.

When he awoke, he noticed the eastern sky around the crown of the mountain taking on a slate-gray glow. He shivered. Stars faded in the east. Dawn approached. The lancers who had straddled the white horses were nowhere to be seen.

"Wake up, Boss," he said, lashing Hastings lightly with the end of a rein.

His friend groaned as he looked blankly over his surroundings. "Are they comin'?"

"Not yet."

Looking across the mesas and barrancas, he expected to see and hear more activity from the Mexican Army. Had not the time for reveille come and gone? He squinted. The campfires that had been kept burning all night long in Santa Anna's camp had dwindled to orange specks. Why would they let their fires burn down? Was this not the hour for brewing coffee?

"Hey, Boss."

"What?"

"It's quiet over there. No 'Viva Mexicos' or 'Viva Santa Annas' this morning."

Hastings blinked hard, twisted his face, looked up at the sky. "The moon has set. It's nigh to dawn. You'd think they'd be beating the long roll about now to come whip our asses."

They sat, listening to a breath of wind passing through the timber down in the ravine. Chamberlain cupped his hand behind his ear. Nothing.

"We gotta go find General Taylor," he said.

"Damn tootin'," Hastings replied.

They reined their tired mounts northward and trotted across the high ground. Coming around the head of a ravine to the Northern Plateau, Chamberlain saw a cluster of men under an American flag, the head-quarters tent, and the colors of May's dragoons.

"That looks like Taylor and Wool, both," Hastings said.

"Yeah, and Taylor's whole staff."

They passed the first of the commands stationed in order of battle on the line. Chamberlain took note of the battle flags of the Arkansas Volunteers—blue fields with white lettering. One said "Rackensack Is in the Field," the other "Extend the Area of Freedom."

As he bounced along on Soldan under a gradually brightening sky, he happened to recognize the big, square boulder he had leaned against the day before yesterday, while sketching the terrain. He scarcely recognized the place now. Craters from artillery blasts pockmarked his surrounds. Wheel ruts left by gun carriages, limbers, and caissons crisscrossed the plain. Down in the gorges, flying lead had stripped branches of foliage as if a cyclone had passed through them.

They trotted by nervous-looking volunteers from Indiana, Kentucky, and Illinois, all standing in line of battle, waiting for the Mexicans.

As they approached Taylor's headquarters, Chamberlain looked over his right shoulder to judge the rosy glow of the sky. Arriving within shouting distance, he saw Major William Bliss setting up a field desk, preparing for the day's battle.

He dismounted, enjoying the feeling of his own feet on the ground for a change. "Major Bliss, sir!" he said.

Bliss looked up.

Chamberlain saluted. "Private Chamberlain, Second Dragoons, reporting from guard duty, sir."

Boss Hastings saluted beside him. "Private Hastings, too, sir."

Bliss strolled over to the two troopers. He returned the salutes. "What have you to report?"

"Sir," Chamberlain began, "last night the Mexicans' fires were burning bright. But this morning they're burnt down to coals."

Bliss narrowed his eyes. "That's your report?"

"Major," Hastings said, "we haven't heard a peep out of them greasers in hours."

"A peep?" the adjutant said, seeming a bit annoyed.

"Or a 'viva' or a jackass braying," Chamberlain said.

"Santa Anna's fightin' cocks ought to be crowin' their asses off right now." Hastings pointed to the reddening east.

"Not a bugle, not a drum, not a whinny," Chamberlain added.

"Sir, we haven't seen a soul, either. No lance points, no fancy feathered hats, no crossed white shoulder straps."

Bliss looked from one private to the other. "Stay right here."

"Yes, sir," they said in unison.

Bliss marched swiftly to his mount and pulled his telescope from his saddle pouch. He peered through it toward the south for several long seconds.

"General Taylor!" he said.

Taylor turned away from General Wool. Both of the old warhorses looked grim, and none too confident, to Private Chamberlain.

"What is it, Major?"

"Sir, the Saint Patrick's deserters have withdrawn from their hill."

Taylor judged the light in the predawn sky. "Are you sure?"

"Yes, sir. Positive." He still had the optics to his right eye. "Sir, there's movement over the far ridge on the road to San Luis Potosi!"

"Movement?" Taylor said. "More of the enemy coming?"

"No, sir. The movement seems to be filing *away* from us, not toward us."

Taylor and Wool looked at each other, astonished.

The drum of hooves from a single galloping rider approached from the Saltillo road.

"Here comes the heroic Colonel May," Chamberlain said sarcastically to Boss Hastings.

"Taylor must have sent him out to scout the enemy lines," Hastings replied.

Black Tom bounded to a stop in front of the generals and Lieutenant Colonel Charles Augustus May leaped from the saddle, saluting as he ran up to Taylor. To Private Sam Chamberlain, May's eyes seemed about to bug right out of his head. And he was smiling.

"Lieutenant Colonel May reporting, sir!"

"Report!" Taylor demanded.

"Sir! The enemy is *gone*! They have packed up and retreated, sir! They are marching south. They're *whipped*!"

Taylor spread his arms and turned to Wool. "By God, we whipped 'em, John!"

The two old veterans fell together in a spontaneous embrace and patted each other's backs as if beating on drums. Around them, Taylor's staff erupted in joyful hurrahs.

"Great day in the mornin'!" Hastings said to Chamberlain. "I never in my born days thought I'd see two generals hug!"

Chamberlain threw his hat into the air and turned to the nearest boys from Illinois. "The Mexicans retreated!" he yelled at the top of his lungs. "We've won the fight!"

All down the line—through Hoosiers, Kaintucks, and Rackensackers—cheers arose and caps flew into the air like leaves in a whirlwind. Batteries fired salvos at nothing, and musket shots peppered the sky.

Chamberlain patted Soldan on the neck. "It's over, ol' hoss!"

The dread that had clutched him the past two days released its grip and allowed a flood of euphoria to envelop him in its stead. He filled his lungs with cool mountain air, turned his face to the morning sky, and let go the nearest thing to a Mexican *grito* that he could muster. It joined forces with some four thousand like ululations that echoed across the ridges and ravines and soared away up high, where Sam Chamberlain thought even the spirits of lost heroes could hear it, feel it, breathe it, and ride aloft on it—all the way to heaven's heralded reward.

Lieutenant
SAM GRANT

Gulf of Mexico
March 1, 1847

Grant stood at the prow of the three-masted packet ship, his hands firmly gripping the gunwale of the vessel. He took peculiar pleasure in the cold spray that splashed in his face and stung his eyes as the ship crashed into wave after wave on the rough Gulf of Mexico.

The freighter, called the *Lassie*, had been built for commerce, not for comfort. For this voyage, she had been contracted by the United States government to move troops from the roadstead of Point Isabel, Texas, at the mouth of the Rio Grande del Norte, to the harbor of Antón Lizardo, Mexico, south of Veracruz. She had no passenger cabins. Officers and men rode down in the hold like so much freight. Some of the immigrant soldiers compared it to the coffin ships that had brought them to America. On this day, the vessel's skeleton crew had furled all but her mainsails and a storm jib, but still she hurled herself across the rough Gulf on a raging northwester.

Lieutenant Grant was hoping the showers of sea foam would somehow cleanse him by dashing away grisly memories of Palo Alto, Resaca de la Palma, and Monterrey. The images from those battlegrounds would come to him at odd moments, for no reason at all.

The one that haunted him the most, even in his dreams, was the recollection of stumbling upon that makeshift hospital in Monterrey. Inside, he had found Lieutenant John C. Territt suffering from a horrible, gaping belly wound. He had promised Territt that he would send help. But before he could find General Taylor to report the room full of injured men, Taylor had ordered the withdrawal of the two regiments advancing on the east side of Monterrey. Lieutenant Territt and the other suffering souls had fallen into the hands of the Mexicans, and they had all died of their gruesome injuries.

He had promised Territt. He had failed. He wondered how Territt had felt, waiting for rescue, only to see enemy soldiers enter the room. For all he knew, the Mexicans might have bayoneted him on the spot.

At night, Territt came to Grant in his dreams, holding his bowels to keep them from spilling out of his wound.

"You promised, Sam. You said you would send help. I waited. No one came. You promised . . . You promised . . . You promised . . ."

Another icy wall of seawater slammed into his face. Someone grabbed his shoulder. Fully expecting to see the ghost of John C. Territt, he wheeled about and recognized the face of his friend Lieutenant Sidney Smith.

"Sam, what in the devil are you doing up here?" Smith shouted over the roar of wind and waves. "Have you gone mad?"

"Yes," Grant admitted. "What but madness would lure a man here?"

His friend smirked and shook his head. "How many days shipboard have we endured?"

"Five," Grant said, spitting out a mouthful of spray that had salted his tongue, "and each day stormier than the day before."

"Five days on soggy hardtack and salt-cured pork. I didn't join the army to be a damned sailor."

Grant braced for the next rolling crest. "I think I should like to sail around the world one day."

"You *have* gone mad."

"Not just to sail, but to see foreign lands. I've always wanted to travel."

"Well, I hear Veracruz is lovely this time of year."

Grant chuckled. Smith's dry wit always cheered him. "It won't be lovely after we get through with it."

"We'll have to take the city before the yellow fever season sets in. I'm afraid *el vomito* would ruin your world travels, Gulliver."

"This is no pleasure voyage, Sidney."

Smith patted him on the shoulder. "I'm going below. Meet me later on the poop deck for high tea."

Grant's smile slid back into a frown as Lieutenant Smith left him. He

swiveled back toward the bowsprit. He had not found a dry enough moment to write to Julia in the five days he had sojourned on this wretched
vessel. Julia was going to worry. Since leaving White Haven Plantation,
Lieutenant Sam Grant had managed to send at least one letter to his fiancée by each mail. He was still days from the end of his odyssey aboard
the *Lassie*, and then the invasion of Veracruz would begin. Julia would
surely think him dead if she did not receive a missive for two weeks.

How he missed her. How he wished this war would end so he could
return to marry her. There had been a moment of euphoria, during the
surrender of Monterrey, when a rumor had spread, announcing an end
to the war. A new U.S. ambassador was on the way to Mexico City, Grant
had been told, to negotiate the terms of peace. But the story had turned
out to be a ruse by General Ampudia to trick General Taylor into agreeing to more favorable terms of surrender.

Later, when he heard of Taylor's victory at Buena Vista, he refused to
believe the renewed predictions of peace. He would not be fooled again.
The Buena Vista news had come to Point Isabel via express riders and
steamboats. Zachary Taylor had pronounced a great victory for the United
States. But Mexican civilian sources reported that Santa Anna also
claimed to have won and had two captured six-pounders and a U.S. battle
flag to bolster his assertion.

Santa Anna would fight on. This war was not ending. It was just going
on and on.

The *Lassie* slammed into another wave, dousing Grant in cold water.
Suddenly he thought of swimming a flooded Gravois Creek. How Julia
had laughed when she saw him in her brother's clothes, too small for his
gangling frame. He had been so afraid to propose to her. And her answer! He would never forget it: "*Married? No! But, Sam, I think it would
be quite charming to be engaged.*"

He found himself smiling into the hard rain that had just begun to
fall. He had a reason to endure: Julia. This war had to end someday. He
would resign his commission with honor. He would return to White Haven to collect his beloved bride. He would whisk her away to a secluded
arbor and take her into his arms, gaze into her eyes, kiss her soft lips.

And then there would be a lavish wedding, peace and a normal life
together. There would be children, honest work to do, a home of their
own. They would have a pet dog and he and Julia would take afternoon
tea on the piazza. He would humor her by listening to her tell of premo-

nitions that came to her in dreams. He would hold her hand and they would talk about the tour around the world that they would enjoy together someday.

And the killing and the bleeding and the dying and the suffering would fade away. The hate and the meanness would sift out of his soul and become a thing of the past. And they would tell their children's children how Grandmother had once said she didn't want to be married but thought being engaged sounded quite charming.

I have a reason to live. I must survive. This war will not deprive me of my love for Julia.

He grasped the gunwale with eagle talons. The bursting crest of a whitecap and a deluge of rain struck him, purifying him. Lightning flashed and cracked. He glared ahead and spat into the wind. His teeth gnashed and he growled. He would never back up. He would move forward. Always forward. He would endure anything and everything for love. And that would make Julia all the more precious to hold.